UNCOVERING Kalyn

UNCOVERING

Kalyn

KALIOPE

CHAPTER

One

JONAH

My instincts scream as my mother materializes out of thin air, especially after she overheard Kalyn and me fucking. After which she made it abundantly clear she was repulsed by our explicit language and believed that *"no respectable woman would speak such vulgar words."* She even went as far as to warn me that I would regret getting Kalyn pregnant, hoping that it was just *"heat of the moment trash talk,"* mentioning filling her pussy with my cum.

A sense of unease settles in the pit of my stomach as I decide to dial security and have them feed me the footage from the courtyard. I see Kalyn sitting on a bench, fidgeting with her fingers and swinging her legs back and forth. She looks so beautiful, as always.

Just as I expected, my mother approaches her. She's so predictable. My jaw clenches as I wait to hear what she'll say. I don't believe in resorting to violence against women, especially my mother, but if she mistreats Kalyn, I won't hesitate to throw her ass out of my house.

Her words pierce the air as she tells Kalyn, "In the business world, men are considered more powerful with a strong woman by their side… with Jenevieve at his side," she emphasizes to Kalyn. Hearing her tell Kalyn she's not my long-term has my heart crumbling in my chest because she's wrong. Kalyn *IS* my long-term. She drones on for a few minutes, and already my patience is wearing thin. It really bothers me that she has ulterior motives for this conversation. At least she didn't dive straight into making threats, which is what I would have bet my money on. I grab my phone and dial Jonathan. I need an outside set of ears to tell me if I'm hearing this bullshit correctly.

"Hey, what's up?" he answers on the first ring.

"Get in my office," I order before hanging up.

Within seconds, Jonathan walks in looking concerned. "You good, Everett?"

I gesture to my computer, and he comes over, leaning on the back of my chair to get a better view.

We watch as my mother spins her web around Kalyn. "I can tell how smart you are. I think we can help each other," my mother suggests.

"Why are you doing this?" Kalyn challenges, hurt evident in her tone.

"I'll send a car for you tonight, dear. Spend an evening with him, enjoy each other's company, take him to bed, release all your emotions, and desert them there. Jonah may be down for a day or two, but he will forget all about you in a couple of days. This is for the best… for everyone. My driver will meet you outside at midnight," my mother concludes and even has the audacity to take

Kalyn's hand and offer a reassuring squeeze, like the plan she just laid out was set forth by the gods of destiny.

I don't need to turn around to know Jonathan's jaw is hanging open.

"Tell Shay to get Kalyn ready for dinner. Reserve a suite for us for a few days and inform Gladys to prepare a dinner in the ballroom for the two of us. Have the staff decorate. I want everything to be perfect."

"Consider it done. What about your mom?" Jonathan asks, exhaling heavily as he straightens.

I pause for a moment, giving myself a chance to calm down. "I know nothing. It's just another ordinary day." I stand from my chair and take my leave. I can't let my mother realize I overheard her. I don't want her to repeat this bullshit stunt later. Luckily, I trusted my gut and listened in. If I hadn't, Kalyn might have actually made it out of here without me knowing.

I don't have to question whether Jonathan will get everything done. That's the thing with him—I can rely on him. He'll handle things exactly as I would.

If my mother thinks she can take Kalyn away from me, she's lost her fucking mind. I have no clue how Kalyn will react to all this. She always surprises me with her actions. My guess is that she won't say a word to me, which means I should actually expect her to tell me what happened. If she does, we can still enjoy a lovely, romantic evening and go to bed as if nothing happened. However, if she remains silent, it will require a great deal of effort to make it through this night.

I head toward the back doors they will be coming from. As I round the corner they're entering, I'm caught even more off guard when I see my mother has her arm wrapped around Kalyn's. She could have fooled me into thinking she actually liked Kalyn.

She approaches me with her arms outstretched and envelops me in a tight hug. I want to squeeze her back, only my intention would be to cut off every ounce of oxygen from her lungs until she falls limp in my arms. But my eyes lock with the most gorgeous eyes, and I soften at the sight of Kalyn. My mother releases me. "I love you, son," then turns to Kalyn with a nod, saying her name and leaving.

My anger is practically rattling my bones by the end of the evening. Even though I pretend to be clueless, I'm seething inside. Throughout the evening, I could see the pain in her eyes multiple times, and I wanted to speak up and let her know I already knew what was happening. But I didn't. I didn't say anything at all.

I invite her to shower with me at the end of the evening, but she turns it down, which I'm somewhat thankful for. Though I love showering with her, right now I need to chill. As she passes by the shower, gently tracing her finger along the glass, my heart aches at how stunning she is. I long to reach out, pull her into the shower, and make love to her right here and now. I restrain myself and even take a longer shower than usual because every time I attempt to get out, my anger intensifies, forcing me to remain under the water longer to calm down once again.

She tells me she wants it intimate tonight, which is different than how we usually have sex. And I'm okay with it. But my mind keeps getting away from me, my anger trying to weave its way in. I have to clench my jaw and squeeze her thigh to keep from taking my frustration out on her while we're having sex.

I embrace her tightly when we're finished. "Right where you belong," I murmur, feeling her body tense. She's at war with herself, but I keep my eyes shut, maintaining a facade of calm, allowing my breathing to steady. I've felt her observing me on many sleepless nights while I, too, lie awake pretending to be sleeping.

Her delicate fingers softly trace my abdomen, tapping each freckle dotting my torso, until she drifts off. Yet, tonight is different. I feel like I'm experiencing time dilation. Every second feels elongated, almost as if we're moving through time at a slower pace than usual.

When she moves, I sense her checking if I'm asleep. Convinced I am, she quietly slips from the bed and pads to the bathroom. Upon her return, she perches on the edge of the bed. "I love you, Jonah," she whispers, her voice trembling.

My chest constricts, and my anger begins churning. It's the first time she's confessed those words, believing I will never know she said them. She exits as silently as she entered. Once the door clicks shut, I dress in the clothes I had already set out.

I shouldn't be surprised when I spot the car actually waiting for her, yet it only adds to my growing disappointment in my mother. Approaching the vehicle, I open the passenger door and smoothly slide into the seat.

"Hey, Geoffrey," I casually greet him, noting his shock. "Here's the plan. Once Kal comes out, you'll get her into the car without letting her know I'm here. Then, you'll take us to this hotel." I hand him a piece of paper with the address hastily written on it. "You're not going to say a word to anyone. Once you drop us off at the hotel, you can call my mother and inform her. Or don't; I don't particularly care. If she fires you, give me a call," I offer, handing over my business card. "I'll have a job ready for you immediately."

"Yes, sir," he responds.

"Where did she want you to take her?" I peer in the side mirror as I ask. He remains silent. Geoffrey has been faithfully serving my parents for as long as I can remember. He's fiercely loyal to them, so I'm not surprised he won't tell me anything.

He maintains his focus straight ahead, so I continue on. "Did she mention who the woman is that you're driving away with?" I inquire, shifting my attention toward him. "She's the love of my life, Geoffrey. I'm going to marry her. My mother can't accept that, and that's fine, but what I can't accept is that my mother convinced her to go along with a plan without even disclosing what that plan is. Can you imagine how scared Kalyn must be right now? Her name is Kalyn, by the way. Did you even know that?"

He shifts uncomfortably in his seat at my words.

I return my gaze back to the mirror, watching as a figure gradually materializes from the darkness. I catch sight of her blonde hair, and my heart plummets. *She was truly going to leave.* I ball my hands into fists. "Alright, here she comes." Without hesitation, he exits and opens the back door for her, allowing her to climb in.

This car is designed for privacy, with a partition separating the backseat from the front. I can't see what's happening in the back, and she can't see me up here, but I can hear her through the intercom, which I lean over and activate while he's getting her situated. It's a two-way system that can be turned on and off, allowing the driver to listen and the passengers in the back to communicate to the front.

There's a button in the back that the passengers can control. It turns red when there's no sound transmission but switches to green when the front seat can hear what's being said. Since she's never been in a car like this before, I know she won't even notice the button or the green light indicating the driver is listening.

The backseat remains quiet until we reach the main road; then she begins crying as we leave the driveway. The sound is almost unbearable. I contemplate ordering Geoffrey to turn back, but I don't say a word and let him continue driving. I can tell how uncomfortable he gets every time her crying starts, and he deserves to listen to the tortured sounds of an innocent woman's pain. I listen to her sniffling for an hour, my anger boiling at the entire situation my mother has created.

She falls silent in the next hour, and I assume she's fallen asleep, only to hear her crying begin again. It's making me want to lash out at Geoffrey, ask him if he enjoys the sound of a woman crying. That he's an accomplice to the bullshit my mother planned. I hadn't even realized that my emotions were evident until Geoffrey silently offers me a tissue. I accept it, wiping away the tears that managed to escape. Taking the tissue felt like the least manly thing I've ever done, but then again, I've never been put in a position like this before.

When the three-hour mark arrives, she suddenly requests that Geoffrey pull over. The road is desolate, with nothing around us other than wild animals, brush, and pavement. He instantly complies, and I hope this is where she asks him to turn around. But instead, I hear her lunge across the backseat, forcefully opening the door behind me. I watch in the side mirror as she tumbles out of the car onto the rough gravel, landing on her hands and knees. She begins to vomit and sob. Every instinct screams for me to leap out and scoop her up—comfort her—but I don't. I choose to remain silent and watch instead. Allowing this pain to fester. It's another step toward loving her more fully and working out how I plan to address this with my mother… if I ever speak to her again.

After throwing up, she collapses onto the ground, her forehead pressed to her knees as she rocks gently back and forth. Her sobs echo in the stillness, her shoulders heaving with each ragged breath. Eventually, she hauls herself to her feet, wiping the dirt from her shorts before beginning to pace the dark road behind the car. The only light comes from the car's taillights, casting an eerie glow over her as she wrings her hands and mutters to herself, dashing away tears. At one point, she stops, tilting her face up to the star-filled sky, and I wonder if she too is wishing an extraterrestrial being would beam her up, the same way I wish they would beam us both up and away from this shitty situation. After a few long minutes, she trudges back to the car, leaning her forehead against the doorframe for a moment before finally pulling it open. She slides into the seat behind me, offering Geoffrey an apology as she does so, her voice sounding utterly broken.

The rest of the drive is the same agonizing whimpers from my baby in the backseat. Glancing at the car screen, I notice the hotel is less than ten minutes away, and a new feeling washes over me.

I'm nervous.

Earlier, I had prepared my clothes and laptop, having Jonathan deliver them to the hotel to make things more convenient for me. He offered to stay with Kalyn and me as a sort of buffer if we needed it, but I declined, expressing my desire for some alone time with her. I did ask him to make arrangements for the private jet to be ready for takeoff in a few days and plan a trip for the four of us to a sunny beach. Jonathan enjoys taking Shay on vacations, and Shay loves going on trips, and being with Kalyn. This will be a good opportunity for us to escape from our daily routines and enjoy a relaxing week away from everything. Maybe give her time to regroup. Who knows? Maybe my home will now be a trigger of bad memories for her, and she won't want to return.

As we pull up to the hotel, I hear rustling from the backseat.

"What are we doing here?" she asks.

Geoffrey doesn't respond, as usual. Despite my anger towards him for his role in this, I see how years of working for my parents have shaped him into someone who tries to fade into the background. I recall how we were never allowed to speak to the staff as children, something that troubled me. Ironically, I grew up to mimic this same heartless behavior with my own staff, walking around pissed off. Repeating the very actions I despised in my parents. It's a wonder my staff doesn't hate me. Quietly, Geoffrey steps out of the car and walks around to open my door.

Let's do this.

I confidently step out of the car, walking over to her door and pulling it open. She looks shocked, her mouth hanging open as she gazes at me with her beautiful green eyes, now even greener from her tears.

"Come on, baby," I say, reaching out my hand to her.

CHAPTER

Two

KALYN

I stare at him in disbelief. *How is he here? Was he in the car the whole time?*

I feel like I'm going to pee out my butt with how embarrassed I am, thinking about him witnessing me sneaking away, puking on the side of the road, and blubbering in the back seat. I can't believe he didn't say anything this entire time! It's humiliating. If he knew of his mother's plan, why did he let me go the entire evening thinking our relationship was over? From the dinner in the ballroom, the dancing, and the conversation on the terrace, he knew exactly what was going on. Was this his way of punishing me for deciding to go?

"Want me to carry you?" His words snap me back to reality.

I somehow manage to get my limbs functioning again and scoot to the edge of the seat, placing my hand in his waiting grasp as I step out, still bewildered by how he got in the car without me noticing. Leaning back in, he grabs my bag, closes the door, and taps on the car's roof. The driver immediately pulls away.

As we enter the hotel, I'm completely dazed. A gentleman approaches us and hands Jonah an envelope, clearly expecting our arrival. Jonah accepts it, then guides me toward the elevator.

Once we reach our room, he leads me inside. We immediately enter a large living room with the lights warmly glowing. He strides toward a set of wide-open double doors and disappears through them. I take a moment to scan the room before following after him.

He wastes no time undressing, placing his shoes neatly by the chair and draping his shirt and pants over its back. Then, he moves to the bed and pulls back the covers.

I find myself rooted to the spot in the doorway, watching in shock as he stands there fully nude.

"Do you need help getting undressed?" He waits beside the bed.

I'm at a loss, unsure of what to do next. Are we really supposed to just forget that, merely four hours ago, I had decided to secretly leave him—and everything we were building together— because his mom told me to? And he clearly knew about it.

"What are you doing, Jonah?"

"I just want to get some sleep, I'm exhausted," he replies, sitting on the bed and running his hands through his hair.

I'm drowning in confusion and sadness. Could he have orchestrated this with Antoinette? What could his motives be in conspiring against me? Surely this wasn't some sort of cruel experiment, right? He wouldn't do that to me. He didn't say a word when Antoinette and I entered the house. He actually sat there looking shocked to see her arm around mine. Yet, here he is, smack dab in the middle of her stupid dumbass plan. My heart aches as I attempt to sort out all these thoughts, feeling both betrayed and utterly lost.

"Why did you come here, Jonah?"

"Because I know my mother too well. I knew she would try to pull some kind of bullshit. And you might think you're a good actress, baby, but the entire evening you were on the verge of tears."

"Were you in on this?" I question suspiciously, folding my arms over my chest in a protective gesture.

"What? God, no." His eyes look so tired but genuine.

"So you just let me think we were done? That I would never see you again?" My sadness turns into irritation.

"Can we discuss this tomorrow? I want to give you my full attention, but I'm mentally at two percent charge right now, babe. I've been awake for twenty-eight hours, and I can't keep my eyes open any longer," he replies, looking up at me almost in a pleading manner.

"Fine," I say, holding back tears.

"Babe—"

"I said fine," I repeat and walk into the room, grabbing my bag from the chair he placed it on and digging through it to find something to sleep in.

He lets out a sigh and lies back in bed. Just as he warned, he's already fast asleep, probably out before his head even touched the pillow.

I lie awake, sleep stubbornly evading me. It feels as though I've been in a trance since leaving the mansion, and his presence now jolts me back to a harsh reality. *How could I have made this decision without talking to him first?* I knew Antoinette was lying when she claimed he would only be sad for a few days before forgetting me. But in that moment, I believed her. A part of me wanted to be accepted by her so badly, I did what she wanted in hopes she would think I did good, seeking praise from a motherly figure. I let myself be swayed by her words, convinced that I was doing what was best for Jonah. Now, the weight of my naivety rests painfully on my chest, slowly suffocating me with how foolish I was.

As he sleeps, I turn to face him, running my fingers up and down his bare chest. He's smooth beneath my touch, his familiar scent enveloping me, intoxicating as ever. I nuzzle my nose against him, taking a deep breath, closing my eyes, and savoring the aroma. I kiss the same spot, holding it there as a single tear rolls down my cheek. My lips part, and my tongue brushes against his skin, relishing the taste of him.

My hand slides further down his chest under the covers, finding his arousal. I press firmly, feeling him respond as my hand moves lower, all while he remains in the depths of sleep.

I shift on the bed, my heart pounding in my chest. Kneeling, I shimmy my panties down my legs, not caring that they'll likely be lost in the bed sheets, only to be found by the housekeeping staff.

Sliding my hand back under the covers, I wrap my fingers around his erection, gripping it gently. I move my leg over him, positioning myself to straddle his lap. It bothers me that I'm so turned on when I just made a colossal mistake. I can't even control myself. He just said he was exhausted less than an hour ago, and here I am selfishly using his body for my own pleasure, overwhelmed by my own desires.

Wake up, Kalyn, I silently plead, wondering if I'm trapped in a dream state.

Guiding him to my entrance, I slowly rotate his member to coat the tip of his crown in my wetness. My skin feels like it's ablaze with electric sparks, every inch of me tingling with fiery sensations. As I lower myself onto him, I feel his girth stretching me wide, and

I exhale a shaky breath. I rise up, then lower back down, my hips moving in a slow, deliberate rhythm.

The first moan leaves my lips, and his eyes remain closed, but his hands move from behind his head to grasp my hips. He squeezes, then releases, using his strength to pull me down as he thrusts upwards. "Baby," he whispers sleepily, his voice husky.

I sink down onto him completely, my hips moving in a frenetic rhythm. I gasp at the feeling I thought I'd never experience again. I had mourned the loss of his touch, and now, being intimate with him again only heightens the emotions. He sits up, pulling my top off and tossing it aside, then leans in to suck on my breast. His tongue dances over my nipple while he gently bites down with his teeth.

Our moans and heavy breathing fill the room as I gyrate my hips on him. I don't even try to prolong this; my body wouldn't allow it even if I tried. A wave of incredible pleasure tightens my stomach, and a sob escapes me. I move frantically back and forth on him, allowing myself to dive over the edge, working my hips on him, feeling each pulsation of my orgasm until he reaches his own climax.

"Fuck," he groans, collapsing back on the pillows and holding my hips against him, lifting his hips off the bed as he releases inside me.

Tears begin streaming down my face as the floodgates of sobs break free, followed by uncontrollable tears. My hands flatten on his chest, my head falling forward, making my hair curtain around my face. My body trembles, and I hate myself for what I did to him. He didn't deserve this, and I didn't deserve it either.

He sits up, wrapping his arms around me. "No, baby, don't cry," he says softly.

"I'm so sorry, Jonah."

He holds me close, running his hand soothingly up and down my back, allowing me to release all the emotions I thought I had already let out on the drive here.

"I don't want to make light of the situation, but you crying like that is squeezing my cock so hard, and it feels fucking amazing."

I let out a laugh, pulling away to look at him.

As he leans back, reaching for tissues on the nightstand, I purposely clench my core around him. His grin grows wider as he sits back up and softly wipes the tissues under my eyes and down my cheeks.

"You feel incredible, baby. You're so beautiful," he brushes my hair back and leans in to kiss my neck.

"Can I have the tissue?" I reach for the folded Kleenex, and he opens his hand for me to take it. I wipe my face, feeling a bit better. "Ready for bed?"

"I am if you are."

I BLINK MY EYES AND SQUINT, TRYING TO ADJUST TO THE BRIGHTNESS in the room. It takes me a moment to realize it's already morning and we're still in the hotel from last night. Everything feels like a blur. I half expected to wake up and find that it was all just a nightmare, but unfortunately, it wasn't. It *did* happen. I really did try sneaking out and leaving our relationship without a word. The pit in my stomach confirms this harsh reality. I can't imagine how it would have felt for him to wake up and find me gone.

Beside me, he has a chair pulled up right next to my side of the bed, engrossed in his laptop. His face carries a serious expression with a hint of sadness. My heart aches at the sight.

Glancing at the clock on the nightstand, I see that it's already 11 AM. The room is filled with a soft light, indicating that the curtains are slightly drawn open. The double doors to the bedroom are open, revealing that the living room curtains are also slightly open. Even though he mentioned he had been up for twenty-eight hours, he can't seem to sleep once the sun begins to come up, which is typically when I like to go to bed. Mulling it over in my mind, I calculate that he must have been sitting here for at least three hours. I also notice that his hair is dry, indicating that he didn't follow his usual morning routine of working out and then showering. This entire situation is throwing off his daily routines.

When a tear slips free, I try to discreetly wipe it away with my hand, but he catches me in the act. His eyes light up when he realizes I'm awake. He quickly gets up and places his laptop on the nightstand before leaning in to kiss me as he sits on the side of the bed.

"Good morning, beautiful," he whispers, brushing away another tear with his thumb and tucking my hair behind my ear. Then he leans down to kiss me once more. "Breakfast will be here soon," he murmurs, running his fingers gently down my arm.

I rise to a sitting position, and he pulls me onto his lap in a warm embrace, wrapping his arms around me securely. He soothingly strokes my back as I nuzzle into his chest. We stay like this until there's a knock on the door, signaling the arrival of our breakfast.

I climb off his lap, and he stands up, taking my hand in his as he guides us out of the room to let the man wheel in the cart of food.

"Thank you," Jonah says to him, placing a folded-up bill in his hand. The guy smiles wide as he leaves.

I struggle to get through breakfast and the shower that he assists me with. It feels like I'm just going through the motions of living without truly feeling anything. What once was pure happiness is now replaced with numbness, trapped in a body I somehow don't belong in, surrounded only by the ruins of what was once the flourishing empire of Jonah and my love. I want to blame Antoinette for stealing my happiness, but deep down, I know it's my own fault. I was the one who fell for her deceitful plan and went along with it.

The seconds tick by, and I no longer even have words to speak. I feel disgusting being here. How can he even stand to look at me or lie next to me? I'm a despicable human, and I deserve to be heartbroken and alone.

I feel like I don't fit in anywhere anymore. Not that I ever fit in in the first place, but I was finally starting to feel like I belonged somewhere. Belonged with someone. I hated my hometown, but it was all I really knew. I never considered leaving because I never had a reason to. However, now that I've left, I can't picture myself going back. Antoinette really caused chaos. Even though things didn't go exactly as she planned, she still achieved her goal in the end. She broke me. She broke me and Jonah.

The day passes, the room transitioning from bright sunlight covering every surface to slowly fading away as the light ebbs down the walls until we are left in the darkness with only the soft glow of the lamps.

Two days pass like this.

Jonah has begged me to talk to him, but every time he does, I just break down in tears.

I half hope he'll realize I'm a lunatic and just leave me here until the hotel kicks me out and I can hitchhike somewhere far away. He brings me food, but I can't even bring myself to eat. When he steps out of the bedroom, I go to the bathroom, making it to the far end of the room. No longer able to stay on my feet,

I sink down the wall until I'm sitting, crying with my head on my knees.

Hours pass by with me crying, stopping, then starting all over again. I've used up almost the entire roll of toilet paper, wiping my eyes, blowing my nose, and tearing the soiled tissue into tiny little pieces. Rolling them into balls, I drop them to the floor. Each piece falls, and it's as if I'm tearing away another fragment of my life and tossing it away.

CHAPTER

Three

KALYN

I didn't hear anyone knock at the door, but I can hear Jonah's voice filter through: "She's in the bathroom." Footsteps echo down the hall, then the bathroom door creaks open. I'm still curled up in a ball, in the same spot I've been in for hours. Shay settles beside me, folding her legs in a criss-cross position facing me, gently resting her forehead against my shoulder.

My stomach ties itself in knots, worried if she's mad at me, disappointed, or if she even knows what happened. If she does know, she must be mad at me—she has to be all of those things. *Did Jonah tell her what I was attempting to do?* If she is here, then Jonathan is too. The thought of letting him down also makes me feel sick. I messed up so badly, and all it makes me want to do is just follow through with the original plan and run away. At least before, I had Antoinette's assistance. Now, I would be completely on my own.

I assumed I had cried all the tears my body was capable of producing, but apparently, I haven't. There are still plenty of them ready to be shed. They start streaming again, leaving wet trails down my face. I lean forward as my sobs build and then burst out.

Shay scoots in closer to me, wrapping her arms around me and pulling me into her chest.

"I'm so sorry, Kal. I know you feel like you did something wrong, but this isn't your fault, and nobody blames you. Even if you had made it out of the house without Jonah noticing, he would have found you and brought you right back. Giles and Gladys think we're all on vacation; nobody else knows a thing. And they won't ever know anything."

Her words only make me cry harder. I feel I'm getting off the hook too easily. I had worked it out in my head that I would never see any of them again. I feel like I've already betrayed them for a lifetime and now feel so unworthy of her time.

"Mr. Everett is taking us on a mini-vacation so we can get away for a while longer. Plus, we need to go shopping," she whispers, her hold on me tightening.

"As you know, I'm very passionate about my feelings for Jonathan. We actually got in a fight one time, and I stormed out of his bedroom. He followed me all the way back to the maid's quarters, telling me to get back here and talk to him right this instant. We fought, and I told him I was done, that we were over, and I was leaving. He was like, 'Over my dead body.'

But then he got called away for work for a couple days, and I had time to stew in my own head, and I packed my bags and left. I had a connecting flight home and was waiting to board the plane when he came and sat next to me. I'll never forget what he said:

'You can be mad at me, you can scream at me, but you can't ever leave me, because there is nowhere on this planet you could go that I wouldn't hunt you down and bring you right back. We need to grow together and realize we can't just cry breakup every time we get in a fight. You are worth fighting for, and I am worth you fighting for me. You are it for me, Shayla. I don't want anyone else, and I'd rather be sullivan the rest of my life than to ever spend a day without you being mine.'

And it was so touching. Then I asked him what 'sullivan' is, and he told me it's where you abstain from having sex. I was like, 'Do you mean celibate?' And he's like, 'Yeah, that's probably the word I meant,' and we still joke about it to this day.

Mr. Uptight Everett didn't say a word to us like he normally would when we had sex in the backseat the entire way back to the mansion. Mr. Everett would rather be sullivan than to ever be with another woman. You're it for him, Kal. You're the end game. Congratulations, you made it through another bumpy part in your long road ahead of yours and his story. But you know what? You're going to come out the other end so much stronger, and one day, you will be telling your daughter during her first fight with her boyfriend about the time you tried to sneak away from her dad, but he brought your cute little butt right back home."

As she talks, my crying settles, and I'm left with heavy breathing while I hang on to her for dear life. I absolutely love hearing stories about her and Jonathan. They are each so genuine, and I can't even count the number of times I have caught each of them admiringly gazing at the other one without the other's knowledge.

"I think we have to be on the plane in two hours or something. I don't remember what Jonathan said, but it's a seven-hour nonstop flight. No rain, just sun, the beach, sand in our toes," Shay says.

As she continues talking and softly rubbing my back, I listen to her calming voice and drift off to sleep while she rocks back and forth with me wrapped in her arms, the same way my mom used to rock me in her arms.

"We're all set. You ready to go?" Jonathan asks Shay as he quietly opens the bathroom door.

"Yep," she responds in a whisper.

"Thanks, Shay," Jonah says, his voice coming closer to us as I hear his quiet footsteps approaching.

I feel strong arms encircle me, lifting me off the ground, his scent enveloping me. I don't even care where he takes me; I just want him to hold me. My body feels weak, my stomach feels like it's eating itself, and I'm thirsty but have no energy to even open my eyes. I can hear footsteps around me, then an elevator door opening, and he steps inside, the temperature feeling like it dropped instantly to freezing.

"The rain won't delay the flight, will it?" Shay asks.

"Nah, we'll leave regardless," Jonathan responds.

"Put my coat over her," Jonah instructs, and I hear movement, then Jonah's coat being draped over my body just before the elevator doors open.

"Your bags are all packed in your vehicle, Mr. Everett. Is there anything else I can do for you?" I hear a man ask as we exit.

"That should be everything, thanks," Jonah replies, just as a cold gust sweeps over us with the opening of the hotel doors. He then climbs into the SUV, still cradling me in his lap. Inside, the warmth of the vehicle engulfs me, and I drift back to sleep without realizing it. I'm only roused when the door opens again, and for a moment, I think we haven't left the hotel. Jonah steps out, holding me securely in his arms, and swiftly ascends stairs with a confident stride.

"Hello, Mr. Everett," I hear an almost flirtatious voice greet him.

He doesn't say anything in response, just keeps walking, and then I'm set down on a heated leather seat.

As my eyes flutter open, I glance around seeing that we are on what looks like a private Jet. All the seats are a light tan, fine leather. The carpet on the floor is swirls of dark red, tan, white, and black, appearing as if nobody has ever stepped on it before now. Next to me is another seat with a table between these chairs and a second set of chairs facing ours. I see a large, long sofa along the other side of the plane and a large, retractable flat-screen TV straight ahead. I don't know why I assumed we would be flying a regular flight, perhaps with upgraded seats to first class, but this never crossed my mind. He never even discussed etiquette with me for this kind of thing. I've never even been a passenger in business class on an airplane, let alone a passenger on a private Jet.

Jonah is talking with the pilot while the two flight attendants chat alongside him. Looking out the window, I see Jonathan and Shay climbing the stairs to the plane. When they enter, Shay spots me and smiles wide as she comes to sit next to me.

"Ready to embark on a relaxing adventure, sleepyhead? Ever joined the mile-high club?" she asks mischievously.

I shake my head.

"I have about a hundred times. Planes make Jonathan horny. Jonathan makes me horny, so I guess planes make me horny as well. The first time we had sex was on a plane," she lets out a sigh as she stares at him.

He has joined Jonah and the rest of the airplane crew at the front of the plane. One of the things I love most about Jonathan is that almost 100% of the time he is smiling. He turns to look over, and his smile doesn't falter as he winks at Shay. I can literally see her melt in the chair next to me, her smile widening as he does this. He notices me awake, nudging Jonah's arm and nods in our direction. I turn my attention out the window, staring absentmindedly at the wide-open tarmac with only Jonah's vehicle beginning to pull away.

He doesn't even need to say anything when he approaches for Shay to get up and clear the seat that she's sitting in next to me. He sits down, leans over, and grabs my seat belt, fastening it and pulling the strap until it's tight. Then he sits back in his chair and does the same to his seat belt.

Shay and Jonathan are somewhere behind us, the sound of their own seat belts clicking into place, followed by quiet words and giggles. While the pilot converses with Jonah once more, the sound of their discussion is muffled by the incessant humming in my head, a noise I struggle to drown out.

I bring my still bare feet onto the seat, wrapping myself as small as I can as I lean against the window and peer out. I wonder whether Jonah carrying a barefoot, unconscious woman onto the plane—destination… who knows—seemed weird to any of the flight crew. Evidently, it doesn't seem odd enough for them to alert the authorities, which doesn't make me feel very confident that if I were being kidnapped, I would ever be rescued. The flight attendants are so smitten with him; they probably didn't even notice he was carrying anything.

When the plane begins to turn, I watch the moment of lift-off: the wheels coming off the ground as we soar toward the clouds. Once more, I let sleep take me away.

When I blink awake, the seat next to me is empty. We're still in the sky, and I glance around, not seeing anyone. Looking back between the seats, I can see Jonah sitting in a chair with his elbows resting on his knees, his hands sunk into his hair, and his head is hung low. He looks defeated. Shay and Jonathan are sitting across from him on a long sofa, talking quietly to him.

It's a sight that makes me feel sick to my stomach. I didn't realize that during my own self-sabotaged pity party, he was silently hurting. He always seems so confident… strong… untouchable. But this, this feels like a man who is all of those things—that is also human.

What the fuck is wrong with me?

Turning back in my seat, I stare blankly out the window.

"Can I get you something to drink? A water or coffee?" the brunette flight attendant asks.

When I turn to meet her gaze, she attempts to look cheerful, but it doesn't quite reach her eyes. I can tell she caught the attention of the other three just behind me because she glances up and looks in their direction.

"Water, please," I say, my voice quiet, my throat dry.

As she goes to hand me the cold water bottle, Jonah takes it from her hand, thanking her, and she hurries off.

"Here, baby," he twists the cap off and hands me the bottle.

"Thank you," I quietly say as I take a drink. Apparently, I needed this more than I thought I did because my body acts like I haven't had water in years, and the second the wetness hits my mouth, it feels even drier than before.

"We land in about an hour," he informs me. "If I have them make you something to eat, will you try to eat?"

Had I not seen him just a couple minutes ago, I would have never known anything was even bothering him. He's masking whatever he's feeling. Is he trying to act strong for me? Maybe this isn't even about me.

Yet, I know that it is.

"I'm okay, thank you," I put the water bottle on my seat beside me.

He picks it up, placing it on the table before standing and moving toward the front of the plane. The flight attendant nods as he speaks with her. Afterward, he turns and walks back to me, sitting down and crossing one ankle over his opposite knee.

He doesn't say anything. He just sits there quietly, and I hate that I can't think of anything to say to him to make him feel better. The silence between us feels heavy, filled with unspoken words and emotions we're both struggling to understand. I stare out the window, wanting to turn and reach out to him, offer some kind of comfort, but the right words—no, all words—elude me.

When the flight attendant approaches awhile later with a cart, Jonah sees her coming and leans over to kiss my arm. "I'm going to go talk to Jonathan," he stands and walks away.

The flight attendant places a tray in front of me. "Here you go," she says, revealing a dish of delicious-looking macaroni. "Let me know if you need anything else."

I nod and thank her as Shay sits next to me, and the attendant gives her a tray with macaroni, too.

"This is the best macaroni," Shay says, scooping up a spoonful and taking a bite. Her eyes instantly roll back in delight. "The best," she repeats as she swallows.

Initially, I intended to resist eating, but the mere aroma makes my stomach rumble, not to mention how amazing it looks. I might be stubborn and bullheaded, but I will gladly set that aside, even for just a single bite of this.

Sitting up, I take a bite of mine, and she wasn't kidding. Airplane food isn't supposed to be good; that's a given. But macaroni shouldn't be this good in general, especially coming from an airplane. It's heavenly. Or maybe I'm so hungry that anything would taste amazing. Either way, Shay eating with me makes me feel more comfortable, and I finish mine before she finishes hers.

The flight attendant collects our trays and reminds us to fasten our seatbelts as we prepare for landing. Jonah and Jonathan sit down across from us, securing their seatbelts. I gaze out the window, sensing Jonah's eyes on me, wishing I could read his mind, hear his thoughts. Then again, maybe I don't want to know.

WE ARRIVE AT THE RESORT AND ARE ESCORTED TO OUR BEACHFRONT suite. Our room opens up to a kitchen-living room combo, with each bedroom opening directly to a sandy beach that leads right to the ocean. A set of chairs sits nestled in the shade, and I find myself sitting here, quietly watching the waves roll in and then recede again. The sand is soft and warm; I dig my toes in, letting them sink deep and remain rooted in place.

I remember watching a documentary on whales and how they can't breathe underwater. Whales and dolphins are mammals that have to breathe air into their lungs because they don't have gills. Their "nostrils" being their blowholes. As in they are quite literally a mammal that can't survive outside of water and would suffocate if they were underwater too long. It's a fascinating predicament of nature—bound to water yet dependent on the air. So, I suppose whales might have it a little worse than I do.

You're such an idiot, Kalyn.

I don't know why I ended up here or what I did so wrong that I was put in this situation. I almost feel I would be better off if he just didn't forgive me. I've never experienced this depth of depression before, and though I would never actually do anything to harm myself, the thought of walking out into the ocean and breathing in a lungful of water—being the opposite of a whale—seems almost appealing.

The sun moves across the sky, and I discern that at least three hours have gone by since I first sat here. During this time, I could feel Jonah watching me the entire time. *All of them* watching me. When I hear the sliding glass door glide open, my mind stays blank. I don't care who approaches me; they will be met with the same silence.

"May I sit?" a familiar voice asks.

When I turn to see Maeva, I'm out of my chair, wrapping her in a desperate hug and immediately breaking down into sobs. She holds me tight, squeezing me and rubbing my back. When she pulls away, she offers me a tissue from the little pack she produces out of her purse, which is such a Maeva thing to do.

"Do you mind if I sit with you?" she gestures to the empty chair next to me.

"Please."

"This is the farthest you have ever traveled," she acknowledges. "The water is so clear."

I watch as she leans forward, scooping up a handful of sand and squeezing it tightly in her hand. She then slowly lets it trickle through her fingers. I almost tell her it feels just as good between your toes but don't. When she finishes, grains of sand remain stuck to her palm. She tips her hand over, and a few more pieces fall away, yet some still cling stubbornly to her hand. I half want to reach over and brush the rest of it off.

"We meet so many people in our lives," she says. "Most come and go; some linger for a while, but others—no matter how hard we might try to push them away—they're here to stay." She extends her hand toward me, showing the grains of sand still clinging to her palm.

"The ones that stick with us are like these grains of sand. They cling to us even when we try to shake them off," she continues, her voice soft and comforting.

I suddenly understand her demonstration. The sand that slipped through her fingers represents the people who drift in and out of my life, while the grains sticking to her hand symbolize those who stick around. Sam… Shay… Jonah.

"I feel unworthy of having such amazing people stick beside me," I admit.

Maeva smiles warmly. "That's okay. It's part of what makes life beautiful and complex. These connections, no matter how painful or joyous, shape who we are. But the key word in what you just said is *YOU* feel. Your feelings are very valid. But they don't trump other people's feelings, and you don't get to decide someone else's feelings."

Her words are harsh but true. I just assumed that if I felt unworthy of anyone caring, it solidified those feelings as fact, and the people no longer deemed me as worthy. But that couldn't be further from the truth.

"Do you think I just like hurting?" I decide maybe I'm more broken than I originally thought.

"You've been in pain for so long that it's become normal for you," she says gently. "I think when you're not hurting, you're unsure how to handle those unfamiliar feelings."

"I don't want to keep hurting," I whisper, as a tear rolls down my cheek.

"I should tell you, Mr. Everett and I had a thorough discussion, so I'm fully aware of the recent events. I can only imagine the sense of betrayal you feel and the abuse you've endured over the past seven months. It's clear you envision a future with Mr. Everett, and in the absence of your own family, you yearn for one that would embrace you as their own. Without that, the pain must be overwhelming. His mother drove a deep wedge between you and Mr. Everett, and it's natural you might feel responsible. But truthfully, you were at a disadvantage from the start. Had she come to you with hostility, you might have seen her motives clearly. But she approached you with the guise of a mother's love, which is why the betrayal cuts so deeply."

I hadn't fully realized that's exactly how I felt until Maeva just explained it perfectly. I did go along with what Antoinette wanted because I desperately wanted her to love me. It makes my chest tighten a little more, knowing she doesn't. She doesn't even want me in her son's life, let alone hers. And that hurts… really badly. However, knowing that Jonah has already informed Maeva on the situation gives me some relief. Otherwise, I would have just pinched my lips together, said nothing, and pretend everything was fine.

"Do you think Jonah will hold a grudge against me for trying to leave?" I ask. "Obviously not right now since he probably feels like he's losing me or has already lost me. But later on, do you think he will hold a grudge against me for all of this?"

"No. There's nothing for him to be mad at you about," she reassures me.

"I left without saying anything."

"You have a big heart. There were no ill intentions in what you were doing. You wanted to make his mother happy."

"I feel disgusting. How can I go on like this never happened?"

"You can't go on like it never happened because it did happen. But you can use this as an opportunity to grow and learn. Think about what's more important to you: a man who will stand by your side through everything or going through life alone, regretting that you tried to leave. He chased after you and fought for your relationship, only to have you still push him aside. Ask yourself, Kalyn: do you love him? Do you want to be with him? Because if you don't, we can walk in there together right now, grab your bags, and leave. But if you love him, you need to stop letting this weigh you down. He's hurting, and I know you see it. Don't let him keep hurting."

CHAPTER
Four

JONAH

Seeing her in such pain is unbearable. I arranged for her therapist—and the therapist's entire family—to come here for an all-expenses-paid vacation just so she could come and talk with Kalyn. She agreed immediately, even before learning about the additional perks, simply out of a desire to help Kalyn.

For the past three hours, I've been standing in the doorway, watching my girl lost in thought as she sits quietly on a beach chair, gazing out at the ocean, completely motionless.

She won't speak to me or tell me why she's so upset with me. All I can do is stand by and witness her suffering in silence.

"How much longer until her therapist arrives?" Jonathan asks, leaning against the other side of the glass door, his gaze also fixed on her.

Glancing at my wristwatch, I mutter, "Maybe thirty minutes," before sliding my hand back into my pocket.

Shay saunters over and leans against Jonathan's chest, and he wraps his arms around her. A pang of jealousy and longing strikes me as I observe their closeness; I miss that kind of intimacy with Kalyn.

"What time do you guys work tomorrow? I was thinking of taking Kalyn to go shopping," Shay mentions.

"Maybe we want to go shopping tomorrow too," Jonathan retorts.

"Maybe we want to go get our assholes waxed," Shay quips back.

Jonathan leans down and nips her ear, playfully saying, "I know for a fact you both are completely lasered, but that's a nice try."

Fuck, I want my girl. Just watching them together makes me reminisce about not too long ago when Kalyn and I were like that, and my dick stiffens.

There's a knock on the door. Quickly adjusting myself, I walk from the bedroom through the living room to answer it. Opening the door, I'm greeted by an auburn-haired woman in a skirt suit, wearing black-rimmed glasses.

"You must be Maeva. Thanks for coming. I'm Jonah Everett," I say, extending my hand in greeting.

"Thank you for calling, Mr. Everett. If you could direct me to where she is," she replies, stepping past the threshold.

I appreciate how she gets straight to the point as we make our way toward the back door. Shay and Jonathan have vanished, and Kalyn remains in the same contemplative state she's been in for hours.

With a deep sigh, Maeva slides open the door, removes her heels, and leaves them on the patio. Anxiety consumes me. I'm second-guessing my decision to bring her here. What if Kalyn resents me for involving her therapist?

Holding my breath, I watch intently as Maeva says something to Kalyn, who suddenly turns. I almost expect Kalyn to turn in my direction and shoot daggers at me, but instead, she springs from her chair and wraps Maeva in a warm embrace.

"Thank God," I exhale, relief washing over me.

For the next three hours, I watch from a distance as they talk, and Maeva persuades Kalyn to walk along the beach. During that time, I step out onto the patio, keeping them in sight until they disappear beyond where I can see from the door.

Jonathan takes Shay out to dinner, promising to call before they return to see if we want anything.

As the evening sky darkens, the soft glow of string lights casts a magical glow from our back patio to the palm trees lining the beach. I admire their beauty, wishing Kalyn and I were nestled together in the hammock, swaying gently.

When Kalyn and Maeva return, they settle back into their chairs. My heart drops as they both turn to look at me. Maeva rises, gesturing for me to join them, leaving me awash with conflicting emotions. Is it happiness or nervousness that overwhelms me?

Without hesitation, I step off the porch and approach them. Maeva shifts her chair closer to where Kalyn is seated. "Go ahead and join us if you'd like," she offers her chair to me.

I look at Kalyn to see how she reacts to this invitation. She responds with a gentle smile, giving me the encouragement I need to take a seat beside her.

Maeva settles on the sand between us, sitting back on her shins. "Kalyn," she prompts.

Leaning forward in her chair, she extends her hands toward me. I eagerly shift in my seat and gently take hold of hers. Sensing a slight tremble, I tighten my grip, silently reassuring her that she's safe.

As she remains silent, my only thought is to give useless facts, knowing she always finds amusement in them. "Jellyfish can re-generate lost body parts. If they get injured or lose a tentacle, it can often regrow the missing part over time. Some species are also capable of producing their own light… bioluminescence."

"Almost like an anglerfish," she replies.

"Exactly," I murmur, leaning in to caress her cheek before pressing my lips to hers.

She tastes divine.

When our mouths part and I look into her eyes, I can see my baby is back.

Maeva clasps her hands around mine and Kalyn's. "If there were ever a perfect couple, you two could be the example. You're going to be so much stronger after this."

"Thanks for being here, Maeva," Kalyn says sincerely.

Maeva picks up a grain of sand from the beach and places it in Kalyn's palm. "Remember what I said," she reminds before standing up.

Kalyn gazes at the sand as she touches it. "Thank you, Mae-va," she stands, giving her a hug.

"Can you walk me to the door?" Maeva asks, and I gesture for her to take the lead.

As we follow Maeva, Kalyn interlocks her fingers with mine, filling me with instant happiness. The double doors separating the two master suites remain open, and Jonathan and Shay have yet to return. I notice a missed call from Jonathan on my phone, but food is the farthest thing from my mind—I plan on devouring my girl for dinner.

Kalyn embraces Maeva, and I shake her hand, expressing gratitude once more for her coming here to help. After closing the door behind Maeva, I turn to catch Kalyn leaping into my arms, her lips seeking mine. As soon as her tongue touches mine, everything else fades away.

I stride across the suite, my anticipation mounting as I make my way to the bed. As soon as I set her down, she kneels before me, her hands deftly undoing the zipper of my pants. I discard my shirt, followed quickly by hers, relishing the sight of her.

God, she's so fucking sexy.

Her small hands tug at my shorts, and I assist her in removing them entirely. My cock thuds out from the weight of it. As I move to grab her shorts, I find her already bent over, her hands wrapping around my shaft. With delicate precision, she softly licks the tip before taking it into her mouth, her wet warmth enveloping the head completely.

Fuck.

She glides back and forth over me, my eyes rolling back at the feel of her.

I need to be inside her.

Sliding my fingers into her hair, I pull her head back. At first, she tries resisting, but her grin grows wider once our eyes lock in a heated stare. I lean in, grasping her by the waist, pulling her up to stand on the bed. With a smooth motion, I slide her shorts and panties down, letting her step out of them before tossing them to the floor alongside my own discarded clothes.

She clings to my shoulders as I explore the softness between her thighs. A sigh escapes her lips as she lifts her leg over my shoulder, her hands holding my hair urging me closer.

"You taste incredible, baby," my voice coming out muffled against her skin as I bury my face deeper into her warmth.

Lowering her leg, she lies down on the bed, her legs spreading wide in invitation. She curls her finger, beckoning me closer.

I climb on the bed, crawling toward her with deliberate slowness. Her smile widens as I draw near. When I reach the space between her legs, I hover above her, taking in the sight of her. She's so captivating, I could bust a load on her just staring at her.

"You better get that big dick in me immediately, Mr. Everett, or you lose the power of being in charge," she teases as she lifts her arms above her head.

"Mmmm," I groan, lowering myself onto her. "My baby is greedy," I smirk, my hand wrapping around my cock as I position myself at her entrance, feeling her arousal.

"Mmhmm," she agrees, her voice filled with blatant need. "I'm horny," she adds in the most innocent voice.

"I can tell," I push the head of my cock just past her folds.

The sexiest gasp leaves her, her smile transforming into pure arousal, and she spreads her legs wider. Penetrating deeper, I lean down until our bodies are nestled together, feeling the heat between us. She wraps her arms around my neck, her nails digging into my back as she bites just below my ear.

"Your pussy is so tight, baby," I mewl, slowing my pace so I don't finish too fast. It's felt like months since I've been inside her, and now that I am, my body pulses with desperate need.

I've missed her so fucking much. My chest constricts as I stare down at her, admiring the way her beautiful breasts sway back and forth with each thrust. Drawing back slightly, I capture her nipple between my teeth, sucking firmly. Her body responds immediately—arching off the bed, urging me to push deeper as she lets out another moan.

"Harder," she pants, wetting her bottom lip as she tilts her head forward to watch me moving into her. I withdraw slightly before plunging back in, slamming into her with force, eliciting a throaty moan from her lips.

"Turn me over and fuck me from behind," she demands breathlessly, trying to reposition herself for even deeper penetration.

I'm clearly not fucking her hard enough if she has the clarity of thought to want to change positions. I guess I need to step up my game. Gripping her hips, I draw mine back, slamming into her so hard, the impact reverberates through us both as she falls back onto the bed, clutching fistfuls of the comforter.

Nuzzling my face into the hollow of her neck, I nip and lick, craving every inch of her. My hands explore her soft skin, tracing a path from her outer thigh, up the swell of her hips, and along the contours of her breast until I reach her delicate throat. With a possessive grip, I claim her, leaning down to capture her bottom lip between my teeth. I watch as her face flushes red, yet her eyes remain heavy-lidded with pleasure as I anchor her to the bed by her throat so her body remains still, absorbing the full impact of each thrust. I want her to feel the intensity long after I'm done with her, to remember why she needs me.

When I finally release her throat, she inhales deeply, her satisfied smile spreading as her body melts into the mattress. Rising to my knees, I slide each arm behind her thighs and lean forward, bending her legs toward her ears as I continue to grind into her from this new, intimate angle. A primal moan escapes her lips as she fists the bedding tighter.

I adjust my rhythm, gyrating my hips to maintain a steady, deep pace. Her body responds eagerly, hips rising to meet mine. I can feel her sheathing me, teetering on the edge of release.

"You feel so good," my voice is thick with need. "Come for me, baby."

The front door swings open, and I hear Jonathan and Shay's voices.

I can feel how close she is, her core stiffening, and I'm right there with her.

"Don't you dare stop," she gasps as Jonathan and Shay enter our room from theirs.

"That's exactly what we're about to do," Jonathan quips, setting two bags on the table. "Dinner," he adds, while I continue my rhythm, moving in and out of Kalyn.

"Get on the bed," Jonathan instructs Shay.

"I want to watch them," she protests in a whiny voice.

"Then get on the bed and face that way," he commands, eliciting an excited squeal as I hear clothes being shed.

A guttural cry rips from Kalyn's throat as she writhes beneath me, her pussy clamping impossibly tight around my shaft as she pants.

I quicken my pace, chasing my own release. With a groan, my cum spurts out, filling her. Her body still pulsates with aftershocks, so I slow my movements, allowing her time to descend while I continue to gently push in and out of her.

As her breathing begins to steady, her hips remain in sync with each of my strokes.

"Well done, sir," she murmurs, her teeth sinking into her bottom lip.

"Thank you, I tried," I say, wiping the sweat from my forehead with my forearm.

She giggles and places her finger under my chin, coaxing me closer until our lips meet.

Gently easing out of her, I lose myself in her inner muscles rippling around me and I revel in the pure bliss of being inside her.

I climb off the bed to grab the food. A soft laugh escapes me when I catch a glimpse of her cupping herself, tiptoeing to the bathroom.

"I'll be right back," she calls out over her shoulder, smiling before she disappears from view.

While she's occupied, I tear open the bags, pulling out our to-go containers. One holds a steak and baked potato, while the other, Kalyn's usual—crispy chicken strips with macaroni. She almost always orders the strips but wants bites of my food too. I open her ranch container and put it down in the middle of her chicken, then watch as she returns from the bathroom.

"That looks so good," her eyes roving over the meal.

"It probably tastes even better," I shoot back, a smirk twisting my mouth as I trace patterns over her bare ass.

Circling around the bed, she climbs onto her side, settling in front of her dinner. Grabbing the remote, I switch on the TV and start mindlessly flipping through channels. Since we rarely watch TV, I don't know what to put on. I continue searching in the hopes of finding something that catches our interest, but so far, no luck.

"These two already watched us; only makes sense we watch them back," she remarks casually, taking another bite of her chicken.

Glancing over, I see Shay on her hands and knees, Jonathan kneeling behind her. Over the years, I've witnessed these two fucking more times than I can count. It used to drive me insane. I would get by just telling myself the novelty would wear off and they would quit boning like rabbits. But they never did. If anything, the frequency only increased. I finally get it now. It takes the right person to understand it.

Cutting off a small piece of my steak, I hold my fork out to her. She doesn't even look in my direction, but her mouth opens, and she moves toward my fork. It's little things like this that make her that much more perfect. She's perfect without even trying.

"That's really good," she says as she chews.

After finishing our meal, I grab the containers and take them out of the room, placing them on the kitchen counter before returning. Shay is pulling on a nightgown as she walks over to our bed and slides in, embracing Kalyn in a warm hug. They hold each other for a while, both of them looking completely content.

Leaning back slightly, Shay plants a gentle kiss to Kalyn's lips. "I really missed you," she murmurs.

If it were anyone else that did that, I would remove their head from their body before their lips had a chance to part. But Shay's gesture carries the affectionate touch of a best friend who was just as pained by Kalyn's state of mind as I was.

"You can have boobie pillows tonight," Shay declares, positioning herself against the pillows and opening her arms. Kalyn's grin widens as she cuddles up to Shay, nuzzling her cheek against Shay's chest.

I chuckle and playfully spank Kalyn's bare ass, then plant a kiss where my handprint is starting to redden. "Want me to get you something to wear?"

"I'm okay," she replies, smiling, and drapes her leg over Shay's while Shay rests hers on Kal's foot.

"Was the steak good?" Jonathan asks, settling into a chair beside the bed and propping his feet up on the mattress.

"Very. Thanks for grabbing dinner," I recline back into the pillows and rest my head on my arm.

"No problem. I used the business account, so thank you."

"Anytime," I laugh.

We spend the rest of the night watching movies. Kalyn falls asleep first, followed by Jonathan.

"Want me to move her?" I quietly ask Shay.

"No," she shakes her head, pulling Kalyn closer. "I missed her. Thank you for getting her help," she adds, her eyes expressing gratitude as she looks at me.

In the morning, I wake before everyone else and head to the resort gym. As I lift weights and run on the treadmill, Kalyn occupies my thoughts entirely. Her presence, her laughter, and the way she unknowingly motivates me to push myself harder. I'm deeply grateful for Maeva's support, knowing that without her, Kalyn's recovery wouldn't have been possible.

Drenched in sweat, sore, and tired, I head back to the room.

"Hey, sexy," a group of girls say as I walk by. I glance in their direction and keep walking, using my discarded shirt as a towel to wipe the sweat off my face. They don't even come close in comparison to the woman I'm going back to.

Entering the room, I hear the shower running and giggles emanating from inside. When I walk in the bathroom, I can see inside the glass shower, catching sight of Shay and Kalyn showering together, talking freely as they wash their hair and bodies. It's the purest sound of happiness. Their intentions aren't sexual and exude a remarkable wholesomeness.

Leaning against the counter, I wait patiently for them to finish, not wanting to rush them.

"Is Shay in there?" Jonathan calls out, his voice reaching the bathroom before he enters. Spotting the girls in the shower, he stops, and his eyes light up with excitement. "They gonna fuck or what?" he quips, walking in and hopping on the counter to watch.

The girls look over and burst into giggles when they see they have an audience. Kal leans over, turning the water off, while they both reach for their towels draped over the glass door, wrapping them around themselves as they step out of the shower.

Kalyn approaches me and plants a kiss on my lips. "We would have gotten out if I knew you were done with your workout," she kisses me again.

I shrug. "It's all good, I'm in no hurry."

"Do you have to work?"

"Just for an hour or so. We're going to take you ladies to get pampered. There's a meeting room next to the spa. We'll hop on our meeting after we get you both settled."

After our meeting, the remainder of the day is filled with taking the girls shopping, sightseeing, and swimming in the resort pool. After a brief nap on the beach, we tuck into a nice candlelit dinner by the shore. Watching Kalyn, I can see her happiness radiating as bright as ever.

CHAPTER
Five

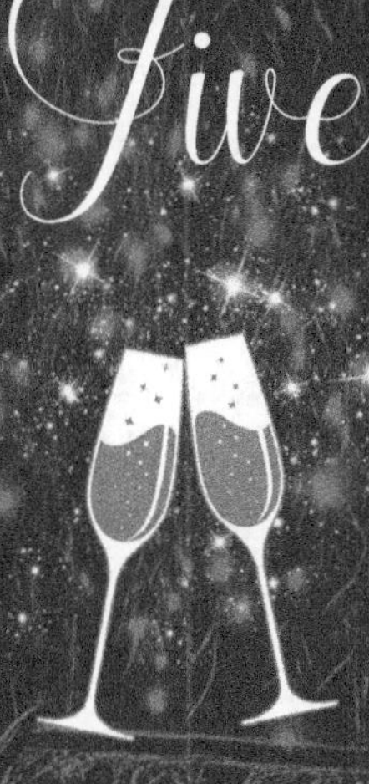

KALYN

We spent a week in paradise.

It's been nine days since I was at the mansion. It feels like an eternity has passed, while simultaneously feeling like I never left. I'm nervous to go back… to go *home*. I know they said and reiterated nobody knows what happened; everyone just thinks we went on vacation… but I know. And I feel guilty over it. After my long talk with Maeva, she helped me understand that I can't punish Jonah for something his mother did. Something his mother coerced me into doing. But I still feel like a fool. My body is a jumble of nerves as Jonathan turns down the driveway.

Out of nowhere, he stops, and Jonah climbs out of the vehicle, pulling open the back door and leaning in to unbuckle my seatbelt. "Scoot over," he says, sliding in next to me.

Once the door closes, Jonathan begins driving again. Jonah pulls me into his lap, so I'm straddling him. Looking down, I take in the glorious man beneath me as he reaches up, grasping the back of my neck and drawing me closer. Our lips meet in a passionate kiss, his mouth exploring mine.

It's only the sound of car doors opening and closing that breaks me away from him. I see we're back in his garage. A quick sweep of the surroundings and my eyes immediately land on Estelle.

"My baby girl," I croon as I swing open the door and hop out, quickly slipping into the front seat of my little beauty. I'm greeted by the familiar scent of *my car* as I lean forward to hug the steering wheel. She's still parked in the same position Jonah left her in when we returned from visiting my family. It's a simple detail, but it surprises me nonetheless.

"Gladys has dinner ready, if you're ready to eat," he says, resting his hand on the top of my car as his head settles against the door frame.

"I'm loving on my girl," I reply playfully, petting my steering wheel.

He stands there supportively, allowing me a moment to ease back into the reality of being back here again… with him. He doesn't rush me—he simply stands there, offering comfort. I've always been an empath, sensing people's feelings without them having to say anything. Maybe it's because I've spent my entire life bottling up my own emotions and noticing everyone else's. Jonah has this presence about him that speaks volumes without words. Right now, all he exudes is calmness, and it reassures me in ways I can't even vocalize.

"Okay, all better. The only thing that would've made this even more perfect is if I had a vibrator with me," I tease as I step out.

I've had my car for four years. It was the first thing I bought brand new, and it feels like my biggest accomplishment because I worked so hard to get her. Even though I spent most of my time walking around town, I still loved having her as an option to get around if I needed to.

I had been saving money while working at Amaryllis because I knew exactly what kind of car I wanted. As soon as I had enough, I bought her, even though I could have used the money to help me get by when I was struggling so much. But I definitely don't regret it. I even remember thinking if I couldn't afford my apartment, I could just live out of my car. Probably not the best way of thinking, but she would be spacious enough for me to sleep in the back with the seats folded down. I'm glad my life never hit that kind of rock bottom.

"I can run up and grab one real quick if you need," he winks at me.

"Maybe after dinner," I pat his chest before stepping in front of him and leaping into his arms. Being carried like this is one of my favorite things—feeling his strong arms as I wrap my legs around his waist. He looks so happy when I do it, which makes me want to keep doing it.

Shay and Jonathan are already seated in the ballroom, chatting with Gladys and Giles. When we enter, Gladys's face brightens even more. Not wanting to give the impression that anything was wrong or raise suspicion that our trip was anything more than a vacation, I return her smile as she hurries over, pulling me into a hug.

"I hope you enjoyed your much-needed vacation," she beams at me.

Maybe Jonah really did tell everyone that we were just on vacation. He's a private man, but maybe in an upset state, he would make a big deal out of the situation. Yet, Gladys seems completely convinced we were away on a relaxing getaway and doesn't suspect anything different.

After we finish eating, Jonah invites me to dance with him. Standing, he extends his hand to me. This man has such a hold on me I'd probably do anything he asked. Honestly, I can't think of a single thing I wouldn't do if he requested it. The one glaring takeaway from this entire situation is how much I love him and how hard I will fight for our relationship.

He draws me close to his chest as we sway to the music. Shay and Jonathan watch us for a couple minutes before they get up and join us. She reaches out, our hands briefly intertwining with a gentle squeeze before letting go, each returning to rest on our men.

"You know this is the calm before the storm," Shay remarks, resting her head on Jonathan's chest. "We can dance now, but after they're finished with us, we might not be able to walk straight."

"I can't wait," I grin.

"Let's spice things up tonight," Shay suggests, glancing up at Jonathan.

"That sounds terrifying. I'm in," he chuckles.

"You didn't even hear what it is."

"I don't care. I'm in," he insists.

"We're going to switch partners tonight," Shay announces, looking up at him.

"Fuck yeah, I'm down," Jonathan eagerly agrees.

"Let's go, Kal," Shay says, holding out her hand to me.

Both guys erupt into laughter, and Jonathan interjects, "Even better."

"You're such an idiot," she jokes, giving his shoulder a playful tap, prompting him to lift her by her waist and spin her around. Their love is so carefree, it's refreshing to watch.

As we leave the ballroom, I tell Jonah I'm really tired and that I'm going to sleep in my room tonight. I don't think I have the energy to spend the entire night with us humping each other.

"Of course, baby," he smirks, while guiding me toward his room.

Guess I'm not getting out of sex tonight. I'll just have to let him do all of the work. I don't think I could muster up enough energy to ride him right now, even if I tried. I'll just let him take me for a joy ride and then go back to my room when he's finished.

As we pass by Jonathan's room, he and Shay don't stop. They keep trailing behind us. "You guys joining us tonight?" I wink. They continue following us, and I start to feel like I'm in the middle of the ocean surrounded by sharks, poised to attack their prey. Yet, strangely—I love it. "You both have a shit-eating grin on your faces, and it's making me nervous."

Jonah stops at the double doors to his room, waiting for me to go first.

"You're all acting weird. Start undressing if we're doing this," I grab both door handles and push the doors wide open.

What I didn't anticipate is what I'm greeted with. His once all-black room is no longer all black. I mean, it's still black, but pops of pink, gold, and silver accentuate everything. The black-framed mirrors that hung above each night table have been replaced with diamond-patterned framed pieces, and the lamps on either side of the bed are… pink. Even the black chairs that used to sit in front of the balcony are now pink, resting on a soft, white rug.

The entire room has undergone a transformation. It's almost unrecognizable as the same bedroom. My jaw hangs open as I step inside and look around.

Shay comes in, grabbing my hand and walking me to the expansive master closet. It's one large area, divided into distinct his and hers sections, with three aisles on each side, all perfectly lit. The large island in the center is neatly organized with Jonah's socks and underwear on one side, where I've always had about four pairs on the other side. However, this time, something's different. While Jonah's side remains immaculately packed with his clothing, my side—typically empty—is now brimming with my belongings, including what I had left behind as well as a lot of new clothing.

"I helped decorate and picked out some new clothes for you," Shay says, scanning all the new items.

"What? How? Is this my room now?" I ask, confused.

"I'm a little salty over this since Shay still refuses to move to my room. Maybe I should do the same as Everett and force her," Jonathan says as he looks at Shay. "Let's go to bed, hun, I want my dessert." Shay giggles as she scampers off toward him.

Jonah saunters into the closet, leaning against the island with an air of casual confidence. "Do you like it?"

"I love it," I reply, taking in the room before crossing to him and wrapping my arms around his waist. I'm actually really impressed with Shay's determination to keep separate rooms until they are married, because I can't stand the thought of spending days without Jonah next to me.

A satisfied smile curls his lips. "Good."

Taking his hands in mine, I step back, slowly guiding him from the closet.

When we return to the bed, I strip off my shirt, letting it fall to the floor. My bra, shorts, and panties follow, discarded in a heap. "I want to show you how much I love it," I work at his belt with tantalizing slowness.

"I know you're tired, but you're too sexy. I need to have you," his gaze fixed on me as I remove his belt and drop it to the floor with a clank.

"Well, you might have to do most of the work, but I can certainly saddle up for a couple minutes," I grin, popping the button on his pants.

He reaches for the collar of his shirt and tugs it over his head, baring his chest, and tossing it aside. His pants and boxers follow, and he sits on the bed's edge, leaning back on his palms. "Climb on, cowgirl."

I straddle his lap, placing one knee on each side and settling back on his thighs, my hands resting on his shoulders. "Every time I see the size of that thing, I'm convinced it absolutely won't fit in me," I confess, glancing down at his erection.

"It was made for you; it has to fit. We're like puzzle pieces."

"It fits extra snug," I wag my eyebrows.

"He likes it snug."

"Does he now?" I trace a single finger down his chest until my hand wraps around his girth. I rotate up and down his length, while my other hand squeezes firmly around the base. We both watch as I stroke him. "Do you have any condoms?" The question is a breathless whisper as I lean in to nibble his bottom lip.

His eyes widen momentarily before narrowing, his eyebrows knitting together. "I got rid of all my condoms years ago. Not ever will a condom be between us," he declares, his voice resolute.

A grin spreads across my face at his possessive words. I sit up and position him in place, gradually seating myself onto him. "I was just kidding," I say as my eyes roll back at the familiar stretch.

Wrapping my arms around his neck, I press my chest to his, reveling in the feel of our skin flush together. I rise and fall along his length, coating him in my arousal as I take him in. I swirl my hips, drawing deep moans from his throat, the vibrations coursing through me and heightening my own arousal.

Rocking back, I glide up his length and sway back down, establishing a languid rhythm that leaves us both panting.

"You've got thirty seconds before I bend you over this bed and have my way with you," he warns, his voice a rough growl.

With that, I accept his challenge. I know I can get myself off riding him in thirty seconds. I cling to him, moving over him with desperate urgency. The sound of our bodies slapping together fills the room as we both cry out in ecstasy. My body tenses, and my skin prickles with bliss.

"Times up, cowgirl," he announces.

"Wait, I'm right there," I groan, continuing my movements, my orgasm seconds away.

With a devilish grin, he wraps his arm around my waist and lifts me, causing me to clench down on him as he withdraws. "That's how you want to play, baby?" he growls, flipping me on my stomach, and climbing onto the bed behind me.

I let out a playful giggle and attempt to crawl away, hoping to entice him to chase me. But he grabs my ankle and pulls me back. Lifting my hips off the bed, he shoves a knee between mine, spreading my legs wide. Instead of the penetration I expect, I feel the surprising sensation of his tongue probing my most intimate area… the back hole I *shouldn't* be letting him touch.

"What are you doing?" I pant, torn between wanting to hate how this feels but absolutely *not* hating it at all. I especially want to hate when I feel him push past the entrance, the soft wetness just barely breaching the outer rim, and yet I moan even louder. *Why am I letting him do this? Did I lose my brain?* I definitely must have since I push back against him, allowing him deeper as he brings a finger to my clit and starts rubbing. My hips rock back, craving him filling all my holes, and I don't even care how.

When he pulls back, I wait, knowing he's positioning himself behind me. He doesn't keep me waiting long before he's pushing himself back inside my pussy. I spread my legs wider, loving how good he feels. My head rests on the comforter, my hips moving in sync with him. I feel moisture on my ass—*did he spit on me?* Before I can process, his finger pushes into me, claiming the same hole his tongue just explored. My fists clutch the comforter as I moan uncontrollably.

"Yes," I cry out as he leans over, thrusting in and out, his digit rocking back and forth inside me.

Bringing his free hand around the front of me, he starts circling my clit, and I completely come undone. My body writhes, tightening in ways I never knew possible. An explosion of ecstasy erupts inside me, and I feel like I'm going to burst. I'm crying out and rocking on him in ways I never have before, every muscle spasming as fluid gushes out of me, causing my ass to shake as it experiences what I can only describe as its own orgasmic response. My body feels like it's past the point of feeling good, and now it's on the verge of breaking.

He withdraws both his penis and finger at the same time, and I can feel the liquid burst out, soaking the bed beneath us. Even as my inner muscles continue to spasm, he slides his finger into my center, penetrating me again, hitting my G-spot, causing more liquid to spill out. Collapsing onto the bed, I feel incapable of moving, my body radiating sensations beyond what a single person should experience.

"We soaked the bed," he remarks, leaning over me to plant a kiss on my shoulder.

"I don't think I can move," I say as my body remains immobile.

"I'll get you cleaned up," he says, getting off the bed. When he returns, he starts wiping me up.

"Sorry," I apologize.

"For what?" he asks, continuing to clean the bedding.

"For coming before you could."

"I came on the bed when I was fucking your ass with my tongue," he smirks.

Sitting up, I turn to see if he's joking, but his gaze drifts down between his legs. Following his glance, I realize he wasn't kidding. He really did come on the bed.

"Why'd you do that?" I question, not understanding why he stopped me when I was riding him. At least then, he would have been able to get off inside me.

"Because you felt incredible."

"Are you planning to rinse your mouth out with mouthwash?" I inquire, meeting his gaze.

"I mean, I always brush my teeth before bed, but I think I'm going to skip it tonight," he winks at me.

"Get your cute little bubble butt in that bathroom right now and brush your teeth AND wash your hands."

"Yes, ma'am," he obediently climbs off the bed and returns a while later, crawling onto the bed and straddling me. Hovering above, he stares down at me.

"What?" I giggle, pulling the sheets up so only my eyes peek out.

He gently blows a cool breath across my face, the scent of mint filling the air. Then, he drags the sheet away and plants a soft kiss on my lips. Rolling onto his back on his side of the bed, he lets out a content sigh.

CHAPTER

Six

KALYN

I wake when Jonah's phone rings. He mutters a curse, silencing it before heading to the closet to change into workout clothes. I bolt upright, rubbing sleep from my eyes as I glance at the clock. 7:30 AM. *Where the heck did the time go?*

"Good morning, babe," I yawn, following him into the closet.

"Good morning, gorgeous," he glances over his shoulder at me.

I scan my side of the closet for my work uniform, but it's nowhere to be found. Hmm. I check the dress section, then the drawers along the back wall. Still nothing. "Hey, baby, I can't find my uniform," I call out, continuing to dig through the dresses in case it got mixed in.

"I can help," he offers, striding over and purposefully opening specific drawers.

"Thanks. I'm gonna be late," I huff, groaning in frustration. I can't even find my work shoes. Maybe they forgot to move them over from my old room. I'll check there next if he can't find them.

He pulls out a matching lilac sports bra and snug workout shorts, setting them on the center island. "Get dressed," he instructs, dropping a quick kiss on my cheek before exiting the closet.

I stand there, staring at the outfit, feeling slightly annoyed that I haven't found my work uniform and this is somehow his solution. But then again, Jenevieve isn't here to reprimand me for being late, and technically, I'm with the boss right now, so I doubt anybody else will say anything to me either.

I change into the outfit he set out for me and walk back to the bedroom, where he's waiting on the bed. He looks up from his phone and smiles when he sees me.

"This isn't my work uniform," I point out, climbing into his lap.

He wraps his arms around my waist, his hands cupping my cheeks. "Mmm, I think we're past that," he murmurs, nuzzling my neck. "Your work uniform is officially retired, baby," he softly nips the other side of my neck.

"Where is it though?" I ask, wanting to make sure I can locate it for tomorrow.

"Hopefully in the trash."

"And now I have to spend my mornings working out?" I laugh.

"That's negotiable."

"Oh yeah?"

"Mmhmm," he confirms, sucking on the flesh where his teeth are clamped down.

"So, I can just say no to working out and you'll let me sleep?"

"You can say no to working out and let me work out on top of you," he counters.

"I like that kind of exercise," I say with a subtle moan, tilting my head to give him full access to my neck.

I'M LOUNGING ON A PATIO CHAIR, MY FEET CASUALLY PROPPED ON THE table, as Jonah plays music and skillfully jump-rope shuffles. It's the sexiest sight—sweat glistening on his shirtless torso, accentuating his chiseled abs, and I'm not the only one who appears to be captivated. A quick glance around reveals several other house staff peering out of windows, equally mesmerized.

He's dressed in black workout shorts, a black baseball cap worn backwards, and black athletic shoes—matching the pair he bought for me for "comfort and support." They remind me of the ones he got for us when we went camping, the ones that made Jenevieve look like she was going to puke from disgust. However, no one would be puking at watching this shirtless, sweaty man.

The song ends, and he skillfully catches the jump rope under his foot, letting it fall out of his hands. He approaches me, planting a hand on either side of my armrest, leaning in close, teasing me with a quick lick of my lips before replacing it with a soft, deliberate kiss. Our tongues meet briefly, and then he pulls back, picking up the jump rope from the table and holding it out to me.

"But I was enjoying the view," I protest, trying to get out of having to participate in the exercise, especially since I like sitting in the shade, and don't want to exercise in the sun. Reluctantly, I take the jump rope, lifting my feet off the table and placing them on the ground. I allow him to pull me up, then he cues up another song.

"Do you need a tutorial," he asks, offering to help.

"I can do this in my sleep," I grin confidently. While I'm familiar with how to shuffle and I also know how to jump rope, I've never done them together. I can't imagine combining them together would be too challenging. It only takes one song for my body and brain to sync. "Like riding a bike," I joke as the song concludes, feeling the sweat trickling down my chest.

He approaches, lifting me effortlessly. His arm encircles my waist while his other hand grips between my legs from behind. Wrapping my legs around his waist, he playfully spanks my backside. "You've got a big booty, baby," he says, his eyes sparkling with mischief.

"So do you," I retort, noting his perfectly round bottom.

"I'm gonna bend you over this table and fuck you."

"I'd probably enjoy that," I wipe the sweat from his brow.

He responds with a throaty hum. I lower my leg, and he gently places me back on my feet. Returning to the chair he pulled me from, he settles across from me, lifting my feet onto his lap and resting his hands on my shins.

"I have to go out of town for business; I'll be away for two weeks," he shares, and a twinge of unease hits my stomach at the thought of him being gone. "I was hoping you'd want to come with me," he adds, a hopeful look in his eyes.

"Jonathan always goes with you."

He nods. "Yes, and he's welcome to still come along if he wants, but I want you to join me, regardless."

I consider this for a moment. "Do I get to come to work with you?" I grin. "Maybe dust off my old business skirts and heels," I slide my legs off his lap and stand. "Maybe get to see my baby in action," I add, my smile turning seductive as I sit down, straddling his lap, my knees fitting neatly under the armrest.

He observes the movement, his eyes roaming over my body. "Do you want to watch me at the office, baby?" he places his hands on my hips.

I lean in and kiss him. "Mmhmm," I murmur.

"Well, looks like we'll have to get you some new clothes. We leave on Sunday," he informs me, giving me a playful spank.

"What if I said no to going?" I lift a brow.

"It was a courtesy pretending you had a choice."

Unable to suppress my amusement, I wrap my arms around his neck, burying my face into the crook of his neck, licking and nibbling on his soft flesh. He reclines, resting his head on the chair while lifting his legs onto the seat I had just vacated. His hands shift, firmly cupping my backside, and he tilts his head slightly.

Moans reverberate up his throat.

"How long until you get to the good part?" Jonathan inquires, pulling out a chair across from us and taking a seat.

Jonah keeps his head leaned back on the chair with his eyes closed. "Patience," he advises Jonathan in a relaxed tone.

"Kal, you should show Shay that vacuum suction thing you're doing on Everett's neck. But I have something better she can practice on," he jokes.

I remove my mouth from Jonah's neck and glance at Jonathan, "Maybe YOU should try it on her first; then she might want to reciprocate," I suggest mischievously.

Jonathan bursts into laughter, placing his hands dramatically on his chest. "Oh, snap. Did you just throw shade at me?" he feigns shock as he points at himself in an exaggeratedly appalled motion.

"Hurts doesn't it," I remark.

"God Kal, that was sexy."

"Put in a call to Tabitha; tell her ASAP," Jonah cuts in.

"On it," Jonathan replies, rising from the table. "I'll do that on my way to find Shay. Got a new idea for something I want to try," he playfully taps the bottom of Jonah's shoe with the back of his knuckles. "Send an alert if you two progress beyond neck sucking," he calls out before stepping into the house and closing the door behind him.

"Who's Tabitha?" I ask curiously.

"The only other woman I allow to undress me," he replies.

TABITHA PRESENTS HERSELF BEFORE ME, SPORTING A SLEEK, BLACK A-line haircut that grazes her jawline, oversized glasses, and bold makeup featuring black lipstick and eyeshadow. Despite the dramatic makeup, her attire is a burst of colors, accompanied by extravagant, vibrant jewelry that almost looks like a child styled her. She assesses me critically while Shay, Jonathan, and Jonah watch from chairs behind me, turning the room into a peculiar spectacle with me at its center. Tabitha circles me, scrutinizing my appearance from head to toe. She takes measurements, grabbing handfuls of my breasts says, 'Firm,' before jotting down notes in her pad.

"Can I try that next?" Jonathan asks, and Shay hits his chest.

He coughs and lets out a laugh. "I want to make sure Tabitha has an accurate description of Kal's chest. I'm trying to be helpful."

"That should do it," Tabitha announces, tucking away her pen and notepad.

"That's it?" I ask, puzzled.

"We leave on Sunday," Jonah interjects, rising from his seat.

"Fine," Tabitha replies nonchalantly, casually striding out of the room.

I turn to Jonah. "That's it?" I repeat, still confused.

"That's it," he confirms with a chuckle. "And you didn't even cry once."

"But she didn't even ask what I like or my shoe size," I express, still perplexed, trying to make sense of the brief encounter.

"Trust the process," Jonah advises, smiling as he drapes his arm around my shoulder, guiding me out of the room.

We barely round the corner when a housekeeper nearly smacks right into us. "I'm so sorry, sir," she says, worried, her eyes darting between me and Jonah.

I still find it odd that I was once in her shoes, sharing the same worries she now experiences. I remember when we worked together, and she was one of the housekeepers who talked about how she wanted Jonah to have his way with her. Now, she stands here looking shy, as if she would rather be anywhere else than right here in front of us.

"Don't worry about it," I reassure her, emphasizing that it's really not a big deal. Just as quickly as she nearly collided into us, she hurries around us with her head down and scurries off down the corridor.

"That was bizarre" Jonah says, looking at me and then back to Jonathan and Shay.

"You, sir, are intimidating," I say, smacking his butt.

It feels odd not working while I watch the other maids and mansion staff move about. Everyone treats me as if I had never been a worker to begin with, as if my place the entire time was Mr. Everett's… I don't know what I am. We're more than fuck buddies, yet we've never established or discussed what our relationship status is.

I've only been back for two days, and it feels… different. It used to feel like a job, but now, it feels like I've found my home. Plus, with Jenevieve being gone, it feels like a permanent vacation. Like the time Sam came to visit while Jenevieve was gone for a week. Vanessa was also let go while we were away. I never did hear the specifics. I'm just glad she's gone, and Erica quit shortly after that. Slowly, all the bad weeds are being removed one at a time.

A new head housekeeper, Yesenia, was appointed. She's worked for Jonah since his mansion was built seven years ago. She has three kids that still live with her in town. Only one of them is under the age of eighteen, while the other two are twenty-two and twenty-five. The twenty-five-year-old has two little kids of her own, keeping Yesenia quite busy with all the kids she cares for. Shay told me awhile back that she's pretty sure Jonah owns the home Yesenia lives in because it's fairly large, and she drives a nice minivan. Shay also mentioned she had overheard Jonah telling Yesenia a couple months after she started that Yesenia should focus on her kids' needs first, and they can negotiate her paying rent later. I'm really glad Yesenia got the position; she's not only worked for Jonah the longest, but she's incredibly gentle and kind.

I recall a particular day when I was walking to lunch and witnessed one of the maids being scolded by Jenevieve. After lunch, I saw the girl sitting tearfully on a bench, comforted by Yesenia's gentle words and embrace. Later, I noticed Yesenia talking to Gladys, likely about the incident, but I never heard more about it.

From an outsider's perspective, Jonah might seem like your typical wealthy jerk. However, he's truly the most compassionate man I've ever met. I've encouraged him to try being friendlier and offering a simple hello to the workers, but he says it feels awkward and he doesn't want to inadvertently make someone feel uncomfortable. He literally has no clue about the effect he has on people. He discreetly extends help to people without seeking any kind of recognition for it. I'm certain if anyone pointed out his kindness, he would brush it off like it wasn't a big deal. Even though, to those he helps, it makes all the difference in the world.

Jonathan retreats to his office while Shay and I follow Jonah into his, occupying two adjacent chairs by the window. His phone rings almost immediately as he sits. I watch him answer it, and he begins talking to the person on the other end of the call. I lean over to Shay and whisper, "Jonah fucked my asshole with his tongue last night." Her head snaps in my direction, her hand clutching my arm.

"Excuse the fuck outta me? What did you just say?" she blurts out.

I shush her and glance over to Jonah, checking if he's giving us a 'you're being too loud' look, but he's still typing, oblivious to our conversation. "It was completely unexpected, and I all but rode it."

"Shut the fuck up! Did you love it?" she asks eagerly, scooting to the edge of her chair.

"I did," I confess, feeling a flush of embarrassment color my cheeks.

"Tell me more," she urges.

"Then he went at me from behind, and it felt like he might have spit on me or something because I felt liquid sliding down my ass. And he pushed a finger in."

"So he was boning you while fingering your ass?" she clarifies.

"Yes, and rubbing my bean."

"I love when Jonathan does that," she sighs wistfully.

"I came so hard I thought my vagina was going to stop working. I soaked the bed."

"You know exactly what he's getting you ready for," she taunts.

"Not even going to think about that," I cover my eyes with one hand and raise the other, motioning her to stop.

"One finger, two finger, three finger… Arizona iced tea," she drawls slowly. "If he plays enough beforehand and uses enough lube, he can ease in without causing any tears. It's not like it's the first time something's gone up there; it will just be the first time something that size has. But trust me, it's heavenly," she adds. "It's even better with a dual-action vibrator that stimulates both the vaginal canal and your clit. You'll lose your mind. It's practically a necessity. Maybe Jonathan and I can help," she suggests playfully.

"Help? That sounds ominous."

"Yes, I'll rub your clit, Jonathan can lie down on the bed while you ride him, and Mr. Everett can finally have his way with the hole he's been craving since camping," she explains excitedly.

The thought of her words instantly turns me on, though I know Jonah would never go along with it, and I doubt Jonathan would either. Plus, I certainly don't want to ruin my friendship with Shay. Even if they all agreed, I don't think I would go along with it. "Cute idea, but never going to happen."

"Never say never," she grins mischievously.

That night, with Jonah peacefully asleep beside me, Shay's words echo in my mind. I try to ignore them, but the tingling between my legs only intensifies. Clamping my legs together makes it worse, as it pinches the bundle of nerves, heightening the sensitivity.

Quietly slipping out of bed, I grab my pillow and retreat to the closet. I set it down on the floor and tiptoe to Jonah's side of the closet, where an assortment of sex toys awaits in one of the drawers on the wall. My hand instinctively reaches for the pink vibrator Shay mentioned, designed to provide simultaneous internal and clitoral stimulation.

Returning to my pillow, I lower myself over top of it, straddling it between my thighs. Envisioning Jonathan lying beneath me, naked. With closed eyes, I lower myself onto the vibrator, relishing the sensation of it filling me while teasing my clit. I imagine Jonathan moaning beneath me as I sink down, not turning it on but allowing my body time to adjust. I move up and back down, holding the vibrator in place on my pillow. *He feels so good*, and I imagine Shay expertly rubbing my clit. With my free hand, I take my middle finger in my mouth, coating the entirety with saliva.

My nipples are peaked, and everything feels electrifyingly good. I imagine Jonathan's hands roaming up my body to my breasts and squeezing, while Shay continues circling between my legs. Panting, I rock my hips on the vibrator, removing my finger from my mouth and bringing it around to my backside, circling the rim before slowly inserting it. Lost in ecstasy, I sway my hips back and forth, each movement sending waves of pleasure through me.

With trembling hands, I push the button on my vibrator, a soft red glow emanating in the darkened room. Struggling to stifle my cries, I surrender to the overwhelming bliss. All three of them—Jonah, Jonathan, and Shay—working me over in unison. Jonah takes me from behind, as I rock my finger in and out of me, he moves my hair to one shoulder, holds my waist, and sucks on my neck. Jonathan continues feeling my breasts, rubbing my nipples, while Shay's hands never cease their tantalizing circles.

Shay shifts her position, sitting directly on Jonathan's face as he brings his hands to her thighs, wrapping around them firmly and sucking between her legs. Leaning forward, mine and her mouths barely touch, melding together.

My movements quicken as my orgasm approaches, the intensity overwhelming. I crash over, coming all over the vibrator and my hand. Moaning softly, I continue to rock until the waves of pleasure subside, the room slowly coming back into focus under the soft glow of the floor lights.

What the fuck did I just do? I question, a sense of guilt washing over me. I feel dirty for even getting turned on by the thought. I shouldn't have ever done that—indulged in those fantasies. I hate how I feel in the aftermath, like I did all three of them dirty. Like I've betrayed them.

Slowly, I slide off the vibrator, my hands trembling as I discard it in the trash under my bathroom sink and wash my hands. The pillowcase, too, is tainted; I rip it from my pillow and fling it into the laundry hamper.

Of course, my mind doesn't want me to sleep either because I go on to dream about the same things. Only this time, the fantasies are even more vivid.

In my dream, I'm full-blown fucking Jonathan. We're a tangle of flesh, our bodies slapping together with heated intensity, taking turns with who is going to ride whom, while Shay and Jonah watch. He lies beneath me, his hands grasping my hips as I ride him, my back arching with each thrust. His fingers dig into my skin, guiding my movements as he groans.

Next, I find myself with Shay, her body soft and yielding beneath mine, while Jonah and Jonathan stand close by, watching intently. Shay's moans fill the room as I kiss her deeply. My hands roam over her curves, teasing and caressing every inch of her. Jonah moves behind me, his hands drifting over my back, as I wait for what he'll do next.

The scene shifts again, and now I'm grinding against Jonathan's face, just as I imagined Shay did. His mouth works expertly, while Shay teases my nipples, pinching and rolling them as I writhe in pleasure. Jonah stands at the foot of the bed, stroking himself as he watches us, his eyes filled with lust.

Scenario after sexual scenario plays out, each more intense than the last. I'm entangled in passionate encounters with each of them, their touches driving me wild. We explore every possible combination, every fantasy coming to life in my mind.

When I wake, I'm covered in sweat. The bed is empty, and I can see it's 10 AM. I scramble to the shower, trying to cleanse away the remnants of all my terrible thoughts. I literally feel like I spent the entire night cheating, and it makes me feel guilty.

Dressing as fast as I can, I decide to do the only thing that could either make me feel better or absolutely worse—going to the stables… to see Brad.

CHAPTER

Seven

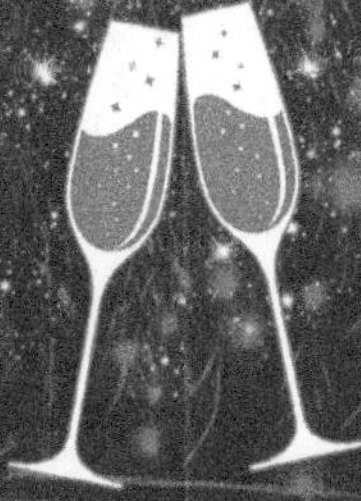

KALYN

I find myself heading toward the stables, seeking out Brad. Walking down the road, I pass the first stable, but Brad is nowhere to be seen. A new hire, working in this area, notices me and raises an eyebrow in surprise. A lot has changed since I last worked here, even though it was fairly recent. The housekeeping staff now focuses solely on cleaning the mansion, which seems obvious. Yet, back then, I was always sent to work in the stables, despite it not being my job. Now, there is staff specifically hired for that purpose.

"Hey, Kalyn. Is there something you need?" she asks, a hint of concern in her voice. I'm a little surprised she knows me by name, as I've never seen her before.

"Do you know where I can find Brad?"

"Why?" she asks defensively. My face must reflect my slight surprise at her question because she quickly starts to back pedal.

"I mean, is there something I might be able to help you with?" she corrects herself.

"No, I'm looking for Brad," I reiterate.

"If I see him, I'll let him know you stopped by. No need to wait out here," she says almost as if she's rushing to dismiss me. This instantly starts to irritate me; she has no authority over where I go on this property. Yet, she acts as if I don't belong here and my presence is bothering her.

"Well, well, well, Wanda, looks like you just can't resist me," Brad chimes from behind me.

I turn around to see him grinning broadly. "Wow, it only took me two seconds to regret coming out here."

He smirks. "Coming to ride a stallion?"

"There are no stallions out here."

"Want me to prove you wrong?" he challenges, leaning against the doorway and crossing his arms over his chest.

As I observe the jealous stare from the worker, it becomes clear that he's slept with her and she's now racking her brain, questioning whether he and I have also been intimate. Some things never change.

When I stand there awkwardly, he turns to her and says, "She found who she was looking for, you can get back to work," without even attempting to be nice about it. She glances between us before walking back down the stable alleyway. She's pretty—incredibly pretty—and I just don't understand why he continues to do this to all these women. Then again, why stop when they just keep throwing themselves at you? Ohhh, I don't know, maybe self-respect and respect for others.

As soon as she's out of sight, I turn back to Brad, who's grinning at me. I've avoided coming out here because I really no longer have any reason to, now that I'm not being forced to work out here and since Jonah and I have gotten together. Brad surely is aware of mine and Jonah's relationship now, and he doesn't appear to be bothered. The last time I was here, I was a huge bitch to him. Though he deserved it, he's never done anything crappy to me personally. I probably would have held my grudge a lot longer, but Amber seemed to move on quite fast after he slept with her and broke her heart. It was about two weeks before she was moving on with that sadness to Sam.

"Wipe that smirk off your face," I match his stance, crossing my arms over my chest.

"It's a smile, Wanda; I'm smiling. You should try it sometime."

"I do smile… to people I like. I guess if you've never seen a smile, that should tell you everything you need to know about how I feel," I eye him up and down, pretending to judge him, which only makes his grin widen. "All jokes aside, I need to apologize for the way I treated you," I admit, regretting being so mean to him. Even though, at the time, I felt he deserved it for sleeping with Amber and not having enough self-control to keep my name out of his mouth while doing so, I didn't need to be so rude. In a weird way, I truly think he means well.

"Did you come to make it up to me?"

"Well, I can already feel the regret in offering an apology creeping in," I counter.

"You never have to apologize to me, Wanda. I already knew you couldn't stay mad at me. You're like a bug drawn to car headlights at night."

"You're so full of yourself. I should just turn and walk away right now," I tease.

"Go for it. Not like it would be the first time I picked your little ass up and dragged you back."

"I'd just kick and scream."

"Yep, you've done that before too."

I remember him doing precisely that: plucking me right off the ground and carrying me out of the stables before I could rip all Vanessa's hair out in true "cat fight" fashion. "I guess I should also thank you for offering up your shower to me."

"Definitely don't need to apologize for that. We both know I got the better deal."

"You're a pervert," I say, knowing full well he enjoyed every second of a naked woman in his bathroom.

"I'm not a pervert. I'm a man, and you're a very well-developed woman, and you bent over and showed me a meal I'd gladly devour."

I roll my eyes. "Unfortunately for you, that meal belongs to someone else," I mirror his smirk.

"Then I dream of another man's meal."

"I'm sure all your dreams are of other men's meals."

He reaches out and boops the tip of my nose. "Wrong again, Wanda."

"Does it bother you that you'll never have this meal?" I step closer and playfully shove his shoulder.

"You wouldn't regret it if you let me have it," he winks.

"Gross," I scrunch my nose at him.

"If you saw me at a coffee shop, you'd absolutely find me mouthwatering."

I refuse to admit he's right. "We're not at a coffee shop, and unfortunately for you, you have a sleazy reputation. Therefore, I'd offer nothing to you other than the privilege of staring at my ass as I crop dust past you."

"Good god, you really have a way with words. You're like a true poet," he lets out a laugh. "However, since we're offering things up, I'd like to offer you the story of how I got to do the honors of firing Vanessa."

"Wait, what!"

"Oh yeah. Security found interesting footage of her planting jewelry in your room. Everett said to get her ass out. I asked to do the honors, and he was happy to oblige."

My jaw drops open. "She planted the jewelry in my bag! She literally told everyone she saw me stealing it!" I can still feel how I felt in that moment when Vanessa accused me of stealing Antoinette's jewelry, especially in front of other maids, Jenevieve, Antoinette, and Jonah. I was mortified at even the thought, let alone someone thinking I would actually do something like that.

"Her and Jenevieve had a little chat in the hall, then Vanessa was like a little raccoon stealing the diamonds. So, we concluded Jenevieve put her up to it, but Vanessa's sticky ass fingers are the ones to commit the crime."

"What'd she do when you fired her? What'd you say to her? Where was I?" My questions are coming out faster than he can answer.

"I kicked her ass out the day you and Everett left for vacation."

Though Jonah has never given me a reason to doubt him, the fact that everyone really does believe we were just on vacation makes me feel a lot better. I feel like I was made to look like a fool by Antoinette, but when he said he didn't tell anyone what happened, he hadn't said anything other than we went on vacation.

"I need more than that," I finally say. "I need details. A play-by-play."

"I paid her a surprise visit to her room, asked if she was ready to get busy, and then told her to pack her shit and get out. She tried protesting, but with the video footage of her planting the jewelry and entering and leaving your room, she knew she was done." He shrugs like it's no big deal.

"I should be so happy over this yet I kind of feel... I don't know, bad,"

"Don't feel bad. Her entire goal was to get you fired, Wanda. She got what she brought upon herself."

"Doesn't it feel weird to you though? You used to sleep with her," I say, feeling a twinge of awkwardness at the mere thought of it. Imagining him having to escort her out makes me want to nervous stretch. She doesn't seem like somebody who would be embarrassed by that; if anything, she was probably too furious to have cared about the fact she must have looked so pathetic.

"She didn't have a golden pussy and she was a shit person; I don't care," he shrugs. "The only thing that would have made it better is if security escorted her out while you and I got it on on the porch—a farewell, if you will."

"Yeah, and then she would walk away knowing that after we finished, you'd ignore me," knowing that's exactly what she would have expected. Brad doesn't get serious with anyone, and he would have happily moved on to the next woman willing to spread her legs for him.

"I'd never ignore you, Wanda; you're an equal contestant to my snark."

"The second someone shows you attention, you slink away," I roll my eyes, knowing this to be fact since I started here. He sleeps with anyone willing to sleep with him, then treats them like they shouldn't dare talk to his royal highness.

"Wanna test that theory?" he quirks a brow.

"I 100% do NOT want to test anything with your slutty ass," I laugh.

"You're breaking my heart, Wanda," he grabs his chest, then pushes himself off the wall. "Come with me," he motions toward the golf cart and pats the seat next to him as he climbs in.

Staring for just a moment, I decide getting in the golf cart with him sounds like a breath of fresh air compared to going back to the mansion and inevitably running into Jonah, Jonathan, or Shay. With a sigh, I walk over and climb in next to him. He watches with the biggest smirk on his face, then pushes his sunglasses from the top of his head down to his nose and moves along the road that encircles the horse track, heading towards the building across from the main stable where Claire always told us if we needed anything she would be working in there. He drives inside past plastic coverings hanging at the door, presumably to keep the cold air inside, and parks by the doors, then climbs off. While I've never been in here before, I know this is where Claire grooms the horses. It must be nice to work in here during the summertime, feeling the coolness after being outside in the heat. Jenevieve never cared when we were half an inch from death with heat exhaustion. She probably would have preferred that for us—me for sure.

We walk to a large area where a horse stands by the wall, her belly severely swollen. She gazes outward with a look of misery and discomfort. It's clear she's pregnant. Despite the pleasant coolness inside, I can't imagine how uncomfortable it must be to carry such a large baby.

Brad unlatches the gate and steps inside. "This is Winona. She's due in three weeks," he introduces, walking over to her and affectionately petting her. Winona responds with a gentle neigh, leaning her head closer to him, clearly enjoying the attention, her ears swiveling back and forth. She appears comfortable in his presence, suggesting he has cared for her or spent considerable time with her here.

The more time I spend around horses, the more fascinated I become. I would have thought a pregnant horse would only want the company of her caregiver or someone she trusts. If that's true, then Brad must have bonded with her. It's intriguing to witness Brad in this role—gentle and caring towards a mother horse. It contrasts sharply with his usual demeanor, particularly his casual disregard for women.

"Would you like to come pet her?" he asks.

Hesitantly, I respond, "Will she be okay if I do? I don't want to stress her out."

"Get in here, Wanda," he motions for me to open the gate wider and step inside.

"Hi Winona," I greet uncertainly, holding out my hand tentatively, debating whether to let her sniff me first before trying to touch her.

She takes a step towards me, and I lean in, gently brushing my hand down her muzzle.

"Can you already determine the baby's gender?" I inquire, observing Brad tenderly caress her belly.

"Yes, she had an ultrasound, so we already know he's male."

"How do you know when it's time for her to deliver? Does she receive an epidural?" I ask, curious about the birthing process.

"We have everything prepared for her in here. Hopefully, she won't require any medical assistance and will be able to give birth naturally."

"Yikes," I grimace, my face reflecting discomfort. That sounds terrible.

"Wanna find out?" he wags his eyebrows. "What it feels to give birth without an epidural."

"Oh yeah? Are you gonna attempt to impregnate me with your tiny little clit?" I quip back.

He stifles a laugh, mindful not to startle Winona. "Well, I see you haven't run low on sass lately."

"Only the best for you, Bert. You did say your name was Bert, right? Is that short for anything? Bertha perhaps?"

"Nah, it's an acronym actually. Buff Erotic Rendezvous Tonic. I'm an aphrodisiac, Wanda."

"The fact that that rolled off your tongue so easily kind of grosses me out," I widen my eyes. Brad is witty, I'll give him that. I'd say it makes sense why women seem to love him, but I know he doesn't let many see this funny side of him.

"You love it," he quips.

"Okay, what's mine?" I challenge.

"Sorry, you're not special enough to get one," he shrugs.

"Okay, smarty pants, make one up," I insist.

"What do I get in return?"

"You can get a knuckle sandwich or me hurling horse shit at you," I grin widely.

"Well, you already offered to hurl horse shit at me the day we met, so let's switch it up and go with a knuckle sandwich."

"You're stalling," I accuse.

"Maybe."

Crossing my arms, I tap my foot impatiently, making sure to exaggerate the movement.

"...Wildly... no no, Wet... Alluring... Naughty... Dick... Ass," he says, seeming so proud of himself.

I slowly shake my head. "You're such an idiot." I try to hold back my laughter but fail, letting it out after a moment of keeping a straight face.

"Thank you," he joins in. "That was pretty good though, right?"

"Not even a little bit. It was quite lame. But you can have a do-over. I'll let you tell me it next time I see you," I offer.

"Next time, huh? Already planning a second date."

"Have you ever in your life actually taken someone out on a date?"

His face curls up into a grin and he just stares at me.

"What?"

"I can't answer that; you'll just get jealous of the women I've taken on dates," he says, leaning over to kiss Winona's belly.

Watching him do that leaves me briefly stunned. It was in the moment and the purest thing I've ever seen him do. I love giving him shit, but this—I don't even want to bring attention to it because I want him to always continue doing things like that without realizing he's doing it.

"Not jealous; I feel bad for the women," I smirk.

"I think I've figured out your love language… you're so mean to me, Wanda, it's actually turning me on."

My eyes glance at his crotch, and I know he doesn't miss it but doesn't mention it or even make a joke, so I try to breeze past it. "Do you wake up every morning and think to yourself how exhausting you're going to be to everyone who has to interact with you?"

"I wake up every morning thinking about you."

"Yuck."

"Not yuck at all. It's quite satisfying," he bites his bottom lip and lifts his brows.

"You should be arrested for violating me in your dreams," I muse.

"Got handcuffs?" he winks.

Coming out here is exactly what I needed. It keeps my mind occupied for hours. After spending over an hour with Winona, we move to a bench swing on the opposite side of the building, just outside the back doors. We talk about everything and nothing for another hour. When I finally tell him I need to head back, he drives me to the back of the mansion on the golf cart.

I step off and catch him staring intently. Placing my hands on the top of the golf cart, I lean my forehead on my arm, searching for the right words. "Thank you" is all I can manage to say. What I don't voice is thank you for forgiving me so easily, thank you for keeping my mind busy for hours of the day that I would be confronted with the memories of what I did last night and the people I thought about with them, and thank you for being such a good friend. But all I say is "thank you."

"You're welcome," he replies with a smile.

"We leave tomorrow for a couple weeks, but when I get back, maybe I'll stop by and pick on you some more."

I notice a flicker of disappointment when I mention leaving again, but he quickly masks it. "I look forward to it," he says, saluting me before pulling away.

CHAPTER

Eight

KALYN

We arrive on the tarmac and step out of the vehicle. A private jet awaits us, and a laugh escapes my lips as I observe its size—it's even bigger than the first one we flew in.

"Shall we?" Jonah invites, extending his hand to me. Instinctively, I take it, and we walk toward the stairs of the plane. I don't know why I'm so nervous. We just did this a couple days ago. Maybe my anxiety stem from the way the flight attendants treated me last time, and I can already see them standing at the door, smiling and waiting to greet Jonah. This is probably the highlight of their day.

As we board, two different, attractive flight attendants greet only him with giddy waves and giggles, completely ignoring me.

As he guides me past them, I offer a courteous nod but receive disapproving looks in return, just like the attendants before.

I inwardly muse, '*This is going to be uncomfortable,*' as Jonah guides us to a pair of leather seats in the middle of the jet on the right-hand side. Just like last time, he buckles me in before fastening his own seatbelt.

The pilot approaches Jonah, discussing our departure in the next ten minutes.

"How long is the flight?" I ask, feeling my palms grow clammy with nerves.

"Two and a half hours, but it will go by quickly," he reassures me, resting his head on the headrest but turning to smile at me.

The plane doors close, and the two flight attendants buckle into their seats at the front of the cabin, while the co-pilot shuts the cockpit door. I notice the attendants whispering to each other and glancing in our direction. Jonah seems completely unfazed, but it's all I can focus on. As the plane taxis on the tarmac, my stomach twists—I hate this part. I watched *Final Destination* with Sam and his sister and have hated flying ever since.

As we prepare for takeoff, I wipe my sweaty palms on my dress. Jonah gently grabs my cheek, turning my face toward his, and presses his lips against mine. Caught off guard, and all my previous worries vanish in an instant. There must be a word for what his mouth does. He possesses a silver tongue—not only can he entrance people with his words, but when he kisses me, my brain turns to complete mush. He moves in ways that make my panties drip with jealousy, leaving my mouth torn between wanting to hold him in place and wanting to relinquish that tongue to my pussy.

His lips part from mine, and as I open my eyes, they lock onto his beautiful blue gaze.

"I don't even have to look to see your third leg made it on the flight," I say, glancing down at his rock-hard erection straining against his pants.

"Thank god," he whispers. "I was worried I may have left it at home."

"What ever would we have done?" I whisper back.

"I'm certain we would have found a way to manage. But since we all made it on the flight, want me to show you what we can do with it?" His hand rests lightly on my thigh, sending flutters through my belly. As his fingers trace a path up my leg toward my panties, my arousal intensifies, and my thighs part involuntarily.

"Yes," I whisper, my voice trembling.

I hear his seat belt unclasp, and his free hand returns to my face, pulling me in for another kiss, reclaiming my lips, and with the first brush of his hand on the outside of my panties, my legs spread wider for him. Jonah has never been one to tease without following through. I'm so turned on; all I want is to be on him, skipping the foreplay and going straight to the part where I get to ride him.

I reach down, struggling to unclasp my seatbelt, fumbling with the unfamiliar mechanism that Jonah fastened. His lips curl up as he secures the strap more firmly around me.

Between ragged breaths, I manage to get out, "I want to ride you."

His fingers slide my panties to the side and effortlessly glide between my wet lips, slowly beginning to rub. My hips lift towards his touch, craving more pressure, and I begin to rock against him, eager to speed up the process.

His grin deepens as his tongue continues to work wonders. I'm desperate for more; I want him to penetrate me. Placing my hand over his, I try to guide it deeper, but he shakes his head.

When I realize he's not going to give me that yet, I hike my leg up, reaching down so I can get my own fingers in me. We can work together to accomplish the shared goal—my orgasm. I almost make it when he stops rubbing me, catching my hand before it reaches my entrance.

"What are you doing?" I whisper, my eyes opening to meet his.

"I've got this under control."

"Either your fingers, my fingers, or your cock are going to fuck me. You're taking too long."

"You're being impatient, baby."

Reluctantly, I try to relax and enjoy this while he's giving it to me, but all I want to do is hump him. My chest rises and falls as he shifts my panties aside again, resuming his delicate circles. His lips find my neck, placing a tender kiss before his teeth softly bite down.

"I have very important work tomorrow, babe. Don't give me a hickey."

"That, you do," he murmurs. "I'll be good." His initial nibbles turn softer, tracing lower along my neck.

His touch is slow, igniting a trail of anticipation until he grazes my entrance, teasing the outer edges with tantalizing strokes. "Payback will be a bitch if you fuck with me—" The words die on my tongue, trailing off into a breathy gasp as he stretches two fingers deep inside, skillfully finding the ache in my core and appeasing it.

My eyes flutter closed, head tipping back as he moves with a confident rhythm, his breath hot against my cheek, sending delightful shivers down my spine. "Were you trying to talk shit to me, baby?" he questions, his voice low and sultry, his touch quickening.

"Yes," I moan, unable to resist the urge to grind my hips against his hand for more friction.

I pant louder, my sounds intensifying as he finds my G-spot and rocks perfectly. "Maybe I should go slower," he suggests, his voice a whisper in my ear.

"Don't you dare," I gasp, my desperation evident as I plead for the release that only he can give me. "I need to come."

His grin widens, his fingers momentarily slowing.

"Jonah," I growl, my teeth clenched in frustration.

"Yeah, baby," his amusement evident in his voice. Then I feel my seatbelt release, and his fingers pick up their pace, moving faster and deeper until my entire ass comes off the seat. The orgasm doesn't creep in; it crashes over me explosively, wringing moans from deep within as I squeeze my eyes shut, my body quaking with aftershocks. My hips move fluidly against his hand until I'm trembling in his grasp, my senses overwhelmed by the pleasure.

"Jonah," I pant.

"Yeah, baby," he chuckles softly, his voice laced with satisfaction.

My breathing is uneven as my body begins to come down from the high and relax again. As the last waves of bliss fade, I slowly start to settle back into the seat while he withdraws his hand until I fully collapse down, completely spent with a satisfied sigh.

Jonah snaps his fingers imperiously, summoning one of the flight attendants to our side. The woman hurries over, a bright smile plastered on her face. "Yes, sir, how can I help you?"

"A towel. Now," he demands sharply. She quickly scurries away, returning moments later with a pristine white towel. He snatches it from her hand, his movements abrupt as he dismisses her. The contrast between his brusque treatment of the attendant and the gentleness he shows me is somewhat intriguing.

We settle back in our seats; he pulls out his laptop to reply to emails while I gaze out the window.

A flicker of satisfaction fills me in the fact he just finger banged me practically in front of the flight attendants, and I hope they understood that as he is *mine*. Yet, as that smug thought flutters across my mind, it's replaced by images of him touching them with the same intimacy. I try to shove the thoughts away but a nagging voice in the back of my mind insists they're not merely fantasies. The way the women stare at him—with familiarity, with longing—makes my stomach twist with jealousy. I sneak a glance at them, finding them engrossed in hushed conversation at the front of the cabin. They don't notice me watching because they're so fixated on him.

I want to ask him if he's slept with either of them, but the question feels like a dangerous Pandora's box. I'm not sure I'm prepared to hear his response. Instead, I turn back to the window, watching as the landscape unfurls beneath me. The pilot had warned of potential turbulence earlier, but I hadn't noticed any. If there was any, Jonah finger banged me through the entirety of it.

Grabbing my purse, I pull it open and retrieve my cell phone. I have a new text from Shay, a picture of her and Jonathan on the private jet we flew on the other day. Shay's holding her phone out, smiling, while Jonathan leans into her, sticking his tongue out at the camera. They are so adorable; I can hardly stand it.

I open the camera app on my phone, hold it out, and smile, making sure Jonah's in the frame, oblivious as he types away on his laptop. I capture the photo and send it off to Shay.

KALYN:

[IMAGE] Where are you two off to?

I had no idea they were traveling too. I assumed they were staying home while we were away. Now I understand why we have a bigger private jet—they have the smaller, yet still enormous one. I instantly get a text back. Shay's scowling, disapproving, while

Jonathan rests his head on her shoulder, eyes rolled back dramatically.

SHAY:

[IMAGE] Mr. Everett can't even look at the camera for 2 seconds? Shame Shame

KALYN:

In his defense, I didn't tell him I was taking the picture

SHAY:

No excuses. Punish him. *wink*

Raising my camera again, I hit record, holding it out as if to take another picture. "Baby," I say, looking at the phone screen. He looks up from his laptop, then at the camera, and instantly straightens, leaning in with a smile. "It's a video. Shay says I have to punish you because she and Jonathan sent a cute picture, you weren't looking at the camera in ours," I explain, turning to him.

His face remains cheerful. "I didn't know we were taking a picture," he admits, still looking at the camera. "Sorry, baby," he adds, resting his chin on my shoulder and softly kisses my jaw before refocusing on my phone.

"What about Shay saying you need punished?"

"I completely agree with her," he replies casually.

Smiling at his response, I ask Shay on the video, "Okay, Shay, he agrees. How would you like me to do it?" I end the video with a smile and send it off to her.

He sets his laptop on the table in front of us, then leans back into me. "Sorry, baby. I wasn't trying to ignore you."

"I know. Look how cute," I say, pulling up the first picture they sent and showing him our conversation, along with the picture I took.

"You're so beautiful," his gaze softens as he looks at the picture.

I show him the last picture they sent just as a new video message comes in. Jonathan leans over the armrest, saying, "Give him a blow job," with a shudder as if the idea is top-tier punishment.

"I agree. Give him a blow job and make sure you use all teeth. Men go crazy for it." Shay turns to watch Jonathan's reaction, and his face contorts in disgust, making her burst into laughter.

"Fuck that," he tells her.

"I thought you loved that?" she teases innocently.

Jokingly, he says, "Yeah, I probably would. Good luck, Everett."

"Take off his belt and wrap it around his neck. Let's see those reins, baby," Shay teases before the video ends.

I turn to Jonah, curious about his reaction. "There's a bedroom in the back," he winks.

I stand, taking his hand, and lead him toward the rear of the plane. Pulling up my camera, I take another picture and send it to Shay so she can see we're going to the bedroom. Inside, I place my phone on the table by the door, then turn to watch Jonah as he grins while he removes his belt and drapes it over his shoulder. Stepping closer, he slips off my dress and throws it aside. "You can either take off your panties, or I'm going to rip them off," he warns, and I stand there smirking at him.

He steps closer, and in one quick motion, he turns me around, tightening his belt around my neck before pushing me onto the bed. I land on my hands and knees, catching sight of us in the mirror on the back wall. He's so dominating and sexy. I watch as he wraps the belt's end around his hand and pulls, forcing me up onto my knees, the leather biting into my skin in the most delicious way.

My face reddens as a tingling sensation spreads across my skin, and my breath becomes shallow. "Is this what you had in mind? Reins, right?" he murmurs, his voice a low growl. I gasp when my panties are torn away, the sound of tearing fabric heightening my arousal. My arm instinctively reaches up to encircle his neck, feeling the heat of his body against mine.

He loosens the belt slightly, allowing me to suck in a desperate breath before grabbing a fistful of my hair and shoving me back down onto the bed. His knee presses between my legs, and I part them for him, feeling the cool air against my wetness. I glance into the mirror and see him undoing his pants, revealing his glorious, throbbing cock.

"Is this how you wanted to punish me?" he asks, adjusting the belt again and ramming his cock into me with forceful precision. "You want my belt around my neck?" he questions, cinching it tighter. The pressure makes my vision blur, but the pleasure is intoxicating.

I tilt my head back as far as I can, trying to lessen the constriction, but this only makes his eyes gleam with a dark satisfaction as he slams into me. When he loosens the belt, I cry out, my screams filling the room as he moves in and out, relentless and unyielding.

"Tell me you want me to choke you," he pants.

I look in the mirror, watching him. I see his eyes fixated on his cock sliding in and out of me, his lips slightly parted. "Choke me," I pant, and the belt tightens again.

My body responds eagerly, my core contracting as a wave of heat spreads through me. I'm getting really good at this whole expelling-all-the-fluid-inside-me thing because I can already feel my body preparing for it. He pulls the belt so tight my vision starts to blacken, and it becomes harder to breathe, yet I love it—I crave it.

When he releases the belt, I feel the part he was holding land on my back. His hands grab my hips, pulling me into him as he slams into me with such force that, if he weren't holding on to me, he would send me flying across the bed. My body instantly spills over, crying out with orgasmic bliss. He shoves me down flat on the bed and straddles my legs, his hips pumping in and out, his hands braced on either side of me on the bed as he groans. His relentless thrusting prolongs the aftershocks of my own orgasm until he finally slams into me and stays buried, his cock pulsating as he spills inside me.

He collapses over me, his face in my neck, until the pulsing stops. We lie here, letting our breathing steady. He sits up, gently removing the belt from my neck and leaning down to kiss my shoulder before slowly pulling out of me. As he withdraws the last inch, he slaps my ass, sending a final jolt of pleasure through my exhausted body.

Rolling over, I smirk up at him. "Pretty sure that would be considered a punishment to *me*."

"I felt so punished," he grins, standing from the bed. He slides open a door to the left of the bed, and the light flickers on. "Come clean up," he says, walking inside.

Relieved to see it's a bathroom, I sigh, glad I won't have to walk out there naked. "Do I just go pantyless now?" I ask, grabbing my dress from the bed.

"Yes," he fastens his belt then slaps my ass again. "Did you see your neck?" He points.

Leaning over the bed, I look in the mirror at the head of the bed and see the glaring red mark his belt left on my pale skin. "Cute," I say sarcastically, as I stand to put my dress back on.

There's a knock on the door, and I hear one of the flight attendants. "Sir, we will be landing soon. We need to buckle up."

I walk to the door, and he holds out my phone for me to take. Sliding the door open, I catch the attendant's eyes drifting to my neck and back up, jealousy flaring in her gaze. Smiling, I take Jonah's hand and walk past her back to our original seats.

I sit down, and as always, he buckles me in before fastening his own seatbelt. I notice I have four new messages and three Face-Time calls from Shay, so I pull them up. The first picture is of her looking shocked. Scrolling past her messages, I find the last message I sent. Apparently, the last one *I* sent was a video Jonah took. The actual last one I sent was of me leading Jonah to the bedroom. Shay's response is a zoomed-in picture of the background, where the two flight attendants look angry.

SHAY:

[IMAGE] HA HA HA HA! If looks could kill

KALYN:

[VIDEO]

I click on the video, and Jonah's face fills the screen. "Is this what you had in mind? Reins, right?" he says, leaning in, holding the camera out to show the belt around my neck, fisting it as my face turns a deeper shade of red. Then, he tears my panties off, making me gasp. This is actually really sexy, and damn, my tits look good. We could star in a porno, and I'd happily watch it on repeat.

"That was sexy," I say, glancing at him as he leans over to watch the video with me. "Want me to send it to you?"

"I already sent it to myself," he grins.

"Nice," I say as I go to the next message.

SHAY:

YESS!

SHAY:

Facetime

SHAY:

Mr. Everett answer the Facetime

SHAY:

You suck!

I laugh at her persistent messages and the fact that she tried to Facetime us. Holding my phone out, I click record again. "I think we did that wrong," I lift my chin to show the red marks on my neck. Bringing the phone closer, I whisper, not wanting to be heard—like anyone could hear us anyway, "I don't even have panties on now," and Jonah grins beside me. I end the video and send it to her.

Jonah is still leaned over in my chair, and I lean back into him. "Do I get like a certificate or a pin or something?"

He looks confused.

"Pretty sure I just joined the mile-high club, or whatever that is Shay was talking about," I explain.

His head falls back and he lets out a hearty laugh. I playfully hit his chest, making him laugh even harder. Reaching down, he unlatches my seatbelt, and I stand, pinching his cheeks between my fingers before kissing him. "C'mon, Romeo," I say, heading toward the front of the plane. He hurries after me, slinging his laptop bag over his shoulder.

The flight attendants stand by the exit, their expressions almost snarling as they attempt to appear cheerful. "Thank you," I offer sweetly as I exit and climb down the stairs.

"Mr. Everett, sir, hope you had a smooth flight," a gentleman in a suit says, holding open the door to a sleek black SUV, similar to the one Jonah has back home.

"Thanks, Royel," Jonah replies, holding his hand out to help me in.

My nose is practically squished against the window the entire drive. I've never been in a city this big before. It feels intimidating yet exciting.

CHAPTER Nine

KALYN

The thirty-minute drive feels endless due to heavy traffic, leaving me increasingly nervous as we approach our destination. Everything here feels so different. At the mansion, we're secluded in a fairytale—it felt right. But here, we're stepping into the real world. This is where Jonah reigns as CEO, commanding billions that allow everyone back home to live in luxury. It's an intimidating concept. Though he's still the same man, he seems so much larger here. My nerves are jumbled, similar to the way they were the first time we kissed. I felt nervous and out of place, yet I needed him. Now, even though I know him, it still feels terrifying.

The elevator doors open on the 35th floor, revealing a lavish hallway. We step out, and I glance down both sides, taking in the elegance. Jonah takes my hand and leads me to the left. At the end of the short hallway is a large door. As he swings it open, I'm greeted by the jaw-dropping sight of his high-rise condo. The foyer has marble floors so shiny they appear wet, and soft, recessed lighting that lends a warm glow. The walls are lined with subtle artwork, and I glance at each piece as we pass it.

We move into the open living room, which has Jonah's style written all over it—modern and classic. Cream-colored furniture, floor-to-ceiling windows giving a breathtaking view of the surrounding skyscrapers, and a sleek fireplace is at the front of the living room. Attached to the living room is a large, open-concept kitchen with stainless steel appliances and custom cabinetry, centered around a large marble island.

Casually, Jonah gestures toward the kitchen, nonchalantly stating, "Kitchen," and then points to the living room, saying, "Living room." Without missing a beat, he leads me down the hall to a pair of double doors. Swinging them open, he reveals the master bedroom, smaller than the mansion's, but it still dwarfs any room I've ever had. My eyes are drawn to the oversized custom bed dressed in high-quality linens—linens that, I suspect, he won't even mind ruining when he inevitably has his way with me on them. This room also emits soft lighting, which instantly makes me feel more relaxed.

There's a large fireplace situated between the bedroom and the bathroom to the right. Two walls on the opposite side of the room are almost entirely glass, with floor-to-ceiling windows. The curtains are gracefully drawn back, cascading down to the floor.

Pulling me toward the master bathroom, I quickly take in its generous size. A large soaking tub and a glass-enclosed shower are set on a marble floor, flanked by marble walls. Two long counters run along the walls, suggesting a convenient his-and-her setup. Typically, a woman wouldn't want to share a bathroom space with a man because they tend to be messy, leaving hair shavings and globs of toothpaste in the sink. But Jonah is clean clean—like, really clean. While I'm guilty of sometimes being the one to leave toothpaste in the sink, he ensures everything is spotless. I've watched him meticulously clean up after shaving, never leaving a trace behind.

Connected to the bathroom is the master closet, a large walk-in space with custom-built shelves and drawers. A large mirror is lit up in the corner, perfectly positioned for a final outfit check before leaving for work in the morning. The closet is well-organized: one half filled with Jonah's varied wardrobe, while the other half neatly displays an array of high heels, business attire, and casual wear, alongside sections of workout attire, pajamas, and other clothing.

My eyes linger on the clothing, pleasantly surprised to find that everything appears to be my size. "Tabitha?"

"Yes."

"Dang. I didn't realize she would have it all done that fast," my eyebrows lift in shock. "She didn't even ask my shoe size." I pick up the first pair of heels, and my eyes grow wide as they are my size.

"I did mention trust the process," Jonah remarks, flashing a confident smile, watching me peruse my new wardrobe.

I sift through the outfits, thoroughly impressed. "Yes, yes you did," I reply, still bubbling with excitement. As I continue looking, intrusive thoughts begin to creep in. "These are all for me, right?" I ask, a bit worried that perhaps they belonged to Jenevieve or another woman he might have brought here. However, what would be the chances we all wore the same size.

"They're all yours," he assures me. "They've never been worn before."

Relief washes over me. Trying to shift my focus, I ask about the plans for work in the morning. We never did discuss his work schedule. "What time are we leaving tomorrow?"

"Dinner should be arriving any minute, and I'll give you a rundown of the day," he replies, extending his hand.

We make our way to the kitchen, where I settle at the island while Jonah opens the door for our meal delivery. Bringing in the food, he places it on the counter and begins arranging the meal setup, gathering dinner plates, silverware, and fancy napkins. With a practiced hand, he proceeds to prepare plates for each of us. This entire sight is sexy and odd. It's as if he's done this every day his entire life—completely laid back and comfortable in a kitchen—yet I'm willing to bet he's done this only a handful of times.

As we eat, he walks me through his daily routine on business days. He explains that most of his day is filled with meetings, which are detailed in an email from his personal assistant the night before and reviewed again once he arrives at the office. He also takes a lot of phone calls and answers a lot of emails, which he's always doing back home, so that doesn't seem out of the ordinary.

"Will I be in the way if I'm there tomorrow?" I ask, feeling a twinge of concern that I will be more of a distraction. The notion of accompanying him to work seemed exciting because I wanted to witness how sexy and commanding he looked in his powerful role. But now, the reality of his immense authority and influence feels overwhelming and too intimidating for me to be prancing around getting turned on. It also makes me start to feel that I'm in over my head with him. At the mansion, I can bury my head in the sand and indulge in the illusion that he and I are equals. But with so many people here in a big city like this, all these people under his command, I feel inconsequential. Jonah has never made me feel this way, but the intrusive thoughts creep in, making me doubt my place beside him. He's built an empire with his brilliant mind, while I have nothing comparable to offer.

I actually don't think many people realize just how intelligent Jonah is. Beyond being a shrewd businessman, he possesses a genius-level IQ, reads faster than anyone I've ever known, and retains information with remarkable precision. Sometimes, I wonder if he has a photographic memory, though he's never mentioned it. He often downplays his intelligence, rarely showing just how smart he truly is.

He dabs his mouth with the napkin, then places it on the counter. "Of course not, babe," he reassures me. Standing up, he collects both of our plates.

"No, please, let me," I insist, rising to reach for the dishes.

"Not today, Cinderella. Go relax," he commands, nodding toward the bedroom.

"Let me at least help."

"I've got it. Go," he nods again, putting the dishes in the sink and grabbing a towel, playfully whipping it at my butt, eliciting a laugh from both of us. After a brief moment of resistance, I give in, realizing he isn't going to back down.

I make my way to the bedroom and head straight for the closet, familiarizing myself with my new wardrobe. Selecting from an assortment of pajamas, I choose a soft silk nightgown and matching panties. Glancing at my reflection in the large mirror, I appreciate how perfectly the nighty hugs my curves, accentuating my well-shaped breasts and sitting a bit shorter than it should in the back, showcasing my rounded bottom.

Moving to the bathroom, I head toward the counter that is obviously mine. It's a similar setup to the bathroom back at the mansion. Jonah's counter is almost bare, aside from a couple modest decorations. My counter has a bouquet of flowers as well as a rhinestones-encrusted tissue holder. Pulling open the top drawer to locate a brush, I run it along my hair, loosely braiding it over my shoulder, then brush and floss my teeth before returning to the bedroom.

One noteworthy observation I've made about Jonah is his insistence on sleeping on the side of the bed closest to the door—a quirk tied to his concern about potential intruders and keeping me safe. Even though there are advanced security measures—key cards needed for the elevator, an elevator attendant, security cameras, and security systems on this floor—he remains adamant about protecting me and still wouldn't let me sleep closest to the door. As I glance around the room, a wave of sadness washes over me at the thought of him staying here alone. Although Jonathan usually accompanies him on these trips, he stays in his own condo down the hall. The thought of Jonah being here by himself seems so lonely. Yet, I lived in my apartment all alone. And, well, it was really freaking lonely.

I stroll over to the large windows, gazing down at the active city below—a stark contrast from the quietness of the mansion. Though I don't mind it here, a subtle yearning for the familiarity of home creeps in.

Lights illuminate the city, and I watch the cars below, my thoughts wandering to the condos across the way. Despite the distance, I can still see inside their windows. With a telescope or binoculars, I could see in perfectly. It looks like the perfect setup for a suspense movie. *Can they see in here?* The thought of sleeping with people potentially watching me makes me uncomfortable.

Catching sight of Jonah approaching in the window's reflection, it feels like we have swapped places from the night of the thunderstorm at the mansion when I approached him in his office.

We've come a long way since that night. I turn my head to look at him. "Hello, Mr. Everett."

He wraps his arms around my waist from behind me, placing a gentle kiss on my cheek. "You look sexy," he whispers, as his fingers run across the hem of my nightgown.

"Thank you. I also used your toothbrush. I hope you don't mind," I grin to show off my clean teeth.

"That's sweet of you. You warmed it up for me," he quips.

"Why are you not bothered by that?" I question.

"My tongue was in your assh—"

"Okay, okay, point taken," I interrupt, not needing to hear those words. I'm well aware of the places in my body his tongue has ventured, but not being in the heat of the moment, I'm embarrassed to hear it.

"These pajamas are nice, but putting them on was a waste. I'm going to take them right back off," he whispers seductively in my ear.

"Is that so?" I echo his seductive tone. "Before you do… can they see in here?" I point out the window to the condos on the other side of the road.

His gaze follows where I'm pointing. "No, we can see out, but from their viewpoint, it's reflected like a mirror. You think I'd let someone else peek at you naked?"

"I mean, you let Jonathan and Shay see me naked all the time."

"It's Jonathan and Shay; they're our best friends. They don't count," he says as he leans in to pinch my ear between his lips.

"Okay, that's true. Back to you telling me more about taking off my pajamas," I wrap my arm back around his shoulder while my other hand softly covers his, gently rubbing over my stomach.

He releases his hold around my waist, and through the window's reflection, I watch as he begins to undress. His shirt lands casually on the floor before he proceeds to undo his pants, slipping them along with his boxers down his thick, muscular thighs. Though obscured from my view as he stands behind me, I can sense his growing arousal even before his touch.

He wraps me in a hug again, and as expected, I feel the undeniable hardness of his member against my back. Our reflections meet in the window, and he spins me around to face him, effortlessly lifting me off the ground. A small laugh escapes me as I'm carried to the bed and gently laid down. However, as soon as he settles on top of me, my breathing turns heavy.

Lowering his lips to mine, he delivers a soft kiss before pulling away to gaze at me, only to return for a deeper kiss. As he pulls away for the second time, I decide to inject some humor, suggesting, "Maybe we should just get some sleep for a good night's rest before work tomorrow," attempting to sound serious.

He sits back on his shins, lost in thought, then bends down, gently biting my nipple beneath the nightgown. The sensation elicits a hitch in my breathing. Moving to the other side, he repeats the action before sitting up once more, decisively pulling my nightgown off and tossing it to the floor. "No more jokes?" he inquires as he descends to my now bare nipples.

"No," I whisper as I wait for his soft, warm tongue to make contact. He leans back down, gently sucking, eliciting audible moans from me. "Wait," I say breathless, and he sits up. I raise my hips off the bed, sliding my panties down to my knees and lifting my legs for him to remove them. "Before you try to rip them off."

He complies, pulling them off and kissing my leg before gently parting them back on either side of him. He runs his hands down my thighs, up my belly, and grabs two handfuls of my breasts, giving them a firm squeeze. "You're so sexy," he murmurs before releasing them and lowering himself onto me.

I spread my legs wide, eager for him to fill me. He smiles at the gesture. "You want me inside you, baby?" he asks as he kisses me.

"Yes," I breathe out.

His hand moves down between my legs, gripping his shaft as he guides it to my entrance. He swirls the tip around, then gently pushes the head inside, holding it there while maintaining contact as he brings his lips back to mine. The partial penetration has me trying my best to draw him in deeper.

Biting my lower lip, he asks, "Do you need more?"

"Yes," I plead, rolling my hips upward, yearning for him to go deeper.

The technique proves effective as he retracts his hips before ramming them back into me, creating a rhythmic rocking motion until he's fully stretched himself deep inside me.

He slips his hand under my bottom, lifting me off the bed as he continues to impale me even deeper. Gradually slowing his pace, he withdraws completely.

I anticipate being placed on his lap, but instead, he flips me over onto the bed, positioning me on my hands and knees. "What are we—" is all I manage to say before he spreads my legs wide. I glance back at him as I lean forward on my forearms, my backside lifted in the air.

His face lights up as he spanks my ass, tensing his jaw and grasping his shaft before pushing back into me from behind. Firmly holding onto my hips, he begins to slowly and deliberately thrust.

I lower myself onto the bed, spreading my arms flat above me, my face and breasts pressed into the cool bedding. "Damn, baby," he groans, his voice dripping with desire as he continues the rhythmic pumping in and out of me. Each stroke ricochets waves of pleasure through my body. I start rocking my hips up and down, matching his rhythm with my own movements, twerking on him while he stays buried deep inside me.

His hand slides around to the front of me, skillfully maneuvering between my slick folds, expertly rubbing. The sensation is electric, eliciting loud moans from my lips. I instinctively clutch his hand, ensuring it stays in place. "Yes!" I scream out, bouncing urgently on his shaft as my climax builds. Frantically, I grab at the bedspread, my body trembling as the intense waves continue to ripple through me.

Jonah's other hand reaches up, lacing under the back of my braid at my nape and forcefully pulling my head back. Simultaneously, I feel him emptying inside me. He brings his face to mine, sliding his tongue into my mouth, engaging in a frenzied, passionate kiss as we gradually descend from the peaks of our orgasms.

"You're amazing," I exhale as he withdraws. My body collapses onto the bed, lying on my stomach. He leaves briefly and returns with a towel.

"You're gonna be leaky," he says, noticing my reluctance to move.

I laugh and feel his fluid starting to seep out. "There it is," he teases, helping me clean up. He's on the side of the bed and invites me to join him. Standing on the bed, I walk over, wrapping my arms and legs around him as he carries us into the bathroom for a shower.

In the bathroom, he sets me down gently and turns on the shower. The steam begins to fill the room as he pulls me into the warm spray, the water cascading over our intertwined bodies. His hands glide over my wet skin, soaping and massaging, rekindling the embers of our encounter just moments ago. His touch is both soothing and arousing, each caress igniting a renewed desire.

Our mouths find each other again, the kiss deepening as the water washes away the remnants of our lovemaking. He backs me against the cool tile, his body molding to mine as his hands explore every curve and contour. I can feel his arousal growing once more, pressing insistently against my stomach.

I wrap my fingers around his shaft, lifting on my tiptoes guiding him to my entrance. He hoists me up effortlessly. With a slow, deliberate motion, he slides inside me again, the water creating a slick, sensual glide. We move together under the spray, our bodies perfectly synchronized in a dance of raw passion.

Our moans echo in the steam-filled space, mingling with the sound of the water. I cling to him, my nails digging into his back as the overwhelming intensity consumes me. His hands grip my hips, holding me steady as he drives into me.

Just as I feel myself teetering on the edge, he pulls me closer. "Come for me, baby," he whispers, his voice a low growl. The command is all it takes for my body to convulse in a shuddering release. He follows moments later, his own roaring through him.

We stay locked together, our bodies trembling in the afterglow, the water still pouring over us. Finally, he withdraws and softly sets me on my feet.

"Are your legs steady?" he asks, leaving his arms around my waist.

"I'm good," I assure him, though my legs feel wobbly. His arms release me, and we each wash our bodies. Then he turns off the shower, wrapping us both in a large, fluffy towel. He carries me back to the bed, laying me down gently before climbing in beside me.

As we lie there, entwined and utterly spent, I stare at his profile, wondering how such a flawless man was created. "You're truly incredible," I murmur, as his fingers trace lazy patterns on my damp skin.

"So are you," he replies, smiling contentedly, drifting off to sleep.

CHAPTER

Ten

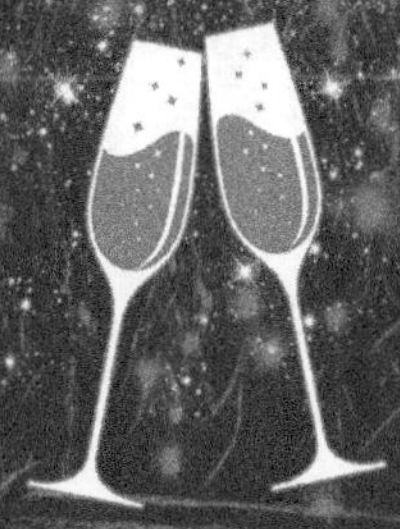

I stand before the expansive closet mirror, absorbing the image before me and taking in my reflection with a mixture of satisfaction and confidence. I'm dressed in a black pencil skirt that hugs the curves of my hips, accentuating my bottom. I've paired it with a red lace top, tucked in to highlight my full breasts. The ensemble is completed with matching red heels that elegantly lengthen my legs. I feel myself again in this attire, and a content smile graces my red-stained lips. My hair falls in perfect curls, and though my makeup is subtle aside from my lipstick, it enhances my green eyes.

Thank goodness Jonah didn't leave any visible hickeys during the flight, though traces of the belt marks are still noticeable, and I've managed to conceal them with makeup.

He enters the room, occupied with tying his tie. Unexpectedly, we find ourselves unintentionally matching, both wearing the same shade of red—his tie mirroring the color of my top, heels and lipstick. As he adjusts the knot, his eyes lift, and he comes to an abrupt halt, mouth slightly agape, eyes intently tracing my figure.

"Holy shit," he exclaims, his appreciation and shock evident on his face.

"Alright, Prince Charming, close your fly trap," I saunter over and lazily rest my wrists on his shoulders.

"I'm gonna bend you over the dresser and fuck you before we leave," he whispers.

"No, you won't, Mr. Everett," I reply playfully, trailing my hand down his tie. "But if you behave today, I might just grant your wish on the way back."

A grin appears on his face. "Deal," he agrees, leaning down to kiss me.

As we exit the condo, he grips my backside with both hands. "You've got a voluptuous ass, baby," he comments through teeth gritted.

"Same to you, apple bottom," I quip.

Arriving to the large building, Jonah clasps my hand and states, "Baby, once we step through those doors, business begins." His tone suggests that the reputed serious businessman I've heard stories about will come to the forefront.

"I understand. I've lived in this world too, as you know," I add with a wink, acknowledging his familiarity with my past.

Leaning in close, he whispers provocatively in my ear, "I'm going to fuck you so hard tonight," leaving that enticing promise hanging in the air. Stepping out, he adjusts his tie as he walks around the car to open my door. Holding his hand out, I take it, praying it hasn't been too long since I've worn heels that I end up breaking my ankle and eating my teeth.

We walk confidently towards the building, and I take in its imposing size. The expansive structure stands majestically against the city skyline, with glistening glass panels capturing the sunlight and creating a striking visual effect. Impressive columns, adorned with detailed patterns, frame the entrance and guide us into a lavish lobby. Inside, the space features marble floors, cascading chandeliers, and carefully designed furnishings.

A striking brunette, clutching a black binder, shoots me a disdainful look, her eyes traveling from head to toe as she notices I'm *with* Jonah. She had been waiting at the entrance when we arrived, so she saw us get out of the same vehicle together. Knowing Jonah's penchant for privacy, I realize she likely has no clue about me or our relationship, so she's probably completely clueless why I'm here. He seems intent on maintaining that anonymity, evident in his businesslike demeanor and the deliberate lack of handholding, which I understand and respect.

The woman seamlessly falls into step beside Jonah. Around the room, people warmly greet "Mr. Everett." The woman accompanying us engages Jonah in rapid conversation, covering a variety of topics, and even presents him with a cup of coffee.

"I'll take tea today, Bridget," he says, declining the coffee but accepting the binder she offers, scrutinizing the documents. While riding up the elevator, I maintain a forward gaze, but it's impossible to ignore Bridget's continued disdainful, sidelong glances in my direction. She has long, pin-straight brunette hair and a slender figure, accentuated by a form-fitting, mid-thigh dress paired with black heels, showcasing her tan skin and killer legs. No wonder her dress is so short; she's definitely trying to showcase those assets.

Ascending to the top floor of the building, we step off the elevator amid a symphony of chatter. Three receptionists stationed at a sizable desk promptly rise, their faces brightening with anticipation upon seeing Jonah. Simultaneously, they greet him, before their gazes shift in my direction and I observe disapproving looks from all three of them. *That's one way to be greeted.*

Progressing down the broad hallway, we pass by glass-walled offices where individuals work in a fishbowl, offering greetings to Jonah as we pass by. He remains oblivious to the friendly gestures.

Passing a spacious, wide-open room filled with focused workers, I peer around, noticing how everyone takes note of Jonah's arrival, their heads swiveling in our direction. Even as we continue along the corridor, I make eye contact with several people, acknowledging them, while Bridget persistently discusses business.

We even pass Jonathan's office; I spot the nameplate 'Jonathan Harper,' and a smile tugs at my lips. Seeing his name evokes a sense of home and warmth, linking him to Shay. I love her so much. And Jonathan—Dick—why hasn't he proposed to her yet?

At the far end of the hall, Jonah swings open the door to his office. I knew it would be his because it automatically feels intimidating. Isn't that the point of a boss's office?

Entering behind them, he nods at Bridget. "Thank you, Bridget. Please close the door behind you." Her parting glance at me is a piercing assessment. Ignoring it, Jonah rounds his massive desk, pulling out his chair just as his phone rings. "Everett," he answers gruffly.

Glancing around the room, I absorb its sleek and spacious ambiance. His uncluttered desk sits at the center of the room, flanked by floor-to-ceiling windows reminiscent of his condo, offering a sweeping panoramic cityscape. Two chairs sit opposite his side of the desk. To the right, a light gray rug complements a spacious black leather couch, a pair of leather armchairs, and a glass coffee table. A well-stocked bar counter near the door displays an array of liquors and pristine glasses. I've never seen Jonah drink, so it seems out of place. Does he ever actually drink in here? I can't picture it.

As he immerses himself in a heated conversation, I take the opportunity to explore the room. Eventually, I gravitate toward the window, drawn to the breathtaking view. My old office at Amaryllis Firm didn't offer anything close to this; stuck on the seventh floor, my view was limited to the neighboring building. Being back in an office setting feels surreal, especially as Jonah's shadow on this business trip. He brought along his traveling pussy on business with him. Even though I'm sure he could take his pick of any of the women he's surrounded by here, to take home for the night.

Why did he bring me here?

Hello, intrusive thoughts.

"Good thing you aren't afraid of heights," he murmurs in my ear, wrapping his arms around my waist. "I have a meeting soon. Would you like to come?"

"I do love coming," I tease, "but I think I'll stay here and snoop around."

A low hum of amusement rumbles in his throat. "Mmm, let me know if you stumble upon anything intriguing," he suggests.

"Absolutely." Leaning in, he kisses me, promising a quick return before playfully swatting my bottom.

"See you soon," he says, then strides purposefully toward the door. Swinging it open, he departs, Bridget waiting attentively. She promptly hands him another black binder filled with a stack of papers, launching into more business talk as they make their way down the hallway.

I walk over to his imposing desk and settle into the commanding chair, metaphorically stepping into his shoes. I reach for one of the folders neatly stacked on the corner of his desk. Familiar with deciphering financial reports from my tenure at Amaryllis, I deftly open the folder and begin perusing the contents. The initial reports look promising, instilling a sense of reassurance. My optimism falters, however, as I delve into the fourth folder; the numbers don't align, prompting a more thorough examination.

Convinced of discrepancies, I seize the opportunity to access Jonah's computer. He left a sticky note with his neatly written password on the keyboard. I've seen his handwriting countless times, but for some reason, being in a new setting, it dawns on me he has the kind of handwriting you would see in an old love story where lovers wrote letters to each other in fancy script. It's beautiful. I'd love nothing more than to get a love letter from him in this impeccably beautiful handwriting.

A spreadsheet materializes on the screen after a few clicks, and I diligently input the numbers, discovering a significant error amounting to hundreds of thousands of dollars. I input the numbers three more times to ensure accuracy, and each time, the results come up the exact same.

Shit.

Rising from the desk, I secure the folder and exit Jonah's office. Spotting the first gentleman in my line of sight, I approach him and inquire, "Excuse me, sir, where can I obtain past reports?"

Surprised, he greets me with a smile, exhibiting eagerness to assist. Presenting the folder, I specify, "I need the reports for the last three quarters of this company."

His enthusiasm is palpable. "I can get those for you, and if you require any further assistance, I'll be right here at the first desk—at this desk—this is my desk right here," he informs me, awkwardly leaning against it.

I respond appreciatively, urging him to proceed. "I'll be in Mr. Everett's office," I inform him before turning and walking back.

Ten minutes later, he returns to Jonah's office. Though the door is intentionally left open for him, he politely knocks. "Please, come in," I say, gesturing him inside as I rise from Jonah's desk. "Do you have the reports?"

He nods, holding up the files. "Right here," he says, handing them over.

"Excellent, thank you, Mr..." I pause, anticipating his introduction.

"Mr. Miles... Miles... just Miles," he stutters, sounding somewhat nervous.

"Thank you, Miles," I express my gratitude.

"You're welcome. I will help you with anything you need. With folders—if you need more folders—I know where to find them."

"Fantastic," I acknowledge.

As anticipated, each report deviates significantly from the expected figures. Despite meticulously scrutinizing the numbers on each report within a spreadsheet, the undeniable truth remains—they are inaccurately presented. Printing off the spreadsheets for all quarters, along with the numerous times I recalculated the numbers just to ensure I didn't make an error, I patiently wait for Jonah to return. It doesn't take long; he enters the room, and I settle into one of the chairs opposite his desk. Bridget follows him in, informing him of his upcoming phone call in twenty minutes. As she exits upon his dismissal, he greets me with a casual, "Hi, baby," loosening his tie as he takes a seat.

I hesitate, then decide to address the issue directly. "These re-ports," I gesture to the pile on his desk, "what's the process for them ending up here?"

"Businesses my company has acquired maintain control of their operations and send over quarterly reports. These reports undergo multiple stages of audits before eventually reaching me," he explains.

Seeking clarification, I ask, "If they're here, you haven't re-viewed them yet?"

"I never check them. Bridget places them here after the fi-nance manager has checked them for accuracy, but they always go right back to the finance manager and are filed away. Why do you ask?"

"This company," I convey, handing him the folders, "is not providing accurate reports." I assert as I navigate around his desk. "Initially, I suspected it might be an isolated error, so I requested the gentleman outside to fetch the previous three quarters, and all of them exhibit the same discrepancies." I inform Jonah while he looks over the reports. "I've created a spreadsheet for each quar-ter… multiple spreadsheets to double and triple check my work," I add, handing him those papers as well, which he accepts and reviews. "However, the numbers are significantly off. I can't deter-mine the extent without all the files, but I'm more than willing to look over every quarter if you can arrange to have them brought up to me."

Jonah continues examining the papers, then reaches for his phone, tapping a few buttons. He sternly instructs the person on the other end to come to his office immediately, hangs up, and drops the folders onto his desk. Turning his chair toward me, he fixes his gaze on me.

Feeling a twinge of regret, I quickly interject, "I'm sorry, Jonah, I didn't mean to overstep." He stands up abruptly and kisses me, a hard and unexpected gesture.

"Fantastic work, baby," he commends me. I'm taken aback, expecting him to be upset, but he appears to genuinely value my findings. A knock at the door prompts Jonah to invite the visitor in.

Bridget announces, "Mr. Hinkley is here, sir." And the gentleman enters.

"I'll step outside," I tell Jonah, standing from my leaning position on his desk.

"You'll stay," he asserts.

I acknowledge with a crisp, "Yes, sir," and turn my attention to Mr. Hinkley as he approaches.

Jonah delves into the revelations with Mr. Hinkley, his displeasure evident in his tone. Mr. Hinkley is visibly shaken, offering a flimsy defense rooted in personal struggles, citing long hours and marital issues as reasons for neglecting the reports. He reacts with disbelief, relying on the absence of prior issues to assume there wouldn't be any now.

At an appropriate moment, I interject, "If I may, I'd like a list of the business reports from the past month—all those that have crossed your desk. I'd like to randomly select a few for a thorough review, just to ensure that further errors aren't occurring." I direct my request to Mr. Hinkley but seek Jonah's approval.

"That's not something I can produce," Mr. Hinkley replies.

"You can and you will," Jonah demands, and Mr. Hinkley, still visibly shaken, reluctantly agrees with a simple, "Yes, sir."

Jonah dismisses him with a stern, "Get out." Mr. Hinkley startles, then scampers toward the door with beads of sweat trickling down his forehead.

We sit in silence momentarily before Jonah breaks it. "You're definitely getting fucked tonight," he declares, lifting me onto his desk.

Leaning in, I grab his tie and pull him closer. "If I continue being useful, can you promise to fuck me hard?"

Seeing him in this element, so authoritative and demanding, is so sexy that sitting down on a chair could send me directly into an orgasm.

He responds with a muffled "mmhmm."

The remainder of the day flies by. Jonah is in and out of meetings, while I get Miles to bring me more reports. Mostly content with my findings, I do uncover minor errors in several more reports, which I promptly bring to Jonah's attention. The more errors I find with Mr. Hinkley's work, the more I want to look into every single report that has crossed his desk.

As we prepare to leave for the evening, I find myself developing a newfound admiration for Jonah. Despite being aware of his constant work at the mansion, today's experience offers a revealing glimpse into the specifics of his endeavors. It's an eye-opening realization and undeniably sexy.

Jonah graciously opens the door for me, and I slide into the backseat of the SUV. He walks around and enters from the other side. The instant the door slams shut, he crosses the seat and passionately presses his mouth to mine, initiating a fervent kiss. My arms encircle his neck, and he shifts one hand, squeezing my breast, then pulls down my shirt, exposing it. His mouth leaves mine only to resume the same teasing action on my now-revealed nipple.

My breath catches, and my hands intertwine in his hair, responding to the intensity of the moment. The ride back to the condo doesn't take long and the driver discreetly waits for us to conclude our private exchange.

Jonah withdraws from my nipple, delicately covering it back up with my shirt. Exiting the SUV, he circles around to open my door, taking my hand and guiding me inside the building to the elevator that ascends directly to his floor. Once inside, he backs me against the elevator wall, resuming our kiss.

As the doors open and a security guard awaits, we reluctantly part, walking to his condo. However, the moment we step inside, he swiftly removes my shirt and his own, leaving them discarded on the floor beneath us. Hiking my skirt to my thighs, he lifts me, carrying me to the kitchen counter where he gently sets me down, proceeding to remove his pants. I lean back against the cool counter as he discards my skirt, leaving me wearing only my red high heels.

True to his promise, he fucks me, and he fucks me hard. Half the time I didn't know if I was screaming from pain or pleasure. Despite the incredible sensations and the remnants of blood between my legs, I refrain from mentioning the severe cramping I'm experiencing in the aftermath. As per usual, he cleans it up and even gets Tylenol for me "just in case."

I inform him that I'd rather have our dinner in bed tonight, telling him I'm 'too comfortable to get out of bed,' without disclosing that I didn't think I could walk from the pounding my pussy just received. We've been *'rough'* before, but never like this. He was slamming into me with such brutal force at one point I thought I was going to puke. I've never cramped so badly in my life, even during my period.

Upon waking in the morning, I find that my pussy still aches—no, my pussy throbs—accompanied by persistent cramping so intense that I doubt I'll even be able to stand up straight. When I ask Jonah for permission to take the day to rest and "sleep in," he easily agrees.

As soon as he leaves, I run myself a hot bath, hoping to alleviate the pain. The warm water soothes my aching body, offering only a very brief amount of relief. But as soon as I step out of the bath, the cramping returns with a vengeance. Midway through the day, I FaceTime Shay, sharing details about my office revelations and the beating my pussy endured as a reward.

"I wish Jonathan would ravish me like that," she remarks, reclining on her bed with a sigh. "He used to. Actually, one time he had to take me to the emergency room after we had rough sex. He's never been quite rough like that again, and it was one of my favorite experiences.

"I've never experienced anything like it," I confess, recalling how good it felt, even with the pain while doing it. "It was incredible," I add, relishing the memory. "My body is such a wimp. She's so accustomed to gently being fucked that one little pounding leaves her bleeding and achy… actually, that isn't true. We've had rough sex before, so I have no idea why this time was so different." I curl into a ball on the bed, my insides hurting so badly I just want to go back to sleep until the pain subsides.

"I wonder what it would take for Jonathan to punish my pussy like that?"

Over the next several hours, Shay does her best to keep my mind occupied, but as the pain persists, she gets Jonathan and lets him know what's going on. He places a call to someone, arranging for some essentials to be delivered to me. Shortly after, a well-dressed gentleman knocks on the partially open bedroom door, carrying a bag.

"Here you go, miss, all the requested items," he enters looking uncomfortable, placing them on the bed before exiting. Upon inspecting the contents in the bag, I discover heat patches for menstrual cramps, immediately applying one to my lower belly. There are also pads, tampons, Midol, some candy, and ice cream.

I dispose of the heating patch wrapper in the trash and head to the use the bathroom. "Annnnnd there she is," I mutter, noticing the blood.

I organize the remaining items and head back to bed, curling up in the fetal position as I gradually drift into sleep. The mattress dips as Jonah joins me, and his delightful scent surrounds me.

"Hi baby, I'm home," he greets, planting a gentle kiss on my cheek. In my drowsy state, I offer no audible response. He disappears into the bathroom, and when he reappears, he kneels by my side of the bed. "Baby?" he whispers, brushing hair off my face.

I manage only a quiet "hmm" in response.

"I've got Dr. Mary Reed here; she's going to check on you, okay?" he says, sounding concerned.

"Hello, Kalyn, I'm Dr. Reed," she introduces herself as she approaches my side of the bed. Jonah steps back, giving her more room to work, and she sets her medical bag down, placing a stethoscope on my back, proceeding to listen to my chest and abdomen.

"Can you tell me where you're feeling discomfort?" she asks, still using the stethoscope. I glance at Jonah and then back at her.

"It's okay, babe," he reassures me.

"I'm fine; I just started my period," I explain.

Dr. Reed asks gently, "Would you be okay if I perform a pelvic exam?"

I agree, silently grateful for not having used a tampon. After completion, she removes her gloves. "Does it hurt to walk?

I look at Jonah, not wanting to hurt his feelings.

"Answer truthfully, baby," Jonah encourages.

"Yes," I admit.

"Is it intense cramping? Or does it feel like a sharp pain?" She questions.

"Incredibly intense cramping," I correct, lowering my eyes.

She places a bottle of pills on the nightstand. "Well, good news. I come prepared. These are for the pain. Your cervix is dilated and incredibly inflamed, causing most of your discomfort. Typically, under different circumstances, activities like last night wouldn't have been an issue. However, the pressure and force on your cervix for an extended period of time irritated your body. Give it a week, and you'll be good as new," she assures, smiling at both me and Jonah.

"Does that mean no sex?" I ask as she stands.

She appears slightly confused. "Do you think you could handle it?"

I couldn't. I know I couldn't. Just the thought makes me feel like I'm going to pass out. I don't even want to spread my legs open to shove a pillow between my knees for sleeping. But for Jonah, I would let him continuously pound my pussy even with me hurting. "If that's what you want," I say softly, looking up at Jonah.

"No, baby, that's not what I want," he leans down to kiss me, then stands back up. "Thank you, Dr. Reed. I'll walk you out," he extends his arm as a gesture for her to lead the way. I hear them quietly conversing as they exit.

Jonah returns a short while later, slipping into bed and enveloping me in his arms. "I would have come home sooner if I had known you were in pain, baby," he says, trying to be helpful.

"Thanks," I respond, opting not to take the route of my preferred choice, which would involve telling him that if I needed him to come home, I would have asked him to.

Unfortunately, my period is triggering insane emotions, causing my initial response to his every comment to lean toward being rude. Fortunately, I manage to keep my self-control intact, refraining from voicing anything disrespectful. As the night continues, my intrusive thoughts intensify, allowing typically insignificant matters to seep in and stir up a myriad of emotions, making small issues much more frustrating than usual.

It's been raining, and I've been facing the window since Dr. Reed left, watching the raindrops slide down the glass, tracing the paths of the previous droplets. Jonah has been on his laptop typing away, and the rapid clicking of his keys is driving me nuts. Normally, nothing he does ever bothers me, but right now, I want to take his laptop and throw it against the wall. Yet even that noise would inevitably annoy me.

I never even looked around his condo to see what's down the other long hallway or what's upstairs. He must have a guest bedroom somewhere. Maybe I should go sleep on the couch. Anything sounds better than listening to his incessant typing. He has to type at least two hundred words per minute. Who types that fast? I don't even think I can read as fast as he's typing. Is he actually typing words? Maybe he's just trying to be annoying.

Convinced he's doing it on purpose, I turn to look at his computer screen. Boy, was I wrong. He's typing so fast, and they *are* actual words. He's completely absorbed, oblivious to my gaze, his fingers flying across the keyboard without a single mistake or spelling error.

What is he, a robot?

"Have you had sex with anyone from the office?" I blurt out.

The thought of his big ass cock penetrating another woman makes me want to rip it off and punch it into the mattress. Images of wet, salivating pussies flash in my mind, with him sitting naked and women climbing onto his lap, bouncing up and down while screaming his name.

The typing on his computer stops immediately, and I can hear the wheels turning in his head as the question catches him off guard. I turn to look at him, and the answer is evident on his face by his startled expression.

"Well," I prod, keeping my gaze locked on him.

"Yes," he replies openly, turning to look at me.

"Who?" I ask, a nauseating feeling creeping in. Receiving no response, I probe again. "Bridget?" I ask and hold my breath.

"Yes," he responds.

Of course he's slept with Bridget. She's beautiful, but this revelation hits me like a punch to the gut, finding myself now being the one completely caught off guard. Honestly, when I asked the question, I never anticipated his answer would be yes. I think I wanted to be mad about something, but I figured I would ask the question and get nothing to fuel my anger, so I would just have to drop the subject and be mad about his fast typing. I want to ask why he still has her employed—maybe so he has easy access to pussy anytime he gets lonely? Or maybe he's still sleeping with her when he comes for business trips. At this point, I'm really just trying to hurt my own feelings.

"The receptionists?" I question, still reeling from his admission to having sex with Bridget.

The way Bridget looked at me was one of *'have you been with him also?'* Like she was trying to figure out our relationship while maintaining her composure. The receptionists all stared at me the same way. Though he gave no indication he had ever been sexually involved with any of them, they either have an unhealthy infatuation with him or they have a warranted infatuation with him, knowing firsthand how good his dick feels, therefore making any other female that comes around feel unwelcomed by giving them the cold shoulder.

"Yes," he replies once more.

"All three?" I ask, astonished.

"Not simultaneously, but yes," he admits.

"So you slept with each of them on separate occasions?"

"For the most part," he responds.

"For the most part? As in what? What does that mean?"

"That most of the time I slept with them one at a time," he doesn't even look uncomfortable answering these questions. He more so looks annoyed.

"So there are instances where you slept with more than just a one at a time?" I'm asking questions I have already decided are my period brain's nonsense, only to be met with answers I wasn't expecting. And this question I know what the answer is about to be, and I feel the bile making its way up my throat.

"Yes," he responds candidly.

"You had a threesome?! Was it at the office?" I ask, shocked. Why am I asking these questions if I don't want his honest answer?

He lets out a sigh. "Yes."

"You and two other women from the office?"

When he just sits there, my stomach sinks even further.

"Jonah," I persist.

"Yes and no," is all he replies.

"What the fuck does that mean? You had a threesome with a girl and a guy?"

"Yes," he states simply.

"Who?" My hands begin shaking, and he stays silent. "Jonah, who?"

"Jonathan and Bridget."

My mouth falls open. "You fucked Jonathan?!"

"No. I fucked Bridget. While Jonathan also fucked Bridget," he corrects, as if this question, of all my questions, is what really sets his annoyed meter off.

"What the fuck does that even mean?" I ask, though I'm not sure why. I was just imagining this exact scenario the other night with my vibrator and finger. And now I'm not only mad she fucked Jonah, but I'm mad she fucked Jonathan. And I know for a fact Shay would have never allowed that. Did they both put their dicks in her vagina? Just the thought of this makes me want to clamp my legs together and never spread them again. Especially with Jonah's size. And I have seen Jonathan's dick too, and he's almost as long and just as girthy as Jonah.

He lets out a sigh, putting his laptop on his nightstand and leaning back on his pillows.

"You better explain what the fuck that means," my voice trembles, and I know just how unhinged I sound but can't seem to reel my emotions in.

"Her pussy was on his dick while I fucked her ass. Why are you asking all this?" His irritation seeps into his words.

Okay, so exactly like I was fantasizing the other night.

"Did you wear a condom?"

"You are the first and only person I haven't worn a condom with," he says, his expression sincere.

"How does something like that even happen? Are you attracted to Jonathan?"

"No. She wanted to fuck, we were all at the office late and it happened."

"And you and Jonathan just decided it would be a good idea to both fuck her at the same time? Did you only fuck her ass?"

"I just told you I've had sex with her many times."

"Oh right… how could I forget," I reply sarcastically. "I'm meaning that night. Did you only fuck her ass?"

"No, we switched off."

"That's disgusting. And I'm pretty sure that can cause infections, so you and Jonathan just decided to get that dirty shit all over your dicks?" I'm so mad I feel like steam is billowing from my head.

"We were wearing condoms," he says dryly.

"What a classy woman… or rather classless," I retort. "And the flight attendants? They seemed to also hate the sight of me. Did you fuck them too? Did you and Jonathan do a nice little bang train on them too?"

Again, without missing a beat, he responds, "Yes."

"Yes to which part?"

"All of the above," he sighs.

"You had threesomes with the flight attendants too?"

"Yes."

"Jonathan cheats on Sh—" I can't even get the words out.

"No," he insists. "Jonathan hasn't entertained another woman since he and Shay got together. Jonathan is obsessed with Shay, worships the ground she walks on. He treats every other woman like they don't exist."

"Have you fucked every pussy that has ever come near you?" I ask, knowing I'm being a little irrational now.

"A lot of them, yes," he admits.

Okay, that certainly is not what I was expecting him to say. I want to punch the shit out of him, but I have no real reason to. "So is this what my life is going to be, Jonah? A series of seeing all the women you've fucked?" I ask, exasperated. "Because let me tell you what, it's pretty lame. You have all this pussy here; you definitely didn't need to bring your back-home pussy along for business."

"Back-home pussy? I didn't bring you here so I could get laid. As you so kindly pointed out, I have pussy waiting on a silver platter whenever I want. I brought you because I want to be near you. I have a past, babe. I can't change it."

"No, you can't. But did you ever consider how it might make me feel? Going on a business trip with you, only to be scrutinized by half the staff because you've slept with all of them?" My frustration evident in my tone. "The sheer thought of you putting your penis in all the women I have to see when I go to work with you has me wanting to scream."

"I can tell," he acknowledges.

"Why keep them employed at the office?" I ask, puzzled by his decision not to dismiss them.

"I keep competent staff," he asserts bluntly.

I let out a disbelieving laugh. "Fantastic. How much staff would remain if you remove everyone you've slept with?" I question.

"Definitely every male," he responds. Seeing my anger, he adds, "Baby, I'm joking. A terrible, terrible joke," he holds his hands up in surrender.

"Is this a joke to you, Jonah? Am I just a joke to you?" Tears fill my eyes, and before a single one falls, I rise from the bed, grabbing the pillow that's meant for between my legs and throw it at him, not even checking to see if it ever hits him, and retreat to the bathroom, locking the door behind me.

An hour later, I cautiously open the bathroom door and slip back into bed. Though I sense he's still awake, he remains silent.

CHAPTER
Eleven

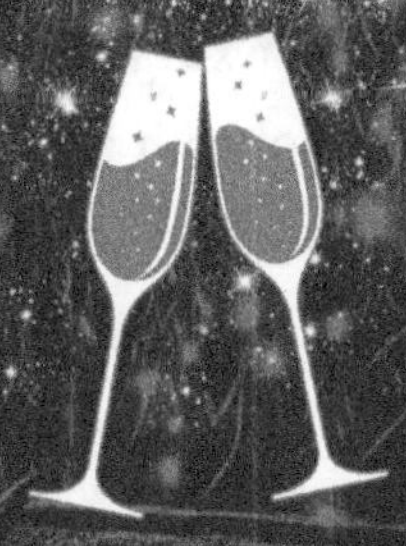

JONAH

She is pissed.

I was completely blindsided by her line of questioning. Before we left, Jonathan brought up the possibility of this being a potential issue, especially considering how possessive Bridget can be at times. I didn't think it would actually be a problem. Bridget is aware I would fire her immediately if she caused any trouble, but apparently, Kalyn is perceptive to even micro facial expressions—ones I hoped she hadn't noticed.

I keep my personal life private. No one at the office knows about my infatuation with Kalyn or that I always left work trips early so I could go see her. I don't care how others react to her, but I do care about how she's treated. I noticed the way Bridget and my receptionists glared at her, and I will address that. I don't want Kalyn to feel uncomfortable anywhere she goes.

I'm not ashamed of the number of women I've been with or that my best friend and I shared many women at the same time. But I hate that the knowledge of it hurts Kalyn. She asked, and I wasn't going to lie to her.

If she asked me to fire every employee I've slept with, I would do it. I would lose over a hundred good employees, but I'd do it if it would make her feel more at ease.

Jonathan has never mentioned anything about telling Shay. She's never been to the office, though she has been on business trips with us before, but she stays at Jonathan's condo. The women from the office who have slept with Jonathan know he has a girlfriend now, and he's put them in their place since him and Shay became exclusive. Now they know not to even try. I guess I need to do the same.

Kalyn is smart. She's so incredibly smart. I'm not the least bit surprised she picked up on the vibes from the female staff. Despite noticing, she held herself with confidence and didn't let it show. She's also mature, so I never thought she would do anything rash. But now, given her heightened mood shift from her period, I'm not sure how she will react. She's never started a fight with me like this before, and to be honest, I don't know how to respond.

I want to go to the bathroom and kick the door in just so I can hold her. But I could see her ripping the toilet from the floor and smashing it over my head with her Hulk-like anger right now. Anger I'm not sure stems from the conversation we just had, her period, or the vigorous appreciation I showed her for uncovering the errors in the financial reports. She discovered millions of dollars in mistakes. The companies are now being audited and will pay back every penny they have lied about and didn't account for.

I negotiate generous deals with every company I partner with. The only reason to lie on reports is for their own financial gain.

Most of these companies were on the brink of collapse, which is why I was brought in. My investments are crucial for their survival. I don't tolerate thieves or those who take my generosity for granted.

Yet, even with that situation, I again find myself more bothered by the fact that she's mad at me.

Mr. Hinkley has worked for my company for nine years, and I never thought he would let anything shady happen under his watch. But I must acknowledge my own culpability; I've been so enthralled with my girl that I stopped keeping a close eye on every part of my company. With Kalyn by my side, my business could become unstoppable. On the other hand, if she asked me to quit working, I'd gladly give it all up for her.

I need a hundred Jonathans. He's loyal, smart, and always gets the job done. I can rely on him for anything. If I were to step back from working so much, he could easily take my place and do as good of a job as me. He also just goes along with whatever the fuck I say. He's the kind of friend who would help you move a body without hesitation or question.

We've been planning a vacation for ourselves and the girls. Jonathan finally designed the ring he's going to propose to Shay with. I offered to cover the expenses so they could go enjoy themselves, but he insists that Shay would want Kalyn there and he would like my support.

I started the process of having Kalyn's ring made after the third time I saw her. It's been ready for years now. I look at it often, imagining my baby wearing it. Retrieving it from my nightstand drawer, I lift the lid of the box. A 2.7-carat oval diamond sparkles even in the darkness. Intricately set along the slender band are smaller diamonds wrapping just to the sides. From the top, it looks like they surround the entirety of the ring, but the jeweler recommended against encircling the entire band for comfort. It's etched in tiny print inside the ring: "Jonah & Kalyn Everett."

She was cemented in my heart the moment I laid eyes on her. I've known for the past year I would be proposing soon. I would have already, but I don't want to steal Jonathan's moment, and he wants to propose to Shay as soon as possible.

We've planned the details of the trip. While Kalyn and I are away, Jonathan and Shay are taking the opportunity to visit her family. Since Shay's family is traditional, Jonathan wants to show respect to them and has requested a private conversation with her father—who's overly excited about the meeting. Since Shay's dad loves fishing, they're planning to go to his favorite fishing spot tomorrow, where Jonathan will ask for his blessing to marry Shay, which he already knows he has it. In three weeks, Shay will have Jonathan's ring on her finger, and he plans on having the wedding within two months after that.

We already have wedding planners ready to start preparations in a month. We don't want to take over everything; we just want to be prepared when the time comes. I'm certain Jonathan will reach out after he secures her father's blessing. It's practically a formality at this point. Her family has been eagerly waiting for them to get engaged. Every time she visits, her mother instantly looks at her hand, only to be disappointed when she doesn't see a ring.

I'm genuinely happy for them, but I do feel a twinge of envy knowing they'll be engaged soon while Kalyn's ring sits untouched in a box. I hear movement in the bathroom and close the lid to her engagement ring, sliding it back into the drawer, then roll onto my back. I can hear her blow her nose, and I know she's finished crying.

These moments are a double-edged sword. I could intervene and try to mend things, but that might just make her angrier, possibly ending with her yelling at me to leave anyway. Or I could stay put and let her go through emotions of hating me, probably wanting to kick my dick off, thoughts of breaking up, and then realizing it's her period causing her emotions to run on overdrive.

We've never been in a fight before, and I'm adrift in uncharted waters. I'm not even entirely sure if this is a fight. It certainly feels like it is with the way my stomach is churning. I hear the bathroom door unlock, and my eyes shut. By the time she opens the door, the light is already off, plunging the room into darkness. She silently closes the door behind her, crosses the bedroom, and slips into bed beside me. I half expected her to make a point and sleep on the couch, in which case I'd probably end up on the floor because I can't sleep without her.

She retrieves the pillow she threw at my face earlier, quietly placing it between her knees. I want to reach out and pull her into a hug, but I'd probably end up with a broken nose. She silently pulls a tissue off her nightstand. I don't hear her blow her nose, so I can only assume she's wiping her eyes. After what feels like an eternity, I finally fall asleep.

DR. REED ALREADY ORDERED KALYN TO REMAIN HOME FOR THE REST of the week. My alarm goes off at 4:30 AM, and I slip into my workout attire before heading down the hall to the gym at the other end of the condo floor. Off the elevator to the left are 2 condos: mine is 3,800 square feet, while Jonathan's next door is 3,000. The rest of the floor features a swimming pool, a gym, and two other condos reserved for guests.

Emerging from my grueling hour-long workout, I'm drenched in sweat but feel a measure of tension melting away. Typically, after arriving at the office, I'd start my day with a full-body massage to work out the knots, but I'm trying to avoid any unnecessary contact with others right now—even if it's purely professional. I take a hot shower, get dressed, and by 6 AM, I'm ready to head to the office early, planning to leave early as well. Walking to her side of the bed, I lean down and kiss her cheek, then head out.

The day at the office drags on. I find myself checking my phone repeatedly, thinking I hear a text from her coming in. Yet, not a single one comes. By noon, the soreness from my workout catches up with me, prompting me to have Bridget arrange for a masseuse. I emphasize that I need them to be strong. Preferably someone older.

Within a half hour, a masseuse arrives, sets up her table in my office, and firmly instructs, "Undress and lay down." Bridget lingers, staring as I begin to undress.

"You can go," I dismiss her. She nods and exits, closing the door behind her. I do as the woman commands, undressing to my boxer briefs and lying down on the massage table.

As soon as she starts working out the knots on my shoulders, she mutters, "Jesus," and I can feel exactly what knot caught her off guard.

She thoroughly works me over for the next hour. When she has me roll onto my back to work through the knots on my quads, she seems slightly confused.

"I'm not looking for that kind of massage," I clarify, keeping my eyes closed.

She immediately resumes massaging my legs without hesitation.

"Is there anywhere else that still feels stiff?" she asks. I sit up, rotating my neck.

"I feel much better. Thank you," I respond, getting off the bed and dressing again.

After paying her, she hands me her business card, mentioning she's available whenever I need another session. Although I appreciate her offer, I sensed her disappointment when I clarified the nature of the massage, so she won't be coming back. I don't need my dick sucked. Strike that, *I do* need my dick sucked. But only by one person, and she's currently ignoring me.

Meanwhile, the audits on the fourteen companies that Kalyn flagged for financial discrepancies are in the beginning stages. These companies know they fucked up because they did all they could to try and stop the audits from happening, promising no errors in next quarter's reports. I already know there won't be—my baby will snuff them out if there are.

By 3, I haven't heard a word from her, and it's driving me crazy. I need to hear her voice. I will set my pride aside and be the one to reach out. Dialing her number, I hover over the call button, contemplating if calling her will piss her off more or make her happy. Maybe she's sleeping.

Pressing "call," I listen to it ring—and ring—before it diverts to voicemail. I recall the day we recorded it: my voice starts, "This is Kalyn Evere—" only for her laughter to interrupt, "Give me that. This is Kalyn *Bell*, you know what to do," while I try to say 'Everett' over her 'Bell.' Then comes the beep.

"Hey baby, I miss you. I'll see you soon," I say and hang up.

Immediately, I want to take the voicemail back. But it's already out there. I spend the next three hours in business meetings, checking my phone every ten minutes, wondering if I missed a call. Still nothing.

JONAH:

Hi, baby. Thinking of you.

Nothing.

I'm aware her read receipts are on, yet it only shows 'delivered.' Maybe she's just sleeping or caught up in a conversation with Shay. After one final meeting, I plan to leave.

As I head to the elevator, Bridget falls in stride with me.

"Are you leaving already?" she asks.

"Yes," I reply.

"It's barely five."

"Do you need something, Bridget?" I ask as I push the elevator button.

"No, you just never leave this early."

"My girlfriend is sick, and I want to get home to her," effectively ending her questions. "Have a good evening," I add as the elevator doors close. '*Jesus Christ,*' I sigh, slightly irritated as I notice her eyes fill with tears.

When I get home, Kalyn is lying down on the couch, reading a book. "Hi, baby," I greet her, attempting to guage her mood. She merely turns a page, continuing to read without acknowledging me. Walking over to her, I lean down to kiss her cheek, but she rolls her head, avoiding my kiss without a word.

With a heavy sigh, I stand and walk to our bedroom. Her phone rests on the nightstand. Tapping the screen, I see no new messages. Swiping up to unlock it, I click on the messages icon and see she has a new, unopened message from me. My voicemail remains unplayed, and when I check her call log, I see that she and Shay FaceTimed for five hours. That was a long conversation, probably spent bashing my dumbass.

After my shower, I change into shorts and a T-shirt. Marietta, my cook, housekeeper, and personal shopper, is due to arrive soon. I asked her to wait until I was home to come so I could introduce her to Kalyn.

Exiting the bedroom, I hear the murmur of voices. When I enter the living room, I see Kalyn in the kitchen, chatting with Marietta and helping her take items out of grocery bags.

"Mr. Everett," Marietta beams when I enter.

"Hi, Marietta. I see you've met Kalyn." I settle onto a stool at the counter.

"Oh yes, she's wonderful," she replies, her eyes twinkling.

I didn't realize how much I needed to see Kalyn's happiness until I just seen how relaxed she was with Marietta. A pang of jealousy stabs at me—my dick twitches in agreement.

Marietta won't let Kalyn help her cook but tells her to sit at the counter so they can continue their conversation. Over the next hour, Kalyn and Marietta talk as if they were longtime friends catching up. When Kalyn excuses herself to the bathroom, Marietta's eyes widen, and she holds up her ring finger, wagging her eyebrows.

"Already have the ring."

"Good man," she says, then turns her attention back to Kalyn as she reenters the room.

As Marietta starts dishing up two plates, Kalyn insists she must eat with us. I can't tell if it's because she wants to keep their conversation going or if she doesn't want to be left alone with me.

"I have much to do, I'll take a little to go. Now eat your dinner," Marietta pats Kalyn on the back before she exits down the hall.

Kalyn pulls her book over to her and resumes reading as she eats. The deafening silence feels heavy in the room. "How was your day, baby?"

She continues to eat and read, unresponsive.

"How long are you going to ignore me?"

Nothing.

"Kalyn," I say, growing more frustrated, "put your book away while we're eating."

She snatches her napkin from her lap, tossing it on the counter as she steps down from the stool. Book clutched in her hand, she walks away without a word.

"Kalyn!" I call after her, but she doesn't break stride as she heads for the bedroom.

I drop my head, drawing in a deep breath in an attempt to calm my irritation. Following after her, I find her already in bed, her knees drawn up as she pulls the blankets up over her lap. I stand in the doorway, watching her, but she gives no indication she even sees me. Walking to her side of the bed, I sit down, pulling one knee up on the bed as I stare at her. "Kalyn, talk to me."

Her eyes continue to move across the words on the page, and I feel my patience waning. "Wanna fuck?" I ask, finally getting a reaction. Her eyes snap from the pages of her book, and she gives me the most disgusted look before returning her gaze back down. "I'll take that as a yes," I grab at the blankets on her knee, and she slams her book down on my hand.

"Leave. Me. Alone," she bites out.

I'm not sure how long her period lasts, but from what I've gathered, it's about two days of heavy flow and then one day of not really anything. Just to be safe, she should be over it in two more days. I'll give her space until then.

CHAPTER

Twelve

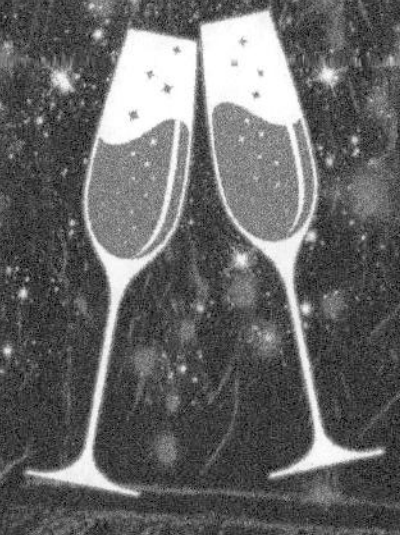

KALYN

It's Friday, and my period has decided to overstay her welcome, keeping my irritation on high alert. Just thinking about going to the office makes me mad, especially knowing that Bridget will spend her entire day waiting on Jonah hand and foot. So pretty much every time Jonah has went away on business to come back to the city, he's spent all his days surrounded by gorgeous women fawning over him. Maybe I should stay home another day, but then I would do what I've done the last three days and sit here making myself even more mad. I almost want to go to work just to ask about every single woman we pass by: "Have you slept with her? What about her?" I sound like a stage-five clinger, which is definitely not a good look, Kalyn.

Deciding it's time to be an adult again, I get ready for work while Jonah is exercising. We don't exchange any words on the ride to work, and then, just to purposely be annoying, I deliberately slow my pace as I exit the vehicle and walk toward the building. Jonah, with his long strides, usually has everyone scrambling to keep up, but he adjusts to match my speed without comment.

I've set up my workspace at a conference table near the large windows in his office, working from a new laptop he had set up for me. It's sufficient for most tasks, but there are moments when two monitors would be easier. I've considered using Jonathan's office for that, but my annoyance with him dissuades me. Plus, I'm finding satisfaction in the glares Bridget gives every time she walks in here and sees me.

I have Brownshire Corp pulled up and have gone over their last six quarters of financials, finding errors in each. Judging a book by its cover, I hate what the founder looks like—he just looks slimy. Though that's no way to run a business, I brush aside the sinking gut feeling and make my way across the room to Jonah's desk. Since he's in a meeting in a conference room on another floor, I can run numbers faster, having access to both his computer monitors.

I spent forty-five minutes combing over everything with the company and all the financial documents that were provided, and the conclusion I've come to is that I really hate this founder more by the second. Taking a break, I decide to snoop. I did tell Jonah my first day that's what I planned on doing. I click from folder to folder, looking to see what all he has on here. He's such an incredible businessman, and his computer is like the rest of his life: really well organized.

Leaning back in his chair, I stare at the picture of him and me in his kitchen back home, displayed on his computer screen. We're both smiling—he's so handsome. Plus, my tits look phenomenal in the picture. Probably why he has it as his desktop background.

Leaning in closer, something about the image catches my eye—my nipple seems… I don't know… not flush with the rest of me. I swipe my knuckle on the screen, wondering if maybe there's a smudge. But it's still there. Curious, I use the mouse to hover over the area. Nothing changes. I double-click, and suddenly, a password prompt appears.

Why do I instantly feel like I've hit the jackpot while simultaneously feeling like I'm doing something I'm not supposed to? Then again, he's the one trying to hide whatever this is… in *my* nipple.

I try the password he wrote down for me, but it doesn't work. Then I try a couple more, and still nothing. On a whim, I enter my name and the date of the gala… it works!

For the most part, it appears boring. Folder after folder, hundreds of folders filled with what seems to be leverage on people. The files are cryptically labeled with initials, dates, and random names. He obviously has a system for organizing this information.

As I browse the different titles, I stop when I see "J.J.B." That shouldn't have any significance to me, yet my heart plummets when I read it. Breathing in and holding it, I double-click on the folder. My heart might have literally stopped beating in my chest. I trusted my gut, and now my guts are going to be on the floor any minute. J.J.B. Jonah. Jonathan. Bridget.

There are multiple videos, over twenty. Clicking on one that shows the still image of Jonah sitting on the couch in his office. I watch as it starts. It's on tits. Big fake tits. I can hear Jonah and Jonathan talking as the tits move closer. Then the camera is set down and the angle is adjusted.

Jonathan, in typical Jonathan fashion, has a smirk plastered on his face. "What's up."

I fast-forward through the video, watching in sped-up time as she sits on Jonah's lap, wrapping her arms around his shoulders and crossing her legs. My breathing grows heavier as they begin kissing. Speeding it up faster, I watch as she stands and undresses all while he watches her. Then she leans down, unbuttons Jonah's shirt, and turns at something Jonathan says to her. She moves away from Jonah and starts undressing Jonathan, while she keeps glancing back at Jonah, who never takes his eyes off her.

My eyes well with tears as I witness exactly what I envisioned when he told me about their threesome.

I stop the fast-forward and let it play in regular speed. Jonathan lies back on the pillows on Jonah's couch, and she mounts him, letting out—I hate to say it—a sexy moan as she lowers herself onto him. She supports her hands on his chest as she bounces up and down. He reaches up, grabbing her tits and squeezing them, just like I envisioned him doing to me. When she eases herself all the way down and turns to Jonah, who is sitting in his chair watching, the first tear escapes my eye.

"Come here," she says, reaching her hand back to him.

He downs the rest of the liquor in his glass, places it on the coffee table, stands, undoes his belt, then unbuttons and unzips his pants, lowering them. He fully removes them and sheaths himself in a condom, positioning himself behind her. Letting spit drip from his mouth to her backside before he uses his thumb to move it around, then buries himself into her ass. They thoroughly rock her. Both of them slamming into her with such speed my core hurts. She's screaming so loud that ten floors down could have heard.

I want to puke, while at the same time, my body betrays me as I feel moisture between my legs. Damn it, body. *This is Jonah with his dick in another woman; you know that, right?*

Exiting the video, I click on four more, all showing her recording him fucking her. Some of them are so rough I wonder why she didn't press charges against him, but she keeps coming back, begging him for more.

I find the videos of him having threesomes with the receptionists, and that makes me more mad than him fucking Bridget. They took turns sucking his cock and balls, then he fucked each of them in their pussy and ass while the one getting railed went down on the other girl.

What the fuck kind of freak-show circus is this place?

My bones are rattling with anger. I close out of all the screens, re-lock his computer, and grab my laptop. Walking over to Miles, I set my laptop down on his desk and pull up a chair.

"Hey, Kalyn… Miss Bell, I mean," he says, appearing nervous.

"Will it bother you if I work right here?" I ask, not waiting for a response.

"Are you okay?" he questions, pulling a couple tissues from the box on his desk and handing them to me.

"Thanks," I reply, taking the tissue and blotting under my eyes.

He doesn't mention my crying again, and I can feel when my face regains its normal color. Every time I cry, my already full lips get even puffier, so I pull up my phone camera to check them. My lipstick is still perfectly intact, and to anyone who doesn't know me, my lips don't look swollen. However, I can tell they are, and I know Jonah would notice too.

Going over more financials, I ask if he understands numbers.

"I'm the number guy," he says happily.

Walking him through what I'm seeing, he plugs in different figures into his computer. He appears concerned too when he gets the same numbers I'm getting.

I hear giggles and whispers and glance up to see girls all around the room looking behind me. I don't even have to turn to know it's Jonah they're all staring at. Though I try to stop myself from looking, I can't resist. I glance behind me and see Jonah staring at a binder with Bridget and two other men, all walking toward his office. My mind instantly replaces the image with Jonah and Bridget naked, her bouncing on top of him.

"Miss Bell?" Miles asks, waving a hand in my face.

"Sorry, I didn't hear you," I turn to face him.

"I said we should go to records and have them pull additional quarters."

"Great idea. Lead the way."

We walk away with armfuls of files and head directly to the cafeteria. We settle at a table with great natural lighting, overlooking the floor below with more seating and food options. After getting our food, we sit back down and start inspecting the documents.

"How do you think these discrepancies are being reported?" I ask Miles. Just then, the chair next to me scrapes across the floor, drawing everyone's attention within earshot to Jonah, who plops down in the chair holding that stupid fucking leather binder and reading it. He doesn't say anything, he just sits there and continues reading.

Miles looks at me wide-eyed, but I just continue discussing the numbers in the first folder.

We continue talking for another thirty minutes until I check the time. Miles had mentioned he leaves work at 2 on Fridays. "It looks like it's time to wrap up. Thank you so much for all your help," I initiate us gathering our things as I stand and begin collecting our folders.

We walk to the Elevator, and Jonah strides right along beside me.

As we reach Miles' desk, I begin collecting my things. "Thank you again, you've been a huge help. Have a good weekend," I say, waving as he slings his bag over his shoulder.

"You too, Miss Bell. Mr. Everett," he nods and walks off.

"I know you like to stay late, Mr. Everett, I'm going to head out. I don't feel the need to put in the long hours you do."

Before I can move past him, Jonah says, "I'll call you a ride."

"No need," I respond, walking around him, heading towards his office. As I pass Bridget's desk, she eyes me up and down. For good measure, I give her my best fake, toothy smile.

I put the files down on the table I've been working from and prepare to leave.

"I have three more meetings; I can't leave right now," Jonah says as I head toward the door.

"I don't recall offering for you to leave with me," I retort.

"Your 2:00 meeting is ready in the conference room," Bridget announces from the doorway.

"See ya later," I say to him, as I walk past her.

He follows after me, and I can hear Bridget's heels clicking right alongside him. When we reach the elevator, Jonah presses the button before I can. Standing here waiting feels so awkward. I can feel the receptionists staring at us, and there are clients sitting in chairs waiting for an associate to come get them, and they too are staring in our direction. When the elevator doors finally open, Bridget strides in first, and Jonah holds his hand out for me to go. I walk in and stand directly in front of her while he stands next to me. He presses the button for the main floor and another four floors down. Obviously, the floor his meeting is on. When the elevator stops on that floor, Jonah strides out, and Bridget bumps into me as she passes.

"Excuse you," I snap.

Jonah stops and turns around, looking at me and then Bridget.

"Sorry, that was my mistake," she says to me.

"I know it was," I maintain eye contact with her as the doors close. But not before I hear Jonah ask, "What did you do?" I don't hear her response, but I can see her giving me a disgusted look.

Royel was waiting for me when I exited. I honestly planned on flagging a taxi, but this works out better.

Back at the condo, I shower, then grab my book and head to bed. That's what I love about reading—it transports me to another reality where time works differently. I don't even realize it's seven o'clock until I hear the front door closing.

Jonah strides into the room, sets his laptop bag down next to the bed, and heads to the bathroom. After his shower, he reenters the room. I try to ignore his presence, but I can't.

"Well, let's talk about it," he says.

"Talk about what?" I ask, plugging my phone in.

"You know what," he replies, his voice deeper.

"Why don't you stop with the cryptic bullshit and use your words? I'm not in the mood to play guessing games with you, Jonah,"

"The videos," he says bluntly.

I freeze. How did he know I saw them? Did he have cameras in his office watching me? I thought I deleted the history.

You know what, fuck this. He should explain why he kept those videos, especially on his work computer. That's incredibly inappropriate and unprofessional. "Yeah, let's talk about them. Which one do you want to tell me more about?" I turn and look at him. "You're always on your laptop; maybe you can pull one up and give me a play-by-play. That sounds super fun. Go ahead. Get one ready." I snap, then turn back to my book.

My rage burns hot when he climbs on the bed and yanks my book from my hands, throwing it across the room. "Quit being disrespectful. We're talking. Give me your attention," he demands.

I feel like I'm being scolded, and it makes me feel small. But at the same time, I was only purposely reading to try to piss him off. So I can't be shocked when it worked.

"You threw my book," I state the obvious, as I stare in disbelief at my discarded book in the corner of the room.

"I'll buy you a new fucking book."

"You asshole," I snap, starting to climb out of the bed.

He grabs my arm, holding me in place.

"Let go of me," I bite out, trying to move again. But he pulls me back, positioning my legs on either side of his lap and pushing me against the headboard.

"Talk to me," his voice is deep but pleading, his eyes glancing back and forth between mine.

"I don't want to talk to you. I can't even stand the sight of you." My chest heaves, my anger feeling like it's going to burst out of me.

"What is making you so mad? That you asked if I have fucked other women and I told you the truth? That I have videos on my computer of fucking other women? That I didn't lose my virginity to you?" He sounds so annoyed with me.

I was on board with his questioning until he said that last part. "Fuck you. Take your stupid computer and your stupid pillow and get out."

"That won't solve anything."

"It will make me feel an ounce of happiness right now." I glare at him as the words come out.

"You'd want me back the second I walked out that door. You wouldn't say it, but you'd feel it."

"Let's call Bridget, maybe she will come fuck you in this bed. Who am I kidding. She undoubtedly already has. We know she's already mounted you in every square inch of your office." I bite out.

He shrugs. "She does enjoy other people watching me fuck her… kinda like you do."

My eyes widen at his words. "You fucking assh—" He catches my arm as I raise my hand, ready to slap him.

"Big mistake," he says, clenching his jaw and grabbing me by my neck. He twists us around until I'm flat on my back, with him planted between my legs, his weight crushing down on me.

"Get off me!" I yell as I struggle beneath him. "I don't want you, Jonah. Get the fuck off of me." My anger escalates as my body betrays me, wanting him… badly.

His lips curl up in a sinister smile, and he climbs off of the bed, just as I told him to. Yet, I instantly feel irritated that he got off me. What kind of dumbass mental games am I playing.

"Yeah, run away," I laugh, and when he still seems unbothered, I get even madder. "This is your condo. I'll leave." I bite out, climbing off the bed.

"Not like you have anywhere to go," he says, grabbing his pillow.

"Oh, trust me, it will take all of five seconds to find a man to go home with," I snap back.

His head snaps in my direction, and he stares for a minute before shaking his head as if he can't believe what I just said, then walks out of the bedroom.

As soon as he's gone, my heart aches. I started a fight and am mad that he isn't fighting back. I want to understand why he kept videos like that. It feels like I caught him cheating on me over and over again, even though those videos are from almost five years ago.

CHAPTER
Thirteen

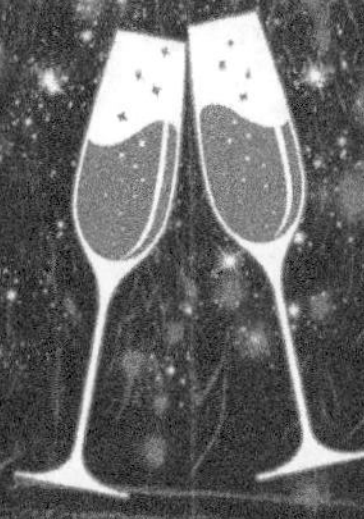

KALYN

I spend the entire night tossing and turning, unable to find any rest. Every time I would finally drift off, I wake up hoping it was just a bad dream, only to see his pillow is gone and his side of the bed is cold and empty.

In the morning, he's already gone. I know he's down the hall at the gym, like he is every single morning. I wait around for an hour past when he would normally return, thinking I might try to talk to him. But as each minute passes and he doesn't come back, my anger builds all over again.

Getting dressed, I quickly braid my hair and leave the condo. The elevator ride downstairs feels interminable, each second stretching out as I try to steady my racing thoughts. When I step outside, the city greets me with its usual chaos. Fitting for how I'm feeling right now. I don't know where I'm going; I just need to escape the suffocating confines of his condo and clear my head. Walking aimlessly, I find some comfort in the rhythmic sound of my footsteps against the pavement as I count each step.

"Hi, can I get a room, please," I ask the woman behind the counter.

She's friendly and checks me into a room with no hesitation. With my key in hand, I take the elevator up to my floor. Once I'm settled in my room and the adrenaline starts to wear off, I turn on the TV and close the blackout curtains completely. The room transforms from bright daylight to a pitch-black night in a quick sweep of the fabric.

I settle on cartoons until I fall asleep.

My chest constricts with anxiety, making it feel impossible to breathe. The overwhelming need to apologize to Jonah consumes me. I have to tell him I'm sorry. Driven by desperation, I rush back to his condo, my heart pounding as I swing the door open.

"Jonah? Jonah," I call out, not finding him in the living room. My ears catch on to faint noises coming from the bedroom, making my pulse quicken. Slowly, I approach the slightly ajar door, each step feeling weighted down as if vines are coiling around my ankles, trying to hold me back. My mind races with doubts and fears, flashes of walking in on Wyatt and the intern start to flicker with each step closer, gnawing at my confidence.

I push the bedroom door open and freeze in horror. Jonah is completely naked, holding Bridget in his arms, thrusting into her against the window. The scene is raw and intense, their bodies glistening with sweat in the bright light.

"Jonah," I say shakily, tears streaming down my face. "How could you?" Despite my presence, he doesn't stop. His hips continue to move rhythmically in and out of her. Bridget's screams grow louder, her eyes locking onto mine with a triumphant snarl.

Rushing toward them, I attempt to intervene, but it's as if an invisible barrier holds me back. My fists are clenched, ready to strike him, but they never make contact. Jonah's movements become more forceful, his grip on Bridget's hips tightening. The sound of their bodies colliding fills the room, mingling with his deep grunts. He just keeps fucking her, fast and hard, and all I want to do is strangle him. Yet my hands can't make contact. He turns to look at me, and they both start moaning louder.

"You feel so good, Bridget," his voice drips with pleasure as he still maintains eye contact with me.

"Jonah," I plead, trying to reach out one more time. My fingers brush the air, never quite connecting with his skin. Desperate, I try again to break through the barrier, but my hands remain uselessly suspended in the air. Bridget's back arches as she clings to him. His eyes are so dark with lust and determination, I clutch my stomach trying not to puke. I hate him. I never want to see him again.

They both begin laughing, the sound echoing in my ears like a cruel taunt. The scene becomes surreal, as if I'm watching it unfold from a distance. Their laughter fades, and the room feels like it's spinning. My vision blurs, and the noise around me seems to tunnel away, becoming more distant with each passing second.

Suddenly, my eyes shoot open, and I gasp for air, jolted awake in the hotel room I had fallen asleep in. The cartoons still play on the TV, the only familiar comfort in the disorienting aftermath of my nightmare. I glance at the clock on the bedside table and see that six hours have passed. My exhaustion from the previous night finally caught up with me, but the haunting image of Jonah and Bridget lingers in my mind, making it difficult to breathe.

Shoving the blankets off, I scramble from the bed, rush to the curtains, and frantically jerk them open. Unlocking the patio door,

I swing it open and step out onto the balcony. The gentle breeze is instantly refreshing, and I take deep breaths, trying to calm myself. That was probably the worst nightmare I have ever had to date. I would take a Wyatt nightmare over anything to do with Jonah and another woman any day. I would rather relive the day I walked in on Wyatt screwing the new intern than ever have a dream of Jonah with anyone else.

Sitting in a chair, I just look out at the city, watching the people walking around and cars driving by, taking in the noises and the air. Everyone has somewhere to go, something to do. They have thoughts, hopes, dreams, and ambitions. It's weird to think about how small we all really are. Like a higher being could look down on us and see we are all just insignificant. That in the blink of an eye, everything could just be gone. Maybe we are a science experiment in some alien's petri dish. Or maybe I'm the star of *The Truman Show*, showing everyone I'm a complete fool.

Perhaps this is why I've always been alone. Maybe my brain knows I'm a lunatic who shouldn't let people in because this is how I treat them. Jonah has been nothing but wonderful to me, and last night I treated him like garbage. But he said hurtful things too. And even though I regret what I said, I brought it all on myself. I'm the one who questioned him. I wanted to know if there was something that happened in the past with him and Bridget. Asking about everyone else was just prompted by his response to him and Bridget.

I'm nothing special. I see all these gorgeous women he's been with and don't understand why he's choosing to be exclusive with me. Actually, I don't even think we are exclusive. I don't really know anything anymore. Why am I even here? I don't want to go to the office and have everyone know what it feels like to have his dick inside of them. Why did he sleep with so many women? Why am I so jealous? This is a very unattractive trait. I'd be putting me on a plane and shipping me back to the mansion to pack my things and get out if I were him.

He's probably relieved I'm gone, if he's even noticed. Well, he's obviously noticed. He doesn't have me nagging in his ear constantly. Why do women have to get so hormonal? I can't even help it. Even when I try to calm down, I'm fired right back up and ready to brawl at all times.

Okay, Kalyn, you have twenty minutes to play out a scenario in your head with you and Bridget.

Fine.

"You stupid bitch," is how I would start. "You just think you can fuck my man? You put your disgusting pussy on his penis."

"Yeah, and it felt so good."

Well, I didn't necessarily want to hurt my own feelings with this.

Maybe I won't add in her commentary.

Taking a deep breath, I allow my mind to start over. I would walk into the office, right up to her where she always waits for Jonah.

"You stupid bitch," I begin once again.

No Kalyn, you are the stupid bitch, I scold myself. I can't even play out the fantasy of ripping into her because she did nothing wrong. The only wrong thing in this picture is my brain running away from me.

Is this how relationships measure who cares more? By tormenting themselves with imaginary scenarios about their partner's past relationships? I can't imagine Jonah ever giving this much thought to any of my past relationships. He probably hasn't even considered the idea of me with another man. Yet here I am, obsessing over all the times he's been with other women. I could probably look down at the people walking below and see at least ten women who have slept with him. Maybe I should yell down, "If you've slept with Jonah Everett, raise your hand." But then I'd probably hurl myself over the balcony when every woman's hand goes up.

I wonder if the other women who have slept with Jonah feel it was as amazing as it is when him and I have sex. It never felt like just sex with him—it felt like so much more. Like our souls became one in ways so indescribable that no one could ever grasp the magnitude of our connection. Now, I'm pretty sure that was all in my head. What a lovely thought. Each touch, each kiss, felt as if no other touch or kiss from either of us were ever meant for someone else. That they were strictly for the other. The way his hands move over my body, as if he's memorizing every curve, while simultaneously already knowing on a soul level each curve of me. It all made me believe we were connected on a level beyond the physical.

The first time he and I were together sexually, I felt an electric surge. I felt like we were so deeply rooted in chemistry, and it wasn't just about the pleasure. I remember the way both of our breaths hitched at the feel of our skin-on-skin contact. Time could have stood still, and not a single other thing in the world mattered except for the two of us in that moment.

But now, I wonder if it was ever real. Or maybe it was just one-sided. Because it was real for me. I have so many doubts and insecurities, replaying every moment he and I have shared for signs that it was special to him too. And now that I've been a big giant crazy lady, how do I even go back? Do I walk in the door and just apologize? Do I walk in and ignore him? Maybe I'll get back, and the doorman won't even let me go up. He'll say I'm not allowed back.

I can see myself standing there, my heart pounding, rehearsing my apology, trying to find the right words to convey my regret and sorrow. But what if he doesn't want to listen? What if he's already decided that I'm too much, that my insecurities are too overwhelming? The thought of losing him terrifies me, but the fear of not addressing my feelings is even worse.

"You're not planning on jumping over, are you?" a Scottish man's voice from the balcony next door asks, startling me.

I look over and see him in a bathrobe and a fisherman's hat, lighting up a cigar as he sits in the chair on his balcony. He looks to be in his forties, with perfect skin. Then again, he's staying here, so of course he has money to make sure his skin remains unblemished and unwrinkled. Yet, he's smoking, so, kind of defeats the purpose.

"No," I scoff.

"Good, because I'd have to hurry and beat you to it," he snickers.

Ignoring him, I turn back to gaze at the park across the way, observing people chatting and playing frisbee, dogs chasing after balls and joggers passing by.

"The only reason someone people-watches for this long is to try to escape their own thoughts," he continues.

"Cool. Escape your own thoughts quietly," I snap before I can even process how rude I'm being. "Sorry," I sigh, leaning forward, crossing my arms on the balcony railing and resting my chin on it.

"No need to apologize. A stranger is interrupting your day-dreaming. I'll keep my trap closed."

I turn my head to the side, peering over at him. "Smoking is so bad for you, and that reeks," I say, lifting a brow to him.

Smiling, he puts his cigar out in the ashtray. "Sorry 'bout that," he says, leaning back and putting his bare feet up on the banister.

I let out a laugh when I see his toenails are pink and sparkly.

"I can't fathom what you could be laughin' at. I know it's not my polish. I can tell you where I got it done, but you'd never be able to get yours done as pretty," he says, wiggling his toes.

"She must be in high demand."

"Aye, she is. She's only five, little firecracker with red hair, just like her mama," he smiles. "Had to leave home to come for business. My daughter did it just yesterday before I left."

"I see. Well, I suppose you're right, I won't be able to get the same perfect pedicure."

"That's right, ya won't. Very unfortunate for you, lass," he says.

I copy his move and kick my feet up on the railing nonchalantly so he can see my dark red glittery nail polish, acting like I'm oblivious to him seeing them.

"Yikes, mine definitely look a hell of a lot better than that," he leans over, squinting to get a closer look at my toenails.

"Yeah, I agree. Unfortunately, she kept the polish just to my nails. Your pedicurist clearly went above and beyond, polishing your entire toe," I lift my foot slightly to give him a better view.

"It was a surprise for me too. I had to pay her in extra kisses and bedtime stories. Worth every bit."

"Do you have a picture of this one-of-a-kind, talented artist?"

"Aye," he replies, pulling his phone out of the pocket of his robe, unlocking the screen, and then proceeds to scroll through his gallery.

Standing up, he walks to the edge of the balcony, and I do the same to meet him from my side. He holds his phone out to me, and I take it, looking at the precious little curly red-haired girl, a stunning redhead woman with striking green eyes, and a baby who doesn't quite have two hairs on his head yet but is smiling wide nonetheless in his dad's arms.

"What a beautiful family," I say softly, a genuine smile spreading across my face. I must look like a total creep staring at his family's photo and quickly hand his phone over.

"And you?" he asks as he takes it back.

"No kids," I settle back down in my chair.

"Not yet, or not ever?" he probes.

"I don't know. I kinda suck at being an adult. Can't imagine trying to parent a child."

"Kids are arseholes," he jokes, "but the best kind."

"I've never really been around kids," I admit.

"And your boyfriend?" he asks, his tone casual.

I turn to look at him, arching an eyebrow. "Is this a creepy way to find out if I'm single so you can try to talk me into coming to your room because you convince me it will be the best decision of my life all so you can get your rocks off while you're away from your wife and kids? Because if so, I can hold your robe to make it easier for you to nose dive off the side of your balcony."

"Ouch," he raises his hands in mock surrender. "You read too many fantasy books. I love my wife and kids and don't need to have a one-night stand to get my rocks off. I'm satisfied at home, and she sends me off with all the pleasure I need to hold me over while I'm gone. I only ask because I know the look on your face. You seem sad, but only a temporary sad because your aura is still so bright."

I look over and laugh. "My aura?"

"Aye," he says with a playful grin. "Yours is pink and yellow."

"Interesting."

"You might not see it, but you have a serious glow. It's vibrant but flickers and then bright again. My guess is an internal struggle," he shrugs. "But you aren't someone who's going to let whatever it is keep you down."

"You're so insightful," I tease.

"I have perfect vision, never worn a contact in my eyes or glasses. I was blessed in all the ways a man could be blessed."

"I'm on my period," I confess abruptly, reclining in my chair, letting out a heavy sigh.

"… okayyy," he drawls, sounding slightly puzzled why I gave out that information, but also slightly amused by my sudden admission.

"I'm on my period and I'm emotional. I asked my boyfriend if he's ever slept with his assistant, and I got the answer no woman ever wants to hear," I admit, feeling a strange sense of relief for having said it out loud.

"Did he cheat?" he asks, leaning forward slightly.

"No, it was over five years ago. It just feels… like he cheated," I say, knowing I sound ridiculous but unable to shake the feeling.

"Why'd ya ask?"

"Because his assistant was giving me death glares when I went to work with him." I huff, crossing my arms in frustration.

"He can't take back the past, and the only reason she would be giving you eyes is because she never got him the way you have him," he offers.

"He slept with his receptionists too… and his flight attendants… and every other female in the city. Your wife isn't in the city, right?" I turn and look at him.

His grin widens. "No lass, she's home in Scotland."

"Good," I reply, not meaning it to be funny, but he laughs anyway, a deep, hearty laugh that somehow makes me feel a bit lighter.

"So he was quite the ladies' man but must be killer in bed now, aye," he winks at me.

"Unfortunately, he's unbelievable in every aspect of life," I admit. "But I just want to throttle every woman who's put their stupid vagina anywhere near him. Ughh!" I exclaim, more aggressively than I intended.

"He only slept with that many women because none of them felt 'right' to him. At least he kept giving it a try until he found the right one."

"Keep going," I urge.

"It's like finding the perfect dress and then searching for the shoes that complement it. You try on flats, but they feel awkward and look a bit off. Then you attempt heels; they're beautiful, but after wearing them, your feet ache and may blister. So, you keep trying different styles, colors, and fits, hoping to find the perfect match. Until one day, you discover the ideal pair of heels. They match your dress flawlessly, as if they were made together. Snagging the last pair in your size, you slip them on, and it feels like walking on clouds. Each step is like a sweet kiss to your toes, and at the end of the night, you reluctantly take them off, longing for that cloud-like comfort. You find yourself reaching for them again and again, realizing they're the only shoes you ever want to wear."

"What color were her shoes?" I ask, referring to his wife.

"I'll become any color shoe she needs me to be. Your guy tried on all the shoes, and you were the only one that fit. And all those women know it. And if I'm being blunt, he's really feelin' like shiet right now, knowin' he fucked up and doesn't know how to fix it. He did all that before he knew about you, and he's being punished for it."

"He keeps all these women employed at his company. His assistant follows him around like a lost puppy. Then he invites me to come along, where I'm mean-mugged every second of the day. I literally spent one entire day at the office, then he takes me home and fucks me so hard I quite literally couldn't walk for a week. I start my period and start a huge fight with him, then sneak out while he's exercising and am hiding out in a hotel, people-watching, wondering if they all have it easier than me. And I have it pretty damn easy," I say exasperated.

"Fucking hard is good. Assistant might just be good at her job, obviously not good enough in bed to keep him wanting more. I can't imagine anyone being prettier than you," he says sincerely.

I turn and look at him. "You're married, remember."

"I'm not talking about for me. I'm talking about for him. He brought you to work with him to show you off."

"To show me off to all the women who know what he looks like naked. He has the biggest dick I've ever seen in my entire life. I could come just thinking about it. And all the women in the office have also come all over it. That makes me nothing special. He made me squirt, you know that. Like full-blown all over his bed the first time we had sex. I legit thought he was pushing on my bladder so hard it was going to make me pee all over him and his bed. The sheer thought of another woman squirting on him makes me feel murderous," I say, clenching my teeth.

"Not all women squirt, ya know," he says. "He's good in bed, yes, but not every woman he's been with is squirting all over his rod. And I'll bet he didn't put in nearly the effort he puts in with you with them. Especially if he's having sex with them at the office. Those are usually just quickies."

I ponder that for a moment and realize he's right. I don't think he took any of them back to his condo. I guess I don't really know. But I almost don't even dare ask. Can't imagine the revelation I would find with more questions.

"I got here and took a nap, and dreamt I returned home and walked in on him and Bridget having sex in his bedroom. And when I woke up, I was sad, depressed, and turned on," I confess with a sigh.

"Don't be getting hung up on a lass named Britches," he says, sounding taken aback.

I laugh. "I like Britches better than Bridget."

"You look better when you smile," he relaxes, kicking his feet back up. "Does the thought of him having sex with another turn you on?"

"No… maybe… I don't know. The thought of him doing it now doesn't. But the thought of past him doing it… kind of, I guess. His assistant is really pretty. Sexy even. And she knows it. She wears these sexy little outfits that border on being inappropriate, and she has these huge fake boobs that look perfect in her tops, that she doesn't wear a bra with. I picture her and him having sex when I see them interacting in his office. But now knowing they did, I want to strangle both of them."

"You're quite angry, lass. How long does this period last?" he chuckles.

"I don't know. Hopefully just another day." I glance over at him giving him a grumpy look at the thought.

"Does he get squeamish around blood?"

"No. I assume you're referring to period blood? The first time we had sex I bled, and he acted like he didn't see it smeared all over our bodies. I wasn't on my period, so maybe that was the difference. But we had sex a couple days ago, and he still didn't seem bothered by the blood. I'm giving you way too many details. I really don't know when to shut the fuck up," I say, really hating how I'm spewing all my problems onto this random stranger, but couldn't find words when I was with my therapist that I paid.

"Do you feel better?"

"Yeah, actually, I do," I turn my head toward him. "Thank you."

"Go home and ride him; he won't know what hit him," he suggests, a smirk forming on his lips.

"I think I'll stay mad awhile longer," I muse.

"Why? You like feeling like shiet?"

"No, I hate it, actually."

"Then stop," he replies, as if it were that simple.

"Want to know what's so lame? I'm most upset that I don't know what we are. Like, we live together, we sleep together, we share a room. But am I his girlfriend? I wouldn't even know how to introduce him to someone. Like, this is my… friend with benefits? My boy friend? How do you even establish that? Maybe you just don't as you get older."

"You could just ask him," he suggests, tilting his head as if it's the most obvious solution.

"Why would I do that? He would probably think I'm a weirdo. Hey, we've been fucking and you like to lick my asshole; are you my boyfriend?" I retort, rolling my eyes.

"Back it up, he licks your balloon knot?"

"I'm having a serious crisis right now, and all you hear is that?" I say, exasperated.

"I hear all of what your saying. I was just taken aback," he replies, trying to suppress his laughter.

"Why?" I question.

"Ya look too snooty for that."

"Well, that fixes all my problems," I throw my hands up dramatically, pretending to be relieved.

"So, how many times has he licked your back door?" he asks, as if trying to solve a puzzle.

"Every time he goes down on me, kinda. I always thought it was accidental, until he put his tongue inside," I say openly.

"Oh, he likes you. And doesn't find you dirty."

"Well, that's reassuring. I never had it in my mind that he might find me dirty, but now that you said that I'm sure I'll be looking for signs."

"No need, he licks your starfish; he don't find a thing wrong with ya. Ask him how many he's licked. Bet he can count on one finger."

"You're very therapeutic," I say sincerely.

"So are you," he says back.

"I'm going to take your advice and head home," feeling like a weight has been lifted off my shoulders.

"It was nice chatting with ya, lass," he says as I stand. He stands as well and walks to the edge of the balcony, extending his hand toward me. With an amiable curve of my lips, I approach and clasp his hand in a firm shake. He gently tickles the inside of my wrist with his pointer finger, sending a wave of unexpected laughter through me before he releases my hand.

"Bet ya won't forget me now," he winks.

"You're absolutely unforgettable," I agree, waving goodbye to him before going back to the room, collecting my purse, and leaving.

CHAPTER
Fourteen

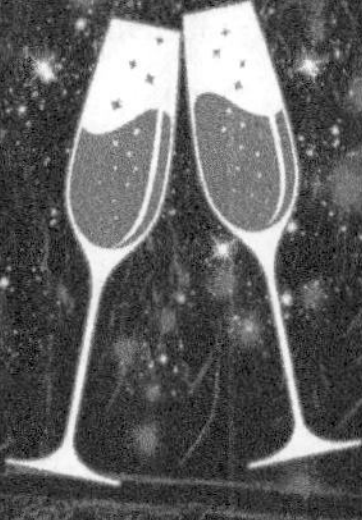

KALYN

Thankfully, the elevator attendant lets me up, and when I get to Jonah's floor, I'm relieved when his door opens. I half expected it to be locked. But the moment I round the corner, Jonah is standing from the couch, a mix of worry and anger etched on his face.

"What is wrong with you?" he demands.

Every bit of calmness I felt before instantly dissipates at his words, and my frustration comes right back. "I think that's pretty obvious," I say dryly, walking past him.

"Don't walk away from me," he orders, but I scoff and keep walking.

"What are you, five? You throw a tantrum and leave. Did you think that would show me? Just really stick it to me while you wandered off to a hotel by yourself?" he continues.

"How do you know where I went?" I turn, narrowing my eyes at him. "Are you stalking me again?" I spit out.

"I know where you are at all times. You think you have freedom… I just loosened the leash. You want to run like a stray, have it your way; I'll rein you right back in," he snaps.

"Whatever that means," I roll my eyes and walk toward the bedroom.

I can hear him stomping after me, so I quicken my pace, trying to close the door and click the lock in place, but he puts his foot out, and the door immediately stops.

"I don't want you in here," I bite out.

He glares down at me. As I release the door, he shoves it back open. "Fine, take the stupid bedroom," I say, irritated. I try to walk past him, but he grabs my arm. "Let go of me," I try pulling my arm away, but he only jerks me in closer to him.

Why does he have to be so sexy?

He threads his fingers through my hair, tugging my head back. "You wanna act like a spoiled brat, I'll treat you like one." In one swift motion, he spins me around, yanking my leggings and panties down, then presses me hard against the wall. My hands rise to brace myself, my cheek crushed against the cold surface by the unyielding pressure of his hand on the back of my head. I hear the sound of his pants unzipping, and my traitorous pussy weeps for him.

She gets exactly what she wants because he doesn't make us wait long. He crushes his face against mine, his breath hot and heavy as he pulls my hips towards him while guiding his throbbing cock into my slick, wet entrance.

I want to be angry. I want to tell him to stop, to get off me. But the truth is, I want his touch.

I need his touch.

He slides along my slit until he's at my center, and pushes inside, not caring if I'm ready. But he quickly finds that I certainly am. I tell myself I won't give him the satisfaction of hearing me moan, but a gasp escapes my lips as he thrusts in deep, filling me completely.

He takes me fast and hard, his grip on my hair painfully rough. His teeth sink into my neck, and I cry out, reaching my hand back to grab his hair, tangling my fingers in the soft, wavy locks, pulling just as hard as he is. He grunts, a primal sound that reverberates through me, then pulls out, guiding me by my hair to the bed.

He shoves me down on my stomach, climbing on behind me. With a forceful yank, he pulls my hips up, spanking my ass hard enough to make me yelp. The sting of it sends a jolt of pleasure straight to my core. He parts my legs with a nudge of his knee, then slams into me.

Aside from the belt, this might be exactly what Shay meant when she suggested putting the belt around his neck. He referred to it as "reins," and it feels exactly like what he's holding onto, controlling my every movement with a dominating grip on my hair.

I will for sure have a headache when he's done with me, but he feels so incredible I don't even care. He's not gentle; he's angry and making sure I know it, and somehow, that makes it even hotter. The front door closes, but he doesn't slow down. Instead, he quickens his pace, slamming into me with a relentless intensity until he finally reaches his climax, pumping every last drop in me. Then, just as quickly as it began, he pulls out and adjusts himself, leaving the bedroom without a word.

This is a complete contrast to our usual sex. Normally, even after he finishes, he would make sure I got off too. But not this time. He leaves me wet, horny and dripping with his seed.

Fucker.

I'm furious by the time I manage to get off the bed. My rage burns hot as I head to the bathroom to clean myself up. The mirror reflects my flushed cheeks and tousled hair, which also pisses me off. After a quick cleanup, I step out of the bedroom, part of me wanting to storm out and drag him back to bed by his ear, but the enticing aroma of Marietta's cooking distracts me, pulling me toward the kitchen. As I enter, Marietta greets me, but her expression fades as she takes in my appearance.

"Miss Kalyn, are you ill?"

"I'm fine, just a little headache," I reply, sliding into the chair next to Jonah. My anger simmers, and my body betrays me by reacting to the close proximity to this big, sexy jerk.

Jonah slides a glass of water toward me and scoots his hand across the counter, concealing something beneath his palm. When he lifts his hand and returns to his computer, I see two pills in front of me. So, he's an asshole, but a thoughtful one. My head throbs, but not as intensely as my pussy is throbbing for him.

"Thank you," I whisper, taking the pills.

As Marietta serves our dinner, I'm about to remind Jonah not to be on his computer during dinner, the same way he told me I'm not allowed to read while we're eating, when I see he has powered it off and closed it. He picks up his fork and begins eating in silence. The tension between us is palpable, and I hope he feels guilty for not letting me come; it was selfish. Then again, why would he want to get me off? I've been terrible to him. I asked him those questions, and he was honest, even though it looked like it pained him to tell me.

Marietta returns just as I stand about to take my plate. "Miss Kalyn, let me," she says, reaching out.

"Marietta, I can do it," I smile at her.

"Let her do her job; that's what she's paid for," Jonah says, and both Marietta and I turn to look at him.

The room feels awkward, and I can tell even she senses it. Handing her my plate, I muster my best smile. "Thank you so much for dinner—it was wonderful."

She returns the sentiment with a hesitant look as I exit the kitchen.

I didn't want to make a scene or do anything that would make Marietta feel even more uncomfortable, even though I wanted to yell at him right then and there. I also felt like crying. This is definitely the most emotional a period has ever made me, and I know it's because I'm in an unfamiliar place, with women constantly making me feel like I don't belong, and Jonah seeming more irritable than usual. Maybe coming to the city brings out the worst in him. Even so, I'm madly in love with this man, even at his worst.

I brush my teeth and put on a nightgown, then go back to the bedroom. There's a chair in the corner of the room on my side, meant for decoration. It looks comfy, so I pull it across the room next to the large windows and plop down in it to read. Instead, I watch the sky darken and the city lights come alive.

My eyes shift from the view outside to the reflection of Jonah coming in and walking straight to the bathroom. When he returns, he walks to the bed, sets his phone down, pulls back the covers, and places the extra decorative pillows on the bench at the end of the bed. As soon as he gets in bed, he pulls out his computer and starts typing. I put my book down, climb into my side of the bed, and lie there for two hours, hyper-aware of his presence.

My skin prickles with desire that I try my best to suppress, but I can't. I still yearn for him after earlier, and I need to feel myself come around his cock. I try to stifle these feelings by thinking about how he embarrassed me in front of Marietta, but my body doesn't care about that. All it wants is to feel him inside me.

I try to calm my breathing and relax, but my rapid heartbeat is literally making my chest heave. I need to get off. I will him to make a move, to come over and take me. I don't even care if it's rougher than before—I just want to be close to him. But he doesn't come; he just continues typing away.

I'm done with this. Done with his typing. Done with him ignoring me. Done sitting here, drenching my panties wanting to have sex with him. I'm done waiting. Tossing the blankets off me, I pull my nightgown over my head and slip off my panties. He doesn't even look over at me, still engrossed in his work. I grab his laptop and slide it to the end of the bed. His head jerks up, and the anger in his eyes vanishes instantly when he sees me before him completely nude.

"Lean back," I command, and he complies without hesitation. I straddle his face, placing one foot on either side of him. "Eat it," I say, and his hands wrap around my thighs, his tongue immediately getting to work. I clutch the headboard, my head rolling back from the intense sensation.

He licks and sucks at me like a starved man. My hips move against his mouth, my hand twisting in his hair, pulling him deeper into me as I ride his face. His grip on my thigh loosens as he makes his way to my center, penetrating me and finger-fucking me while sucking on me. My orgasm builds quickly, and I come hard, all the tension from our fight, the videos, the conversation with the Scottish man on the balcony, and his earlier roughness, flooding out of me as I ride his fingers and face long after the aftershocks subside.

When my hips finally stop moving, he withdraws and softly kisses the inside of my thigh, looking up at me. I bring my leg back over him, bend down to grab my nightgown, panties, and book, and storm out of the room.

Standing from the bed, he follows after me. "Get back in bed."

"No," I snap. "You wanted to fuck me and not get me off. You owed me," I say, walking to the couch.

"Fine, we're even," he snaps back.

"I'm aware," I reply, lying on the couch and opening my book.

"Come fuck me," he says from the doorway.

To make it clear that I'm not going to move, I kick my leg up on the back of the couch. He approaches and leans over, staring down at me. I pretend to be engrossed in my book, even though I can't concentrate. He reaches over, grabs my foot, and softly squeezes it. "Baby, come back to bed," he says gently.

I pause, catching my breath, and I can still feel the ghost of his tongue on my skin. My body is tingling, still sensitive from the orgasm he just gave me.

Fuck it.

Throwing my book to the floor, I stand, walking over the back of the couch right into his arms. His eyes widen in surprise, but they quickly flare with desire as our mouths crash together, as we devour each other.

He walks us to the bedroom, setting me down. I turn and shove him onto the bed and crawl back on, my body moving with a feline grace. His breath catches as I straddle his hips, feeling the hardness of his cock pressing against my wetness.

"You're not finished," I whisper, my voice low and sultry. "Not until I say you are."

"Anything for you, baby," he pants, his hands finding my hips as I lower onto him, gasping as he fills me. I take him in slowly, inch by inch until I'm fully seated on him. We stay just this way for a moment, our eyes locked, the only sound being our ragged breathing.

I start to move, rolling my hips in a slow, deliberate rhythm. His hold tightens, his fingers digging into my flesh as I ride him. My hands splay across his chest, feeling the hard muscles beneath my palms. His eyes never leave mine, a mix of anger and lust swirling in their depths.

The friction is exquisite, my pace quickening, as I ride him harder, faster, my nails scraping down his chest. His hands move to my breasts, squeezing and kneading. I throw my head back, a low moan escaping my lips as the pleasure mounts. His hands travel down to my ass, guiding me, urging me on. I can feel him getting close, his cock throbbing inside me.

With a final, desperate stroke, he comes, his release triggering my own, and I cry out as my body convulses around him, milking him dry. I collapse against his chest, spent and satisfied. I can feel his heart pounding beneath me, matching the rhythm of my own. His hands rub my back soothingly, and I close my eyes.

Sitting up, I don't say another word. I climb off him and walk back to the living room. I grab my nighty and slip it back on, then pick up my pillow and settle back onto the couch. My anger flares up again. I hate how hormonal I am; I usually don't get this mad. I feel like I belong in a straightjacket.

I annoy myself for the next twenty minutes, my brain really trying to piss me off, reminding me of the videos of Jonah and Bridget having sex until I drift off. I'm almost fully asleep when I feel the heat of an inferno curling up behind me on the couch. His arm wraps around me, and his face nuzzles into my back, and off we go, sleep blanketing around us.

I ALREADY KNOW THAT WHEN I GET UP, HE'LL BE GONE, LIKELY DOWN the hall at the gym. Opening the front door, I'm shocked to see two security men standing there with their backs to me.

"Excuse me," I say, trying to push past them, but they don't move. "Am I not allowed to leave?" I ask, but they remain silent. I try to shoulder past them again, but they stand firm. "Move," I demand, but they stay put. "Pricks," I mutter, slamming the door behind me.

So now I'm a prisoner because he's being a jackass?

Within ten minutes, Jonah strides through the front door.

"So, am I not allowed to leave now?" I stand from the couch, asking as he ignores me, walking across the living room to the bedroom.

"Jonah," I call after him, walking fast to catch up. He peels off his shirt as he enters the bathroom and turns on the shower. "You don't want to talk to me, and you don't want me to leave. What can I do?" I ask as he strips off the rest of his clothes and gets in the shower. His body is so sexy my mouth starts to water. "So this is what we're going to do? You beg me to talk to you, and I ignore you. I beg you to talk to me, and you ignore me?"

Fine by me.

"Fuck you," I say as I storm out.

The entire rest of the day, neither of us says a word to the other. I go to bed early and wake when he comes to bed, but I lie there quietly, not letting him know I'm awake. He's just as bothered as I am; I can tell by his breathing that he's awake too. I want to ask him what he's thinking about, but I don't. He'd probably just ignore me anyway. I could fuck him; I know he wouldn't turn that down. But I don't want to reward him. Instead, I stay quiet until I finally fall asleep again.

CHAPTER
Fifteen

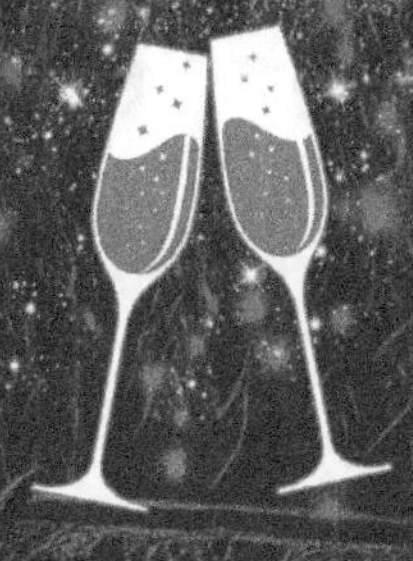

KALYN

We spent the most uncomfortable weekend in silence. If I'm being completely honest, I'm torn about going to work today. On one hand, I know I can be helpful and prove my worth to Jonah business-wise. On the other hand, I dread seeing Bridget. I've replayed in my head over and over how hard Jonah and Jonathan were railing her, her moans waking me every time I tried to sleep. Once, I even woke up whimpering in sync with her. I've never had a threesome; the closest I've come is fantasizing about Jonah, Jonathan, and Shay in the closet. Now, after seeing my fantasy come to life with another woman they were plowing, I feel awkward about seeing Jonathan again, as if he and Jonah had plowed me.

It sucks because Shay is the person I want to vent to about this, but I can't even do that because I don't want to be the one to tell her that Jonah has videos like that saved on his computer. And I'm sure Jonathan has copies.

We dress without exchanging a single word. When I realize that we are once again matching, I decide to switch things up. I swap my blue top and shoes for an emerald green ensemble, then exit the closet. As I'm leaving, I notice Jonah writing on a piece of paper, then folding it up and putting it in his shirt pocket.

That was weird, but okay.

Heading out the front door, I wait by the elevator, which the security guard has already pressed the button for. Jonah exits the condo and joins me as we stand side by side.

"Got a problem?" Jonah asks, and I freeze, thinking he's talking to me.

"No, sir, sorry, my apologies," the security guard next to me says.

What was that about?

When the elevator doors open, I step inside but see Jonah lean into the guard. "Get a hard-on again looking at my girl, I will cut it off and shove it down your fucking throat." His words are so dark and his voice is so deep my eyes bulge.

"Yes, sir, I'm sorry," the man stammers, clearly rattled by Jonah's threat.

At the office, Jonah promptly exits the vehicle and strides to open my door. Stepping out, I notice he has switched his tie to perfectly match my emerald green outfit. It's in this moment, I realize it hasn't been a coincidence that he and I end up with matching outfits—he purposely matches with me every day.

Entering the building, we find Bridget already in her usual spot, waiting for Jonah. Her eyes reveal a desire that I hadn't fully noticed before, but now it smacks me in the face. "Good morning,

Mr. Everett," she greets, handing him his leather binder and immediately diving into business.

During the entire elevator ride up, I periodically glance over at her, imagining how her boobs bounced while she rode Jonah's dick, how his large hands caressed them, and how Jonathan laid on the couch in Jonah's office while she rode on top of him, with Jonah putting his giant cock in her ass. Two best friends fucking the same woman. I knew they were close; I just didn't realize how close. I know for a fact Shay has no clue about this because if she did, either Jonathan would never come to the office again without her, or Bridget would find herself jobless.

When the elevator doors open, Jonah holds his arm out to keep the door open and gestures for me to go first, cutting Bridget off. "Baby," he says, indicating that he wants me to go. The immediate satisfaction I feel with this only grows when I glance at Bridget and see a death glare plastered on her face. As soon as I walk through the doors, he falls in stride next to me, leaving Bridget scrambling after him. I want to laugh but keep my expression serious.

Moving down the lengthy corridor, I spot Miles standing in the doorway of an office two doors down from Jonah's. "Miss Kalyn, I got all the files we requested. I placed them on your desk," he gestures toward the office I've never been in.

"Good morning, Miles," I say as I stop next to him, peering in the room he's pointing to. I stand frozen as he points to the nameplate on the door: Kalyn Bell. My mouth falls open, and I turn to look at Jonah, who glances at me, his face serious as he winks before entering his office.

I step into the office space and am utterly captivated by its beauty. At the center is a pristine white desk with two computer monitors, and behind it, another desk adorned with tastefully arranged pink and gold-accented accessories. The room is covered in pinks, silvers, and golds—my absolute favorite. The walls are painted in a gentle blush hue with subtle gold trimmings enhancing the elegance. The office sparkles with glittering accents that catch the light, infusing a touch of glamour. A pink, fluffy area rug graces the floor beneath a white couch and a glass coffee table. Overhead, a stunning crystal chandelier hangs from the high ceiling, leaving me nearly speechless.

Wouldn't that suck if it fell on my head while I was working?

As I take in the exquisite surroundings, I notice the impeccable design has to be Tabitha's work. There's no doubt in my mind that she created this stunning office.

Just as Miles mentioned, a cart filled with neatly organized folders has been wheeled in and placed next to my desk. "Wow," I exclaim softly, genuinely taken aback by the office.

"The decorator worked over the weekend. Actually, she was here all week in the evenings," Miles explains.

"Thank you for everything, Miles," I say gratefully. "Could I have your phone extension in case I need further assistance?"

"Absolutely," he replies, quickly jotting it down on a post-it and handing it to me.

"You're the best," I compliment.

Taking a few more moments to absorb all the intricate details of the office, I find myself particularly drawn to the large windows. Finally settling into the comfortable chair at my desk, I beam, "Well, how do I look?" asking Miles though I don't expect a response.

"Breathtaking," he blurts out. Then, as if noticing he said that out loud, he clears his throat. "Professional, you look professional," he stammers. "I'll be at my desk," his face flushes, and he hurries off.

I reach for the mouse, prompting the computer to come to life instantly. The picture of me and Jonah smiling in the kitchen is set as my right computer monitor's background. Funny, my nipple looks perfectly peaked in this picture. He didn't want to add a hidden folder on my computer? I inwardly scoff.

The left monitor displays a picture of the camping group, everyone so happy on the day we were leaving. I love this picture. "Sam has his arm wrapped around Amber's shoulder. Shay radiates joy as Jonathan holds her in his arms bridal style, and she holds her arm up as if striking a pose. Jonah stands behind me, his arms wrapped around my chest, my arms come up to hold his forearms. I'm smiling wide, while his is half-assed. Yet he's still devastatingly gorgeous.

During the initial hour, I familiarize myself with my office and then resume meticulously reviewing reports. Similar to previous reports, I uncover several errors in the first few I examine. This raises concerns, as I contemplate the possibility that these discrepancies might provide grounds for Jonah to initiate an audit on even more companies. It's clear the only reason these entities would fabricate their profits would be to steal money.

I've been immersed in the files all morning, so much so that I didn't even notice the day slipping away until Miles knocks on my open door with a tray, explaining that it's already 1 PM and he hasn't seen me eat yet. Grateful, I thank him and begin to eat while discussing the files with him. He confirms the discrepancies I've discovered.

Once I've gathered sufficient evidence to support my suspicions, I grab the files and head toward Jonah's office. Though I don't particularly want to engage with him, I can maintain a professional demeanor and let him know what I found.

"He's in a meeting," Bridget interjects sharply as I approach Jonah's office. Does she spend all her time guarding his office? When does she do anything productive?

Disregarding her, I confidently knock on his door, waiting for a response—a departure from my usual manner back at the mansion, where I typically tap and enter. "I said he's in a meeting," she snaps, grabbing my wrist as I attempt to knock again.

Glancing from her hand wrapped around my wrist back to her, I seethe, "You will wish you were never born if you ever touch me again," jerking my arm free and pushing Jonah's door open. Bridget follows closely behind, casting a disapproving glance at Jonah as if she explicitly instructed me not to enter.

"You can leave," I assert firmly, turning to her, my anger still evident from the way she grabbed me.

Jonah abruptly concludes his phone call, saying he'll call them back, just as I approach his desk, with Bridget hot on my heels.

"You can close the door when you get out," I assert, meeting her gaze. She shoots me a disdainful look before turning to Jonah for assistance.

"Did you not hear her? She said leave," his tone is sharp, causing Bridget to jump slightly as she scurries towards the door, closing it behind her.

Handing him the folders, I proceed to guide him through all my findings, strongly recommending audits for these specific companies. He agrees and promptly makes phone calls to set the additional audits in motion.

"I have a really important meeting in ten minutes that I'd like you to attend. I'd appreciate your input if you wouldn't mind," he says.

"Yes, sir," I reply promptly. "What should I bring?" I ask, preparing to follow his lead.

"Just yourself," he responds, rising from his desk. As we leave his office, Bridget remains in the hallway. "We're heading to my meeting," he informs her as we pass, and she already has his leather binder and her laptop in hand.

Though my issue with her stems from her past relationship with Jonah, I do find she seems to be on top of things work-wise, always having everything he needs exactly when he needs it. Maybe that is the entirety of her job. He did say he keeps competent staff, and I hate to say it, but she is definitely proving to be competent.

Descending four floors, we arrive at another impressive office level and convene in a spacious, sophisticated upper-class meeting room with a large conference table. Five men occupy one side while two sit on the opposite, leaving only three vacant chairs. As we enter, everyone rises.

"Mr. McIntosh, I trust your flight was smooth," Jonah greets, shaking the man's hand. By the time my eyes meet his, my mouth almost hangs open. It's the man in the robe from the balcony. The man I went in-depth with how big Jonah's manhood is. He's the important meeting Jonah has. "This is Kalyn Bell," Jonah introduces me.

"It's a pleasure to meet you," he says, shaking my hand, his pointer finger coming to the inside of my wrist as he softly tickles it.

"Likewise," I smile awkwardly.

"And you are?" he turns to Bridget.

"Mr. Everett's personal assistant, Bridget," she responds confidently, shaking his hand firmly.

"You've got the handshake of a man," he winces with exaggeration, tugging his hand away and shaking it as if she hurt him. This seems to embarrass and offend her simultaneously. He continues giving Bridget a sideways glance as we all take our seats.

They delve straight into business discussions, and Mr. McIntosh frequently glances between Jonah and me over the next half hour. At one point, I can almost sense his thoughts, and I narrow my eyes at him as if to tell him to shut up. He smirks and returns his attention back to Jonah.

After Jonah and his team provide all the important documentation and information to Mr. McIntosh's team, I assume that we'll conclude the meeting, allowing Mr. McIntosh time to deliberate on entering into a business partnership with Jonah. From a business standpoint, Jonah is hands down the best. Anyone would be smart to go into business with him.

"And what are your thoughts?" Mr. McIntosh turns his focus to me unexpectedly once Jonah finishes speaking.

"Me?" I ask, caught off guard.

Bridget attempts to interject, but Mr. McIntosh raises his hand, immediately silencing her. "Nobody asked you to speak. You're the assistant," he states flatly before redirecting his attention back to me. "I can tell you're the head of the company. I want to hear what you have to say."

"Mr. Everett is the epitome of honesty and loyalty. Entrusting your business in his capable hands would be the smartest decision. He possesses integrity and would never lead you astray. I believe you'd be a bloody idiot not to sign the contract here and now," I assert.

"Well, shiet, hand me the bloody pen," he responds, extending his hand.

"We should review the contract first, sir," cautions the gentleman seated to his left.

"This woman would have me on my knees in seconds if she wanted. I'll sign the bloody contract because she said it's a good idea. If she asked for all the money in my bank accounts, I'd drain them just to see her smile," he winks at me.

Jonah's hands tighten visibly on the table, and I see everyone in the room shift uncomfortably.

"Are you married, Mr. McIntosh?" I ask.

"Aye, I am," he admits, signing the first page.

"I don't think your wife would appreciate you talking like that about another woman," I say, shooting him a pointed look to cool it. I know what he's doing—he's trying to get under Jonah and Bridget's skin. And while I appreciate him shutting Bridget up, I don't like that Jonah is feeling threatened.

"Of course, I've just never encountered a woman so beautiful in a meeting," he explains. "I'll bet you have to fend off hordes of admirers," he nods his head to Jonah.

"Not even one," Jonah replies in a low tone.

"You two would make a sexy couple. Maybe you should go on a date," Mr. McIntosh suggests casually. "You'd produce some strong, little lads."

"We do go on dates… often," Jonah replies dryly.

"Aye, good. Well, if you're going to be spoken for soon, I better hurry and set you up on a date with my brother before you're off the market," he quips.

"She's very much off the market," Jonah asserts, narrowing his eyes and grabbing my hand.

"The contract, sir," I remind him, directing his attention back to the papers.

"Right," Mr. McIntosh acknowledges. Flipping the page, he looks confused. "Can you come show me where to sign?" he asks me specifically.

"Just where it's been pre-highlighted for you," I reply.

"I left my glasses at home," he says sheepishly.

Letting out a sigh, I move to stand.

Jonah places his arm out in front of me, stopping me from rising. "Bridget," he says in a stern tone, signaling for her to be the one to help.

"I don't want the assistant helping me. I want the smart one," he nods to me.

"Flattery will get you nowhere here, Mr. McIntosh," I narrow my eyes at him.

"Then let's get it over with," he smirks.

Standing, I walk around the table. He exchanges a glance with the man beside him. "Make room for her, would you? What do you expect, her to sit on my lap?"

I don't dare look at Jonah, knowing he must be fuming. I'm just relieved he hasn't ended the entire meeting prematurely because of this idiot's mouth.

"I'd suggest next time you attend a business meeting, you bring proper eyewear. Although you look to me like you have excellent eyesight. I doubt you've ever even had a contact touch your eyes," I repeat the words he said to me just a couple of days ago.

"You can tell just by looking at me that my eyes are good," he says, smiling up at me.

"The contract," Jonah interjects tersely.

"Aye, sorry, sorry, contract. Got it," Mr. McIntosh pretends to refocus. "So, why two assistants?" he asks Jonah.

Jonah looks irritated, so I cut in. "He only has one. I'm a colleague," I clarify, pointing to the next spot on the paper for him to sign.

Jonah scoffs at my words, and I can tell Mr. McIntosh is getting the exact reaction he was trying to provoke. After the last signature, I gather the binder. As he stands, he stares down at me, our chests almost touching. "It was a pleasure to meet you," he grins.

"We will be in touch, Mr. McIntosh. I look forward to working with you," Jonah says, cutting through the stupid eye glare we are giving each other.

"Aye, me too. I did make a small adjustment to the contract. I'd like Kalyn to handle my account personally," Mr. McIntosh announces.

"Bridget handles these matters," Jonah asserts.

"And I don't need anything from 'Britches'. Kalyn will do just fine. I feel a sort of bond. Her aura is bright and welcoming. Hers is murky, like swamp water," he says, giving Bridget a squinted stare. Then he turns back to Jonah and me. "Now, both of your auras together are almost blinding. Soulmates for sure. Though, you seem angry, lass. I'll bet a romp in the office would make you both feel better," he suggests, shaking Jonah's hand.

Jonah seems momentarily stunned, blinking a few times.

Letting out a laugh, I shake his hand. "Thank you for your business, Mr. McIntosh."

As we walk away, I turn to look at him over my shoulder, and he's smiling wide and gives me a thumbs up, followed by a wink. I smile and shake my head.

Exiting the room, we don't head toward the elevator like I expected we would. Jonah must sense my confusion because he speaks before I have a chance to say anything. "We have another meeting to attend," he gestures toward another conference room just as we reach it.

At one end of the conference room, a projector stands ready for presentations, while the entire table is encircled by chairs with people scattered around. Three vacant chairs are positioned at the far end of the table. Upon entering, Jonah greets everyone, guides me to my seat by pulling out the chair, and then takes his place at the head of the table, while Bridget occupies the other remaining seat.

The meeting kicks off with three men launching into their presentation, but it quickly becomes evident that their pitch lacks careful preparation. The data is incorrect, and the numbers Jonah requested are missing. The shorter gentleman initiates a slideshow and mentions that he doesn't know how half the slides mysteriously disappeared.

They're just winging it at this point.

I notice a woman in the meeting staring and smiling in Jonah's direction. Initially, I attribute it to her likely having engaged in intercourse with him before. However, my thoughts shift as I stare with a mix of admiration—if they have, because I know the wonders of Jonah Everett—but also a sense of sympathy because she's no longer experiencing it.

Lost in thought, I gaze at her and shift my eyes away when I notice Jonah reaching into his shirt pocket and pulling out the folded-up piece of paper he slipped in there that morning. My focus returns to the meeting as I listen to the speaker. Feeling a gentle brush on my leg under the table from him, I reach down, anticipating him wanting to secretly hold hands, but instead, he places the piece of paper in my hand.

Confused, I look at him, but he avoids eye contact, leaning back casually on one arm of the chair, his pen rested thoughtfully on his lip as if deeply engrossed in the meeting. Under the table, I unfold the note, and a rush of emotion grips my heart, making it feel like it's leaping into my throat.

Suppressing a smile, I pinch my lips together and reach over, taking his pen from his hand. I draw a heart in the "yes" box, fold the note back up, and discreetly pass it back under the table to him.

Bridget lifts her gaze over the top of her glasses, her eyes darting between us. For a moment, I feel an urge to stick my tongue out at her like a child but quickly suppress the impulse as Jonah retrieves the paper.

As he unfolds the note, a smile spreads across his face, which he quickly masks with his hand. He then puts on a serious expression, writes something on the paper, and Bridget leans forward in an attempt to peek at it. Just as swiftly, he folds it and returns it under the table.

When I try to take it, he holds onto it, intertwining his fingers with mine, the note held between our hands. We remain like this for the duration of the meeting.

As the meeting begins to wrap up, he releases my hand, flattening the paper into my palm before standing up and moving to the front of the room to speak. Under the table, I unfold the paper, and my eyes well with tears as I read:

I love you, Kalyn

I stare at the words, reading them over and over. Looking up from the paper, I lock eyes with him at the front of the room. He continues speaking effortlessly, a subtle lift at the corners of his lips.

And just like that, every ounce of my anger has officially dissolved.

As the meeting concludes, he exchanges handshakes with everyone, and we make our way back to the elevators. His hand finds mine, our fingers interlacing, while I still clutch the piece of paper in my other hand. I want to get back to my office so I can spend the next hour smiling at it and sending Shay a picture.

The elevator doors open on the top floor, and he glances down at me. Our gazes meet, and he leans in, his lips brushing against mine before he guides me out. The receptionists stare, their mouths agape, but we pay them no mind, continuing on to his office.

All eyes follow us as we pass by. I'm sure they've all been wondering who I am to him—arriving and leaving together, I appeared practically out of nowhere, yet am always wherever he is. If there were any lingering questions about my relationship status with him, they should be answered now.

At his office, he gestures for me to enter first. Once inside, he closes the door behind him and pulls me back, pressing me against the door as his lips claim mine in a passionate kiss. He pauses momentarily, staring deeply into my eyes. "I love you, Kalyn," he murmurs, before his mouth crashes down on mine again.

The week of silence and tension has only heightened the need we both feel between us. He briefly tears his mouth away, his hands lifting my skirt up to the top of my thighs as he hoists me up, my legs wrapping around him. In a few strides, he carries me to his desk, setting me down on the cool surface. My fingers begin working at his belt and unbuttoning his pants, freeing his straining erection.

As I attempt to scoot off the desk to kneel before him, he intervenes. "I don't think so, baby."

Staring up at him, I bite my lip as I scoot back, surrendering to my desires. I recline back on his desk, bending my legs back to offer him easier access. A smile spreads across his face as he observes the view I've presented. I'd skipped wearing panties under my skirt to avoid any visible lines, and now the sight of me bare before him lights a fire of eagerness in his eyes.

His finger trails up and down my wetness, arousing me even more. Aligning himself at my entrance, he gradually eases himself in until he's fully submerged. The sensation is so profound my eyes flutter closed from the fullness.

God, how I've missed him.

He begins to thrust, each one growing harder and more insistent. I cling to the edge of his desk for support as he vigorously pounds into me, the pleasure building with every stroke. My breath comes in short, ragged gasps.

"Does that hurt, baby?" he asks, making sure he's not pushing in too deep again.

"No," I moan in response, my voice trembling.

"Ride me," he commands, lifting me up while still buried deep inside me.

Seated on his desk, I straddle him, wasting no time in grinding my hips against him. My head rolls back, arms draped over his shoulders as I move with abandon. He grips my hips, guiding my movements.

"I'm so sorry, babe. I've been awful to you," I pant out, barely able to form the words. "Forgive me."

"Always, baby," his lips reclaiming mine.

"Sorry to bother you, sir, Mr.—Oh God, I'm sorry," Bridget stammers as she walks in, shock written all across her face. "I've been knocking," she adds, frozen in place.

Breathlessly, Jonah pulls his lips from mine, "What is it?" he asks, continuing to guide my hips back and forth on him.

"Mr. Garrity needs to speak with you, sir. He won't leave a message," she informs him, her eyes darting between us.

"Fine," Jonah replies, lifting me up and laying me back onto the desk, seamlessly resuming his previous actions. She stands there, unsure of what to do.

Tilting my head back, I stare directly at her. "You can transfer the call to him."

Shock renders her immobile.

"Go!" Jonah commands more sternly.

With that, she hurries out of the room, the door clicking shut behind her. Jonah quickens his pace, finishing inside me just as the phone rings.

"Everett," he answers, staring down at where he's still buried inside me.

I listen as he engages in business conversation. My desire for him doesn't wane; it intensifies. I kick both heels to the floor, plant my feet on the desk, and begin rolling my hips up and down on his pelvis. Jonah deftly positions the phone between his shoulder and ear, gripping my hips to assist my movements. His lips part breathlessly as he listens to the man on the line, his thumb finding my clit and gently rubbing in time with my rocking movements.

My orgasm rips through me, and I do my best to muffle my moans in my arm. He allows plenty of time for my body to pulse below him, then leans over, producing a tissue, and carefully withdrawing from me, using it to catch the stray drops of fluid.

Observing me and inspecting for any signs of blood, he displays a satisfied look. The call concludes, and he leans down to kiss me. "No more bleeding," he murmurs, as he disposes of the tissue.

"I know," I remark jokingly, rising from his desk. I straighten my skirt and reach down to slip my heels back on. "I'll bill you for that later," I pat his chest. He pulls me into a hug, and I attempt to pull away, but he only holds me tighter.

"Are you trying to squeeze my eyeballs out?"

"I'm trying to fuse with you, baby," he jokes, his voice filled with affection.

"I thought you needed to bite me?"

"I can do that," he smirks.

As he lets go, I move towards the door, opening it slightly. "Oh, and Jonah?" I pause, waiting for him to meet my gaze. When he does, I add, "I love you, too," before walking out, leaving a beaming smile on his face. Bridget stares in disbelief as I exit, and my grin widens as I continue down the hall to my office.

Halfway to my office, I realize I forgot my note on his desk. Turning back, I see Bridget beside him, discussing a client while he types on his computer. As I approach, he stops typing and looks up.

"Come back for more?"

I reach over and grab the note. "I'll be taking this. Love you," I say, loving how it feels to say those words to him out loud.

He lets out a laugh, "I love you too, baby," and resumes typing.

Back in my office, I open the note again, feeling the same giddy excitement as when I first read it. Not only did I finally receive an actual note asking me to be someone's girlfriend, but it came from Jonah. I'm so excited, I hurry and take a picture of the note, holding it up with a wide smile so both the words and my happiness are visible, and send it to Shay. She knows we've been fighting and we've FaceTimed nearly every day. This will be the first positive update on Jonah and me in a week.

KALYN:

[Image] *hairflip* anyways, I guess you could say things are getting pretty serious. EEEEEP

My phone instantly rings with an incoming FaceTime call. I place it on my phone stand and answer, beaming from ear to ear.

"Shut. The. Fuck. Up! Hold that up," Shay exclaims as soon as she sees me.

I do as she says, holding the note in front of my face with only my eyes peeking over.

"He just randomly gave you that?" she asks.

"What's interesting is, this morning when we were getting dressed, I saw him writing on a piece of paper and tucking it in his shirt pocket. I thought it was some sort of reminder. Later, during a business meeting, the client totally ruffled Jonah's feathers. During the next meeting, I noticed a woman staring at Jonah, and I couldn't focus until I saw him reach into his pocket and pull out the paper. I started paying attention to the meeting again, then felt his hand under the table. I thought maybe he wanted to hold my hand, but he gave me the note instead."

"That is literally the cutest, Kal! I asked Jonathan why Mr. Everett has never said 'I love you' yet when he's loved you for years, and he always shrugged it off and said he would when the time was right. Guess he did good holding onto that wild card." Her gaze turns from the camera. "Come here," she says, and Jonathan sits down next to her, wrapping his arm around her shoulder.

"Whats up, Kal," he grins.

I momentarily forget I'm mad at him. "Pretty sure your best friend wants to marry me," I tease.

"Not wants—he will," he corrects.

"Show him," Shay exclaims excitedly.

"Yeah, show me. Just make sure Everett doesn't see, or he'll cut my eyes out for looking at your tits," he laughs.

I hold up the note again, smiling wide as I watch him read it. His eyebrows lift, and he looks genuinely impressed.

"That was smooth for sure. Couldn't have thought of a better way to ask," he leans back on the couch.

"Did you and Mr. Everett talk about him doing that?" Shay turns to look at Jonathan.

"Of course."

"You guys sit around like little girls, talking about your girlfriends?" Shay accuses.

"We do; our girlfriends are pretty cool," he winks at the phone.

Just then, I see Jonah standing outside my office door, engaged in a conversation with Bridget, who shows him something in a leather binder. He nods, and she glances at me and walks off. He comes in, smiling as he approaches. I point at my phone, and he leans down, one hand on the back of my chair and the other on my desk, peering at the screen.

"Hey," Jonah nods to Jonathan.

"What's up? Kal has a pretty cute note. You should have her show it to you," Jonathan laughs.

"Oh, sorry, it's meant for my best friend and boyfriend's eyes only," I pretend to look sympathetic that he won't have the privilege of seeing it.

"Perfect, I am one and the same," he bends down and kisses me.

CHAPTER *Sixteen*

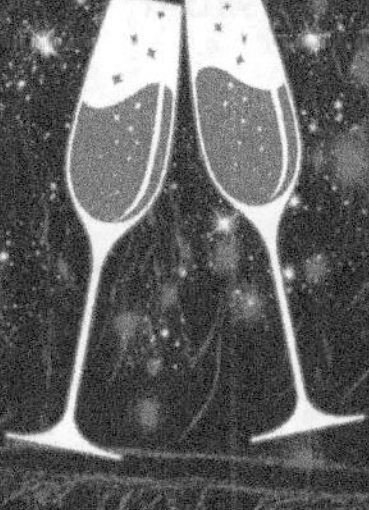

JONAH

I've spent years putting in long hours at the office, taking my work home, and working well past when I should. There was nothing but work to fill the void inside me that was leaving me numb and empty. Now, with Kalyn, I feel alive. For the first time in my life, that emptiness is filled with her love and presence. I no longer need to drown myself in work. I've told Bridget not to schedule any meetings for me after 3 PM, so Kalyn and I can leave by 4 PM and spend more time together.

Today, though, I stay until after 6 PM to wrap up my last late meetings before heading to Kalyn's office. I'm eager to see, making the remaining seconds before I get to her office feel like hours. As I approach, I see her standing up from her desk, grabbing her purse, and putting her phone in it. The sight of her, even in such a simple action, brings a smile to my face.

"Ready to go, baby?" I ask, leaning casually in the doorway.

She looks up, her eyes softening. "Ready."

I made sure to let Marietta know this morning that she didn't need to cook dinner tonight—I've made a dinner reservation instead.

We're seated in a cozy, private corner of the restaurant with a view of the city. She stares out the window, looking heartachingly beautiful. When her attention turns back, she catches me admiring her, and the corners of her lips curve up. I bring her knuckle to my lips and touch a soft kiss to it, then place our hands back on the table.

"Am I officially an employee?" she asks.

I'm intrigued by where this conversation is headed. She never needs to work again in her life if she doesn't want to. If she and I weren't romantically involved, Kalyn has the kind of work ethic I would hire immediately and pay her well above her worth just to keep her. I've never told her about specific times watching her at the diner because the more I divulge, the bigger creep I seem.

One instance I distinctly remember was a man going into the diner and sitting in one of her booths. He looked like he hadn't showered in weeks, and as he passed by, customers gave him disgusted looks. We had seen him earlier, rummaging in a garbage bin near the diner. Despite his appearance, Kalyn approached him with a genuine smile, pulling her notepad from her apron to take his order. From watching her, I got good at reading her lips and saw her say, "Nonsense, get whatever you'd like, on the house," before taking his order. After he left, I watched her pull her own tips from her apron to pay for his meal.

We caught up with the man later and gave him a small amount of money to see what he would do with it. Impressively, he returned the next day to pay for his food. Kalyn smiled, put the money back in his hand, and told him, "Hang on to it; you can buy your meal next time." He never got the chance for a next time because we discovered he was down on his luck and had hitch-hiked his way here. After some digging, we found out his mother had been searching for him, with missing posters four states over. He didn't know. We got him cleaned up and sent to his family. Last we checked, he was doing well—mowing lawns in the summer, and shoveling snow in the winter, and taking care of his mom.

Smiling across the table at Kalyn, the memory of her selfless-ness touches me. "If you want to be official, you can be."

"Well, I do have an official office."

"Then welcome to the company, baby," I bring her knuckle to my lips again.

"And I'd like to discuss terms."

"Pay?" I clarify not understanding.

"Something like that," she grins.

Interesting. "Okay," I smirk, ready to give her any amount she wants, not that she will ever need it.

She leans down, grabs a notepad and pen from her bag, and winks at me as she begins to write. Tearing the paper from the notebook, she folds it in half, and slides the pen and paper to me.

Grinning, I pick it up and open it.

REQUIREMENTS:

Quit matching me (Kalyn Bell)

Work lunch 2x week

4 kisses during the work day

3–20 orgasms a week. (At our discretion)

NEGOTIABLE:

Cuddling in bed without laptop at least 1x weekly

SIGNATURE:

I take the pen and cross out "quit" and write "keep," then draw an arrow to "Bell" and write "for now" above it. Lunch twice a week is doable; I know she and Miles have been having lunch, so I leave that alone. Four kisses? I suppose that's fine, but I draw an arrow to it and write "Ouch." For the orgasms, I draw an arrow and write "During or after business hours?" Not that it matters—I'll give her an orgasm here in the restaurant if that's what she wants.

Then I sign:

Yours always, Jonah Everett

REQUIREMENTS:

Keep ~~Quit~~ matching me (Kalyn Bell) For now

Work lunch 2x week

4 kisses during the work day Ouch

3–20 orgasms a week. (At our discretion)
→ During or after business hours?

NEGOTIABLE:

Cuddling in bed without laptop at least 1x weekly

SIGNATURE: Yours always, Jonah Everett

I slide the paper back to her, and she opens it, her eyes scanning my additions. She holds out her hand, looking at her ring finger, then gives me a side-eye before continuing to read. Folding the paper up, she puts it in her bag, then leans closer, curling her finger at me. When I'm close enough, she touches under my chin and pulls me in, softly kissing me.

"That contract starts when we get home," she says flirtatiously.

"How hungry are you?" I lean in, biting her lip softly before pressing into her mouth. She relaxes instantly, our tongues moving gently against each other.

"Who's ready to eat?" the waitress cheerfully interrupts, bringing us back to the present.

Our lips part, and we both sit up straight in our chairs.

"Thank you," Kalyn says as her food is placed in front of her.

When the waitress walks away, I lean over and whisper, "I have a boner."

Her fork pauses at her lips, and she glances down before looking back up at me with a wink.

"Lets get our food to go," I suggest, my eyes searching for the waitress.

"Absolutely not," she shakes her head and turns to follow my line of sight.

"You're torturing me," I say, pouting playfully.

Sighing, I begin eating. I enjoy food, but I enjoy her more, and the taste of the food replacing the taste of her kiss isn't worth it right now. "Wanna go find a bathroom?" I ask her.

"Jonah," she playfully hits my leg.

"What?" I let out a laugh. "You don't think that sounds exiting?"

"Behave, we're at a nice restaurant," she looks around making sure no one can hear us.

"What if I drop my napkin and accidentally find myself under the table between your legs?"

"You're naughty, babe," she says, her cheeks flushing.

"You're naughtier than I am," I retort.

"Maybe we're equally naughty," she bites her lip, her gaze shifting from my eyes to my lips.

I shake my head slowly, grinning.

"How is everything?" the waitress returns, her tone cheerful.

"Check, please," I say, never taking my eyes off Kalyn.

"Of course," she says, hurrying away.

"I'm not done eating," she whispers, her gaze locked on mine.

"I don't want to wait any longer to start the terms of our contract," I lean over and slide my hand under her chair, pulling her closer. She giggles as our legs brush under the table from our closeness. Her mouth, lips, and teeth are so perfect that I can't help but stare as she talks. I have to push away thoughts of filling her plump lips with my cock.

"I guess we probably should make the contract official by checking off one of the things on it," she nods, our lips inching closer.

My hand comes up to her neck, brushing the soft skin as my fingers wrap around it, pulling her in. Our mouths part as our tongues meet. I feel the waitress return, and I smoothly reach into my pocket, grab my wallet, flip it open, and hand her my card. Moments later, she places the leather check wallet on the table and walks away.

Dinner was exactly what we needed. When we finally get home around 8, she showers and comes to bed.

"Not working tonight?" she asks, resting one knee on my side of the bed.

"I wanted to check on you first," I reply, remembering she mentioned wanting me off my computer at least once a week. I wonder if she was hinting she wanted tonight to be that night.

Climbing on the bed and straddling me, she sits down directly on my dick. "I already like where this is going."

"I just got to the good part in my book," she winks at me.

"Are you wanting to read, baby?" I wrap my hands around her waist and cup her ass.

"Yes," she whispers, smiling innocently.

"Okay," I sit up to kiss her.

We fall into comfortable silence for the next hour, my foot crossed under my leg and her small foot resting against mine. Every so often, one of us pushes softly into the other, just to acknowledge them. When she closes her book and lays it on the bed, she sits up straight, then slumps, propping both hands under her face on the pillow, she sighs.

"I'm still upset over the videos."

I turn to look at her, then push my laptop down on the bed. "I know, baby, I understand. I'm sorry." It has been eating me up. I have to keep the files in case an employee gets fired and tries to blackmail me. I had Dame remotely extract the files from my computer so they can be stored back home, off my work computer. The truth is, I've never watched any of the videos. Mainly because I found it disgusting that an employee would let me or both of us fuck them the way we would. It made me lose respect for them, and I figured if I watched it, I would want to fire them because I'd lose any remaining respect. They would get sent to Jonathan, who would upload them into a shared file we have. He never watched them either.

"I want to talk to Shay about it. I feel alone in this, but I don't want to get you or Jonathan in trouble," she says, looking concerned.

I let out a sigh, grabbing my phone off the nightstand, and call Jonathan.

"What's up," his usual happy voice fills our quiet bedroom.

"Hey. Kalyn found J.J.B.," I say, and there's a long silence on the other end of the line.

He lets out a deep sigh. "Fuuck. Sorry, man. Is she still there?"

"Yeah, she found the folder a week ago," I reply.

"The note must have been the make-up portion? Is Bridget still employed?" he asks, though I know he doesn't really care.

"She's still employed," I confirm.

"Well, fuck, sorry, Everett. Anything I can do?"

"Kal is hurt, really hurt. She wants to talk to Shay about it. She's *going* to talk to Shay about," I correct.

He lets out another sigh. "Understandable. My nuts are going to be in a fucking grinder. Can she hold off until tomorrow?"

I look at her, knowing she can hear the conversation, and she nods.

"Yes," I tell him.

"Kal, I'm so fucking sorry," Jonathan says.

She doesn't respond, just watches our phone call. "Well, good luck. My nuts have been under Kal's heel for the past week. I'm still on my knees groveling."

"Get off the phone so you can continue groveling." She pulls the covers open and straddles my lap, pulling off her top and tossing it to her side of the bed.

"Mmm," I moan.

"Guess I better go get some too before Shay kicks the shit out of me… and probably you and Bridget. Night," Jonathan says and hangs up.

"Guess I better go get some too before Shay kicks the shit out of me… and probably you and Bridget. Night," Jonathan says and hangs up.

CHAPTER
Seventeen

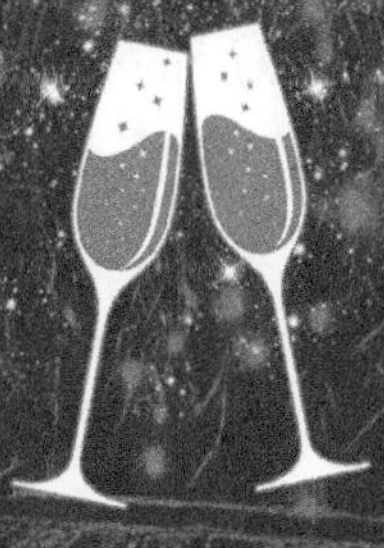

In the morning, we get dressed together, and, well, okay, I kind of love that Jonah always makes sure to match me. He puts on his slacks and heads to the bathroom to shave and brush his teeth while I finish getting ready. When it's my time to brush my teeth, he goes to the closet to complete his outfit. Today, I choose a sapphire blue top with matching heels, knowing he'll pick the same shade for his tie—it makes his eyes pop.

"I'll start picking out my outfit the night before so you can plan your outfit accordingly," I glance over my shoulder at him.

He winks at me as he heads to the closet.

Arriving at the office, it's the same routine. Bridget is waiting at the door, handing Jonah a black leather binder as she dives right into details of the day. As the elevator doors open to our floor, I decide I won't let the receptionists bother me anymore. Jonah holds his arm out to keep the elevator door open, letting me go first. With a broad smile, I greet the three receptionists with a "Good morning, ladies," before they have a chance to ignore me and only greet Jonah.

Momentarily, they all appear stunned, exchanging annoyed glances as we walk past. Jonah falls into stride beside me, squeezing my ass before sliding his hand up to my lower back.

When I reach my office door, I walk in.

"See you in a bit, babe," he says, tapping the door frame as he keeps walking. I'm digging in my purse for my phone when he comes walking back into my office, pressing his lips to mine.

"One," he says, then strides back out.

My smile lingers as I watch him leave, only to see Bridget giving me a disgusted look before turning to follow him.

Bitch.

Walking to the door, I peer down to Jonah's office. The door is slightly ajar, and he's inside with Bridget. I know I don't have to worry about him with her, but it reminds me I wanted to talk to Shay about the videos. Closing my door, I go back to my desk, set my phone on the stand, and FaceTime her.

"Good morning, my lovely," she coos as she answers. It's late morning where she is, and she's already dressed and, from the looks of it, day drinking.

"Where are you?" I ask, noticing her wide-brimmed hat and sundress, her hair softly blowing in the wind.

"Some girlfriends and I came to the beach," she says, sipping on a cocktail at an outdoor restaurant. She flips the camera so I can see the beach and ocean, then turns it back, smiling.

"You're cheating on me?" I feign jealousy.

"Never, my love. How's work?" she asks, taking another sip.

"Just got here. Call me later when you have a second," I tell her, not wanting to dampen her beach trip.

"No, I'm all yours. The girls are on the beach hitting on some guys, so I came to get a drink," she flips the camera again to zoom in on four girls in bikinis talking with a group of guys.

"I snooped on Jonah's computer," I blurt out. Her camera flips back to her.

"And? Anything juicy?"

"I found videos... of Jonah and Jonathan... having sex with Bridget," I tell her, waiting for her to tell me to 'shut the fuck up,' but she just kicks her feet up on the high-top chair next to her, leans back, and sips her drink, unbothered. "Jonah's assistant," I add, thinking she might not know who I mean. "Shay, did you hear me?"

"Quit staring over here, asshole," she says to someone off-camera, then looks back at me. "Yeah, sorry, hun. I've seen the videos," she says.

I sit there, trying to understand why she's so calm, while I just spent a week fuming over the same thing with Jonah. "Wait, what?"

"Jonathan is a fucking idiot. He had them saved on his computer at the condo under a folder labeled 'Private.' Obviously, that's the biggest red flag of OPEN ME NOW."

"Does he know you saw them?

She just shrugs. "Probably not."

She is so nonchalant it catches me off guard. Did she see what I saw? I'm mad that Bridget slept with Jonathan, and he's not even my boyfriend, yet she acts like she doesn't care at all. "Well, you're handling this better than I did."

"I found them like three years ago, and I wanted to murder him. But it happened before me. Trust me, I wanted to wring his neck. But you saw the videos. They weren't respectful with her at all. I half expected her organs to fall out when they were finished with her. She couldn't even stand afterward, and they legit flopped her on the couch, got dressed, and started drinking while she struggled to get dressed. Did Jonah ever treat you like you were just a piece of easy pussy? Because that's exactly how they both treated her—exactly like she is, a cheap-ass raunchy pussy," Shay says, sipping on her straw.

I burst out laughing. I should have talked to her a week ago—it would have saved Jonah and me a week of ignoring each other. Shay keeps me grounded, and it's times like these that I appreciate her even more.

"Jonathan told me about this one time they were at a business conference. Everyone was swooning over Mr. Everett and him, but there were these four girls who made a bet to see who could bed Jonathan. So as they approached him, he was just like, 'Come on.' He didn't give them a chance to lay it on thick. They looked confused but went along with him. He took them to the men's bathroom and told them to bend over the counter and hike their dresses up. He tossed a condom to each of them and told them to have it ready. Then, one by one, he screwed each of them against the counter, purposely messing up their hair as he did it from behind. When he was done, he said, 'If you come to business events to be sluts, you'll get treated like sluts. Get the fuck out of the men's room,' and dismissed them without giving them time to clean up or anything."

"What!" I exclaim. "That's fucked up."

"Yeah, but so is going to a conference with big executives just looking to snag a rich guy. That's how men end up knocking these women up and paying insane amounts in child support," Shay defends.

"What ended up happening with the girls?" I ask, still shocked.

"He fucked up their hair and their pussies. They left immediately after," she shrugs.

"Did Jonah know? Or has he ever done something like that?" I don't know why I even asked that. As soon as the words fell from my lips, I regret them. I'm not emotionally strong enough to hear of Jonah doing something similar.

"C'mon. It's Mr. Everett. He avoids messy situations like that, especially at work. He always stays professional. Jonathan just took one for the team and nipped the bullshit in the bud before they went for the top dog," she winks.

"I'm gonna be honest, if you had said Jonah did that, I would have gone two weeks ignoring him this time," I admit. I couldn't handle another story like the Bridget-receptionist story right now. My feelings are too raw.

"Nope, just my dumbass boyfriend," she takes another sip of her drink as she glances around the beach beyond the phone.

We talk for an hour, and we're mid-laugh when there's a knock on my door.

"Hey, baby, I have a meeting. Come?" Jonah asks, but I can tell he wants me to go with him since he's even offering.

"Alright, hun, talk to you later. Love you," Shay says as I turn back to the screen.

"Love you," I smile and blow her a kiss.

"Do we still have a living Jonathan?" Jonah asks.

I look up at him, surprised, and playfully tell him, "Absolutely, she's known for three years."

His meetings go by quickly, probably because I can't take my eyes off him. He captivates the room effortlessly. Even Bridget can't stop looking at him, her eyes roaming up and down as he speaks. I'm surprised she isn't drooling. I want to tell her to act more professionally, but realize I should take my own advice and mind my own business—though Jonah is all my business. The longer she stares at him like she wants to devour him, the more the inside of my lip gets punished. As the meeting wraps up, a gentleman asks if he can stay behind to bounce an idea off Jonah, and Jonah agrees. I hear Bridget say she's going to the ladies' room, and he nods.

Standing from the table, I walk over to him. "Meet me outside the restroom when you're finished."

"Okay, give me five minutes," he agrees.

No problem at all.

I use my irritation to push me forward as I enter the ladies' room. Bridget is leaning into the mirror, reapplying her lipstick. She looks up when she sees me, stares for a moment, then turns back to the mirror.

"You used to have sex with Jonah, yeah?" I ask. She freezes, then caps her lipstick and turns to look at me.

"Often," she says confidently.

"I assume you enjoy working with him since you've stuck around after five years. Here's a suggestion: stop eye-fucking my boyfriend in meetings, stop side-eyeing me and giving me dirty looks every time you see me. I'm Jonah's girlfriend, and you should remember that, or you will find yourself out of a job. I've kept my mouth shut to avoid confrontation, but I'm tired of you. I don't know you, and I never want to know you. You work *for* Jonah, and that's it. You're an assistant. Quit being a bitch and grow the fuck up or get out."

"Excuse you," she retorts, stepping closer with an air of defiance.

"You heard me right. If you want to continue this discussion, Jonah is waiting outside for me. We can let him in on it. I think we both know whose side he will take," I say, stepping toward her.

She glares at me, her nostrils flaring. "I've seen that pretty smile. I suggest you learn how to use it, because your only option is to fake it toward me or fake it in your next job interview. But I wouldn't list this job as a reference… it doesn't look good that you were part of a bang train with your bosses. You'd probably never work in a corporate setting again. Well, not as anything significant. Possibly the office mattress," I shrug and turn to walk out.

That felt good.

When I step out of the restroom, Jonah is walking toward me. "Ready to go get lunch?" I ask.

"Ready," he replies, extending his hand to me.

Just as we're about to leave, the restroom door swings open, and Bridget emerges, dabbing her eyes with a tissue.

"You okay?" Jonah asks.

She glances at me, then back at him. "Fine, just allergies."

Jonah doesn't dwell on it. He just pulls me toward the elevators and presses the button to go down. "You going back up?" he asks Bridget without looking at her.

"Yes," she sniffles, and he holds the button for up as well.

Our elevator arrives first, and as we step in, I turn and wave. "Have a nice lunch, Bridget."

"I don't even want to ask," he says, glancing up at the numbers descending.

"Then don't."

He lets out a laugh, releasing my hand and wrapping his arm around my neck, pulling me close and kissing my hair.

When we return, Bridget isn't waiting. I almost find it amusing, given how she seems to spend her days waiting for Jonah.

"Did you put the fear of God in her," he jokes as we walk to the elevator.

I shrug. "Not if she's just here to do her job, which, by the way, I do acknowledge she's good at."

We learn from the head receptionist that Bridget needed to go home for "personal reasons."

I pull up Jonah's afternoon schedule on my computer and print it out. He has three more meetings. Each meeting is meticulously detailed with times, locations, and attachments containing all the necessary documents, complete with highlighted portions already marked for signatures.

I print everything for the meetings and then study each company, familiarizing myself with their backgrounds and reading the contracts. In the second document, I spot inconsistencies in the numbers. After some research, I realize the figures don't align at all. I draw up a new document changing the proposed 50/50 split to 35/65 and create spreadsheets showcasing each company's numbers. Jonah's company is significantly more profitable. This guy is delusional if he thinks a 50/50 split is reasonable.

I ask Miles to find me the leather binders Bridget always uses, and he immediately brings me four. I get everything organized, grab my black bag with blue sides matching my top, and empty its contents onto my chair. I place the binders for the last two meetings inside, along with an extra one Miles brought me that contains a notepad and pen. Once I'm satisfied with the organization, I grab the binder for the next meeting and my bag, then walk to Jonah's office. He's wrapping up a business call.

"Your next meeting is in twenty minutes," I inform him, handing him the first binder. He looks slightly confused until he opens it and flips through the pages.

I begin explaining the company and the contract with him. I've even printed a list of attendees with their photos and a brief bio for each person so he knows who everyone is.

"Baby," he says, his eyes widening as he looks through the pages, a smile beginning to form on his lips.

"Let's go. I have everything prepared for all three of your meetings. Bet you didn't know I could be an amazing assistant too," I say as I head towards his door.

The first meeting goes smoothly. I collect the documents, organize them back into the binder, and prepare the next one for Jonah, handing it over to him. We're running behind schedule because the previous meeting overran, so he doesn't have time to review them in detail.

As the meeting progresses, my palms grow clammy. Everyone directs their questions and comments to Jonah, maintaining steady eye contact. When one of Jonah's attorneys poses a question and the gentleman across the table responds, I lean over, flipping the pages in the binder. I point to the tab with the relevant information I found, making sure Jonah sees the issues, allowing him to decide how to proceed. He reads over them, looks at the numbers, and then reaches under the table, squeezing my leg as the men turn their attention back to him.

The same contracts I reviewed prior to the meeting are brought out, and Jonah's attorneys begin examining them. Discussions intensify as each side goes back and forth with the terms.

"Miss Bell, would you like to take point?" Jonah asks, genuinely curious if I would want to.

"Really? Are you sure?" I whisper, my excitement radiating through me.

"Please," he says, scooting the binder over to me.

I stand, pulling out the document I created, and slide them to the gentleman across from Jonah. Then, I hand copies to his four colleagues and our attorneys. I discuss my findings and the numbers, explaining how a 35/65 split is more equitable. We go back and forth, and I gracefully hold my own. These bigwig executives don't intimidate me. Maybe they did when I first started at Amaryllis, but I've always felt comfortable participating in business meetings. In fact, I find something so powerful and feminine about showing up a man who looks down on women. I'm more than willing to do it, especially to a man who tries to take advantage of Jonah.

"Miss Bell," Mr. Dunn begins, adjusting his glasses as he scrutinizes the contract, "your proposal is certainly thorough, but I'm afraid a 35/65 split is simply not in our best interest."

I smile politely, meeting his gaze without flinching. "Mr. Dunn, I understand your concerns, but if you examine the projections on page four, you'll see that the 35/65 split ensures sustained growth and profitability for both parties while, Everett Solutions takes the higher risk."

One of Mr. Dunn's colleagues, a woman with a shrewd demeanor, interjects. "Even with your projections, Miss Bell, we still stand to lose a significant portion of our initial investment under these terms."

I nod, acknowledging her point. "I appreciate your perspective, Miss Turner. However, if you refer to the market analysis on page six, you'll notice that the increased market share we secure with this deal far outweighs the initial investment concerns."

Jonah leans back in his chair, watching the exchange intently. I can feel his support, a silent reassurance as I continue to hold my ground.

Mr. Dunn sighs, clearly not convinced. "What you're asking is slashing 15 percent of our profits directly to you, Miss Bell. We need more assurance that this deal will be as beneficial as you claim."

"That's perfectly reasonable," I reply smoothly. "If you look at the appended risk mitigation strategies, you'll find comprehensive plans to safeguard your investment and ensure mutual benefit."

Another executive, Mr. Hughes, taps his pen on the table. "Miss Bell, the risk mitigation is sound, but the return on investment is still not compelling enough for us to agree to a 35/65 split."

I lean forward slightly, emphasizing my point. "Mr. Hughes, the return on investment is projected to increase substantially within the first two fiscal quarters. By accepting these terms, you're positioning your company to capitalize on market opportunities that would otherwise be missed."

There is a moment of silence as they digest my words. Dunn's eyes flicker over the document once more before he speaks. "We would be more comfortable with a 45/55 split."

I shake my head gently. "I'm afraid a 45/55 split would not adequately reflect the value we bring to this partnership. The 35/65 split is equitable and ensures both parties thrive."

Ms. Turner narrows her eyes. "What if we added a performance-based incentive? If certain benchmarks are met, we adjust the split to 40/60."

I consider her proposal. "A performance-based incentive is a fair suggestion. However, the benchmarks would need to be clearly defined and agreed upon by both parties. We could establish a review period every quarter to reassess the terms based on performance."

Mr. Dunn exchanges glances with his colleagues, then turns back to me. "That sounds more reasonable. Let's outline the specifics of these benchmarks. Then discuss the numbers."

For the next hour, we delve into the nitty-gritty details, negotiating the terms of the performance-based incentives. The back-

and-forth is intense, but I remain poised and assertive, ensuring that every clause protects Jonah's interests.

Finally, as the meeting draws to a close, Mr. Dunn leans back, a weary look on his face. "Miss Bell, you've certainly given us a lot to think about. The 35/65 split with performance-based adjustments just doesn't feel like the split is where it should be."

"Mr. Dunn, I don't want to waste either of our time. I'll be direct, if I may. This is the only and final offer you will get, sir," I say with confidence.

He lets out a sigh, glancing between his colleagues, knowing I'm right, and this IS a fair deal. He scrutinizes the contract and the documentation I provided once more. Briefly, it seems he might reject the deal. He looks at me for a long moment and then at Jonah. "Then you've got yourself a deal," he says, standing and reaching his hand out to me.

I stand and firmly shake it. "Thank you, Mr. Dunn. I believe this partnership will be highly successful for both of us."

"She's a feisty one," Mr. Dunn remarks, his eyes wide with surprise and something close to admiration as he looks at Jonah.

"That she is," Jonah replies, standing and shaking his hand.

We make it to the last meeting, and I'm sure the entire room could feel the sexual tension between Jonah and me. He all but drags me back to his office, and I giggle as I walk with him, keeping up with his urgent pace. As soon as the door slams shut behind us, my skirt is being hiked up, and he's bending down to pick me up.

"That was fucking sexy," he groans, flattening my back against the door.

Without hesitation, I reach between us, undoing his belt and pants. His erection springs free, hot and hard in my hand. I stroke him with deliberate, teasing movements, my own arousal growing with each touch. I don't even want to fool around or wait until we get home—I want him fast and now. Pulling my panties to the side, I line him at my entrance and bring my mouth back to his as he surges upward, pushing his cock inside me with an urgent force.

"Do you like when I'm in charge?" My voice a mix of pleasure and command.

"Yes," he breathes, his hips moving faster and deeper. "You're amazing, baby. You did so fucking amazing."

"I do it for you, Jonah. I do it all for you," I cry out, my hips meeting his thrusts with equal fervor. "Right there," I gasp, digging my nails into his shirt.

"Come on my cock, baby," he growls.

He impales me so hard I tighten my grip on him, my arms clinging around his neck, my core clenching around his girth as my orgasm rips through me. "Oh my god, yes," I gasp.

His head falls in my neck, his movements urgent and frantic until he spills inside me. "Fuck," he murmurs, his breathing heavy as he leans against me, both of us catching our breath.

"You have to carry me to your desk like this," I whisper, my fingers combing through his hair. He leans back, his eyes meeting mine with a mixture of adoration and lust. He presses his lips to mine in a searing kiss before moving from the door, carrying me to his desk without breaking our connection.

Once we clean up, he grabs his laptop, and we head out together. As we open the door, we halt, freezing at the sight of six employees lingering outside. Their eyes widen before they scatter down the hall, their faces flushed.

Once we're in my office, I pull the binders out of my bag, lock them in my desk, and put the items on my chair back into my bag. "They totally heard us fucking."

"Totally," he agrees.

"Let's go home, Mr. Everett," I say, walking past him.

He playfully spanks my ass. "Lead the way, baby."

CHAPTER

Eighteen

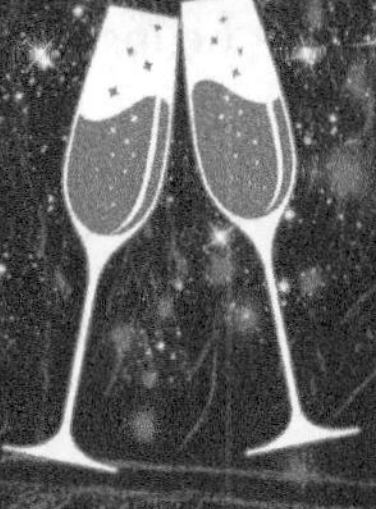

KALYN

Bridget decided to call out for the rest of the week, so I take it upon myself to manage Jonah's schedule. Apparently, we don't just make an amazing couple but also an incredible team in meetings. I ask if I need to adjust anything, and he tells me I've been the best assistant he's ever had. I'll take those brownie points wherever they're being given, especially with the way he pleasures me after a day of good work.

When we get off work on Friday, we come home and find our luggage packed by the door. Jonah doesn't even acknowledge the suitcases; he just walks past them, and two men come in to take our luggage away.

"Are we being robbed?" I ask as I watch them leave, then follow after Jonah.

"We're going away for the weekend. Dress in something comfy for the jet," he says, unbuttoning his shirt.

"Exciting!" I exclaim, clapping my hands and grabbing a pair of leggings and a tank top, leaving my bra and panties behind, thinking ahead for the plane ride.

"We'll be back on Sunday," he says, stripping off his clothes and pulling on shorts.

We arrive at the tarmac, and the larger jet is waiting. I try to get Jonah to go first so I can stare at his ass but also avoid glares from the flight attendants, but he insists I go first.

"You just want to stare at my ass," I say as I walk past him.

He playfully spanks me as we walk up the stairs. To my surprise, both flight attendants greet me politely as I enter.

I stop when I spot Shay and Jonathan sitting on the couch; she's sitting on his lap, and they're kissing. She pulls away, noticing me, jumps up, and rushes over, throwing her arms around my neck.

"What are you guys doing here?" I ask, surprised and not releasing her from my embrace.

"We're going on vacation! You completed your first two weeks of work!" she beams, pulling me to the back so we can sit next to each other. "Mr. Everett, you can sit there. You've had her to yourself for two weeks," Shay points to the chairs across from us.

"Fine, she'll be in the bedroom once we're in the air," he winks at me.

"I've decided I will also be coming to work with you lot," Shay squeezes my hand. "Mr. Everett, you better get an office ready because I'm your newest employee," she grins at Jonah, then at me.

"Done," Jonah replies, putting his laptop bag on the floor by his feet.

"Why the sudden change of heart?" I raise a brow at her, wondering if it has something to do with me bringing those videos back up.

"You," she says matter-of-factly. "I want to be where you are, and you are where he is, and he is where he is," she says, pointing at Jonah and then to Jonathan, back to Jonah.

"I love it," I squeeze her hand back.

We settle into our rooms, and as the sun begins to set, the guys tell us to start getting ready for dinner. Shay and I spend an hour in the bathroom, chatting and getting dressed. They didn't specify the dress code, so we opt for casual dresses. Shay wears a short blue dress, while I choose a white floral print dress that is fitted at the top and flows to mid-shin, with the fabric overlapping in the front to form a delicate slit on the right side.

The guys are also dressed casually in shorts and T-shirts. I'm always still a little surprised when I see Jonathan's tattoos covering his legs and arms in beautifully colored art, and my eyes tend to linger longer than they should at how good they look.

Jonah takes my hand, and we walk to the beach, where a table is set up with a path of flower petals leading to it. Lanterns in the sand and string lights above create a dreamlike feeling.

"Wow." My mouth hangs open, looking around. "This is so romantic," I nudge Jonah.

After dinner, a group of musicians—a man with a guitar, another with a hand drum, a woman with a handpan, and another with a unique instrument clutched in her fist—line up in front of our table off to the side and begin playing and singing. Shay and I exchange excited glances and turn in our chairs to watch. Their performance is mesmerizing. The man and the woman harmonize beautifully, capturing our full attention. I feel Jonah's thumb rubbing up and down my shoulder, so I reach up and lace my hand with his.

As the band transitions to a mellow tune, Jonathan stands and walks around to Shay, holding out his hand. My heart leaps in my throat, and I turn to Jonah with wide eyes. He winks and kisses my shoulder.

"Jonathan?" Shay's face turns serious as she realizes what's happening. Shay has likely dreamed of the day Jonathan would propose since the moment she met him. She claims not to think about it often, but I know she's wanted to marry him and that it must have bothered her somewhat, especially since she insisted on not sharing a room until they were engaged and she knew just how bad Jonathan wanted them to share a room.

We watch with bated breath as Jonathan gets on one knee in front of Shay. He presents the most beautiful engagement ring, speaking words that could melt any heart. Shay's eyes glisten with tears of joy as she realizes the moment she's dreamed of is finally happening.

I wipe away my tears, my cheeks hurting from how big I'm smiling. "That was beautiful," I tell Jonathan when they turn back toward us.

We stand to congratulate them, and Shay falls into my arms, sobbing with happiness as she holds out her hand to show me the ring. I delicately take it to get a closer look. "It's absolutely perfect. It's about time," I say to Jonathan, playfully hitting his chest. He laughs and pulls me into a hug. "Congratulations," I say, squeezing him.

We sit back down, and I watch as Jonathan admires Shay, who's still staring at her ring. He's so in love with her, and she with him. My chest aches with all the love I feel right now.

"Let's go for a walk and leave these two to make out," Jonah teases, walking around the table in front of me.

"Who's he kidding? *We* are going to make out," I joke, standing up and holding my hand out to Jonah as I grin at Jonathan and Shay. Shay's mouth falls open, and I turn to Jonah as I feel something slide onto my ring finger. I stop abruptly, my mouth mimicking Shay's as it falls open, when I see Jonah down on one knee in the sand, holding the same hand he just put a ring on, with a ring box in his other hand.

"Jonah," I whisper, my heart thundering in my chest. Turning to look at the table, I see Jonathan has a knowing smile on his face while Shay's hands are clasped over her nose and mouth.

"What's happening," I ask as tears form in my eyes.

"Baby, I'm so madly in love with you. I would chase you across universes and galaxies, through time and space. You are my heart, my body, and my soul. You are every part of me, and the only thing I need in my life right now is for you to be my wife. Kalyn Wrenley Bell, will you allow me to fuse with you and make me the happiest anglerfish on earth by marrying me?"

Tears stream down my face as I nod. "Yes… yes, yes, yes."

He stands, and I jump into his arms, holding him close and kissing him.

"You didn't even look at the ring," he says.

"I don't care about the ring," I say amidst my tears, crushing my lips back to his.

"I designed it and handpicked the diamonds," he tells me.

"Then I love it," I smile, bringing my hand between us to admire the most beautiful diamond ring I've ever seen in my entire life.

"Five years ago," Jonathan says, then coughs.

"What?" I look between Jonathan and Jonah.

"The third time I saw you, I knew I was going to marry you, so I designed the ring and had it made."

"My creepy, stalker, fiancé," I wipe away tears and stare down at the giant diamond glistening on my finger, mentally thanking Shay for insisting on the mani-pedi. "It's so beautiful, Jonah."

"We're getting married!" Shay exclaims, leaping out of her seat and rushing over to me. Jonah gently sets me back on my feet, and Shay wraps her arms around my neck.

"I'm shaking so bad," I admit to her.

"So am I," she agrees.

We separate and hold our rings out to each other to inspect. Shay's hand looks exactly how I always imagined, with a ring on her finger. The ring was meant to be on her hand.

"Can we hurry and get married so we can push you both off a cliff and be billionaires?" Shay jokes.

"Where you gonna find a dick as big as mine if you kill me, you little horndog," Jonathan wraps his arms around her neck and kisses her cheek.

I lift a knowing brow at her.

"We might be idiots, but treat you like the princesses you are," he kisses her again.

"You want to push me off a cliff too?" Jonah asks, wrapping his arms around my waist and lifting me into his arms.

"Nooo," I drawl. "I'm with Jonathan on this one. Where am I going to find someone who dicks me down the way you do?" I grin, pressing my lips to his.

I hold my hand out and look at my ring again. "It's so beautiful, babe," I wiggle my finger to watch it sparkle. "Well, future Mrs. Jonah Everett requires immediate bed time."

"Yes, ma'am," Jonah says, carrying us back toward our room.

I WAKE UP FEELING DIFFERENT. THE ONLY THING THAT HAS PHYSICAL-ly changed is the huge rock on my finger, yet I feel transformed. I hold my hand out, staring at the ring in awe, still unable to believe that I'm going to marry Jonah. I get to spend forever with the most wonderful man. I think about the day we met in the hallway, the way he sprawled me out on the hall table, how hard he was, and how wet I was. I didn't know the surge of emotions I felt then would blossom into something so beautiful. I remember our first kiss, how the butterflies in my stomach felt like they could lift me off the ground and take me away. Cleaning the tea in his office, sitting on his lap, grinding on his crotch. When he fingered me in the alcove. Our first time having sex, and every time since. Each memory is a piece of our story—the love and care he has shown me, the endless happiness I have felt. I love this man so much.

"You like it, baby?" His muscular arms wrap around me, his voice still groggy from sleep.

I lower my hand, rolling over to face him. "I love it, almost as much as I love you," I wrap my arms around him. "I love him the most." I slide my hand under the covers to rub his erection.

"We're a package deal, baby," he moves in to kiss me.

"I accept the full package," I say between our lips parting and reconnecting.

"Is there any penetrating happening?" Jonathan asks, climb-ing into bed behind me and wrapping his arms around me and Jonah as Shay climbs in behind Jonah.

"Not yet, we were working towards that," Jonah laughs.

"I can literally feel your dick in my ass crack," I turn to look at Jonathan.

"We've already gone at it twice," Shay pushes his shoulder.

"I'm allowed to be happy. I'm engaged. What are we doing today?" Jonathan rests his chin on my shoulder as he looks between us.

Jonah lifts his head and peeks behind me, then settles back down. I watch his movements and then back at him curiously, "What was that?"

"Making sure he has boxers on," he laughs.

"Is this a no-clothes zone?" Jonathan asks, amused.

"For you, it's definitely a clothes zone when you're putting your dick near my girl's ass," Jonah says, leaning in to kiss me.

"Are you getting jealous?" I ask.

"He's not jealous, he just wants to be the first one to put his dick in your ass," Shay quips.

"My dick might be long enough to slide to the front," Jonathan says.

"It's long enough," Shay says knowingly.

"If it were anyone else, I'd cut it off," Jonah admits. "But he's a safe zone."

"Does that mean, since it's just Jonathan, he can do other things with her?" Shay questions seductively, walking her fingers up Jonah's arm and then sliding them down his neck, making him lift his shoulder toward his ear.

"He's ticklish right there," I smirk, watching him squirm as he leans into me.

"Mr. Everett, you're ticklish?" she asks, trying harder to get to his neck.

"I hate this," he laughs as he grabs her hand to stop her.

"We need breakfast," I yawn, stretching my arms and leaning back into Jonathan.

"Breakfast," Jonah agrees, sucking my nipple into his mouth.

"We all want breakfast, not just you," I look down watching him.

"Let's go sightseeing," Shay says excitedly, looking between me and Jonathan.

"Well, this one is going to want to go to the gym," I say, running my fingers through Jonah's hair.

"Breakfast, gym, sightseeing," I announce, laying out our plan for the day. "So, both of you move." I push my butt against Jonathan and place my hands on Jonah's chest so I can get up. Jonah releases my boob with a pop, and everyone laughs as I climb to my knees and start crawling toward the end of the bed.

"Your breakfast is crawling away," Jonathan jokes, and Jonah reaches out, grabbing my ankle.

"Come put that plump pussy on my face," Jonah says, holding my ankle firmly.

I flop onto my stomach, pressing my face into the comforter in defeat. "I'm hungry," I grumble into the blanket.

My ass is slapped, and at this point, I don't even know who did it.

"Get dressed, and we can go get something to eat," Jonah bites the spot that was just slapped before getting off the bed.

"Can we play Barbies, and you dress me?" I lift my head to watch him walk away.

"I will," Shay volunteers, climbing off the bed to fetch me clothes. She returns moments later and tells me to turn over.

"I'm a Barbie, I can't move," I mumble into the bed.

"Flip her over," she instructs Jonathan. He picks me up and flops me onto my back, making us both giggle. My arms splay out to the sides, and he settles back against the headboard, resting one arm over his head.

She slips my panties onto one ankle, then grabs my other ankle, slipping my foot in and works them up my legs. The bathroom door opens, and Jonah emerges, already showered and dressed. He leans against the wall, an amused observer to the nonsense unfolding.

"You wouldn't think playing Barbies would be so sexy," Jonathan remarks to him. Shay and I both laugh at his comment while she does the same with my shorts.

When she gets to my top, she climbs off the bed, bunches the material in her hand, lifts my head, and slips it on. She gets each of my arms in the sleeves and attempts to pull it down multiple times with no luck.

"Okay, Ken, get over here and lift her," she tells Jonathan. He obliges, crawling up my legs to straddle me. His hands slide under my arms, and he easily lifts me into a sitting position so she can finish pulling my shirt down.

Trying not to move my lips, I ask, "What about a bra?"

"Your tits look too good to be in a bra," she declares, then climbs off the bed. She returns moments later with a brush and works through my hair, then braids it. "All done."

"I'm going to release you, your Royal Highness. Now that you're dressed, I think you turned into a real girl," Jonathan laughs as he climbs off the bed, and he and Shay head to their room to dress. Jonah helps me off the bed, and we wait for Jonathan and Shay to get ready.

The days that follow are filled with a perfect blend of relaxation and adventure. We spend our mornings exploring local markets, trying exotic foods, and immersing ourselves in the culture. Afternoons are spent lounging on the beach, with the warm sand between our toes. Evenings are magical as we take long walks on the beach.

On our last night, Jonah surprises us with a private bonfire on the beach. We gather around the fire, its warmth contrasting with the cool night air. We all reminisce about the fun we've had during this trip and Shay and I stare endlessly at our engagement rings.

"So, can we just not go home tomorrow," Shay asks.

"I'm all for that," Jonathan agrees.

"Already trying to get out of your first day of work," Jonah ribs Shay.

"To stay here and relax with my favorite people, yes sir," she grins.

As the fire dies down, we lie on the sand, looking up at the star-studded sky. Jonah wraps his arms around me, and I snuggle into him, feeling a profound sense of contentment. This vacation is everything I needed and more—mainly because we are officially engaged.

In the morning, we pack our bags and spend our remaining hours on the beach. We take one last swim in the ocean. Shay and I collect seashells as keepsakes, and we compare who found better ones.

The flight home was a blur, and I slept almost the entire way. Shay and I curled up together in the bedroom until Jonah gently woke us when it was almost time to land, and he got me buckled into my seat next to him.

CHAPTER
Nineteen

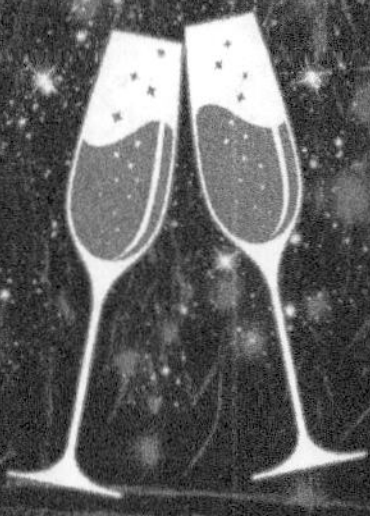

JONAH

We arrive back at the condo, and Shay immediately pulls Kalyn to their condo to show her around. She's gone for about an hour before returning with Shay and Jonathan in tow. Marietta is here, preparing dinner for the four of us, and greets everyone as they walk through the door.

"Hi, Marietta," Kalyn smiles, placing a friendly hand on the counter as she passes by.

"Hi, Kalyn. Did you have a nice time?" Marietta asks.

Kalyn beams as she holds up her hand, catching Marietta's attention. Setting down the knife she's holding, Marietta wipes her hands on her apron and rushes over to Kalyn. I stand from the couch and join them at the counter. Marietta takes Kalyn's hand, her mouth agape. "Mr. Everett," she says, staring at the ring. "Oh, congratulations!" She pulls Kalyn into a heartfelt hug.

Noticing Jonathan and Shay, her eyes lock onto Shay's ring and widen further. "You too!" she exclaims, extending her hand out for Shay to join the hug. "Congratulations to both of you," she says happily. "I didn't know, or I would have made something special tonight," she adds regretfully.

"Anything you make will be perfect," I assure her.

"I'm so happy," Marietta beams, releasing the women from her embrace and returning to her cooking.

"C'mon, baby, let's let her finish," I hold my arm out for her to join me.

We settle in the living room—Kalyn and I on one sofa, with Shay and Jonathan across from us on the opposite one.

"I don't think I have anything to wear tomorrow," Shay realizes, thinking about her lack of business attire.

"You can wear anything from my closet," Kalyn offers. "Let's go look; I need to pick out my outfit anyways," she says, nudging my side and slipping out of my arms.

They disappear to the bedroom, leaving Jonathan and me on the couch.

"Did you two plan that?" Marietta asks, smiling at us.

"It was originally just Jonathan proposing to Shay, but then he suggested we both propose, so we did," I explain. "We had it recorded; we should be getting the video back sometime this week."

"I can't wait to see it," she smiles, continuing her work in the kitchen. "Both of those rings are perfect for those gorgeous women."

"Agreed," Jonathan says, sinking lower on the couch and resting his head back.

"Are you tired, Mr. Harper?" she asks.

"More hungry than tired. I won't miss out on a meal from you," he tells her.

She laughs and says she'll hurry.

The girls return when dinner is ready, and we all gather around the formal dining table. Afterward, Jonathan and Shay head back to their place, Shay carrying an outfit from our closet. Shay and Kalyn both wear size 6 heels, which makes things easier, and they have similar body types. Kalyn's ass is fuller, and she's at least a full cup size bigger than Shay, but Shay has a great figure too, so fitting into Kalyn's clothes won't be a problem.

They could easily convince people they're sisters with their same height, blonde hair, and striking eyes—one with blue and the other with green. Shay has even started growing her hair out, and I overheard Kalyn asking if it was for her wedding, to which Shay replied that she and Jonathan would be a thousand years old by the time he proposes.

As Shay's hair grows longer, she and Kalyn look even more alike. Kalyn has a way of drawing people in, and it's not just men—she has Shay completely wrapped around her finger too. They are inseparable. If she weren't so in love with my best friend, I might be slightly worried about Shay taking Kalyn from me. Shay is bi, which Jonathan told me. Her most recent ex was a woman, something her family never knew. I know she has feelings for Kalyn, and sometimes I think Kalyn feels the same way. It's something I wouldn't mind watching, but I'm not going to mention it to either of them. I also don't say anything to Jonathan because he would definitely encourage Shay to make it happen.

Our relationships and friendships are solid, and even if we crossed certain lines together, I know we would still be okay. On our last day at the mansion, Kalyn had a sex dream about Jonathan. She was moaning his name in her sleep, and while I thought I'd feel rage, I didn't. I watched her writhe until she went silent and still, the dream fading away.

The next day, she spent the entire day at the stables. I found one of our vibrators in her trash in the bathroom, along with her pillowcase in the laundry hamper, which had her scent all over it. I can piece together what happened. I didn't want to embarrass her or make her feel ashamed, so I removed the trash myself to ensure no one else found it. I also stripped the bedding to make it less suspicious for Yesenia when she cleaned the room.

Kalyn is incredibly level-headed, even during her period. Her anger over finding the videos of Jonathan and me fucking Bridget likely stemmed from being upset with herself for dreaming about having sex with Jonathan.

If Kalyn ever entertained the idea of a threesome with Shay or even Jonathan, she's unlikely to let it happen now after finding the videos. And I'm okay with that. I just want her to be happy and am open to trying new things with her that she wants to explore. My only rule is that I must be present, and Jonathan and Shay are the only people I'd ever let her experiment with.

We have a nice routine. Although I go to bed earlier, she comes to bed with me every night and reads until she falls asleep. By the time I wake up in the morning and leave for the gym, she's sound asleep, but doing her hair and makeup when I return. It's an easy flow that we have both adapted well to.

Audits are in full swing over the next two weeks. There were far bigger issues found at the start of the audits, so a team of specialists has been brought in to conduct the remaining audits. I anticipate the tension to be high. While our floor won't see much of the chaos, Kalyn, Jonathan, the legal team, and I will meet with the auditors twice a day to address any issues they might have uncovered.

As I get dressed for my workout, I notice Kalyn has already set out her outfit, and I smile, knowing she did it for me. I grab a red tie to match her top and shoes and place it on the island in the closet where she'll see it. I pull up the cameras in our bedroom while jogging on the treadmill. When I see she's awake, I watch her go to the closet. Her eyes immediately land on the tie, and she runs her finger down the material. Then she takes off her pajamas, puts on her bra and skirt, and heads to the bathroom to do her hair.

"Ready?" Jonathan asks as I slow the treadmill. We set up the weight rack for our lifting session, and I bring up the bathroom cameras on the TV so I can still watch Kalyn. Shay walks in to view, catching Jonathan's attention. He completes his first set, racks the weights, and sits up to watch. We can't hear them, but we see the girls laughing and leaning into each other. We spend the next ten minutes focusing on them, as Shay takes over doing Kalyn's hair. In another life, Shay must have been a hairstylist because she's naturally talented with hair and makeup despite never having formal training. She just enjoys doing it.

We finish our sets and head back to our places to get ready for work.

"Morning," I enter the bathroom, turn on the shower, and go to the closet to undress. I glance at Kalyn as I step into the shower, my eyes roaming up her perfect figure before meeting her gaze in the mirror. She winks and blows me a kiss.

I wasn't planning to start my shower off with a boner, but here we are. Normally, I would just rub one out, but not with Shay here. Turning the water to cold, I finish my shower, clearing away all dirty thoughts, and it works. Getting dressed is much smoother now that I don't have to wait for Kalyn to pick out her outfit. I wondered if she would ever notice that I was purposely matching my outfits to hers. It took her longer than I expected.

As I finish with my tie, Kalyn slips on her heels, grabs her bag, and waits by the door. We stop at the bedroom so I can grab my laptop, then head out. Jonathan and Shay are just leaving their condo, reaching the elevator right before us.

"You look sexy," Shay compliments Kalyn. "Wait, did you guys intentionally match?" She notices my dark red tie matches Kalyn's lace top and strappy red heels.

"HE always copies my outfit," Kalyn nudges me.

"I'm telling Tabitha when she comes to measure me that she has to get us matching clothes too," Shay tells Jonathan.

"Okay," he agrees.

"You two are so fucking cute, I can't stand it," Shay digs in her purse, pulling out her phone. "Scootch together; I'm taking a picture of this."

I place my hand on her waist, pulling her into me. She shifts slightly, resting her hand on my chest so her ring is visible, and we both smile for the photo.

"God, I love you guys," Shay says, looking at the picture before sending it to both of us.

CHAPTER

Twenty

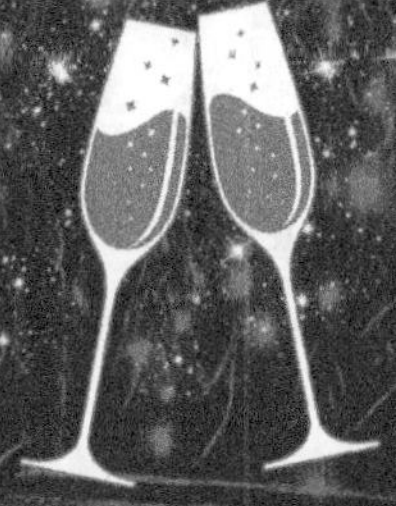

KALYN

I've already decided that if Bridget isn't at work again today, I'll step in and take charge of Jonah's schedule. As we enter the building, she's there, waiting in her usual spot. However, I'll tell you what: the typical disdain I get from Bridget transforms into a look of terror when she sees Shay.

Shay looks her up and down, scoffs, and walks right next to me toward the elevators.

In the elevator, Bridget tries to stand between Jonah and Jonathan. Shay eyes her up and down, then walks toward her until Bridget steps back. Shay Smirks and turns to hold Jonathan's hand. I stand in front of Jonah and look at Shay, who grins at me.

"Who should I talk to about completing the documentation for all of Friday's contracts? I'd like to get those taken care of first thing," I turn to Jonah, wrapping my hand in his. I see Bridget's eyes move to my hand and her eyes widen, then back to Shay's hand and her eyes widen even more.

"Miles should be able to help you," he replies.

"I can take care of them. I'll just grab them when we get to your office," Bridget interjects.

"It's fine, thank you anyway. I'd like to know how to complete the process for when the same thing happens in the future. I appreciate your offer, though."

"You just want to stare at the contract you secured on your own," Jonathan teases.

"That too," I laugh. "Shhh, Jonathan," I point my finger at him like a mother would to her child.

"I'm so proud of you, baby," Jonah says, brushing a knuckle down my cheek.

"Thank you. I momentarily forgot that I successfully negotiated my first deal—I had a big weekend," I smile at him.

We stride out of the elevator, and Shay glances at the receptionists as I typically do, too, but she just keeps walking.

"I'm going to talk to Miles," I tell Jonah, about to break away from the group, but he pulls me back, kissing me before letting me go.

"Good morning, Miles," I greet him as I approach his desk.

"Kalyn, hi! Good morning. How was your weekend?" he asks, smiling when he sees me.

"It was really nice. How was yours?"

"Good, thanks for asking. What can I help you with?" he asks eagerly.

"Mr. Everett said you'd be able to assist me with some contracts. Do you mind coming to my office? I have them in my desk," I say, pointing in the direction.

For the next hour, Miles guides me through the process, revealing it's more complicated than I expected. I wonder if this is something Bridget typically handles herself or if she delegated it to someone else. Either way, I'm relieved she didn't return to a mess after being gone, as I'm sure she was expecting. She was probably expecting to show Jonah how lost he'd be without her. But jokes on her—I doubt he even noticed.

Miles pulls up a chair beside me, and I place the three leather binders from Friday on my desk, opening the one from our first meeting. Miles explains the daunting database system, assuring me, "It's not as intense as it looks. We'll input all this information into the system, upload photos of the contracts so we have them all in one place, and I can show you how to set reminders for each client on the files or on your calendar if you need to follow up with them at specific times, and so on."

I nod, focusing intently as Miles guides me with each step, explaining the why behind everything we're doing. I log into the database, creating a new entry for each client. Miles explains how to input the client's personal information, the details of the deal, and any specific notes. "Make sure to double and triple-check all the figures. Mr. Everett doesn't like mistakes." The words come out, and he instantly looks like he wishes he could take them back. "It's just one small mistake can cause a lot of headaches later," he continues.

"I completely understand and totally agree that double and triple-checking. Accuracy is key to making sure minor errors don't turn into big ones," I tell him, trying to ease his awkwardness.

As we continue through each contract, I notice how methodical and thorough Miles is. His attention to detail is impressive. The process is lengthy, requiring meticulous data entry and frequent cross-referencing with the physical contracts.

After entering all the data, Miles shows me how to create a digital folder for each client. "This keeps everything organized. If these are specific clients you will be managing yourself, I can show you how to make physical record folders. If you won't be managing them, another employee can print the hard copies from the records. If you do end up getting physical records, just mark in the account that you have the physical folder in case another employee needs specific information or updates. Or, in case an employee is no longer employed here, it can be easily tracked down to find the last person in charge of the contract. Not that you would ever not be an employee here."

By the time we finish with all three contracts, I'm confident with my ability to accurately input and create accounts for new clients or business partners.

"You learn really quick," Miles compliments.

"That she does," Jonah says from the doorway. "Hi, baby. I have a meeting at 9, then I'll come talk to you," he walks to my desk to kiss me. "Two," he says, giving me my second kiss of the day for our contractual work terms agreement.

"Okay," I smile.

Jonathan walks in behind him, puckering for a kiss too. "Let's go," Jonah says, patting Jonathan on the chest. Jonathan shrugs and pouts as he follows him out, with Bridget in tow.

"Now that we've completed these, what do we do with the original contracts?" I ask, holding them.

"Shred them. They've been scanned and uploaded to the files," Miles replies, looking at them and then back at me.

"I hate that," I laugh. "Can we just go ahead and create the folders for hard copies instead? I don't feel comfortable shredding them. I can hang on to them in here."

"Yes, of course," he walks me to the copy room to create folders for each client. I like how perfectly organized they turn out.

As we return, Shay emerges from Jonathan's office. "Can I come hang out?"

"Of course. This is Miles. Miles, this is Shay, Mr. Harper's fiancée," I introduce.

We chat until Tabitha arrives, and Miles takes that as his cue to go back to his desk. Tabitha takes Shay's measurements and then leaves abruptly, just as she did when she took mine.

"I think Bridget is thrilled to have me here," Shay teases, crossing her legs in the chair on the other side of my desk.

"That makes two of us. It's hard to look at her without flashes of the videos popping into my head. But I'll give her props; she hides her feelings really well and maintains professionalism."

"Who cares. It'd be fine if she fucked them and moved on, but she recorded it and then treats you like shit, like you somehow were the reason a relationship didn't blossom between them. Mr. Everett was in his tangled mess with Jenevieve at the time, and Bridget still spread her legs for him. Women like that don't deserve respect, and she certainly won't ever get any from me," Shay says, sounding annoyed.

"Well, at least she now knows they are really off the market for good," I glance down at my ring so I can admire it.

"Can you believe that? We're getting married! I hope Mr. Everett was okay with the whole thing. He's wanted to propose to you for so long. I was convinced you guys would be married long before we ever even got engaged."

"Oh my word, no. I hoped you wouldn't be upset that Jonah piggybacked on your proposal."

"You mean, Jonathan hijacked Mr. Everett's proposal. Mr. Everett planned on proposing to you on a beach for years. I thought that's what was happening, so I was stunned when Jonathan proposed the way Mr. Everett planned for you. Jonathan isn't great at planning something sweet. I'm sure Mr. Everett told him to propose first, and Jonathan leapt at the idea. You're my very best friend, I think it was absolutely perfect that we got proposed to on the same night," she reaches across the desk to me, and I grab her hands.

"Jonah planned on proposing to me on a beach?" I smile at the thought.

"Yes, exactly how it worked out. Jonathan kept calling Mr. Everett last week, and I was cracking jokes to him about having a hard time being away from his boyfriend. He just went along with it, saying he didn't know how to function without Mr. Everett. Now, I'm pretty sure they were working out engagement plans."

"Those sneaky guys. I'm surprised Jonah still wants to marry me after I acted like such a lunatic."

"He stalked you for four years. HE'S the lunatic," she retorts.

"Hey, babe, we're meeting with the audit team. You ready?" Jonah asks, peeking in the door.

I wasn't sure what to expect from the audit. I knew some companies would be in trouble for essentially stealing money, but I'm pleasantly surprised by the morning's findings. The audits turned out pretty well. The few companies with several quarters of errors have already been asked to come in. The legal team is working on actions against these companies, and I'm glad I'm not one of their employees. Jonah is intimidating just being himself—I can't imagine being on the wrong end of his scrutiny.

I'm also impressed watching Jonathan. I always assumed he would be more like the "Bridget" in things, but he is equally respected and loved by everyone. Together, he and Jonah are like sour patch kids—sour and sweet.

Our team gathers in a conference room to review each company that has been audited thus far. There are twelve of us in total in here. Jonathan and Jonah stand, looking over the papers. Bridget can't keep her eyes off either of them, and it's clear it's not just about understanding what they're talking about. She has it bad for both of them. I guess I spoke too soon when I said she hides her feelings well.

Jonathan cracks a joke, and Bridget laughs, looking so mesmerized by him. But when she sees me staring at her, her demeanor becomes serious again. I don't blame her— both men are charming and downright sexy. But her attitude toward me because of my relationship with Jonah set the stage for our working relationship.

During the conversation, Jonathan has papers in his hands that pique my interest. I ask to see them, and he walks around the table to hand them to me. He leans on the back of my chair, absentmindedly playing with a lock of my hair while talking to Jonah and the others. As I look them over, my chair shifts, and Jonathan bends over, resting his chin on his arm, studying the documents with me. I glance up, feeling Bridget staring, and her eyes are locked on Jonathan. I'm sure she's wondering if Jonah, Jonathan, and I have the same relationship she did with them.

I continue flipping past pages, growing more annoyed by her gaze. Finally, I stand, and Jonathan straightens up. I move inappropriately close to him and shift my position to make sure Bridget can see us. Playfully grabbing the bottom of his tie, I smile up at him and whisper with barely moving lips, "She's really starting to piss me off."

He grins. "Maybe you'd feel better if I shoved my tongue down your throat? That'd at least give her something to stare at. Or I can have her leave."

"Shay would be mad she didn't get to watch you kiss me. How much longer is this?"

"You wanna head back up? I can handle this, and you and Everett can go blow off some steam."

"That much longer, huh?" I sigh.

"All because of your eagle eyes, love," he says, booping my nose. "If it makes you feel better, Shay is probably going crazy upstairs without any of us. My phone has gone off at least 30 times in my pocket."

"I don't know which is worse; being in the dark or having to witness firsthand the woman you both screwed drooling over you both," I chew on the inside of my lip.

He smirks, wraps his arm around my neck, and pulls me close. "Jealousy looks good on you," he whispers in my ear.

I reach up and pinch his side, making him laugh.

"Shouldn't be longer than a half hour," he says. He pulls away with a smile and wraps his arm around my neck again, this time leading me around the table, positioning me between him and Jonah.

Jonah glances at me and then at Jonathan. I see Jonathan give him a subtle nod, and then Jonah resumes discussing an account with the auditors, his hand gently resting on the small of my back.

When we get back upstairs, Shay is on the phone with Jonathan's mom, sitting in my chair with her phone propped up. Walking around the desk, I lean over and wave at Sienna.

"Hi, honey. I hear congratulations are in order for you too," she smiles. I hold out my hand to show her my ring and she beams. "Stunning."

"Alright, mom, I should give Kalyn back her office. I'll see you tomorrow. Love you," Shay kisses the phone, and Sienna says goodbye.

"My mom and Jonathan's mom are flying in tomorrow. They're eager to start wedding planning and dress shopping," Shay claps her hands excitedly.

"*They* are?" I lift my brow.

"Yeah, *all them*," she laughs.

I FEEL JONAH'S ARMS WRAP AROUND ME AS HE BEGINS KISSING MY neck. Groggy, I let him continue for a moment before opening my eyes and seeing that it's 4:45 AM.

"Go exercise," I mumble, wanting to go back to sleep.

"That's what I'm trying to do," he groans in my ear.

It takes me a minute to comprehend what he's saying, and when I do, I turn my head to look at him. He smiles, continuing to kiss my neck and rolling me onto my back.

"Where's Jonathan?"

"Probably doing this."

"Why are you guys not in the gym?" I ask, confused.

"Because you're off today, and Jonathan and I agreed we'd prefer this morning workout instead. Don't worry; you just have to lay there and look pretty. Go back to sleep if you want," he grins.

Obviously, I don't go back to sleep. Nope. I spend the next hour and a half with Jonah thoroughly working out on top of me. When he's finished and we're both satisfied, he showers and leaves for work. I set my alarm to allow myself two more hours of sleep. When it finally goes off, I check my new messages: a couple of texts from Jonah telling me he loves me, one from Sam, and then I almost jump out of my skin when I see movement out of the corner of my eye. I turn to see Shay laying in Jonah's spot, not looking away from her phone.

"Geez, how long have you been in here?" I clutch my chest.

"Since the guys left for work."

"Couldn't get back to sleep?" I sit up and stretch.

"Nope, too excited," she admits, still leaned back on Jonah's pillows. "Can I do your hair?"

"Yes, please," I eagerly jump out of bed.

Within two hours, Shay and I are ready and downstairs, where Royel picks us up and drives us to the airport. Sienna arrives first, hugging Shay and then me. Jonathan's mom is as sweet as her son, genuinely happy. It's easy to see where he inherited his personality from, though his father, John, is equally as cheerful.

We sit at an airport restaurant, passing time until Shay's mom arrives. Her flight is an hour after Sienna's, so lunch becomes a welcome distraction. Sienna tells us about John accidentally rolling the golf cart while golfing—he took a corner too fast—and how she was so mad at him for it. She hasn't even told Jonathan about it because she didn't want to ruin their engagement weekend.

She shares animated stories, like the ones Jonathan tells, that have us laughing and making the time pass quickly. Once Shay's mom, Valerie, joins us, we head back to the condo so they can settle in. Shay and Jonathan wanted them to stay in their condo, but they opted to share one of the guest condos. We let them know we like to keep our doors open to come and go as we please between condos since nobody is allowed on this floor without permission, and they are free to do the same if they'd like.

Shay and I wait in her condo for them to join us after they get settled in. We hear giggling coming down the hall and smile at each other. When they walk in, Shay's mom has a bag full of magazines and binders of wedding stuff.

"Mom, we have wedding planners to meet with tomorrow," Shay says as her mom starts emptying the bags.

"We can still get started, honey," she says, continuing to unload.

We spend five hours examining them until we hear the guys return home. They come in and greet us as both Sienna and Valerie get up to hug Jonah and Jonathan.

"Hi, baby," Jonah says, softly rubbing his hand down my back as he leans over to kiss me.

"Hi, how was work?" I smile up at him.

"Boring without you. Ready to head back?"

"Yep. I'll see you guys tomorrow," I say as I stand.

"Same workout in the morning?" Jonathan calls to Jonah, who nods in agreement.

TODAY IS A SPECIAL DAY FOR SHAY AS SHE BEGINS HER WEDDING PLANNING, and if all goes well, she will have her wedding dress picked out by the end of the day. She already knows she's going to get married in her hometown at the Catholic church she went to growing up. Her "Nuptial Mass" will be an intimate ceremony, and she's asked me to be her maid of honor, which has me excited, even though I'm the only woman on her side and Jonah is the only one on Jonathan's side.

Thankfully, the bridal shop we're visiting is a one-stop shop. Jonathan and Shay already know they're getting married in two months, and their wedding date is set for July 15th.

Arriving at the top bridal shop in the city, we're greeted by the staff.

"Welcome to Forever and Always Bridal. You must be Shay. We've been expecting you. My name is Clarissa, and I'll be assisting you today."

"Thank you, Clarissa. This is my mom, Valerie, my fiancé's mom, Sienna, and my best friend, Kalyn," Shay introduces us.

"It's a delight to meet you all," Clarissa says, shaking each of our hands. "Please, follow me. We have a private suite prepared for you."

We're led through the boutique, past racks of stunning wedding dresses, each more beautiful than the last. The private suite is an intimate space with cozy chairs, a large mirror, and a raised platform for Shay to stand on while trying on dresses.

"Would you care for some champagne?" Clarissa offers, motioning to a small table where a bottle of chilled champagne and four elegant flutes are waiting.

"Yes, please," Sienna says, glancing at the rest of us, and we all accept.

Clarissa expertly pours the champagne, handing a flute to each of us.

"Here's to finding the perfect dress," Sienna toasts, raising her glass.

"To the perfect dress," we all echo, clinking our glasses together.

"Now, let's get started," Clarissa claps her hands, gesturing to a rack of gowns she has pre-selected based on Shay's preferences. "I've pulled a few dresses that I think you'll love. Why don't we start with this one?" She holds up a dress with intricate lace detailing and a sweetheart neckline.

Shay's eyes widen as she takes in the dress. "It's gorgeous."

Clarissa and two other staff members escort Shay to the dressing room and help her into the dress, carefully adjusting the fabric and fastening the clasps. As she enters the room, we all smile at how beautiful she looks. She steps onto the platform, looks herself over in the mirror, then glances back at us. We shake our heads no in unison.

She tries on the next one, the same reaction. It's beautiful, but doesn't feel right. Over the next hour, she tries on dress after dress, each one stunning in its own way. We offer our input and support, while Sienna and Valerie share stories of how they met their husbands and their wedding days.

"One day, this moment will be the one you tell your daughters about," Valerie says to Shay, leaning in to Sienna.

I'm glad this is something Shay is so excited about. I can tell how much it means to have me and both of their moms here. As I glance around, I wonder what it would have felt like to have my mom here when it was my turn to get married. Maybe that's why I'm not particularly excited for a wedding. Jonah and I haven't really discussed whether we would have a big or small ceremony, and honestly, I hate the idea of a big wedding. I hardly know anybody, so most attendees would be strangers, and a wedding is too personal to have people I don't know watching.

Then I realize I don't even think Jonah has told his parents we're engaged. I don't want to think about how Antoinette would react to finding that out. It would probably be the end of the world to her. Maybe this news is what she needs to finally accept that Jonah and Jenevieve will never be together again. Either way, Jonah is mine forever.

"You okay, sweetie?" Sienna reaches over grabbing my hand, pulling me out of my contemplation.

"Yes, I'm good, thank you," I smile.

"Oh wow," we hear behind the curtain, making us sit up straighter in our chairs. The curtain is pulled back, and my mouth drops open as Shay enters. She is stunning in a classic ball gown with a fitted bodice, delicate beading, and a flowing skirt that makes her look like a princess. As she stands on the platform, look-ing at her reflection, I know that she's found the one.

She doesn't say anything; she just wipes her eyes as she stares at herself. I walk to her side, and we both admire the dress.

"It's perfect," I whisper.

"It's perfect," she repeats, wrapping me in a hug.

"I think we've found the dress," Valerie says as she and Sienna join us.

Next, we meet with the lady handling the wedding invitations. Shay chose an elegant design with exquisite calligraphy. She says she doesn't need it to be over the top, but the invitations she chose still turn out to be the prettiest ones I've ever seen. All that's left is to send a list of names and addresses to the coordinator, who will handle everything else.

Our last stop is cake tasting at the top-rated bakery, that just so happens to be right next door. After Shay selects her cake, the bakery is hired to fly out for the wedding, bake the cake the day before, and deliver it in time for the celebration.

A wedding planner is hired to handle the rest of the wedding, assuring Shay that all she needs to do now is show up for the final dress fitting and the wedding itself.

We get lunch at a diner near the bridal shop, and the main topic of conversation is floral arrangements. Who knew plan-ning a wedding required so much time, effort, and energy? I feel exhausted just hearing all the little details. Watching Shay's ex-citement over every detail, I wonder if I'd be just as excited if it were my wedding. I don't want to be a Debbie Downer or a poor sport because I'm genuinely happy for her; I'm just not the wed-ding-planning type of person. And that's exactly the job of the maid of honor: to support the bride in any way she needs, even if I feel a bit out of my depth.

After lunch, we return to the condo, and I take some time for myself, promising to catch up with them later. That evening, the four of us women enjoy a "girls' night" watching Hallmark movies. It's my first time experiencing such a night with moms, and it makes my heart ache, reminding me that I will never get to share these moments with my mom. I don't mention my feelings to Jonah because I feel stupid for feeling this way, but he senses something is wrong. He's extra affectionate, massaging my back all night as I silently cry for the moments with my own mom I'd never get to have.

Valerie and Sienna stay another day, and after dropping them off at the airport, we go back to the condo. Jonah asks if I'd want to go home early, and I nearly explode with excitement. It's weird because it feels like time away from the mansion seems to drag by, while time at the mansion flies by too quickly to fully enjoy or relax. I don't want to spend my days in the city counting down until we go home, only to blink and be right back in the city.

Even at home, Jonah works a lot—he's a total workaholic. I don't want to work nonstop; I don't feel the need to spend every waking moment consumed by work. Though I would never tell Jonah how to run his business, sometimes I think he should relinquish some control and take time off. But he insists on having a hand in every aspect of the company.

When we return to the mansion, everyone makes a spectacle of Jonah's arrival. I guess I never saw Jonah getting home from being on business, so I didn't realize it was such a big thing. As we enter the main part of the house, the main staff is lined up to greet us. Gladys comes over, hugs me, and then takes my hand in hers. Feeling my ring, her eyes dart to my finger, and then widen.

"This isn't? Is it?!" she exclaims, looking from my hand to Jonah.

"It's an engagement ring, Gladys," he confirms.

"It's beautiful," she says, running her finger over it. "Well, it took you long enough," she winks at Jonah.

"We're here now," he laughs.

CHAPTER
Twenty-One

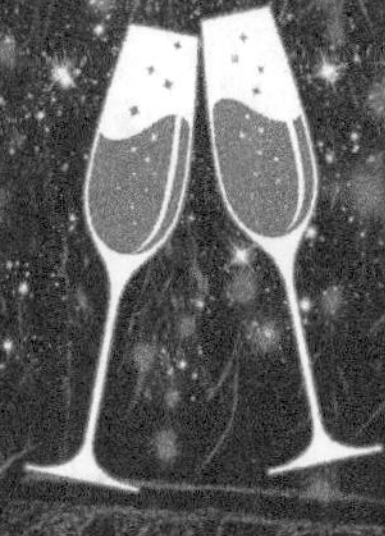

KALYN

"Do you know if anyone is in my old room?" I ask Gladys.

"No, no new maids have been hired, sweetheart. Why?" she gives me a questioning look.

"No reason. Come on," I grab Shay's hand and pull her along with me.

"What are we gonna go do?" She easily follows.

We get curious looks as we walk down the corridor, but I just wave and keep walking. Pushing open my old bedroom door, I step in, the familiar scent of—I don't know… me—fills my nose. I inhale deeper as I step further inside, letting the emotions from this room wash over me. The curtains are drawn open, and sunlight filters into the room.

I walk over to my old bed, pull back the covers, and climb in.

"Are we taking a nap?" Shay asks, though it's less a question and more just going along with whatever I'm doing.

I sit back on the plush array of pillows, the bedding pulled up on my lap, my hands resting on top. Shay sits next to me, lacing her fingers with mine. "So much has happened since the last time you were in here," she says, looking around.

"The first time Gladys brought me in here, I thought I was dreaming."

"And now the entire mansion is yours," she leans her head on my shoulder.

"The day I met Jonah here, he had me so wet on that table from doing absolutely nothing that I would almost bet the front of his black slacks had a wet spot. I could literally feel my arousal dripping down my ass crack," I laugh.

"I couldn't even swallow. When I heard his footsteps, I thought I was going to pass out."

"I'm just glad I didn't start grinding on him right there," I think, reflecting on how badly I wanted to. It's a good thing I had self-control, though now I wonder if that was really the case. I'm still in shock that all that happened; I didn't even know how to react. My boss had me spread wide within seconds of meeting.

"From the first time I saw you guys together, you just looked like you were meant to be, even then. Jenevieve saw it too. It's strange—she felt like you were the reason everything fell apart for her, but you were always meant to be his. At least, that's what I believe," she squeezes my hand.

"I believe that everything happens for a reason, even if they're crappy things. It's all a learning experience. I often wonder what I was supposed to learn from everything that happened with Jene-vieve. I just don't know what I was meant to take away from that, other than trauma and boogeyman nightmares," I sigh.

"Maybe that experience wasn't meant for *you* to learn something. Maybe *she* was the one it was for? Jenevieve will spend the rest of her days blaming you for her and Jonah not ending up together. But if she truly cared about him the way she claimed, she wouldn't have been sneaking around with his brother. Which by the way, have you ever met him?"

"Never. I don't even know what the dynamic is there. I assumed he wasn't part of the family, but I have no idea, and I'm certainly not going to ask Jonah," I shrug.

"God, imagine you meeting Mr. Everett's brother and instantly knowing he was your soulmate or something. That's one of my intrusive thoughts for you."

"Could you imagine Jonah? I don't think either his brother or I would make it out alive." My eyes widen.

"Jonah would tie you down and have his way with you. You'd basically become his permanent bed. He'd probably tie his brother to a chair and make him watch too," she adds that little detail to punctuate her thought.

"He'd impregnate me and have me keep popping out his babies."

"Your babies are going to be devastatingly beautiful, Kal," she looks up at me.

"So are yours," I smile back, meaning every word.

"Did you ever go through a wild party stage?" she asks, switching topics.

"No, I was anti-social, remember?"

"Did you attend college?"

"I completed community college, earned my Associate's degree," I share.

"Did you want to keep going?"

"I wanted out of there as fast as I could," I say honestly.

"Do you hate school?"

"I slept with my professor," I confess, widening my eyes playfully. Her head snaps in my direction.

She sits upright. "Shut the fuck up right now, are you joking?"

I laugh harder. "No, I really did."

She turns to face me, crossing her legs on the bed. "Ohhh, we're doing storytime now," she says excitedly.

"It was my math professor. During my freshman year, everyone talked about the sexy math professor, and a lot of students openly talked about wanting to sleep with him. In my sophomore year, I found myself in his math class. I'd seen him around campus; he was undeniably good-looking and blended in with the students. By the second week of class, I could tell I was going to fall behind because math is not my strong suit. So, I attended a math tutoring session in the library and felt overwhelmed by how hard I found the unit we were working on. The tutor did his best to help me, but I was just emotional, convinced I would never grasp the concepts. My brain simply wasn't processing the information.

The next day in class, my professor asked me to stay after. I thought I had done something wrong and even considered dropping out of school at that moment. But he said he saw me at the tutoring session and was willing to work with me after class if I needed extra help. I thanked him and lied, saying the tutoring session helped and I didn't need any further assistance. Then, I continued going to the tutoring sessions.

In the next class, he asked me to stay after again. This time, he pulled up a chair, had me take out my book, and began working with me on the math unit. Another student came in and said she needed help too, so he helped both of us. But I can't learn like that in a group setting because I get overwhelmed and flustered, so I went back to the tutoring center, and he saw me there once again.

In the following class, he asked me to stay behind again and locked the door so we wouldn't be distracted. We got a lot done, and I was feeling pretty good about the unit.

Then, when we had class next, he asked me to stay once more. I told him I felt I had a good understanding of the assignment, but he wrote a problem on the board and told me to solve it. As I worked on it, I got stuck on some numbers. Then he was just there, right up against me, guiding me through the rest of the problem."

"Don't stop now; you've got me all hot and bothered," Shay remarks.

"His arm brushed against my boob. I wanted him to touch me so badly that I kept shifting to encourage more contact. I lifted my arm over his, pulling him closer. When I turned to look at him, trying to convey that it was okay, his hand moved to the hem of my shirt and slid up, feeling my boobs. Even while touching me, he continued guiding me step-by-step on the problem, and I must really learn when I'm turned on because I understood it completely.

"The next class, he had more problems for me. When I got stuck, he was there again, whispering in my ear, asking if I needed help. I told him yes, and this time his hand slipped into my pants. He fingered me against the whiteboard while explaining the math problem, making me write out what he was saying.

"So for the next class, I ditched the sweats and wore a skirt… with no panties. We had a test and the problem he wrote for me the day he felt my boobs was the first question. The one he had me solve while fingering me was the last question. As he walked up and down the front of the class, watching us to make sure nobody was cheating, I could see him staring at me. I pretended not to notice, uncrossed my legs, and spread them so he could see. And boy, did he see."

"Class ended, and I took my time packing up. When the last student left and I was making my way to the front of the class, he made a beeline for me and… had sex with me on his desk. That continued the entire semester. I went to his house numerous times, and we kept our relationship going during winter break. I didn't have anywhere to go when we had to move out of the dorms. I could have gone back to Sam's, but my professor offered for me to stay with him, so I did. We spent the entire winter break in his bed.

"When we went back for the spring semester, I didn't have him as a professor, but I still went to his class, and we continued having sex. At graduation, he was the one giving out diplomas and told me he was going to fuck me after the ceremony. And he did. Then I packed up all my stuff, moved back to my hometown, and started working at Amaryllis Firm. I changed my number and never looked back."

"Wait, you legit just up and dipped out on your professor?!" she asks, shocked.

"Yep."

"Damn, that's brutal. Did you guys ever establish the relationship?" she asks.

"He told me he loved me."

"Kalyn! And you just up and ditched him without saying anything?"

"I doubt I was the only one he was sleeping with. Every girl on campus wanted to have sex with him. Plus, that student who came in while he was tutoring me was wearing a skin-tight, see-through dress. She was really pretty, and I'm sure he slept with her too. Trust me, he lost no sleep over me leaving. I probably just made it easier for him to bring other women home," I laugh.

"I guarantee you he cried over it," Shay says seriously. "Did he give any indication he was sleeping with anyone else?"

"I certainly wasn't asking him. Every time I felt like I might be catching feelings, I'd overhear another student talking about having him as their professor and something he did, like crack a joke and everyone giggled, but he 'made eye contact with her directly,' and it made me feel like the man I was developing feelings for was using me. So, I decided to use him back. I needed to pass his class, I needed to learn the units, and he was good in bed, especially since I was so inexperienced, and well, he was a teacher after all."

"How often were you guys seeing each other?"

"Almost every day. On the days we didn't see each other, we would text or talk on the phone."

"Do you ever feel bad?" she asks, but not in a judgmental way.

"Well, if that hadn't happened, and I didn't work at Amaryllis, and didn't meet Wyatt and get my heart broken, I wouldn't be with Jonah now."

"Are you curious about what happened to him? Your professor?"

"Not at all. Is that bad?" The truth is, I don't care. At the time, I convinced myself that he was sleeping with every girl who had a crush on him. As my therapist would say, I was "projecting." Though now I know that probably wasn't true, what if me leaving did impact him somehow? I feel like I wouldn't be able to handle those emotions, so I've just refused to look him up since.

"If you could go back and find out you were the only one he was seeing, would you have changed anything you did?"

"No," I shake my head. "I was so convinced he was seeing other students that I wanted to distance myself. For the first week after I left, I kept checking my phone, even though it was a new number, thinking if he cared about me, he would find a way to get my number. I used to watch Hallmark movies, so every time I left my apartment, I would imagine him standing there with peonies, confessing his undying love for me. But eventually, I realized he wasn't going to be there when I opened the door. This wasn't a Hallmark movie, and he wasn't going to come sweep me off my feet and refuse to let me go.

"Honestly, a month after him, I met Wyatt. He came in like a wrecking ball, tearing apart the little bit of life I had left and leaving me so broken that I forgot about my professor entirely. My professor never came for me; he was never my knight in shining armor. But there was a man who came for me, over and over, and secretly watched me while I was working," I turn and wink at her.

"Who else's heart have you broken?"

"I've only ever been with Sam, my professor, and then Wyatt shattered mine. But my dear fiancé pieced me back together."

"You've only been with four people?!" her eyebrows arch in surprise.

"You're like, 'This whole time, I thought you were a lady of the night, taking dick at all hours of the night,'" I tease, pretending to fill in her thoughts.

"No way, I just can't believe only four people have been lucky enough to get with you," she counters.

"Well," I gesture broadly, inviting her to explain her count.

"Oh, my sexcapades would make my grandmother clutch her pearls," she laughs.

"She can clutch them all she wants. You're telling me your body count now," I insist.

"Kal, I sound like I'm as bad as Mr. Everett and Jonathan. I'm upwards of forty, probably. I used to party hard in college," she admits, still chuckling.

"Did you ever play airplane?"

"Uhh, I don't think so. Is it a sex game?" she questions, looking intrigued.

"No, dork," and then I push back the covers and lie flat on my back in the center of the bed, extending my arms and legs into the air. "Stand up and put your stomach on my feet."

She stands up, and does exactly as I instruct, interlocking her fingers with mine. I press upward, lifting her off the bed, and we burst into laughter. She straightens her legs and pretends to steer, then goes toppling to the side of the bed. We explode in fits of giggles.

"My turn," she declares, lying on her back and lifting her hands and feet up. Mimicking her, I position myself above her, but she pushes up quick, like she's eager to have the plane take off, and a grunt is shoved from my throat, and I tumble to the side. We dissolve into hysterics again.

"What was that? The point is for me to stay connected to your feet, not for you to see how much air you can get between us."

"Try again," she says, positioning her feet in the air. I stand and do it again, only this time, I kick off the bed and she almost sends me flying right off the end of the bed. We're laughing so hard, no noise comes out. It looks as if a burst of laughter is caught in both of our throats with no air or sound escaping. By the time sound comes out, we have tears streaming down our faces.

"Your pilot days are officially over," I announce, crawling back up the bed.

She switches positions, propping herself onto her hands and knees. "Did you ever play bucking bronco?" she asks, eyes twin-kling mischievously. "Get on my back, and I'm going to try to buck you off. You have to try and stay on."

I mount her back, wrapping my legs around her waist and grabbing handfuls of her hair, which sends her into another fit of laughter. Her head drops forward as she falls onto her stomach, her face buried in the comforter as I see her body heaving.

"What?" I struggle to keep my balance. "There's nothing else for me to hold onto."

"Grab my shirt."

I do as she says, and she starts trying to buck me off, only I hold on tight and don't budge. We are laughing so hard my back is starting to hurt.

"Imagine if we were horsing around in here and you broke your neck or something. Like how did this happen? We were play-ing airplane and bucking bronco," amusement lacing Shay's voice as she speaks.

"Do you think Jonah has cameras in here?"

"Probably. That man is so obsessed with you he needs to see you at all times. He probably has drones following you around for a live feed of your every move." Exhausted from our antics, we collapse onto the bed, lying flat on our backs to catch our breath.

"What other games did you play?"

"Have you ever played scissors?" She turns her head and smirks.

"No, that sounds terrifying. But I'm up for it," I reply, eager for the next challenge.

"Kal, I'm being a pervert… scissoring, like rubbing our puss-ies together," she giggles.

"Ohhh, right. Well, we were talking about *kid* games, so my mind didn't go there," I nudge her with my elbow.

"Yeah, definitely not. That started in college. Have you ever been curious?" she shifts onto her side, propping her head on her hand.

"I've never really thought about it. Are you offering?" I raise an eyebrow at her.

Her grin widens. "Anytime for you, babe."

"That would have to be a performance for the guys."

"Jonathan would love it—Mr. Everett—he's a wild card. He would either enjoy it or get incredibly jealous that someone else touched you."

"Maybe not, since he knows I'm his," I muse, recalling the videos I saw of him with two of the receptionists. He was enjoying himself. His face certainly seemed captivated watching them, his lips parted, while one of them sat on his lap. He leaned in sucking her boob into his mouth, and her hips began moving again while she continued kissing the other blonde, engrossed in the moment. It seemed no different than what we were discussing—except he wouldn't be involved with us directly. It would just be the guys watching. How could that be any different?

Her phone interrupts us, ringing from the nightstand. She picks it up and then sets it back down. "My mom. I'll call her back," she decides, lying back down.

But her phone rings again immediately.

"It's fine, answer it. I was about to go look for Jonah anyway," I say, sliding off the bed.

"Hi, Mom," she says as we leave the bedroom.

We reach the corridor leading to Jonah's office and our rooms. She waves goodbye and continues down the hall while I turn to head toward Jonah's office.

CHAPTER
Twenty-Two

I overhear Jonah talking to Jonathan about needing Tabitha to have the dresses and tuxes ready in a week. I have no idea what they're discussing, but whatever it is, we'll be dressing up. As I enter his office, they both look up and smile at me.

"Whatcha talkin' about?" I lift a brow.

Jonah turns in his chair, offering his lap for me to sit.

"We were discussing the Gala and what we're going to wear. It's that time of year again. Only this year, I get to have sex on the way to the Gala, at the Gala, and after the Gala," he winks.

"Wow, Jonathan's a lucky man," I grin.

"I'm positive Shay will also put out before, during, and after," Jonah tightens his hold around my waist. "Don't think your little joke was lost on me." He leans in and bites my shoulder.

"I mean, I wasn't properly invited, so I don't need to worry about a dress."

"You've got a smart mouth, baby. Watch it or I'm going to silence it."

I shake my head. "I opt for you silencing it."

"Will you go with me to the Gala?" His voice drops to a low, seductive tone.

"No," I respond, trying to stand up, but he pulls me back down.

He reaches down, grabbing my ring finger. "This is a forever invitation," he murmurs, twisting the ring slightly back and forth.

"My fiancé will thump you if he sees you touch our ring," I smile.

"Is that so?"

I nod.

"I'd like to see anyone try to keep me from touching you."

"Tell me more," I lift a brow.

"Well, I'm a bit possessive and a tad jealous. And I like you just a little," he holds up his hand with his thumb and pointer finger slightly apart to indicate a small amount.

"Only a little?" I repeat, clearly doubting his words.

"Only a little," he agrees with a nod.

"I seem to recall someone stalking me for four years. Would you like to tell me which part of that is only a little?"

"I don't know—you were a cock tease. Giving me boners and never getting me off," his eyes drift to my lips and back to my eyes.

"Maybe you should have made a move," I challenge.

"I did," he grins.

"Oh yeah? When you put your fat-ass dick on my vagina in front of the staff?"

"That's the time."

"You really needed to drag out your suffering, huh? Who knows, maybe we'd still just be strangers had I not wound up with a flyer on my door."

"I was working up the courage, baby. It's called patience."

"You, my love, had the patience of a saint. What if I started dating someone while you were busy taking your sweet time?"

"He would have ghosted you," he says casually.

"And you know this how?"

"Because I would have been the reason nobody ever seen or heard from him again."

"Oh yeah? You would what—kill him?"

He nods and moves closer, our lips parting so our tongues can play.

"You two make me sick," Jonathan laughs.

"Oh, Jonathan, you're still here," I remark playfully.

"I'm not going anywhere," he settles back in his chair.

"I'm telling your fiancée that you're a pervert," I quip

"She knows. Who do you think I learned it from?" Jonathan retorts.

"Without a doubt. But that's what makes her so lovable. So, about the Gala, what am I expected to do?" I lace my fingers with Jonah's. I don't want to admit that the thought of going makes me sick, as images of Jenevieve describing that night with her and Jonah flash in my mind. She told me how he fucked her at the SUV, and the reminder makes me want to vomit.

I can't tell if he notices my hesitation, but his response suggests he must have. "We can always ditch the Gala, and I can spend the evening buried inside you," he whispers, nibbling on my ear.

"Aren't you required to go?" I giggle as he moves down to kiss my neck.

"I'm not required to do anything I don't want to do," he murmurs.

"Gladys says dinner is ready," Shay announces as she walks up behind Jonathan, wrapping her arms around his shoulders and squeezing him.

"Hell yeah, I'm starving," he says, holding onto her arms.

"You're always starving," she retorts, kissing him.

"Did you get an invite to the Gala?" I ask her, knowing she doesn't know anything about it either.

"The Gala? No, I don't think I did. What day is it?" she asks.

"Saturday," I reply.

"Saturday. No, I didn't get an invite, but that's fine, I already have plans for Saturday," she winks at me. "Don't tell me you already forgot about our plans?" Her expression signals me to play along, even though the guys know she's just messing with them.

"Ohh, that's right! Well, it's a good thing we didn't get invites," I say, climbing off Jonah's lap. She releases her arms from around Jonathan and holds her hand out to me. He jumps up from his chair, grabbing her outstretched hand and wrapping his other arm around her neck.

"Nice try, honey," he squeezes her, and she playfully punches him in the chest.

Jonah pulls me back, and I turn to face him, jumping into his embrace. I wrap my legs around his waist and my arms around his neck as he drums his hands on my butt.

AFTER DINNER, THE GUYS MENTION THEY'RE HEADING UPSTAIRS TO play poker with some of the other staff in Jonah's literal casino, and Shay chooses to join them.

"I'm gonna go out to the stables," I tell Jonah, giving him a kiss.

"Okay, baby," he says, watching me as I leave.

Throwing on some pants and boots, I make my way out. There's a slight commotion, and I instantly know in my gut Winona is giving birth. Following the workers as they rush to the main building, I join the group of stable hands gathered around. Pushing my way through the crowd, I see Brad and Claire inside the stall with Winona.

Winona's lying on her side on the ground, while Claire and Brad are preparing for the birth. Over the next hour, we all watch in awe as Winona delivers. And when I say she gave birth to the most beautiful foal I've ever seen in my entire life, I mean he's stunning—completely black with a white mane and tail. He's utterly breathtaking.

Brad looks up, wiping sweat from his forehead, and does a double take when he sees me, his expression transforming from a look of shock that I'm back—which he must not have known we had returned—to a smile spreading across his face. Nodding his head to the side, he extends an invitation for me to come inside.

Smiling, I unlatch the gate and step in. "The ultrasound was correct. It's a boy," he tells me.

"A boy," I whisper, stepping softly next to him. "Can I pet him?"

"Of course," he replies.

I gently kneel next to the baby and stroke his muzzle. "Hi, sweetheart." My voice trembles as tears escape my eyes. I wipe them away and look up to see Brad watching me. I expect him to comment about me crying, but he just smiles and looks back down at the sweet little guy.

"He has your hair," he jokes, making me laugh.

"He's amazing," I say, softly petting him.

"Definitely unique. People will pay a lot of money for him, that's for sure," he comments.

My head snaps up. "No. He can't be sold. Absolutely not. He's mine," I declare possessively.

Brad smiles. "Then yours he is. He'll need a name."

"Kodiak. His name is Kodiak."

"Perfect," Brad agrees.

"Does someone need to come check on mama?" I ask, glancing at Winona.

"The vet will come stay with her," Brad assures me.

"I don't want to sound stupid, but will us petting him make her reject him?"

"That's not a stupid question. It's actually recommended to have contact with a foal while they're young to familiarize them with humans. Especially since this little guy is going to be smothered by his owner," he grins.

"You have a little jealousy spilling from your lips," I wipe the side of my mouth.

"Dang, Wanda, you don't have to blast me on front street like that," he jokes.

When the vet finally arrives, we leave the enclosure to allow space for him to work and do a full check on Winona.

"I'll drive you back to the house," Brad offers as we go to the front of the building.

"Would you want to go for a walk for a bit?" I ask awkwardly, unsure if he would even be interested. He grins, and I instantly know he has something smart to say. "Never mind." I say, pushing him playfully and walking toward one of the golf carts.

He reaches out and tugs at my arm. "C'mon, I'll show you my favorite spot to each sandwiches."

Shaking my head, I follow him. He leads me down a narrow, winding path that meanders through the forest behind the stables. It must be a trail that is used frequently enough that actual stone pathways were put down to guide the way. Lanterns hang from poles, their soft, flickering lights casting dancing shadows on the trees.

"This is beautiful," I whisper, glancing around.

As we continue, I see the trees begin to part and open to the lake. Its surface reflects the twinkling stars like a mirror. Rocks of various sizes line the shore, offering perfect spots to sit. There are also benches scattered sporadically, but I follow him as he walks to a group of rocks. He climbs up on one and takes a seat, then pats the large flat rock next to him for me to join him.

We silently stare out at the lake. Out here in the dark, we can see so many stars twinkling in the sky.

"You know, you would be a siren's worst nightmare. You seem like the kind of man who, if a siren swam up to the rocks and sang her song to lure you in, would somehow be lured up here by you on the rocks just so you could have sex with her and throw her back to sea."

"Fish is my favorite meal."

"I'm sure it is, you dirty man."

"My dad used to take me crab fishing with him, and there were times I thought our boat would never make it back to shore, that we'd end up at the bottom of the ocean. He'd tell me stories about sirens and how it's better to have rough nights than quiet ones because it's the quiet nights when you can hear the sirens' songs, luring sailors and fishermen to their doom. Of course, I always thought it was his way of trying to calm me during the harsh storms we'd get caught in, but even back on shore, he swore the stories were true."

"That's eerie," I shiver, running my hands up and down my arms. "Did he ever say he heard them himself?" The idea of sirens luring men to their doom seems so fascinating to me. Just the idea of a "mermaid" having so much power that she could entice a grown man to walk directly into the water seems incredible. I've watched videos online of people claiming to have caught footage of real sirens, but these days, with Photoshop and special effects, it's hard to tell what's real and what isn't. I wouldn't believe any mermaid or siren footage unless I saw it with my own eyes.

"He claimed he did once. He was out late on deck and thought he heard something, so he looked over the side and could hear a mesmerizing song coming from the water. He said it was so enchanting he wanted to get closer to see where it was coming from, and he almost fell overboard. Two crew members grabbed him and pulled him back, snapping him out of whatever trance he claimed to have been in. He says that's why he quit going out on the boats after that."

"That's a great story. Do you believe in sirens?" I'm completely fascinated.

He shrugs. "Not in the sense you're thinking of. I don't believe there's a mermaid in the water that mysteriously drags men to their deaths, but I believe there are women who have that kind of power over men, even when they don't realize they hold that kind of power at all," he says, staring intently at me.

We fall into silence, the tale of sirens weaving a spell over the night. My mind pieces together scenes of the moon casting a glow across the lake and a beautiful woman emerging from the water in the distance, her fin keeping her afloat as she hovers above the surface. She dives back below, only to reappear even closer.

"Your dad sounds like a really great storyteller. Maybe one day, you will be out here alone and find yourself in the arms of a siren. Then you can come back and tell me all about it." I lean over, playfully bumping into him.

"Because I'd somehow be the one to make it out of a siren's deadly clutches?"

"Yes, you. Of course it would be you," I nod. "What other stories do you have up your sleeve?"

He leans back on his arms, stretching his legs out in front of him on the rock. "See that tree across the water? The really big one?" He points to the large silhouette of a weeping willow, its branches gently swaying in the breeze, illuminated by the moonlight. "There's a story that says the tree has magical powers. It was planted by a woman centuries ago who was madly in love with a man from town. They were having an affair, and he promised to leave his fiancée for her, but day after day, he only ever had excuses as to why he couldn't. Right before the wedding, the woman ran into a witch in the forest who told her if she planted this magical seed, she could make one wish from it, and then she just had to fully bury the seed for it to come true. But she had to dig a hole six feet deep. As she finished digging, she climbed out, holding the seed in her hand, ready to make her wish. But was struck on the back of the head and was never seen or heard from again."

"Was it the fiancée who killed her?" I ask, unable to take my eyes off the tree.

"Thats what the story claims. The fiancée knew about the affair and heard through the grapevine that the mistress was pregnant, so she got rid of her before she started to show. She buried the mistress in the hole she had just dug, along with the tree seed, which eventually grew into that weeping willow. It's believed that the mistress became the tree. Now, it's said if you sit under the tree and tell her your deepest desires, she'll grant you your wish."

"Well, does it work?" I lift a skeptical brow at him.

"Not as well as I'd hoped."

"And… what did you wish for?"

"I can't tell you, Wanda. I'm still holding on to hope that she'll grant my wish," he grins.

"And what does the tree expect in return? I'm sure she doesn't just give out wishes from the kindness of her—heartbroken heart?"

"I don't know. I haven't thought that far into the story yet," he laughs.

"You're such a loser. Did you literally just make that up?"

"Yes," his face is serious and then he bursts into laughter again.

"You had me going for a minute."

"It made for a good story, though, didn't it?" He glances out at the tree again.

"Yes, except now I want to go see it just to feel if there are any spirits near it," I say, watching the tree.

"Maybe we can go sometime, but only if you're comfortable enough to fight off any crazed spirits, because I'll trip your ass and high-tail it out of there."

"I would expect nothing better of you," I joke.

"Thank you for always keeping your standards for me so low," he grins.

"Yeah, no problem. It's easy when you had the bar so low it never made it off the ground."

"Well, now that you've made me feel all warm and fuzzy inside, are you ready to head back?" He stands, extending his hands to help me up.

"Sick of me already, huh?" I take his hand and let him help me down from the rock.

"Nah, just creeped out by the tree story," he says.

"You scared yourself with your own story?"

"Yep," he says, popping the p for emphasis.

"Can we check on Kodiak before you take me back?"

"You're so bossy, Wanda." He guides me back along the winding path. As we enter the stable, we approach Winona's stall again. She stands protectively over Kodiak, who is resting peacefully on the straw.

"He's so beautiful," I whisper, watching the little guy sleep.

He allows me a moment longer to admire Kodiak before he pushes off the gate quietly. I turn to see him nodding for me to follow him.

"You're the bossy one," I retort as we head toward the golf cart. "Thank you, by the way, for allowing me the chance to go in and meet Kodiak and also for telling me made-up stories about weeping willows and sirens."

"Of course. But the siren stories are true."

It's dark out, and Brad drives us around to the side door by the garage.

"Thank you again. I'd ask if I can come back out tomorrow, but I *will* be coming back out tomorrow."

"I look forward to it. See you tomorrow then, Wanda. Sleep well."

"Goodnight, Bert." I wave as I walk toward the door.

CHAPTER
Twenty-Three

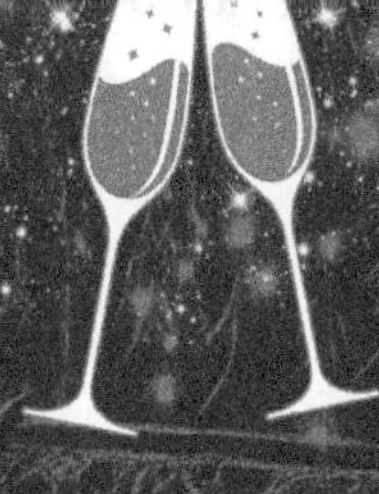

KALYN

The night of the Gala arrives, and I can feel the nerves dancing in my stomach. I'm not one for wanting to be the center of attention; in fact, I'd rather just blend into the background. However, this night is a big deal for Jonah's company, and I feel a mix of excitement coursing through me with a larger undercurrent of dread. Perhaps it's because the last time Jonah attended the Gala, he was with Jenevieve. The thought instantly annoys me. I wonder what the likelihood of her being there will be. All the top business execs will be present, and the last thing I want is to see her. Taking a deep breath, I push the thought aside and focus on the evening ahead.

I stand before the mirror, adjusting the straps on my form-fitting, sparkly red lace dress. The straps form a deep V, plunging down to my sternum and showcasing my breasts. The back of the dress is equally daring, open all the way down to just above my ass. A slit up the left side reaches the top of my thigh, and I know Jonah will appreciate how it fits.

Shay styled my hair in an elegant curled updo, each strand perfectly placed to create a sophisticated yet effortless look. She does my makeup, highlighting my features without overwhelming them. Typically, I avoid wearing jewelry aside from my engagement ring, but tonight Shay insists on more. She places an elegant diamond necklace around my neck and hands me a matching set of diamond earrings—their sparkle complementing the shimmer of my dress.

Shay herself is wearing a black sparkly dress that's form-fitting like mine, with an open back. It always amazes me how she manages to do both our hair and makeup so quickly, but she's told me numerous times that she loves to practice on anyone willing to let her.

The Gala is being held at a hotel just a couple blocks from the condo, so we don't have far to go. In case things get out of hand, I can just sneak away and scurry home. Though I doubt Jonah will let me out of his sight for long.

The men are waiting in the living room for us to finish. We had shown Tabitha our dresses, and she was tasked with finding matching ties for the guys. Being the miracle worker she is, we know she did it flawlessly. Shay specifically told Tabitha that Jonathan's tie needed to be black and sparkly like her dress, and she insisted that Jonah's tie should sparkle too. I told Tabitha she didn't have to find him a sparkling tie, but deep down, I knew Jonah would want his tie to match my dress.

"Are you guys ready?" Shay calls from the bedroom.

"Been ready for the past five hours," Jonathan calls back.

As Shay opens the door, she motions for me to go first. I walk out, and Jonah stands up from leaning on the counter, his mouth hanging open as he scans me from head to toe.

I manage to walk all the way to him, with him standing frozen.

"Holy shit, Kal," Jonathan says, his eyes widening.

"Well?" I ask, waiting for Jonah to say something, as I smile and twirl to show off the back of my dress.

He audibly gulps. "Fuuck, babe."

"Do you like it?" I ask shyly, walking up to him and grabbing the lapels of his suit jacket.

"I have never in my life seen anyone as breathtaking as you. I can't believe you're mine," he says, looking me up and down once more.

"I like your tie." I gently run my hand down the front of his sparkly red tie.

His eyes shift up, so I turn to follow his gaze and see Shay walking out of the bedroom. Jonathan points at her. "Turn right back around, my love. Your ass is getting bent over their bed," he picks her up and spins her around.

"Do you like?" She kisses him.

"Me likey," he agrees, putting her down.

"Shall we get going?" I ask.

Jonah bites his lip, slowly shaking his head. "No, absolutely not. We should go to the bedroom, and you can ride me while you wear that," he murmurs, his fingers delicately tracing down the bare skin of my chest.

"You look sexy as fuck, Kalyn," Jonathan says, approaching us with his arm draped around Shay's shoulder.

"Yeah, she does," Shay agrees. "We have a surprise for you both when we get home. Kal and I are going to hook up, and you guys get to watch," Shay adds as Jonah opens the front door.

"Wait, for real?" Jonathan asks, looking between us. "If you're being serious, we aren't going to the Gala," he pauses at the elevator with his hand hovering over the button.

Shay and I both laugh at Jonathan's eagerness. I push his finger into the button to call the elevator. "Down, boy," I tease.

As we walk toward the front doors, a large black hummer limo waits outside.

"Ever been in a limo before?" Jonah asks as I slow my pace.

Shay eagerly grabs my arm, pulling me toward the limo, not giving me a chance to answer.

"Why are we taking a limo when it's only two blocks away?" I ask, genuinely surprised. I thought we'd be walking since it's so close.

"You'll be on those pretty little feet a lot tonight; let them rest on the way there," Jonah says, settling in beside me at the back of the limo.

It's my first time in a limo, so I don't know what to expect. Swirling lights dance on the ceiling, and soft music plays. Surprisingly, not as loud as I would expect. It feels sexy, and now inside, I instantly feel turned on, and become hyper-aware of the man next to me. It must have the same effect on Jonathan and Shay because she's already lying on the bench with her legs spread, and he's between them.

"I don't want to mess up my hair or makeup," I tell him, not taking my eyes away from them.

"Okay," he drapes his arm around my shoulder and softly traces a path with his thumb.

When we arrive in front of the hotel's grand entrance, I grow impossibly more nervous. The red carpet is rolled out, guiding guests into the lavishly decorated ballroom. We wait for Shay and Jonathan to situate their clothes before we step out of the limo.

Flashes of lights bombard us, and people shout, "Mr. Everett, over here," as more photos are taken. He takes my hand and guides me inside without a word.

The ballroom is filled with the city's elite, the ballgowns and jewelry sparkling as much as the chandeliers above. Men in sharp tuxedos stand with gorgeous women, engrossed in conversation, making me feel like an outsider in a world to which I don't belong.

Jonah gently squeezes my hand, grounding me amidst the total intimidation around the room.

"You're doing great, baby," he whispers, his voice soothing my frazzled nerves.

We mingle, and thankfully Shay has been right by my side. Jonah and Jonathan are naturals at engaging people. Jonathan makes everyone laugh, while Jonah listens intently, and when he speaks, everyone hangs on to his every word. As I take in the room I can see different crowds of people all socializing, periodically glancing in our direction and it just looks like everybody is waiting for the perfect opportunity to approach Jonah. I forget how high he is on the totem pole because to me, he is no longer Mr. Everett, my boss, me his housekeeper. But I am now Kalyn, his fiancée.

Jonathan whispers in Shay's ear, and her face lights up. She winks at me as he pulls her away. I know exactly where they're going, and I wish Jonah was taking me along with them. Having sex right now would definitely ease my nerves.

Jonah is deeply engaged in a conversation with a group of men. Looking around the room, I spot the bar. So far, the only beverage that has been offered has been alcohol, but all I want is water.

"I'm going to the bar to get some water. I'll be right back," I discreetly tell him, stepping away.

"Can I get a glass of water, please," I ask the bartender. He nods and pours water from a bottle into a glass. I guess I just thought I was going to get tap water. Had I known it would come in a fancy bottle I wouldn't have asked for a glass. This probably makes me look high maintenance… over water.

"Thank you," I pick up the glass and take a sip.

"You look beautiful, Kali," a voice says, making my skin prickle and my blood run cold. That nickname… that voice.

Setting the glass on the counter to steady my trembling hands, I take a deep breath. His familiar scent hits me as he leans on the counter beside me, making me instantly want to vomit. I can't even bring myself to look up. I stand frozen, screaming internally at my legs to move, to carry me away from here, but I can only stare at my trembling hands.

"Hi, baby," Jonah chimes in, softly tracing his hand down my bare back, stopping where the fabric of my dress begins just above the curve of my butt.

Relief washes over me. I straighten my spine and lift my glass again, my confidence slowly coming back. Turning with my head held high, I meet Wyatt's gaze. He straightens from his leaning position on the counter. A devilish gleam sprawling across his idiotic face.

"Wyatt," I say flatly, my voice steady while my insides are anything but.

His eyes roam down the front of me, lingering on my chest, his grin growing wider.

"Jonah," Jonah breaks the tension extending his hand to Wyatt.

"Wyatt Broderick," he shakes Jonah's hand back, making sure to say his entire name, thinking he's a big fucking deal.

It feels like a pissing match as neither one of them lets go, yet I can see Wyatt's hand turning red from how hard Jonah is squeezing it.

"Okay, babe, let's go," I prompt Jonah to finally release Wyatt's hand, though he doesn't break eye contact.

"Are you two here together?" Wyatt questions with a look of amusement.

"Here and everywhere. We live together," Jonah's gaze remains fierce.

For a split second, Wyatt's mask almost slips, nearly revealing that this upsets him. But just as quickly, it's back in place. "It was great seeing you, Kali. We should get a drink sometime and catch up," he says to me. Then, for good measure, he adds condescendingly, "With your permission, of course. I know how wild this one can be. Don't want to get her in trouble."

Hold the fuck up. What the hell was he insinuating? HE was the one who was 'wild' in our relationship.

"My fiancée doesn't require my permission for anything," Jonah fires back, his eyes burning into Wyatt.

I had always assumed Jonah knew about Wyatt. He knows everything else about me, but he's never mentioned him. It's clear now that Jonah does indeed know who Wyatt is.

"Fiancée?" Wyatt raises an eyebrow at me, the muscles in his jaw flexing, before shifting his attention to Jonah. "Wonderful, I'll reach out soon."

As Wyatt saunters off, I feel like all the oxygen has been sucked out of the room. I watch as he approaches a cluster of gentlemen, his charisma undiminished. They greet him as he joins their circle, and he regales them with lively chatter. His eyes flicker to mine, a devilish glint on his stupid ass face.

"Come on," Jonah urges, grabbing my hand and steering me through the crowd.

I'm so thankful he doesn't mention what just transpired. All this time, I've been worried about the possibility of running into Jenevieve; I completely overlooked the potential for a Wyatt encounter. Though logically, why would I ever expect to see him here? He has no reason to attend this event. Unless, of course, he's been promoted at Amaryllis, but I can't fathom why anyone would deem him worthy of advancement. He barely lifted a finger to do his own work, instead delegating all his work to other employees, like *ME*, while I was there. After I was gone, I'm sure the new little intern inherited not only his workload as well as his dick, until he did the same thing to her that he did to me—fucks a new hire and gets her fired.

Jonah navigates the social landscape effortlessly, seamlessly integrating himself into various conversational clusters. In one particular group, an older woman's eyes land on my ring, and she gasps, "Dear heavens, is that an engagement ring?" Her hand presses to her bosom as she radiates happiness, and she turns to her husband.

"Yes," Jonah announces proudly.

"May I?" the woman requests, extending her hand for a closer look.

"Of course," I acquiesce, placing my hand in hers.

"Exquisite," she says, admiring the ring before studying Jonah and me with interest.

The other women in the group swarm around, eagerly examining the ring until they've all had a look.

"What's everyone so fascinated with over here?" a new woman asks, as she inserts herself into the circle.

"Your son's engagement ring," one of the men explains. As the women step aside to allow her entry, I freeze as Antoinette and Beaumont appear.

My heart pounds erratically, threatening to leap free from my ribcage. Antoinette falters as she looks between Jonah, me, and the ring on my finger. This is the first time I've seen her since everything happened, and I'm uncertain how this will play out. I'm annoyed with Jonah for failing to forewarn me of their attendance.

"Engagement ring?" Antoinette repeats between gritted teeth.

"We'll catch up with all of you later. We need a word with our son," Beaumont states, a broad smile on his face as he subtly dismisses the group.

"Son?" she parrots, her expression flat.

"I thought you said you couldn't make it tonight," Jonah accuses, his eyes narrowing at his mother.

"Well, my own son refuses to return my phone calls—" she begins.

"Not the time or place, dear," Beaumont interjects, his voice hushed as he discreetly surveys the room.

"Would you like a closer look at Kalyn's engagement ring, Mother?" Jonah asks, his eyes narrowing accusingly.

I watch her chest rise as she takes a big inhale of breath and slowly lets it out.

"Antoinette, dear. Let's get you a drink, shall we? You haven't had anything to ease your nerves," Beaumont suggests, gently guiding her away. She shoots Jonah and me a glare before stalking off. Beaumont places a hand on Jonah's shoulder, giving it a reassuring pat as he follows her.

"This night just keeps getting better and better. When will Jenevieve show up?" I ask dryly, scanning the room for Shay.

"I'm sorry, baby."

"Did you not think to tell me who all might be here?" I feel a surge of annoyance.

"My father texted me a week ago saying they couldn't make it. I didn't think I needed to double-check."

Before I can respond, a group of men approach Jonah and start conversing. Their companions soon join, and everyone mingles happily. My heart drops when I see Mr. Weaver, the asshole that fired me from Amaryllis, approaching with Wyatt.

"Mr. Everett, I'm Mr. Weaver. I wanted to introduce myself and discuss a potential business venture that could benefit us both."

Wyatt's face registers shock when he realizes Jonah is *the* Mr. Everett. It's almost comical. Wyatt and Mr. Weaver are goldfish turds in the ocean of sharks. They don't even deserve to be in the same room as Jonah.

"You can direct all inquiries to my fiancée, Kalyn Bell, practically Mrs. Kalyn Everett," Jonah states, his gaze affectionate as he looks at me. "She's the brains and beauty of my operation." It's clear now Jonah definitely knows my past. I'd usually make a lighthearted comment about how that's not my last name yet, but I understand his intent. He wants to show all of them that they fucked with the wrong person.

"Yes, of course. Do you have a business card, Katelyn?"

Mr. Weaver doesn't even remember who I am. I was clearly so insignificant to the company that he doesn't even realize how many sticky situations I got his little bitch ass out of.

"Katelyn? I worked for you for two years, remember? The one always cleaning up your sloppy messes, and you don't even have the decency to call me by the correct name? Are you trying to belittle me or just showing Mr. Everett your incompetence? No need to contact me. I don't want to do business with a company run by idiots," I bite out and walk away.

My nerves are a jumbled mess, and I'm sure everyone is staring at me, but I don't care. I'm so angry I storm outside, welcoming the cold breeze. The gala isn't over for another two hours, which means we've only been here for two, though it feels like ten. Our limo driver is just up a ways, parked at the curb and leaning against the limo as he talks on the phone. When we make eye contact, I head straight for him, and he hurries to open the door for me.

I'm so angry I could scream. Instead, I sit in the limo, listening to music, stewing in my frustration to avoid causing more scenes. I kick off my heels and prepare to lie down when the door opens, and Jonah climbs in.

We don't speak; we just stare at each other. Then, he shrugs off his jacket and moves across the seat, our lips crashing together frantically. He pushes my dress up my legs and pulls me onto his lap as my hands fumble to remove his tie and unbutton his shirt. He reaches down, undoing his pants, and the anticipation between us explodes into a passionate embrace.

"Fucking assholes," I mutter, continuing to undo his shirt.

"Yes," he agrees, his lips reclaiming mine.

My dress didn't leave room for panties, making this task easier. Lowering myself onto him, I glide up and down, sinking deeper each time until I'm fully seated. All the anger I was feeling inside instantly evaporates as I begin rolling my hips back and forth. He feels incredibly big, and my moans ring out without a care who might hear us. I don't even care how much the limo rocks from the outside—fuck them all.

He lets me release my aggression on his dick until I'm coming hard. Not allowing me time to descend, he holds me close as he lays me down, getting me off again before licking between my legs, sending me into spiraling pleasure. Before long, I'm climbing back onto his lap. He pulls my dress down my arms, sucking my peaked nipple into his mouth.

Leaning back, I place my hands on his knees, rolling my hips on him, my head falling back as I chase another release. The door swings open, and Shay and Jonathan climb in.

"You made quite the exit, Kal. You embarrassed the shit out of the dorky, bald, clown-band, redhead in there," Shay says as she settles into the back seat.

"Fuck him," I groan, not stopping my movements.

The limo begins to move, and soon the sounds of Jonah and me are joined by those of Shay and Jonathan. We must have taken a long way back because we have sex for at least thirty minutes once we leave, allowing us time to clean up and situate our clothes before we arrive back up to the condo.

After we get out, Shay, Jonathan and I stand by the entrance while Jonah talks with the driver.

"What happened?" Shay asks curiously as Jonathan holds her in his arms. She reaches out to hold my hand, and I take it.

"Well, my ex was there. Haven't seen him since I caught him with the intern. Then Antoinette tried killing me with her dagger eyes when she and Beaumont heard Jonah and I were engaged. Then my ex-boss, who fired me because my ex was cheating on me, literally had no clue who I was and called me the wrong name in front of Jonah and all the other business execs. So I called his ass out. I probably embarrassed Jonah, and I feel shitty about it, but it felt so good," I say, turning to look at Jonah.

"Embarrassed him? Everyone thought you were a total badass," Jonathan declares.

"It's true, they did," Shay agrees.

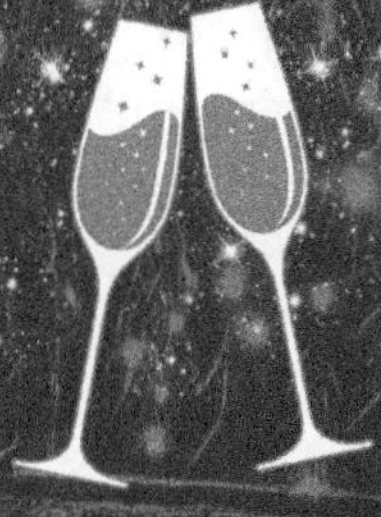

KALYN

It's been three weeks since the Gala, and word spread quickly about my confrontation with Mr. Weaver. Apparently, he really had no idea who I was and had to ask around until it finally clicked.

Lilly, Amber, and I have been planning Shay's bachelorette party for the last two weeks, mostly via text since we've been away for work and Amber moved in with Sam. It's still strange that she lives in my hometown, but she says she loves it. They often go to Milo's diner, and she keeps me updated about Milo asking about me, telling her and Sam I need to visit again soon. She completely caught me off guard when she mentioned that every time Mr. Milo praised me as his best employee and offers for me to come back anytime I want, she tells him she'll take the position instead if he needs a waitress. I know she doesn't mean anything by it, but it makes me feel like she's trying to *be me*.

We've been home for a week, and finding time to discuss plans without Shay around has been challenging. Tonight, we're heading back to the city to celebrate her. Amber is flying in to meet us, and we'll pick her up from the airport.

Jonah got us a suite at the hotel where the nightclub is, giving us VIP access for a proper girls' night out without the guys around. Despite Jonah and Jonathan insisting on joining us, we firmly tell them it's a girls-only weekend.

"I can't believe we're going on a private jet," Lilly exclaims as we climb the stairs.

We sit in our usual spots, Shay and I side by side with Lilly across from us, eagerly looking around. "Isn't there a name or something for having sex in the air? Have you guys done it?" Lilly's eyes widen as she asks.

"Mile-high club, and yes, I've done it," Shay answers, turning to look at me with a grin. "What about you, Kal? I just picture—I don't know—something about a belt."

"Hmm, I don't know," I laugh.

"You'll have to invite Theo to the wedding, and you two can also join the mile-high club," Shay wags her brows at Lilly.

Jonah finishes talking to the pilot and then walks over, scooting past Shay to sit on the knee-high wooden table in front of us. He places his hands on my legs and starts fastening my seatbelt. "Are you good?" he asks, checking if I'll be okay without him sitting next to me, especially since I'm a nervous wreck during takeoff.

I hesitate, unsure how to tell him I'll need him to distract me, but Shay interjects. "I've got her; she'll be fine," she assures, grabbing my hand.

Jonah keeps his eyes fixed on me, then nods and leans in to kiss me. He takes a seat diagonally from us, in a two-seater spot with single chairs facing each other and a table between. Jonathan sits with his back to us, while Jonah positions himself where he can keep his gaze on me.

Lilly chatters excitedly, staring out the window, as Shay secures my hand in hers. But all I can focus on is Jonah, our eyes locked. His presence comforts me, even from a distance, easing my nerves.

The flight goes by quick as we talk. Before we know it, we're landing in the city. We collect Amber as planned and all ride to the hotel together. Jonah and Jonathan escort us to the suite Jonah reserved, and it's absolutely stunning. There are two bedrooms, each with king-sized beds and their own bathroom, along with a living room, and a kitchenette. We plan to stay in tonight and go dancing tomorrow night.

"Kal and I can share this room," Amber offers. I immediately notice Jonah and Jonathan exchange a sideways glance.

"No, Kalyn and I are sharing a room," Shay corrects her.

"It's just, you see her every day. I was hoping to catch up," Amber replies.

"You don't see me or Lilly every day either; why not share a room with Lilly?" Shay challenges.

"I'm not dating Lilly's best friend or living in Lilly's hometown," Amber says, visibly annoyed.

"It's also not your bachelorette party," Shay retorts, looking like she can't even believe Amber is arguing about this.

I interject, "It's just for sleeping. Shay and I share a bed all the time, so it makes sense for us to do it now too," trying to sound neutral and ease the tension, even though Shay is definitely the person I feel most comfortable sharing a bed with.

"Kal, I wanted to talk to you," Amber almost pleads.

"And we can, it's just for sleeping, Amber."

"We can FaceTime Sam in bed. I'm sure he would love to see you before bed."

"This conversation is over. Kal is sleeping with me. Plus, I don't think I could fall asleep if we didn't grind our pussies together like we always do," Shay adds with a smile, walking to our newly claimed room.

"You guys have sex?" Lilly asks, intrigued.

Jonathan chuckles and follows Shay. I trail behind them, with Jonah at my heels.

As I step into the room, Shay hovers just out of sight of the door. "What the fuck was that?" she mouths to me.

"Somebody's jealous," Jonathan remarks, swatting Shay's butt.

"Me or her?" she fires back.

"Both," Jonathan shrugs.

"Out. Both of you," Shay orders, pointing to the door. When neither of them moves, she points at each of their crotches. "Penis and penis. NOT a penis party. Take both of those out of here." She grabs Jonathan by the arm and guides him out.

I take Jonah's hand and follow after them. "Love you." I stand on my tiptoes to kiss him.

He scoops me up, wrapping his arms around me. "I love you too, baby," he kisses me softly, then places me back on my feet.

We gather in the living room in our pajamas, laps full of snacks, catching up on all the recent life events. Shay brings out her iPad and pulls up the video of the guys proposing. We show Lilly and Amber the video, and all the emotions from that moment come flooding back. I love Jonah more than anything, and I had a front-row seat to our best friend's big moment too.

"That was so sweet," Lilly places her hands over her heart. "Did they plan it that way—to propose at the same time?"

"Yes," Shay responds excitedly, crossing her legs on the couch as she stares at the still image from the video of all of us hugging.

"I can't believe how much has changed since you first arrived, Kalyn," Lilly says dreamily.

"I know. Sometimes I can't believe it either," I lean my head back on the couch. "Some days I feel like I have impostor syndrome. Like Jonah is going to wake up and be like what are you doing in my bed."

"Do you get bored going to work with Mr. Everett?" Amber asks.

"Not at all, I stay busy while I'm there."

"He has you working?" Lilly exclaims.

"No, I choose to work," I clarify.

"I stopped by Sam's work to bring him lunch, and they got weird about someone stopping by."

There's no reason for that to make me feel any sort of way, but her casually mentioning going to Sam's work makes me almost uncomfortable. It's a painful reminder of my past, a place she probably visits and feels excited about. Pushing those feelings aside, I do my best to focus on the present.

"While we were back home, we visited my great-grandparents' graves and brought them flowers and a windmill. Did you know people go to cemeteries and steal flowers and gifts left for loved ones? That should be an automatic year of community service, picking up trash, and a kick to the dick. I thought cemeteries paid people to watch for that kind of thing," Shay says, irritated. "I told Jonathan if anybody steals the flowers we left, I'm going to push them into the nearest hole that was dug and fill it with dirty myself."

"It probably depends on the groundskeeper. I know Lavern watches out for that kind of thing," Amber says knowingly.

Sitting up, I feel the color drain from my face. "How do you know that name?"

Amber looks like she realizes she might have messed up. "It's the groundkeeper's name for the cemetery near town."

"I'm aware. Why were you there?" I question, feeling my stomach knot.

She looks like she's trying to figure out what to say, her cheeks reddening as I stare. "Sam—"

"Sam, what? Sam doesn't have family there," I cut in.

"I just try to make sure your parents have visitors and flowers."

"You're visiting my parents?" I ask, shocked. I knew what she was going to say before she said it, but hearing her admit it makes my truth—true.

"Kalyn, your parents passed away?" Lilly asks, her eyes widening with shock.

Trying to calm my nerves, I do my best to breathe in and out. "Yeah, I'm the single living person in my family. Neat, right?" I say coldly, then turn my attention to Amber. "Amber, I'm saying this with as much respect as I can. Don't visit my parents' grave. Quit bringing them flowers or whatever else you're doing. You're going around to the places where I grew up, trying to get a job at my old work, talking to my old employer, and going who knows where else from my past. I'm sure you mean well, but it's really not coming off very well," I bite out, then stand up and walk to the bedroom, closing the door behind me.

Grabbing my phone, I go to the bathroom and pull up Jonah's contact. My finger hovers over the call button, trying to decide if I should call. But honestly, he's the only person I want to talk to right now. Pressing call, I hold the phone to my ear.

"Hi, baby," he answers on the first ring.

I know my breathing is shaky, so I don't say anything at first.

"Babe?"

"Tell me I'm being overdramatic," I say, and wait.

"Okay, what's going on?"

"Amber is visiting my parents regularly and trying to get a job at Milo's diner. Am I being a baby for telling her that's out of line?" I slump down onto the floor and put my forehead on my knees.

"No, baby. If you feel it's out of line, your feelings are justified. Want me to come get you?"

"No. I'm here for Shay; I don't want to bail on her," I sigh, and we fall into silence. "I'll let you go. Thanks for listening."

"Love you," he says softly.

Amber wouldn't intentionally hurt me, and I know that. I think part of me is envious that she's close enough to my parents that she can go see them more than I'm able to—more than I did when I lived so close to them.

A gentle knock on the door has me looking up.

"Hi, hun. Mr. Everett is at the door and wants to talk to you. Sam called Amber, so she's in the bedroom talking to him," Shay says quietly.

Relief washes over me, and I stand, brushing past her. She softly touches my shoulder in a comforting gesture.

When I open the door, I find him leaning against the wall, his hands in his pockets. As I approach, he stands, wrapping his arms around me. He lifts me effortlessly, and I bury my face in his neck, tightening my hold. He leans me against the wall, just cradling me in his arms. He doesn't say anything; he just holds me like that.

There's always a looming feeling reminding me of my parents' absence. Most days, it's easier to push back and cope, but right now, it feels unbearable. Growing up without a mom to confide in has been really crappy—someone to talk about the little things, like the way Jonah stares at me when he doesn't think I notice, or the way he loves me so unconditionally.

I don't remember the sound of my mom's voice. I remember that she would always sing, but not how it sounded. My grandma didn't have any videos of my parents, so their voices exist only in my dreams, pieced together from fragments of memories, but never enough to feel satisfied.

I push back the sting of tears threatening to escape, knowing if I let one out, I might not be able to reel them back in. This is when a mother's guidance would be helpful—offering love and understanding. I've faced each new milestone practically alone and have gotten pretty good at it. But sometimes, it would be nice to have someone else carry my burdens for a while. Jonah would gladly do that, but it's an emotion I can't even put into words. He's my anchor, my safe place, but he provides a man's touch and a man's comfort, though he does his best to be everything I need.

I hate when I throw pity parties for myself. I hate when I feel weak or blindsided by something. It makes it harder to remain strong when I just want to crumble.

Shay opens the door quietly and informs me that it's been 45 minutes, asking if I'm ready to go to bed. I let out a sigh and relax my hold on Jonah's neck. "Thank you for coming," I whisper.

"Of course. I love you," he whispers in return.

Pressing my lips to his, we linger in the kiss before I finally pull away.

"Love you," I murmur as he sets me gently on my feet and Shay and I re-enter the room.

"Do you want to talk about it?" she asks quietly as we lay here silently.

I turn my head to look at her, not wanting to talk about anything. "No, this is your weekend."

As we descend the grand hallway with its red and gold carpet toward the club, the booming music guides our way. There's a long line waiting to get in, but we walk beside it to the front. Jonah assured us mentioning my name would grant us entry.

"Hi, I'm Kalyn Bell. I should be on the list," I shout over the music. The bouncer checks his clipboard and then scans me up and down.

"You're not on the list, but I might be persuaded to let you in," his gaze roams up and down me again.

"Kalyn Everett," Shay interjects from behind me. The bouncer looks at his list again, finding my name this time. He drinks me in one last time then moves the red rope aside, ushering us inside. A girl in a dress shorter than mine leads us through the crowd to our private table. A bottle of champagne is brought to us, the woman pouring each of us a glass.

"I can't believe you and Jonathan are finally getting married," Lilly beams at Shay, taking a sip of her champagne.

"I know," Shay admires the diamond on her finger.

"You too!" Lilly says, turning to me. "You've bewitched Mr. Everett."

As the night goes on, we migrate to the dance floor. The music is loud, and colorful lights swirl all around. Men try to smoothly insert themselves, their arms attempting to wrap around us, but we manage to evade their advances. One particularly handsy man doesn't seem to understand what "no" means and keeps trying to touch me, which got annoying after we kept moving away, only for him to shimmy his way back in.

"Get the fuck away, bald-ass bitch," Shay shouts at him. He looks embarrassed and offended but moves away from us, clearing off the dance floor entirely. After an hour of dancing, we decide we've had enough and retreat to our table. I don't know why women wear such high heels to these kinds of things when all it does is make our feet ache the next day. Sitting back on the VIP bench, I let out a sigh of relief as my feet finally get a break.

Shay leans in, shouting over the pulsating music, "Are you rubbing my feet when we get back to the hotel?"

I let out a laugh. "No, you're rubbing mine."

"But it's my party," she whines.

"Fine, we can rub each other's feet."

Her eyes shift behind me, and I hear *his* voice a moment later. "Kali, can I talk to you?"

I freeze, just blinking at Shay before turning to face him.

"No," I say coldly.

"Please, Kali," he persists, edging closer.

"Why are you even here, Wyatt?!"

He drops to his knees at my feet. "I love you, Kali. Please talk to me."

The audacity. This son of a bitch is doing what I prayed he would have done years ago. And had he, I wouldn't have Jonah.

Rolling my eyes, I turn back to our group with a look of disgust as he continues pleading. "Kali, just hear me out."

"How did you even know where we'd be? Are you stalking me now?"

"Amber told me." He gestures to her. Surprise and guilt flicker across her face. That's Wyatt—always willing to throw someone else under the bus to save his own skin. This time, Amber's the one he's making a human speed bump with.

"You what?" I demand, thinking I must have heard him wrong.

"It was an accident," she stammers, looking stricken.

"An accident? You accidentally told my ex about Shay's party?"

"We were having lunch and—"

"Excuse me," I cut her off, my head falling forward in disbelief. Now I know I'm more drunk than I originally thought. Did my friend just say she was having lunch with my ex?

"Kali, baby." He reaches out, brushing his fingers down my leg.

"Get the fuck out of here, Wyatt!" I yell. Instantly, two bouncers appear.

"Everything alright, ladies?" one of them ask.

"No, this guy is harassing us," I glare down at Wyatt with disgust.

"Let's go," the bouncer says, grabbing Wyatt by the arm and pulling him up.

"Get your hands off me," he snaps, adjusting his suit coat defiantly. "This is my girlfriend," he tells them.

The bouncers look at me for confirmation. I shake my head and hold up my hand. "I'm engaged to Jonah Everett. You wish you were my boyfriend."

This infuriates him, and he tries stepping toward me, but the bouncers jerk him away.

"Please don't let this ruin our night," Shay whispers in my ear, resting her hand on my thigh. "Please."

I stare down at where she's touching me, focusing the anger and hurt I feel on how good her hand feels against my skin. A tingling radiates from the spot she's touching, right to my core, and all I want to do is pull her hand between my legs. "Okay," I say, finally looking up and forcing a smile.

We stay for another hour before heading back to the suite. The shots have taken their toll; alcohol-fueled laughter bubbles up as we stumble through the door, arms intertwined for support.

Once we're in our room, Shay and I help each other out of our dresses and into the shower to wash off our makeup and clean our sweat-soaked bodies.

Emerging from the bathroom, I stumble, clumsily wrestling with my clothes, then collapse onto the floor in exhaustion.

"Come on," Shay encourages, pulling on my arms. "Let's get in bed."

"I'm coming," I slur as I start to crawl toward the bed.

I wake abruptly, startled by something covering my mouth. My eyes widen in confusion and terror as a shadowy figure hovers over me, pinning my arms with their legs and silencing me with... their hand. I'm paralyzed with fear, unable to identify who it is, but my body instinctively knows that I'm in danger.

"Please just talk to me, Kali," Wyatt whispers urgently.

"Get off of me," I try to say, but my words are muffled.

"I was assaulted that day in the copy room." I wonder how long it took him to think up this new version of what happened. I struggle beneath him, trying desperately to throw him off, but he flexes his legs, locking me in even more. "I just need you to listen to me, okay? I don't want to hurt you, but I need you to come with me."

Doing the only thing I can think of, I kick at Shay. I can't move my head, but the lamp on her side clicks on, and she rolls over toward me. I can partially make out her eyes widening when she sees Wyatt restraining me on the bed.

She reacts immediately, leaping out of bed, grabbing her phone, and calling Jonathan within seconds. He answers on the first ring. "Babe! Kal's ex broke in and has her pinned to the bed," Shay's voice shakes. Wyatt's head snaps toward her, looking furious. He grabs the phone from my nightstand, wrenches it from the wall, and hurls it at her, his face flushed with rage.

She ducks out of the way before it can hit her, and he yanks me from the bed, "Let's go, Kali," he demands. My feet tangle in the blankets, and I crash to the floor, bringing him down with me. He quickly regains control, climbing on top of me and pinning me down again. Everything happens in a blur, too fast for me to process.

Shay rushes across the bed, wielding a lamp high above her head. With a loud crash, she smashes it over Wyatt's head. He yells in pain, clutching the back of his head. "You bitch!" he shouts, sitting back on the floor. I remain frozen in place until I find my legs moving, scrambling away. But he grabs my hair, pulling me back towards him.

CHAPTER
Twenty-Five

JONAH

We secure a room directly across the hall from the girls. They'd be pissed if they found out, but we want to make sure they're safe after all the drinking. Just as we're settling in, the club owner contacts me about a man harassing them. When I receive a picture on my phone, I see it's Kalyn's ex-boyfriend. Before we can even make it out of our room, the owner informs us the situation has already been handled.

We hear the girls return and watch on the hall cameras as they giggle and fumble with their suite key. Once they're in bed and we're certain they're asleep, we finally manage to fall asleep ourselves.

I'm startled awake when Jonathan's phone rings, and he answers it immediately. All I hear is Shay's panicked voice yelling that Kalyn's ex is in their room. We exchange a single, alarmed glance before sprinting across the hall and using the key to their room that we procured earlier to let ourselves in.

Inside, we find him looming over Kalyn, pinning her arms to the ground, and pleading with her to listen to him. Then Shay darts across the bed and smashes a lamp over his head with a fierce battle cry. It's probably one of the most badass things I've ever witnessed. The impact sends him sprawling off Kalyn, but he snatches her by her hair, yanking her to his chest. My body vibrates with barely contained fury.

"I just want to talk to her," he begs, holding his hands up as if he means no harm.

"Let her go," I calmly reply, not wanting to rattle him.

"Let me talk to her first," he insists.

"Baby, why don't you come here," I extend my hand to her, careful not to make any sudden moves in case he has a weapon.

"Okay," her voice trembles as she nods.

As she tries to get up, he clamps his arms around her.

"I just want to talk to her!" he repeats, holding his hand out to keep me from moving closer.

"And I am telling you now to let her go and peacefully leave," I keep my voice calm.

"I love you, Kali! I want to marry you! I'll be so much better, I'll treat you how you deserve to be treated," he pleads, his face close to hers.

"You cheated on me! Then got me fired! I lived in misery because of you. I want nothing to do with you ever again," she snaps, and he becomes even more enraged.

"That's so like you, holding grudges and never letting anything go."

"Yeah, okay," she scoffs, as a tear trails down her face.

"We were so happy, you're not letting yourself remember because you think you saw something that you didn't actually see," he insists.

She laughs incredulously. "You're going to sit here and gaslight me?"

"I'm not, I promise. Just come outside and talk to me, okay? You're going to come with me so we can talk." His arm tightens around her neck, desperation creeping into his voice.

"Just talk?" she answers skeptically.

"We can do anything you want. We can do that thing you like so much," he whispers, pressing his nose to her ear. He's trying to rewrite history, to make her doubt her own memories and pretend her feelings are inaccurate, that the years of her pain and suffering were all due to delusions and false memories. These mind games make me want to toss him off the balcony.

Her eyes flick to mine, and I subtly shift my head to signal her to look at him. She instantly picks up on this and turns to face him.

"Kali, all I'm asking for is a chance," he says, staring into her eyes.

He's so entranced he doesn't notice me approaching until his eyes widen as I lift him off the ground by his throat.

"Stay the hell away from *my* fiancée, do you understand?" I demand, his feet dangling. His face begins to turn purple, and I tighten my grip, wanting to feel the life drain from him.

Kalyn gets up and runs to the bathroom, slamming the door behind her. I look back, torn between dealing with him and chasing after her.

"I got it," Jonathan makes my mind up for me, smiling as he rips him from my hold.

"He threw a phone at me," Shay spits, throwing the broken phone on the bed.

Jonathan stares at it, then his face curls up in a devilish grin, and I know Wyatt is fucked.

"I'll go check on her," Shay says, starting to head that way.

"No, I will," I cut in, and she instantly halts.

Entering the bathroom, I see Kalyn on the floor in front of the counter, her knees curled to her chest.

"How did you get here so fast?" she questions, lifting her head to look at me.

"I have the suite across the hall," I admit.

"Why?" she bites out.

"Does it really matter? If I had gone home, I wouldn't have made it here as quickly."

"So, now you're stalking me?" she accuses.

"You think it ended when we got together? I'm always watching you. You think there's not a camera from which I can see you from at all times?"

"You're a creep," she climbs to her feet, her eyebrows knitting together in anger.

"And you're mine."

"I'm not a piece of property, Jonah," she says, stepping closer.

"If you're looking for an apology or for me to say I'll quit watching you, you're not going to get it, Kalyn. I'm not ashamed of my love for you."

"Maybe I don't want to be watched all the time."

"Too bad."

"Get out of my way," she tries to push past me.

I lean back against the door, crossing my arms to block her exit.

"Move, Jonah." She reaches around me, grabbing the handle and tries to pull the door open. "Move!"

I'm not letting her leave this bathroom while she's mad at me. It's probably just going to make her more upset, but I'm not leaving. I stare down at her, watching her struggle with the handle and smile. Her eyes snap up to meet mine, burning with anger.

"Asshole," she mutters, pushing my chest. I grab her arms, and she tries to pull away, but I keep a firm hold on her. She struggles, then stares at me, her eyes darting between mine, and suddenly jumps into my arms, kissing me hard.

Her hands move down the front of me, pulling my shirt up until it's completely off. Our lips immediately rekindling.

"Pull your pants down," she whispers, and I set her on her feet. I barely have them tugged down when she fully removes hers and tosses them aside. "Sit," she orders.

I slide down the door, my pants tangled around my ankles, as she straddles me. Her lips claim mine again as she reaches between us and grips me.

"You want it?" she whispers.

"Yes," I pant.

"What if I told you, you can't have it?" she slides my length between her folds.

"I can't help myself, baby. I want to fuse with you and be with you all the time," I groan. If it were socially acceptable to handcuff her to me, I'd make sure she was never out of my sight. It's unhealthy what I feel for her, and I will never try to control it. It's better she realizes it now than after she marries me.

"You don't have enough self-control?" she asks as her hips begin to sway.

"Not with you."

"And when my belly is big and round with your child?" she asks, positioning me in place.

"I'll be worse," I admit through gritted teeth as I grab her hips and thrust into her. A moaned yelp escapes her as she slumps over on my shoulder, her nails biting into my skin.

I keep a firm hold on her, remaining fully buried as I push her hips back and forth. Her movements take over, and I clutch her to me. When she starts bouncing, I place my hands under each cheek to help guide the movements until we're both coming undone.

Our breathing is ragged as we stay entwined, her forehead resting against mine while we share a lingering kiss. Her body trembles in my embrace. Gradually, our breathing steadies, and she pulls back slightly, her eyes meeting mine with a satisfied grin. "Thank you once again for your services, Mr. Everett. Now, off you go." She slowly stands, letting me glide out of her.

I watch her perky ass walk across the bathroom to clean up. *I'm the luckiest man alive.*

By the time I'm dressed again, she's walking out of the restroom, smiling.

"What?" I smirk.

"Nothing," she says, bending down to grab her shorts and top.

When we leave the bathroom, Jonathan and Shay are sitting on the bed, Shay holding an ice pack to his knuckles. Kalyn's eyes land on his hands, and she walks over, pulling the pack up to reveal Jonathan's bloody knuckles.

"Jonathan," she exclaims, grabbing his hand to examine it. "Are you okay?"

"Fine. You should see the other guy," he winks.

"What if he calls the cops?" she asks, concerned.

"He won't. We had a nice chat. I got you, girl."

"Sorry you got hurt," she says, putting the ice pack back in place.

"You gonna nurse me better?" he grins at Kalyn, and Shay smacks him on the back of the head.

"She already had a traumatizing night, don't make it worse, idiot," Shay scolds him.

"Amber told him where we would be," I whisper to Jonah.

"Why would she do that?"

"No clue. I didn't even know she knew Wyatt. But somehow, they knew each other enough to have lunch together. Anyway, you guys can go. We're going back to bed. That's enough excitement for one night," she tells us.

Jonathan smiles and lays back on the pillows, making sure he's right on the edge of the bed. "Hop on in, ladies," he invites.

Shay looks at Kalyn, raising a brow. "There's no way they'll leave us now."

We all settle in, the adrenaline from the night slowly ebbing away. The exhaustion from the events takes over, and I'm out like a light.

In the morning, I wake up to the soft light filtering between the curtains. Gently rousing everyone, we all slowly get dressed and begin gathering our things in preparation for the journey home. As we move their bags toward the door, Lilly and Amber emerge from their room.

Looking at me and Jonathan, Lilly asks, "I thought this was a girls' trip? I saw you both sleeping in there last night," she says accusingly.

"Well, after Kalyn's ex broke in last night and assaulted her, we needed protection," Shay says aggressively, glaring at Amber.

"What!" Lilly gasps. "Kalyn, are you okay?"

"No, she's not. She woke up with a crazy man on top of her, pinning her to the bed. And now my fiancé's hands are banged up from having to deal with him. Maybe from now on, people need to stay in their own damn lane—or perhaps get their own life and stop trying to live someone else's," Shay directs her words to Amber.

"Kalyn, I am so sorry. I didn't mean to cause all these problems," Amber says as her voice begins to wobble.

"I don't want to talk about it right now, Amber. Give me time to cool off, and we can, okay?" Kalyn responds as we head to the elevator.

The girls were supposed to fly home alone today, but there's no way I'm letting Kal out of my sight. We drop Amber off at the airport to catch her flight, and she continues trying to apologize from the sidewalk. I step out of the SUV and pull her luggage from the back, setting it down next to her. "Time to go, Amber. She'll reach out when she's ready," I tell her, climbing back in the SUV and closing the door, leaving her standing there, staring after us.

I don't know much about Amber other than she's the girls' friend, was employed in my house, and is dating Sam. With her absence, the strain between everyone dissipates.

Jonathan's truck is waiting for us when we land. He drives, Kalyn sits between us in the front, and the other two occupy the back. During the drive, Kalyn absentmindedly traces her fingers up and down mine. I smile at her unconscious gesture. When she catches me watching, she does a double take.

"Hi," she says shyly.

"Hi, baby."

"Thank you for being creepy," she murmurs softly, kissing me.

"Thank you for accepting my creepy. Did you have a nice time?"

"Yes, did you?" she nods, leaning closer.

"I did. Especially your bathroom; it was remarkable."

"Mmm, tell me more about this remarkable bathroom," she nudges her nose against mine.

"Are you guys going to start talking dirty to each other?" Shay interjects, resting her arms on the back of Kal's seat, looking between us.

"We were going to until you interrupted," Kal jests.

"Well, don't let me intrude. Carry on," she laughs, making no move to sit back.

"You were saying?" Kalyn grins at me.

"I was saying… the floor was really cold, but a wet warmth suctioned onto me, and I was no longer cold. In fact, I got overly hot and sweaty."

"I like you sweaty."

"Maybe you should come over here and make me sweat again."

She leans closer, her hand cupping my groin. "I like that idea," she bites her bottom lip.

"Hello?" Lilly answers her phone suddenly. After a moment, she holds it out to Kalyn. "Sam needs to talk to you."

"I'll call him later," Kalyn dismisses, pressing her lips to mine.

"He says he's called you nine times and you haven't answered," Lilly informs her.

"I'm trying to be intimate with my fiancé."

"I don't want to be in the middle. She'll call you later, Sam. Bye," Lilly says, hanging up abruptly.

I release her hand, and she looks over at me, but I just wrap my arm around her neck and kiss her temple. I work my way down her neck, and she lets out a soft laugh as she tries to pull away. I tighten my hold and draw her back.

She giggles and slaps my thigh. "Stop…" a sexy sigh breaks free from her lips.

I move just below her ear and start to suck gently. This time, she relaxes into me, wrapping her arm around my neck. I trace my fingers up her bare leg, leaving goosebumps in their wake. When I reach the edge of her shorts, I slide my hand under the fabric, softly trailing back and forth.

Her free hand guides mine, encouraging me to move under her shorts. Her lips part slightly as she watches my hand.

"How long till we're home?" she breathes out, turning to Jonathan.

"Fifteen minutes," he responds.

"I have some work I need to take care of," I tell her.

"You can take care of me first."

Back in the garage, everyone heads inside, and I hop out of the truck and turn back to her. She's already at the edge of my seat, and I undo the button on her shorts, tugging them down. She willingly lifts so I can pull them off.

She pops the button on my pants, freeing my already throbbing cock. She wraps one hand around my neck, glancing down as I snake my arms under her knees, drawing her nearer and breaching her already-soaked center until I'm fully inside. Her hips rock against my every thrust, her core gripping me firmly.

I plant one foot on the truck floor and lean forward inside, pulling her onto my lap so she can ride me while I stand. She eagerly takes over, gyrating frantically, our moans echoing in the large space.

I press my mouth on hers, sucking on her tongue until I feel her body tense and her movements grow unsteady. Her legs tremble as she tightens her hold on me. I bury myself fast and hard until I still, leaving my semen deep inside her, neither one of us moving until our breathing steadies.

"Get that fat dick outta me, Mr. Everett, and get to work."

We both stare down as I slowly withdraw. She's so small, my dick looks almost comically big when next to her. Once I'm fully out, I watch my semen trickling out of her, filling me with a deep sense of satisfaction. I grab her bottoms and help her back into her panties and shorts, buttoning them up.

"Keep them on for an hour, and I'll fill them up some more when I'm finished with my meeting," I say as I assist her down from the truck.

"Nope, I'm going to shower."

As we round the truck, I see all the bags have been brought inside, likely by Giles at some point.

I'm about to demand she not shower until after my meeting, but Brad appears at the perfect moment. "Kal, wanna come see Kodiak?" he calls, walking by the open garage.

"Yes, I'll meet you out there. I'm gonna go shower real quick."

I slap her ass. "No need, go on, baby," I smile down at her, loving the idea of my seed seeping out of her.

"You can't smell any worse than a horse," Brad jests.

She turns and hits my stomach before walking to Brad.

CHAPTER
Twenty-Six

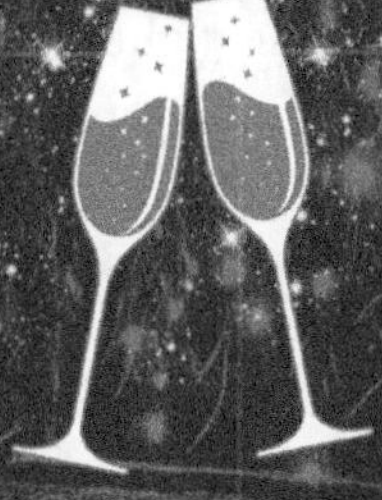

KALYN

"Why'd you need to shower? You a stinky girl?" Brad asks as I approach him.

"My vagina is filled with his semen," I reply with a sideways glance.

"Maybe you should go back and shower," he chuckles.

"Nope, I offered, and nobody cared, so now you all will suffer with me."

"You'll be the only one suffering. You're gonna be sloshy. I'll wait if you want to shower, or we can stop at my apartment. You can use my shower anytime you want."

"You just want to see my asshole again," I quip.

"It's a nice asshole," he shrugs. "Did you have a nice time?" he asks as we walk down the paved road to the stable.

"Obviously. Sex feels good."

"God, Wanda, I was talking about the bachelorette party. I don't want to hear about Everett plowing you." He shakes his head, trying to erase the images from his mind.

"Yeah… until my ex showed up at the club, got escorted out, then decided to break into our hotel and attempt to kidnap me," I say sarcastically.

Brad's entire demeanor shifts immediately. "Are you serious right now?"

"I'm so serious. It was so bizarre."

"What's his name?" The tightly leashed fury in his voice makes me want to deflect, to steer the conversation toward a different topic altogether.

"What are you gonna do, Bert, kill him," I nudge him with my elbow.

"Yes, absolutely yes," he says seriously.

"Shut up," I say playfully. "Anyways, Amber was the one who told him where I would be, so that felt even better. And the baby-back bitch ripped the hotel phone from the wall and threw it across the room at Shay! I don't even want to ask Jonah what kind of charges he got for the damages since Shay smashed a lamp over his head."

"What?" The word rips from his voice so fast it startles me. "I'm serious, Kalyn. What is his name? And why does Amber always wind up in the middle of shit?"

"Kalyn? You just Kalyn'd me? This is serious. Don't worry about it, though. Jonathan handled it. Wyatt quite literally got knuckle sandwiches. So many in fact, Jonathan left half his knuckles with Wyatt. It's fine now."

I can tell how mad he is because he begins walking so fast I almost have to jog next to him just to keep up.

"Can I at least get a piggyback ride if you plan on sprinting the whole way back?" I joke.

He abruptly stops, turning toward me but not meeting my eyes, swiping his hand down his face.

He turns his back. "Get on," he gestures his hands for me to jump up.

Smiling, I run and jump on his back, gently tugging on his ear before wrapping my arms around his shoulders. This time, when he starts walking, his pace is slow.

"How's my sweet boy?"

"I'm fine," he smirks, continuing to walk.

"You wish you were my sweet boy," I laugh.

"He's doing well. A couple of visitors have put in offers to buy him when he's older."

"You said no, right? He's not for sale. He's mine!" I say defensively. The thought of my little guy getting sold off makes me sick. Who visits a stable to ride horses and tries to buy one? Is that normal behavior?

"Of course, I told them no. Mom and Dad aren't willing to sell him."

"Are you implying that you're my precious baby's dad?" I ask playfully.

"No implication needed. I *am* his dad."

"Not possible. He doesn't have a dad."

"Okay, we'll see who he comes to when we get out here," Brad says confidently.

"No, that's not fair, you've spent more time with him," I protest.

"Doesn't matter," he insists.

"Yes, it does. He needs time to remember me."

"I thought you said you were his mom. He shouldn't need time to remember his mom."

"I AM! But mommy has been gone," I joke.

As we enter the building, Brad sets me down, and we walk over to the large stall Kodiak and Winona are in.

"Hi, Kodiak," I say gently. His ears twitch, and he trots over to the gate. "Hi, baby," I murmur, petting his white mane. Turning to Brad, I smile. "You were saying?"

"You cheated," he replies softly, leaning on the gate beside me and stroking Kodiak.

"Oh yeah? Tell me how?"

"It's the hair color," he teases.

"That makes sense," I nod sarcastically.

"Wanna take him for a walk?"

"Yes!" I exclaim eagerly.

Brad retrieves the leather halter from a hook on the stable wall and opens the gate to the stall. He slips the halter over Kodiak's head, making sure it fits snugly but comfortably. Kodiak stands patiently, his ears twitching with curiosity. Brad fastens the buckle under Kodiak's chin and attaches the lead rope, giving it a gentle tug to make sure it's secure. Kodiak shakes his head slightly, adjusting to the feel of the halter.

"You'll get used to it, buddy," Brad strokes down his muzzle reassuringly.

"Don't you think it's odd that wealthy people come out to the middle of nowhere to ride horses? Surely Jonah's horses aren't any better than others, right?" I glance around as we walk along the horse track. I appreciate the beauty here, but it seems strange for people to visit such a hidden town just to ride horses.

"I think people sometimes just want to escape the bullshit of what's going on in the world. It's like a little slice of paradise that not many know about. The townsfolk are friendly and welcoming... unless you try to move here. Everett owns all the land. People have tried to come and buy pieces, but he doesn't sell. Locals enjoy visitors but also enjoy when they leave."

"But wouldn't the town struggle without out-of-town visitors?" I ask, genuinely curious.

"Most locals don't want to leave. Not even for shopping. That's why Everett pays well to keep the stores stocked. It costs a lot to bring supplies here. Once a month, he has a jet full of goods brought in. Store owners place their orders by the third week of the month to have them delivered and stocked by the first. They pay for the items and a small fee to help with the cost of flying items in, and Everett covers the rest. The town knows how much he does for them, which is why they treat him like a celebrity."

"Do they realize how much he works? Like that's all he does."

"Yeah, we all know how much he works. You know he'd give it all up for you, right?" Brad says, looking at Kodiak before turning to me.

His words take me by surprise. "I wouldn't change a single thing about him."

We walk in silence for a while, absorbed in our thoughts, and I appreciate how, even when neither of us have anything to say, the quiet doesn't feel awkward or weird.

"So, Bert, why do you choose to live here? Do you love horses that much?" I ask.

"I stay here," he corrects.

"What does that even mean?" I ask playfully.

"I have a house and property on the other side of town," he replies.

This shocks me. I literally had no idea he ever stayed any-where else. I always thought he was just in his apartment when he disappeared for days, watching TV or something."

"What?!" I exclaim.

"You thought I just lived in that tiny apartment?"

"Uhh, yeah," I reply.

"Believe it or not, Wanda, I'm quite a catch."

"I believe you have potential."

"Potential? I'm the whole package."

"Why do you treat women the way you do?" I ask, knowing he won't like me saying that. "I know you have a kind heart, but what you do isn't kind, and it makes me think something led you to be that way. And don't give me a bullshit response. We can talk with honesty sometimes too. We don't always have to give each other shit."

He takes a deep breath before speaking. "I was in special ops overseas. I was gone a lot, and my wife started to become distant. I loved my job but loved her more, so I decided to end my tenure and fly home to surprise her and let her know I would be taking a local position for her. We'd been together since eighth grade, mar-ried right out of high school. When I got home, there was a car in the driveway I didn't recognize. I knew it wasn't good. I walked in and heard noises only I should be making her make. I found her in bed with another man. She was irate that I came home and didn't tell her I would be coming back early. I left for a couple of weeks, drowning myself in alcohol. When I went back, I caught them again. This time, I lost it and beat the shit out of the guy. The ambulance had to come for him. While waiting for the cops, I went to the kitchen and saw ultrasound pictures on the fridge. My wife was pregnant with another man's child. I filed for divorce, and she took half of everything.

After that, married women started throwing themselves at me. I slept with them, hated myself for it, and then began hating them. It became a twisted game to see how many married women I could sleep with, testing if there were any decent women left. Not once was I rejected. It was like they had no regard for the damage they'd cause. My rage blinded me to the fact that I was the real problem. So, I sought out Everett, knowing he lived in a remote location. He flew me out, and I've stayed ever since. If they want to be fucked, I don't turn them down," he finishes with a heaviness in his tone.

I'm shocked by his confession—and heartbroken for him.

He looks at me, his eyes softening. "I'm destined to be alone."

"You're destined to be a Casanova."

"Something like that," he smiles.

"Well, maybe one day, you'll feast your eyes on the most beautiful woman and realize we aren't all bad. Then, you can give her a fair chance."

"Maybe."

"Maybe, if you would take the time to get to know a woman before sleeping with her, you might get somewhere. Everyone you sleep with is incredibly pretty, so you clearly don't have an unfortunate face," I admit.

"Unfortunately for me, it doesn't work out for me."

"Because you sleep with them before talking to them," I jest.

"I don't waste my time. I don't care about friendships, I don't do small talk, and if I'm talking to someone, it's either a necessity or I want something."

"I call bullshit."

"Why's that?"

"Because you harassed me and never tried sleeping with me, so you obviously knew I was so awesome you forced a friendship," I grin.

"No, Wanda, that's not what it was." He trails off.

"You saw me as weak and wanted to pick on me like everyone else?"

"I thought you were the most beautiful woman I had ever laid eyes on. I had to talk to you, and within minutes of me talking to you, you threatened to throw horse shit at me, and I fucking ate that shit up," he laughs. "But you never gave me the time of day. I thought maybe if I sleep with you, the feelings would just go away. But I couldn't bring myself to even try. I respected you too much. Then I saw you naked and thought my heart was going to give out. It ramped up my need for a release, so I was fucking anyone who threw themselves at me. Then I saw you with Everett and I realized you were the one he had been chasing for all those years. I wanted to throw my fist through the wall. I felt like I was finally being punished for all the wrongs I'd committed, and karma was coming back to bite me in the ass in the form of you. I knew about Everett's obsession with the mystery woman from hearing Gladys and Giles talk. I figured one day a woman would run the Mansion, and that would be my cue to leave. I imagined someone like Jenevieve. But when I realized it was you, I didn't ever want to leave, because if I could see you, even with you being with another man, I'd accept it."

"Well, thank you for not trying to have sex with me," I smile.

"We have sex every night in my dreams, Wanda."

"That's fine. I hope I suck, and my pussy is nice and dry for you."

"Like a desert," he grins.

"And I hope my bush is so big and untamed that you can't ever get your dick in because of all the hair."

"We both know I know you there is no big, untamed bush," he quips.

"I would have," I say, turning to look at him.

"Would have what?" he meets my gaze.

"Slept with you… if you had tried. I might have turned you down the first couple of times, but I would have, and I thought about it. Especially after the bucket incident," I admit.

"Why the hell would you tell me that now?" he says, letting out a laugh.

"I don't know. I didn't plan on it," I shrug. "I know how you feel, by the way. I walked in on my ex with the new intern in the copy room, and he got me fired the same day."

"The guy who broke into the hotel?" he asks.

"The one and only," I sigh. "Tell me who married Brad was."

"Married Brad was still a douche. But I was loyal to a fault. Never cheated. Got screwed over in the end, so I said, 'screw it.'"

"There's still hope for you, even if your sex count is in the thousands," I quip.

"You never had a slutty phase?"

"I've been with four people, is that not slutty?" I joke.

"Wow," his eyes widen. "I would have never guessed."

"That's rude. Are you stereotyping me as a slut?"

"Not at all. Someone inexperienced wouldn't have constant whispers about the sex you and Everett have," he says.

"How would people know what kind of sex we're having?"

"You guys do it in his office with the door open. Every staff member has taken a peek."

"And you? Herbert the Pervert."

"I've heard a second of it before I left as fast as I could. Hearing another man fucking you does nothing but piss me off," he shrugs.

"You're jealous?!" I laugh.

"Uhhh… yeah, you're like that 'take one for the team' girl," he jokes.

"So atrocious you have to play rock-paper-scissors, hoping you're not the sucker who has to take me home for the night."

"Yeah, but I'd be willing to take one for the team and take you home forever just so my friends can sleep with the pretty girls," he says, and we both crack up.

"And here I thought you had no redeeming qualities. Guess we can list 'true friend' as your only one."

"Never heard that one before. But I'll take it."

"You said you were in the special ops. What kind of job is that?"

"A job that keeps you on your toes and away from home," he says distantly.

"Okay... what part of your job were you good at?"

"You don't want to know," his eyes focus on a distant point as if replaying something from the past.

"Do you not want to talk about it, or you think I'll judge you? Because I won't judge you, and I wouldn't ask if I didn't actually want to know."

"I don't want you to look at me differently."

"The way I look like I always want to puke?" I grin.

He stares at me, then inhales deeply. "You would actually puke."

"Tell me," I say, slowing my pace.

"I hurt people to get information."

"Like tying them to a chair and beating them up?" I try to recall scenes from movies featuring mobsters and drug lords to imagine what they did.

"I tortured them."

"When my ex destroyed my life, I would lie in bed and think of all the ways I wanted him to suffer, like tying him down and putting some sort of flesh-eating bugs on his dick, or locking him in a really hot room and only feeding him really hot meals with really hot coffee."

"Now there's an idea," he smiles.

"Let me know if you ever need new ideas," I tease. When he stays silent, I continue, "I don't want you to think I'm making fun of your job or your past. I think you're so strong, and I can't imagine what you must have gone through."

"I'm good at reading people—controlling situations, understanding their fears and the things that make them tick, and using it to my advantage."

"What's your read on me?"

He smirks. "I won't ever try to read you, because once I do, I'll lose my reason to keep staring."

Jonah leans against the fence, watching us. As we approach, he smiles. I didn't even see him there and feel a pang of guilt for admitting to Brad that I fantasized about us having sex.

"Hi," I smile at him as we near.

"Hi, baby. How's your horse?"

"Umm, he's precious as ever," I reply. "Mom and Dad took him for a little walk."

"I'm dad," Brad clarifies.

Jonah lets out a laugh. "Okay, Dad. Can you take your son back to his milk Mom so I can take this one back to the house?"

"No problem," Brad responds.

"Well, Bert, be good. I'll come back to see our son soon," I say, then kiss Kodiak and pet his muzzle. "Love you, my sweet boy." I climb over the fence and fall into Jonah's arms, kissing him.

As we walk back to the mansion, I glance back and see Brad walking Kodiak. Our eyes meet briefly before he focuses back on Kodiak.

That night, I find myself unable to sleep, thinking about everything Brad said. It finally makes sense why he is the way he is, and I have a newfound respect for him. I know I would have slept with him if he had tried. Had we crossed those lines, where would Jonah and I be then?

We are cuddling in bed, and I can tell Jonah is turned on, but I'm a million miles away. He senses it and hasn't made a move.

I hate that Brad tried to ease his hurt by hurting others. But I hate even more what his ex did to him. I can't imagine coming home to find out she was not only cheating but pregnant with another man's child and happily displaying it on their marital fridge. I wonder if he knows anything about her now or if he's hurt that she had another man's child.

Jonah eventually falls asleep, but I lie awake, lost in my thoughts.

I glance at the nightstand clock: 2:48 AM. Everyone is asleep; I'm assuming even Brad. But I need to talk to him. I hate how much his past bothers me. It's like all the puzzle pieces have finally come together, revealing the full picture of Brad's behaviors. Quietly, I pull back the covers, ease into my slippers, and head to the stables. Knowing Brad has a house now, I'm unsure if he's even here. But I have a feeling that my return might have kept him around.

As I walk up the stairs to his apartment, I debate whether I should turn back around and go back to bed. My knuckle hovers over the door, hesitating if I should even try. I start to walk away, making it to the bottom of the stairs, but then turn back and climb up again. What's the worst that could happen? I intrude on him having sex with someone? That would actually be incredibly awkward and cause unnecessary gossip. Or maybe he's not even here? Resolved to leave, I start down the stairs again, reaching the last step when the door opens.

"You know there's a gym at the house with a stair stepper, right?" Brad yawns.

My heart leaps to my throat as I whip around. "Brad, hi. Did I wake you?" Obviously being the clear cause of his disrupted sleep.

"Brad? This must be serious. Is everything okay?" He rubs the sleep from his eyes, looking so innocent and childlike.

"Are you alone?"

"Uh, yeah, it's 3 in the morning."

"And you're a man whore," I retort.

"I have sex with women; I don't let them sleep with me. C'mon, Wanda," he holds the door open for me to come in.

Sighing, I walk back up the stairs past him, leaving my slippers by the door. I sit on his couch as he closes the door and sits down opposite me.

"Is everything okay?" he leans forward with his elbows resting on his knees, a worried look in his eyes.

"I don't know. I'm bothered by what your ex did to you," I admit, rubbing my hands together to ward off the cold. It's freezing outside and even colder in here. Does he not turn the heater on?

He stands up, grabs a blanket from the corner of the couch, and offers it to me.

"I'm fine," I lie, gesturing that I don't need the blanket, even though I'm shivering. He keeps holding it out, not backing down, his gaze dropping to my chest before returning to my eyes, insisting I take it.

I left the house wearing just a tank top and shorts, not realizing how cold it was. Jonah always radiates body heat, almost to the point of making me sweat, so I was overheated when I left the bedroom. It quickly hit me when I stepped outside that I should have changed.

"Oh, sorry," acknowledging him wanting me to cover up. I take the blanket and wrap it around my shoulders, tightening my grip around the material. "Funny how nipples can be so distracting to you when you've seen millions of them."

"Yours are distracting," he corrects.

"Because mine are off-limits to you."

"Because yours are connected to you, Wanda," he clarifies.

I don't know how to respond to that. Normally, I'm quick with the comebacks, but all I can think about is how to ask him if he's ever gotten mental help for how to cope with what his ex did, without coming off as nosy or rude.

"Well, since I know you didn't come all the way out here just to make good on your sexual fantasies about me, what's on your mind?"

"As if. I don't fantasize about you," I retort defensively. His lips curl up playfully, and I realize he was purposely trying to get a rise out of me. Damn, I'm really off my game tonight. "Did you ever talk to a therapist after what your ex did?"

He laughs like I said something funny and shakes his head. "No."

"If I had my therapist call you, would you speak with her? She really helped me after everything Wyatt did."

"I don't need therapy, Wanda."

"What do you need?" I ask softly.

"You know I can't answer that."

Letting out a sigh, I sit back on his couch and stare at him. "You're gonna give me gray hairs."

"They won't be noticeable with your already white hair," he smiles.

"That's good for me. However, I've noticed all the grays popping up in those curls up there," I tease, pointing at his hair. He doesn't even have a single gray hair that I can see, but Brad is vain enough that a jab at his ego might do him some good.

"And every one of them is from that smart mouth of yours," he quips back.

"Do you ever miss her? Your ex? Honest answer."

He holds back all sarcasm and releases a deep breath. "No, not her per se. I miss coming home to the woman I love, sharing a bed, and waking up together. But it's not her I miss—just the feeling of being married as a whole."

"Are you lonely?"

His eyes soften, and he looks like he would rather crack a joke than ever admit he's lonely.

"I've been lonely my entire life," I say, cutting off any chance for him to deny himself being lonely. My admission catches him off guard, and he subtly shakes his head, surprised by my words.

"I was in a car wreck when I was six. I survived, but my parents were killed. My grandma on my dad's side took me in, but she didn't like my mom. She used to tell me I looked just like her, which, obviously knowing she didn't like my mom, definitely didn't feel like a compliment. She was a heavy smoker and got lung cancer, so I was often with my best friend's family.

Sometimes I'd be overwhelmed with sadness and didn't know how to handle it. I was always by myself. Both my parents were only children, and I quickly lost everyone. I started sleeping with my best friend while staying there as a way of self-coping, which made things weird. It felt like I burned the last bridge to anyone, and when my grandma died, I was completely alone.

I still sort of had Sam's family, but I was 18 and left for college. Clearly, I never learned anything because I moved on to sleeping with my professor. After I graduated, I moved back home and never talked to him again. Then I got a job and started dating a higher-up until he cheated on me.

My life has been shit on top of shit, and now that I'm here, sometimes I just want to run away because I think I somehow preferred when my life was hard. Does that even make sense?"

"I had no idea, Kalyn. I'm so sorry."

"Yeah, and now look at me."

"I see you. I see an incredible woman. All those struggles made you stronger. That's why you were so resilient to Jenevieve. Her bullshit was minuscule compared to what life has thrown at you. If it were anyone else, she would have run them off the first week," he says.

"Do you plan on staying here forever? Is this your endgame?"

"I don't even know what I plan on doing the next week. I just take it one day at a time."

"Do you want kids?"

"I did. Not anymore. What about you? Planning to pop out devilishly handsome children, Wanda?"

"I just might."

"Do you feel better?" he asks.

"Somewhat."

"Let me walk you back," he stands and stretches his arms above his head.

"I'm just going to sleep on your couch if you don't mind. I don't want to walk that far back," I adjust the blanket.

"You and Everett fighting?"

"No, not at all. He was sleeping when I left."

"Okay, I'll get you a pillow." When he returns, he's carrying two pillows and a much larger blanket. He lays a pillow at the end of the couch, and I thank him as I make myself comfortable. He takes the blanket I was using and swaps it for the bigger one.

"You don't have to sleep out here," I tell him as he places the other pillow on the couch and lies down, using the blanket I had been using.

"I have to keep an eye on you. I can just tell you want to rummage in my panty drawer and steal all my lacy thongs," he winks.

"You collecting women's panties, pervert?" I tease.

"They are all mine," he turns his head to look at me. "Night, Wanda."

"Good night… Do you work tomorrow?"

"I do, so power your brain down and go to sleep."

I turn to look at him, and even though he doesn't look back, he smiles.

CHAPTER

Twenty-Seven

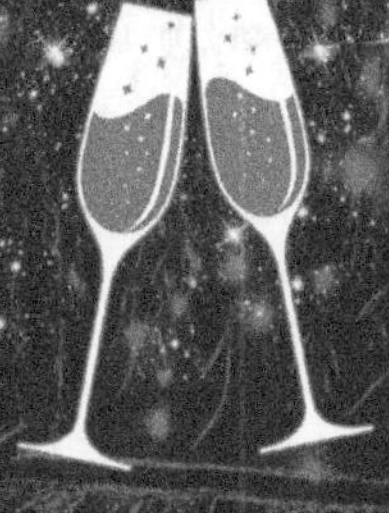

JONAH

I wake to an empty bed. Kalyn is nowhere in sight. I get up and check the bathroom, but she's not there either. Returning to the bed, I grab my iPad and flip through the security cameras, but still can't find her. Pulling on shorts, a T-shirt, and running shoes, I head to Jonathan and Shay's room. They're getting it on but turn to look at me when I ask if they've seen Kal. They haven't, so I leave without another word.

I ask Gladys and Giles, but neither of them has seen her. As I start to search the house, I pass the large windows at the back, and my feet carry me toward the stable, certain she's there.

I see Brad moving bales of hay. "She's in my apartment," he calls.

"Is she okay?" I ask. I know she seemed distant last night, but we were good when I fell asleep. Did I somehow misread her body language?

"Yeah, she's fine. She just wanted someone to talk to and didn't want to wake you."

"Thanks, man," I head to his apartment, taking the stairs two at a time. I open the door and see her lying on the couch. As usual, she has the blanket, now balled up between her knees. I sit on the coffee table and watch her sleep. She's so beautiful.

"Good morning, baby," I say, brushing her hair out of her face.

"I'm tired, can you be on top," she murmurs, rolling onto her back and kicking her leg over the back of the couch.

I gently take her hand in mine. "Baby, let's go back to the house."

Her eyes open, and she looks so tired but gives me the most breathtaking smile. Then her eyes look around, realization dawning of where she is. She sits up. "Where's Brad?"

"It's 8. He's just downstairs working. Come on, let's get back." I stand, holding my hand out to her.

She takes it, and I pull her to her feet. I grab the blanket she was using, fold it, and place it on the couch, setting the pillow she was using on top of it.

At the door, she looks like she's still trying to wake up. "Here, baby, I'll carry you," I say, turning and lifting her up. As we leave the stable, we pass Brad.

"Good morning, sleepyhead," he calls.

"Good morning, Bert. I'll be out later," she says, then turns her attention back to me, laying her head on my shoulder.

"See you in a bit," he calls.

"You coming to bed with me?" she kisses my neck.

"I'm going to take you to bed and make love to you, yes," I smile, and she squeezes my neck.

WE LIE IN BED, TANGLED IN EACH OTHER. MY FIRST INSTINCT IS TO get dressed and go work, but how can I, when she chose to talk to Brad in the middle of the night rather than wake me up with whatever was bothering her? I hate that she knew someone else would be there to listen. That should be my job, yet she didn't come to me.

I quickly text Brad, telling him he can take the day off and I'll still compensate him for staying up to talk to her. But he immediately replies that it was his pleasure.

I bet it was.

"Are you tired?" I ask, trailing my fingers up and down her bare side.

She turns her head to look up at me and shakes her head. "No, are you?"

"No," I say, watching her kiss my side. She then tries to sit up, but I hold her to me. "Where do you think you're running off to?"

"You have to work, don't you?" She looks at me, confused.

In this moment, I realize I've been working too much. She's taking what time she can get with me, not complaining, and instead, forming a friendship with Brad. I don't feel jealous, but I do feel like I'm letting her down, and she doesn't deserve that.

"Would you like to go for a walk?" I barely finish the sentence before she's excitedly climbing onto her knees.

"Yes!" she exclaims.

I lead her to the back of the mansion, on the side of the house, to a nearly hidden entrance that opens to a beautifully paved path. The cobblestone walkway winds among tall trees, forming natural tunnels. Sunlight filters between the leaves, casting dancing shadows on the ground. Birds chirp, their songs echoing through the trees. Bridges cross over ponds and creeks, their water reflecting like mirrors. Water lilies float on the surface, their pink and white petals floating delicately. Benches are placed along the trail, giving people who walk them a chance to take a break or what I plan to do with Kalyn on them—fuck her.

"How did I not even know this was here?" Her eyes fill with wonder and happiness as she looks all around.

"The trails wind off in different directions, creating a bit of a labyrinth, but if you cover each trail, it totals about ten miles."

She takes in the vibrant colors of the flowers and shrubs lining the path. The peonies, dahlias, and other various flowers are in full bloom, their vivid hues contrasting with the deep green of the ferns and ivy that blanket the forest floor. Butterflies flit from flower to flower, and Kalyn points out each one.

We walk hand in hand, and I point out each type of flower we pass. Peonies are her favorite, which is why they were planted out here.

The trees open up ahead, where the trail runs parallel to the lake. The water is a deep blue, calm and inviting, stretching out to the horizon.

"Could a shark survive out there?"

I glance out at the water. "No, a shark couldn't survive here."

"Good… Why not?"

"Sharks are saltwater creatures. The lake is freshwater, and the two environments are vastly different. Sharks need saltwater to maintain the balance of salts and water in their bodies. Their bodies are adapted to the ocean's salinity levels, which is crucial for regulating their bodily functions."

"What would happen if a shark were put in this lake?"

"Without the saltwater, a shark's body would struggle to function properly. Their cells would begin to take in too much water and lose salt, which would disrupt their physiological processes. Essentially, they wouldn't be able to maintain the right balance of fluids and salts, leading to serious health issues, and ultimately, they wouldn't survive."

"Is this water safe to swim in?"

"Yeah, are you wanting to swim in it?"

"Not at all, I hate open water," she admits.

This is something I didn't know about her. "Why?" I ask, intrigued.

"I don't know. You can't really see what's under the water. Like some sort of monster could be just below you, tonguing your toes, and you'd have no idea. The thought is so creepy."

The path winds back through the trees, revealing new sights. There's a secluded gazebo draped in wisteria and another bridge. She stops in the middle, glancing over the edge at the pond below, where koi swim beneath the surface.

"How do koi fish survive out here?"

"It's a bit of a process. The koi were brought in and introduced to this pond because it's a controlled environment. Once a week, a team comes out to clean the pond and check on the fish. They make sure the water quality is perfect, testing for things like pH levels, ammonia, and nitrates. They also ensure the filtration system is working properly and clean any debris that might have accumulated."

She nods, watching a particularly colorful koi glide past. "So they get a lot of attention."

"Definitely. Koi are pretty hardy, but they still need a good environment to thrive. The team also feeds them. Koi have specific dietary needs, so they get high-quality pellets that provide all the nutrients they need. Sometimes they get fruits and vegetables, too."

"Excuse me?"

"They like it," I assure her.

"They sound like a lot of work," her eyes widen.

"They are, but they're worth it."

"What makes that much work worth it?" she quirks a brow.

"How intrigued you seem by them. I'll find a way to put a shark in the lake if it will keep you this interested in anything I have to say."

"I'm always intrigued by you," she squeezes my hand.

We continue walking, climbing up stone stairs as the trail winds on.

"Do you ever find something so cute you want to squeeze it really hard, but to avoid harming it, you clench your teeth instead?" she asks randomly.

I look down at her, and she meets my gaze, serious at first, and then she smiles.

"You," I admit.

"Me what?"

"Every time I look at you, I want to squeeze you until your eyes pop out, but instead, I clench my teeth."

"Okay, I thought I was the only one," she says, her jaw tensing. "Sometimes I have intrusive thoughts where I think you are so handsome, I want to unzip your skin, climb inside, and wrap you around me like a warm, gooey blanket."

I stop walking and my head falls back as I laugh. "I love you, baby. If I could unzip my skin and let you climb in, I'd gladly do so."

When we begin walking again, I slow my pace, and she turns to look at me. I adjust my hand in hers, then spin her around before pulling her back to my chest. I dip her backward, holding her securely. Our faces are inches apart as I glance between her eyes. "I love you," I whisper.

"I love you too," she whispers back. "So much."

As we start walking again, she moves in front of me, walking backward while holding both of my hands. "Did you know we're going to get married? Then you'll never be rid of me."

"Correction, you'll never be rid of me. I like to let you think it's all your choice, but I'd never let you leave even if you wanted to." I tighten my grip on her hand slightly, and she mirrors the gesture.

"Good, because I'd rather us both be dead than ever be apart. If I died, you better climb into my coffin and die with me," she jokes.

"Deal. And you?" I wait for her to say she will also climb into my coffin and die with me if I go first.

"Oh, babe. I can't. Me and all my next boyfriends would honor you by showing up weekly to have sex on your grave," she smiles and tries to take off running, but my arm wraps around her shoulder, pulling her into me as she laughs. I pick her up and spin her.

"You think that's funny," I nibble at her neck.

I move us to the grass, gently laying her down and straddling her as I pin her to the ground. I tickle her sides, making her squirm and laugh uncontrollably. Taking her hands, I hold them above her head, leaning down to bite the crook of her neck.

"You better not give me a hickey, or Shay will murder you for ruining her wedding pictures," she sighs, her arms relaxing as she turns her head to give me full access to her neck.

"I think Shay would approve of what we are doing."

"I think she would too," she subtly nods.

Sitting up, I look down at her, then climb to my feet, holding out my hands to help her up.

"No, come back down here," she protests.

"Absolutely not. You'd just imagine all your boyfriends," I grin as I pull her to her feet.

"Yeah," she nods, sliding her arm around my waist. "I want to pretend it's them taking advantage of me out here." As we start down the steps, she asks, "Do you want to be buried or cremated?"

"Whatever you're going to be," I tell her.

"But I want to be whatever you are going to be," she looks up at me. "If I got to choose, I'd want to be cremated so my coffin isn't taking up a bunch of unnecessary space in the ground. I wouldn't even care if I was cremated and my ashes were dumped in the trash," she laughs.

My mouth hangs open as I look down at her. "Cremated, we can be. Dumped in a trash bin, we will not be."

"Why? We would never know."

"Babe, are you serious?" My eyes widen at her admission.

"Yes, what's the point of taking up so much space when, a couple generations down the line, nobody will even know who we are?" Her words make sense, but I can't imagine the most important person in my entire life being merely dumped in the trash as if everything they did and were was just tossed away. "Maybe we'll die together, and they can put us in the cremator together. Can't you picture our souls standing outside, watching our bodies burn? It's eerie to think about," she says, making a disgusted face.

"We all have to go through it, whether it's watching our body being lowered into the ground or being pushed into a crematorium," I say.

"What do you think happens after all of this?"

"Well, you and I will die in our 90s, and if I die before you, I'll be on the other side of wherever, waiting for you," I say.

"And if I die first?"

"You tell me, are you going to go wait for me or find someone else on the other side? We've already established on this side; you would find many others." I pinch her side, and she squirms and giggles.

She steps closer, resting her chin on my chest staring up at me, "I'll wait for you always. Even if we're just stardust drifting through the universe, I'd find you."

"If we're stardust, we can finally really be one. I'll dust myself all throughout your stardust." I kiss her.

We reach the final stretch of the path, emerging the same way we came in. It's noon, and by now, Gladys will have lunch ready for us.

OUR DAYS BLEND INTO A COMFORTABLE ROUTINE. I FORGO WORKING in the mornings, choosing instead to take walks with Kalyn. These morning strolls with each other have been our special bonding time. We share quiet moments by the koi pond, and Gladys brings our lunch out to the patio around noon when we return.

As the days turn into weeks, Kalyn spends her afternoons with Shay, discussing wedding arrangements, and her evenings out at the stables with Brad and Kodiak.

On the eve of the wedding, our bags are packed as we prepare for an early flight, double-checking everything we need for the ceremony tomorrow. Shay and Jonathan are a bundle of nerves, oscillating between excitement and anxiety. In less than 24 hours, they will be Mr. And Mrs. Harper.

CHAPTER
Twenty-Eight

KALYN

The day kicked off to a fantastic start. Weddings in movies are often depicted as high-stress events, but today feels completely different—relaxed. We arrive at a spa bright and early to get pampered. After an hour-long massage for Shay, her mom, and me, we're led to a serene room where we sip champagne while getting our hair and makeup done.

"Your hair is amazing," the stylist comments as she brushes my locks.

I thank her, feeling a bit awkward with compliments about my hair. I've always had long, thick hair, but it always felt weird to me to acknowledge that I, too, really like my hair. I didn't want to come off as stuck up or conceded.

"How are you feeling?" I ask Shay, turning my chair to face her.

"I'm so happy, Kal. I can't believe we're actually getting married."

"Looks like he was ready to plant his ass down and deal with any future issues, huh?" I grin at her.

"He doesn't have a choice now."

"You deserve all this happiness, Shay. I'm truly so happy for you," I tell her earnestly.

"You better not forget that I demand to be your maid of honor in your wedding," she warns, playfully pointing a finger at me.

"That's a given," I reply.

"The day Jonathan and I met, I was waiting at the airport because I missed my flight and got on the next available one. I had about a four-hour wait. I was sitting alone, and this guy sat across from me and kept staring. I took my earbuds out and asked if he needed something, and he said no. So, I was like, then stop staring. He apologized but continued staring. I was already annoyed and wasn't going to deal with that. I gathered my stuff and moved to a different section of the airport, and this guy came and sat right next to me again. I thought, this can't be happening.

I moved again, and as I was walking to find a new seat, these two guys tried talking to me, and it freaked me out. I went to the bathroom, and when I came out, they were still by the door. I panicked a bit because the airport was full, and almost all the seats were taken. I saw a man sitting alone at the end of a row with his backpack and coat on the seat next to him. He was either alone and didn't want to be bothered, or he was saving the seat for someone, but desperate times, call for desperate measures.

These guys wouldn't leave me alone, so I grabbed this man's bag, sat down, and put it on my lap. The men approached, and the guy looked like he was going to object when he pulled his headphones off. I said, 'Thanks for holding my seat, honey,' and then looked at the men. They asked, 'Is she with you?' and he wrapped his arm around my shoulder and said, 'Obviously.'

The men stared, and finally, the man with his arm around me said, 'Do you guys have a problem?' They said, 'We just didn't see her with anyone for the last two hours.' He replied, 'Cool, bye,' and they walked across the room but kept staring. He said, 'Well, girlfriend, they aren't leaving, so make yourself comfortable. My name's Jonathan,' and he smirked at me. I looked at him to say thank you, and my God, Kal, he was the sexiest man I had ever seen. And now I'm marrying him," she becomes teary eyed.

"None of that," I tell her with a smile.

"Sorry," she blots under her eyes.

Valerie and Shay finish getting ready before I do, and Shay looks stunning. Since my hair takes longer, the stylist who worked on Shay's hair steps in to help curl mine. Once they finish pinning it up and completing my makeup, they turn me toward the mirror. My eyes widen—I look as good as when Shay does my hair and makeup, though this time, the makeup is more prominent for pictures.

"Let's get you in your dress," the stylist says. "You should have left ten minutes ago."

They rush to get Shay in her dress while I slip on my light turquoise bridesmaid dress. It's an elegant, floor-length gown, form-fitting on the top with delicate straps that hang gracefully off my shoulders. The bodice is intricately adorned with lace, a sweetheart neckline accentuating my collarbones, and the dress cinches at my waist, creating a flattering silhouette. The skirt flows down smoothly, hugging my hips before flaring out slightly, allowing for easy movement.

"Oh, Kalyn, you look lovely, honey," Valerie smiles, already dressed, with Shay beside her in her gown.

"Can we get one picture before you ladies leave?" the stylist asks, and we agree.

They take us to a beautiful decorated wall, snap a few pictures, and promise to email them to us.

A white limo waits for us outside the spa, ready to take us directly to the Catholic Church.

"I'm so nervous," Shay says, grabbing my hand.

"You aren't going to leave Jonathan at the altar," I quip.

"You're right. That man is never going to be rid of me."

As we step inside, we get a few sideways glances, telling me we have caused a slight delay—oops. It was my thick hair that took so long. We follow the coordinator down the softly lit hallway, leading us to the waiting area. This moment feels so special: it's Shay's dad's first time seeing her in her wedding dress.

When he catches sight of her, he becomes teary-eyed. His hands tremble slightly as he reaches out to embrace her, overcome with emotion.

Jonah stands by the chapel door, appearing almost nervous. As I approach, I tease, "Were you starting to think you had a runaway bride on your hands?" His eyes meet mine with a hint of relief, then travel down my body and back up.

"God, baby, you're… sexy," he breathes out.

"I'm a lady of the lord, babe. You can't talk to me like that… and we are in His house… so you double can't talk like that."

He grins mischievously. "We *are* in His house of worship, and I will worship you right now if you allow it."

I shoot him a "don't you dare" look as the doors open. The packed room turns to look, and the music begins to play. Jonah offers me his arm and says, "I love you so much, baby."

"I love you so much back."

We start down the long aisle together, and Jonathan's smile broadens as we near the front. He steps forward, wrapping his arms around me and kissing my cheek. "You look beautiful, Kal."

"And you look dashing, Mr. Harper. I'm so happy for both of you," I return the kiss on his cheek before taking Jonah's arm again. He escorts me to my place, then steps in line behind Jonathan.

Shay's three-year-old niece, the precious flower girl, steals the show as she begins her walk down the aisle. She wears a fluffy white dress with tiny blue flowers and clutches a small basket brimming with petals. With each step, she carefully drops petals, her tiny fingers scattering them in a delicate, haphazard pattern. She glances up, her eyes wide taking in the sea of smiling faces, and she beams with innocent pride. The guests chuckle softly at the undeniable cuteness. As she reaches the altar, she looks back at her handiwork, then shyly walks over to her dad and mom, Shay's brother and sister-in-law, pointing to show them what she did.

The organ begins to play the processional hymn, and the congregation rises, turning to watch the bride. Shay appears at the doorway, her arm linked with her father's. As they begin their walk down the aisle, the room fills with a collective sigh of awe, and I stare at her as if it's my first time witnessing how stunning she is.

Jonathan's hands come up to his mouth, and tears begin to fall as he watches his entire future walking toward him.

When Shay reaches the altar, she whispers, "Don't make me cry," and laughs softly. I stand behind her, gently adjusting her veil as she takes a deep breath. As I straighten, my eyes lock with Jonah's, my heart tumbling with somersaults with the intensity of my love for him. His gorgeous lips curve up, sending warmth cascading within me and grounding me in the chaotic swirl of emotions surrounding the ceremony.

"I love you," he mouths.

"I love you," I mouth back.

Shay turns and hands me her bouquet as the ceremony proceeds with traditional Catholic rites. The priest begins with the Sign of the Cross, leading the congregation in prayer. Shay and Jonathan, now standing hand in hand at the altar, listen intently to the readings from the Bible. The priest reads passages on love and commitment, his voice echoing through the grand cathedral.

After the readings, the priest addresses the couple directly, speaking of the sanctity of marriage and the importance of mutual respect and unwavering support. Shay and Jonathan exchange glances, their eyes shining with emotion.

The priest then invites Shay and Jonathan to profess their vows. Their words are filled with heartfelt promises to love, honor, and cherish each other for the rest of their lives. Shay's hand trembles slightly as she slips her vows back into her bouquet, her eyes locked on Jonathan's.

The priest nods, signaling Jonah to step forward. Jonah offers Jonathan the rings. As Jonathan slips the ring onto Shay's finger, he whispers, "With this ring, I thee wed," his voice steady. Shay repeats the gesture, her eyes never leaving Jonathan's. "With this ring, I thee wed," she says, her voice breaking slightly with tears of joy.

The priest continues with the Nuptial Blessing, asking God to bless this union and fill their lives with love and happiness. The congregation responds with a resounding "Amen," their voices echoing through the cathedral. I feel a swell of emotion as I watch my best friend pledge her life to the man she is madly in love with. The priest invites Shay and Jonathan to join him in the Eucharist, a symbolic sharing of bread and wine. As they kneel at the altar, the priest prays for their unity and faith, blessing their marriage in the eyes of God.

"May the peace of Christ be with you always," the priest concludes.

"And also with you," the congregation responds.

Finally, the priest announces, "I now pronounce you husband and wife. You may kiss the bride." Jonathan lifts Shay's veil, and they share a tender kiss, sealing their vows. The congregation erupts in applause, the sound filling the vast space of the cathedral. Jonah and I exchange a look of pure happiness, knowing we've witnessed something so special.

As Shay and Jonathan walk back down the aisle as husband and wife, Jonah extends his arm for me to take, as we follow close behind. The church bells ring out in celebration, marking the beginning of a new chapter in Shay and Jonathan's life together. The wedding party exits the church, stepping into the bright sunlight. Shay turns to me, and I hug her tightly, my eyes brimming with happy tears. "You did it!" I exclaim.

"I couldn't have done it without you."

Jonah claps Jonathan on the back, a proud smile on his face. "Congratulations, man."

"Thanks, Everett," Jonathan responds, his gaze fixed on Shay. "I should have done this years ago."

The newlyweds prepare to head to their reception, ready to celebrate the night away with friends and family. The wedding reception takes place at a high-end hotel. The ballroom is transformed into a wonderland of twinkling lights and lavish decor. Tables are draped in pristine white linens, with lush floral arrangements in shades of turquoise and ivory.

When it comes time to cut the cake, all eyes are on Shay and Jonathan. The multi-tiered cake is a masterpiece in itself, with intricate sugar flowers and scrollwork. "If you smash that in my face, I will bite your nuts off," Shay whispers to Jonathan, and he chuckles, carefully feeding her a bite, making sure not to get any on her face. Shay shows him the same respect, careful not to get any on his face. The room erupts in applause, cameras flashing to capture the moment.

As the evening winds down and the crowd begins to thin, I find a sofa in a corner of the room. Leaning back, my feet ache from hours of dancing and the day's constant activity. Shay, still radiant in her wedding dress, slumps down next to me with a blissful sigh.

"Hi, Mrs. Harper," I greet her as we lean against each other.

"I'm Jonathan's wife," she beams, holding out her hand now glistening with her wedding band.

"Did you sign a prenup?" I ask.

"Nope," she replies. "He never mentioned one. But the only way he's getting out of this marriage is one of us in a casket."

"I wonder how you go about getting one?"

She looks at me, lifting a brow. "Mr. Everett would never make you sign a prenup," she laughs.

AFTER THE WEDDING, THE FOUR OF US RETURN TO OUR CONDOS. First thing Monday morning, Shay and Jonathan head out to the city office to legally change Shay's name.

Jonah sits on the couch, talking on the phone, while I lie with my legs draped over his lap, his laptop propped on them as he types away, handling work-related business. We are packed and ready to head home, just waiting for Jonathan and Shay to return.

When we hear the elevator open, Jonah wraps up his call. I stand from the couch and walk to the door. "Oh hey, Harper clan," I say as they walk into our condo.

"I am officially Shayla Harper," she announces, holding up her driver's license.

I reach out and snatch it from her hand. "That's a great picture."

"Agreed," Jonathan smiles.

"Everyone ready?" Jonah asks, slinging his laptop bag over his shoulder.

"Ready," we all respond in unison.

We get back to the mansion by four. Jonah heads straight to his office, and I follow him, sitting in a chair on the opposite side of his desk. The book I was reading before we left is still there, so I pick it up and continue where I left off.

"Kal," Shay whispers, walking toward me.

Jonah glances up briefly from his computer before returning to his work. Smiling, I stand and walk over to her, and she grabs my hand.

Whispering, she says, "We combined all our bank accounts… Jonathan is rich. Like, rich rich." Her eyes widen in astonishment.

"Well yeah, he works for Jonah."

"He joined our bank accounts like it was no big deal."

"Yeah, you're married. Now that you realize you're rich, are you going to move out?" I ask, feeling slightly bummed at the possibility she'd say yes.

"Heck no, I'm never leaving. Plus, we're going to be like sister wives, but with our own dynamic where we have our own husband and our own kids, but we share the responsibility of caring for each other's kids."

"Okay, wife, get your ass to our bed," Jonathan commands, walking up behind her and grabbing her by the neck, crushing his mouth to hers.

She squeals with excitement and follows him out.

Laughing, I turn back and walk to Jonah's desk. "Can I do the same to you?" I ask, approaching him. Reaching over, I softly grab his neck and press my lips to his. "Get your ass to our bed," I repeat the words Jonathan just said to Shay, only they don't sound as sexy or demanding coming from me.

He sits back in his chair. "Oh, ehh," he says, pulling his mouth back as if there's an issue. "See, I'm turning over a new leaf. I can't have sex with you until we're… married," he whispers the last words, feigning concerned sympathy.

"Oh, is that so?" I sit on his desk.

"Yeah," he nods.

"Well, that's a shame… you're a good time," I lean back on one hand and prop my bare foot on his desk, spreading my legs so he can see my lace thong. Biting my bottom lip, I bring my other hand between my legs, softly tracing my middle finger from my center up my slit and then back down.

This time, when I reach the top, I don't stop. I slide my hand to the edge of my panties and slip it inside, slowly moving down until my finger glides between my lips. Pressing on my sensitive bud, I begin to circle slowly, my head rolling back at the exquisite sensation. Letting out a sultry moan, I rock my hips, reveling in the heightened thrill of him watching me.

I hear a zipper and open my eyes to see him, still leaned back in his chair, watching me, his now-hard cock in his hand as he strokes himself.

"Does that feel good?" I shift my thong to the side so he can see me spread open for him.

"Yes," his grip tightens as he strokes himself slowly.

"Good," I circle my clit again.

As my fingers slowly trail to my center, he watches intently, his movements quickening. "Fuck yourself, baby," he pants.

I push my middle finger past my folds, letting out whimpers of pleasure, more to get a rise out of him. It works; he's fucking his fist faster as I rock in and out of myself, gyrating my hips with the movements.

Sliding my finger out, I replace it with two and continue working them inside me, feeling how wet I am.

"Jonah," I pant, my hips moving faster.

Readjusting my position, I keep pleasuring myself, bringing my other hand to my clit and circling it.

"Tell me how good that feels," he demands.

My chest heaves, breaths becoming labored. "So good."

His eyes darken with desire as he leans forward, his gaze never leaving my fingers. "Show me more," he growls, his voice thick with lust.

I slip another finger inside, feeling my wetness coat them as I pump in and out, my thumb circling my clit. His hand moves faster on his cock, matching the rhythm of my movements.

"Fuck, that's so sexy," his says, his eyes locked onto mine. "I want to see you come."

The intensity of his words has me working faster. "Jonah," I gasp, my hips bucking as I chase my release.

"That's it, baby," he encourages, his strokes quickening. "Come for me."

With a final cry, I shatter, my orgasm ripping through me, leaving me trembling. He groans, his hand moving in a blur until he finds his release, hot and thick, spilling over his fingers.

Breathless, I look down at him. "I'm going to clean myself in the bathroom if you'd like to join," I offer as I stand from his desk and sashay towards the door, throwing a glance over my shoulder.

Gripping his cock with one hand and holding his other beneath it to catch any stray semen, we walk to the bathroom just outside his office. It's our usual cleanup spot after we mess around in his office.

"Shay wanted to go bowling upstairs, but if she and Jonathan aren't finished, I think I'll go out and see Kodiak," I mention, flushing the toilet and heading to the sink to wash my hands.

"They won't be done for a while. I can let her know you're at the stables," he offers.

"Thank you," I reply, kissing him softly. "I'm going to change and head out."

CHAPTER
Twenty-Nine

KALYN

I throw on shorts, a comfortable tank top, and the sparkly cowboy boots Tabitha got me, then head to the stable. The same girl from before spots me, her expression a clear indicator that my presence is still not appreciated.

"Hi," I greet her with a wave, catching her gaze as it travels from my face down to my boots and back again. Her displeasure shifts to outright distaste. I can feel her gaze on me as I walk around the horse track to the building across from her, only relaxing once I can feel her eyeballs are no longer on me.

"Hi, baby," I coo, reaching Kodiak's stall. Both Winona and Kodiak approach the fence, Kodiak eagerly jumping over. "Wow, that looked really cool, buddy," I smile as I gently stroke each of their muzzles, when I suddenly feel a light whip of a towel against my leg. Startled, I turn to see Brad grinning at me.

"Nice boots, cowgirl. You entering a rodeo pageant?"

"Laugh all you want at my boots now, Bert. But you won't be laughing when you're shitting rhinestones for a week after I shove my boot up your ass."

"That boot is toddler-size; I probably wouldn't feel it."

"I can believe that. You have a face that looks like it's made a lot of men shove their boots up your ass."

He lets out a laugh while reaching for Kodiak's harness.

As we step onto the track, Kodiak stomps the ground, adjusting from the firmness of concrete to the softness of dirt. Brad glances over at me. "How was the wedding?"

"You would know if you went. You received an invitation."

"Weddings aren't my thing." He shrugs.

"That's shocking. Weddings are prime real estate for hooking up with women. I'd think you'd be chomping at the bit to attend one." I wonder if the last wedding he attended was his own. Maybe he hates all weddings now because it reminds him of what his ex did.

"Maybe I want more," he says, his tone suddenly serious.

I stop in my tracks, my mouth hanging open.

"That was a joke, Wanda. Let's go," he laughs, shaking his head as he looks back at me.

"You're lame," I mutter, catching up to him.

"Wanna help train him for riders?" Brad nods toward Kodiak, who is softly padding alongside us.

"No one is going to ride my baby," I say firmly, stroking Kodiak's mane.

"One person is…"

"Who?" I squint at him, challenging him to say he's planning to ride him.

"You."

I scoff at the absurdity. There's no way I'm getting on Kodiak's back, especially not with everyone saying he's growing so fast—he'll be enormous when he's fully grown. "No… absolutely not. I don't ride horses," I object.

"You haven't yet, but you *will* be riding this one," he insists proudly.

"No, I couldn't" I protest, shaking my head.

"Wanda, he trusts you. He'll let you," he reassures me.

"You can't ride a baby," I argue. His poor little legs probably couldn't withstand the weight of a saddle plus a rider.

"No, you can't. But in two years, you can," he says confidently.

"Plenty of time to come up with an excuse to get out of it then."

"You'll be fine. I'm a good teacher, I'd never put you in danger."

"Ohh, so you're the one who's going to teach me how to ride a horse?"

"The *only* person who is allowed to teach you how to ride a horse," he corrects.

"Then you better be good at it, or I'll find someone else to teach me."

"Wanda. Don't. I'm putting my foot down. I demand to be the one to teach you. I haven't gotten anything I wanted from you. Let me have this."

"Then I shall put my trust in your hands and allow you to teach me to ride my precious boy when he's old enough," I agree.

"Thank you. I'm confident that my training abilities will have you looking like a badass riding around on him." He seems so sure of himself, and I absolutely trust that he's just as good as he seems to think he is.

"Well, duh, have you seen my boots?" I point down at my sparkling footwear catching the sunlight.

"Are they genuine ostrich?" he asks.

"Yeah, three payments," I wink at him. "I'm just goofin'… new boot goofin'."

He stops walking, and while I've heard Brad laugh before, this is the first time I've heard him laugh this hard. His laughter echoes around the track, drawing the attention of a few stable hands who look over, curious.

As he tries to catch his breath, he wipes the corners of his eyes. "You're something else, Wanda," he shakes his head.

"Glad I could make you laugh."

"Why did the Rooster go to KFC?"

"Is this a joke?"

"Yes," he smirks.

"I don't know, Bert, why did the rooster go to KFC," I ask, raising a brow.

"To see a chicken strip."

I sit there for a moment, pondering why a rooster would want to see a chicken strip, and wonder if this is a cannibal type joke. Then, the absurdity of it hits me, and I burst into laughter. "I hate that that was so funny," I say, wiping under my eyes as tears spill from the corners.

I always find it awkward and uncomfortable when someone tells a joke and you have to pretend to find it funny, even though it's not. Thankfully, his joke genuinely makes me laugh.

"I'm gonna have Miguel's son tell me jokes every day if that's all it takes to make you laugh." After a moment of silence, he speaks again. "When do Shay and Jonathan leave for their honeymoon?"

"We leave later tonight. Jonah is wrapping up work things."

"We? You and Everett are going?"

"Yeah, they insisted. And I love celebrating them."

"How long will you be gone?"

"You already missing me, Bert?" I jest.

"I always ache for you," he winks.

Though he plays it off as a joke, I sense there's some truth behind his words. Choosing not to broach that subject, I answer his question. "A week at the office, a week on vacation, and then back here for the festival."

He seems to be lost in thought as he mulls over the plans for the next few weeks. "Do you like going to the office?"

"I do. I—"

"Say that again," he cuts me off.

"Say what again?"

"The first two words you just said."

I don't even remember what I said. I was going to tell him I've worked in a corporate setting... and then it dawns on me. "Is that what turns you on?" I move in front of Kodiak until I'm walking backward in front of Brad. "Kalyn, do you take Brad to be your lawfully wedded husband?" I pause, watching his expression turn serious. Leaning in, I whisper, "I do," then playfully shove his shoulder. "Was it everything you hoped it would be," I tease, as I take my place back on the other side of Kodiak, giving his muzzle a gentle scratch.

"It was perfect," he says, and I see him subtly adjust his pants.

"I worked in the corporate world, so I don't mind going. It feels natural to me. Except, you know, dating the boss—people don't try to bully me."

"You know why they do, right?" he asks.

"Because of my dashing good looks and witty sense of humor?" I bat my lashes.

"Because you're fucking gorgeous, Wanda. It's threatening," he replies.

"Well, for the first time, I don't feel worried every second of my day that everyone is going to start a rumor about me that will get me fired or that I'm going to walk in and find my boyfriend screwing another employee. Aside from the fact that every employee has already been with him," I add.

"Well, none of them managed to get what I'm sure every one of them wanted—the fat boulder on your finger," he smiles.

"And yet, they all still know what his dick feels like inside of them," I say, feeling a surge of anger.

"I never took you for the jealous type. But it's a penis; they all do the same thing."

"They most certainly do not. And if you recall, Erica made sure to let me know how amazing you are in bed."

"I admit, I am. It's this secret technique I use. I stiffen like this and shake my head," he stops walking and demonstrates by stiffening his entire body and shaking without almost moving, his eyes wide.

"I literally hate everything about what you just did," I push him playfully.

"You couldn't handle my moves, Wanda. I'm a freak in the sheets."

"Yeah, I can tell." I laugh. "Did you practice those moves on women or learn them from watching porn?"

"I make them up as I go."

"You should make a sex guide. I think it would be a total hit."

"What makes you think I don't already have one?" he counters.

"Wait… do you do porn too?" I ask, pretending to be shocked. "I've been so worried people would find out that I have videos out there." He stops again, and I keep walking. Turning to look at him, I shake my head, "You're too easy, Bert."

"I was about to cut this walk real short," he jests.

"Yeah? How much should we bet that there's still a small part of you wondering if I actually have any videos online, and you're going to search for them when you get home?" I playfully challenge.

"I'm a thousand percent going to search for them when you leave," he admits.

"And if you found one?"

"Depends. You by yourself or another female, I'd take a month off work and fuck my fist for the foreseeable future. You with another dude, I'd get the video removed, and I'd have no choice but to find the guy and flick him in the forehead."

I laugh at the thought of someone as tough as Brad flicking another man in the forehead. Wyatt recorded us one time having sex, and when we watched it back, he was all for it until the video was from the backside. He said the angle was weird, and after watching that section of the video a few more times, he commented that the size of my ass made his dick look disproportionate. I think that was the first time he realized just how small his dick was.

He used to hump me like a jackhammer and ask me repeatedly if he was hurting me or going too deep. It especially ramped up after the video incident, and he would fixate on the idea that he was penetrating me too deep and would seem overly concerned. After so many times of him doing this, I told him it wasn't possible for him to hurt me with his size.

As I think this over, I realize it was only a week after that he was in the copy room railing the stick-skinny, no-ass intern. I must have really damaged his ego. I wasn't meaning to be rude; I just didn't want him thinking he was hurting me because he went on endlessly about it, which seemed so comical.

"Do you know how to cook?" I subtly change the subject.

"I can grill. Come to my house when you get back, and I'll grill for you," he offers.

"I don't know if I can be alone with you. You give off panty-snatcher vibes," I give him a disgusted look. "You'll probably lock me in your basement and try to suck on my toes, too."

"I'd find myself with a Russian necktie at the hands of your boyfriend before I could get your toe in my mouth," he laughs.

"What is a Russian necktie?"

"You don't want to know," he admits.

"Fine. Now that I know you know my man will snap your pencil neck, I accept your offer to poison me by way of your charred grilled food," I grin.

"Charred? Wanda, you are going to eat your words."

"I half hope you're as good at grilling as you're bragging about, and half hope you suck so I can keep teasing you."

"You know, if I'm bad at grilling, you can't actually make fun of me anymore. You can't joke about things that are real," he points out.

Even though he's absolutely right about that, I still like to give him shit. "Says who?"

"Common sense, Wanda."

"Something you know nothing about, Bert." I retort.

"Correct. I put all my eggs into a single basket. Common sense and book smarts were not either basket—"

"Yeah, you put all your metaphorical eggs in any puss that comes near you," I tease. "What are you going to do if you end up catching STD's or something?"

"I wear condoms always. No exceptions. And get tested every three months, or more if I take home someone from a sketchy place."

"That's so disgusting," I crinkle my nose at him.

"Thanks, Wanda. That's a nice way to make someone feel good—telling them how disgusting they are."

"You already know I hate your antics."

"Quit filling your cup with haterade and coming to see me right after."

I roll my eyes but can't help the smile tugging at my lips. We complete our lap around the track, with Kodiak trotting calmly beside us, his ears flicking now and then as he listens to our chatter. Once we arrive at the stable, I lead him back to his stall, giving him a gentle pat on the neck and a kiss on his muzzle before saying goodbye.

Brad waits by the gate, watching me, amused. "You really love that horse, don't you?"

"Of course. He's my big guy," I reply, smoothing Kodiak's mane one last time before stepping out of the stall. We walk together to the edge of the stable drive.

"See you when you get back, Wanda. Have a good time," he waves, his usual smirk replaced by a forced smile.

"See ya later, Bert," I reply, holding up a peace sign above my head as I continue walking. I glance back once, catching a glimpse of Brad standing there, hands in his pockets, watching me leave.

CHAPTER
Thirty

KALYN

Two weeks fly by in a whirlwind of activity. The first week is spent at the office, diving back into work and catching up on everything that piled up during our brief absence. The second week is a blissful escape, celebrating Shay and Jonathan finally getting married. But now, we're finally back home, settling into the familiar rhythm of our lives.

Jonah sleeps in until around ten, which is unusual for him. He's jolted awake by his phone ringing incessantly. By the time he gets out of bed, I can hear a voice on the other end of the line, sounding urgent. He looks irritated as he gets dressed, kisses my cheek, and rushes out the door within a matter of minutes.

Shay and I sit outside Jonah's office, listening intently as he yells at people over the phone. Jonathan joins him, bringing his laptop and a sense of purpose. The tension is getting to Shay as she fidgets beside me.

"I want to be nosy and go eavesdrop," Shay admits, glancing at the door.

"I'm sure they'll tell us when things settle."

We sit quietly, trying to catch snippets of the heated conversation through the thick office door. An hour later, Jonathan exits, looking slightly weary but composed, and heads back to his office.

"Honey," Shay calls to him, and his face softens as he turns to her. She approaches him, and he leans in to kiss her.

I stand and walk to Jonah's office, hesitating for a moment before softly opening the door and peeking in to see if he has calmed down. He is furiously typing away on his computer, scowling.

"Hi, babe," I say gently, not wanting to add to his frustration. "How late will you be working?"

"Apparently, I shouldn't even take time off since shit gets fucked up whenever I do," he snaps, still focused on his screen.

I know he's not mad at me, but the harshness of his tone catches me off guard. I turn to leave, deciding not to engage.

"Baby," he calls, his voice softening as he stands from his desk. "I'm sorry. I'll have to work late to get things sorted out."

"Brad was going to BBQ, so I'm going to his place. I'll just have him bring me home later," I respond, wanting to get away for a while.

"Okay," he agrees, leaning in to kiss me.

I head upstairs to change into shorts, a tank top, a lightweight cardigan, and sandals. I loosely braid my hair, then make my way to the stables. Brad's truck is in the parking lot, but he's nowhere in sight. Inside the building, I still can't find him, so I head to Kodiak's stall.

"Hi, baby," I say as he approaches the gate.

I spend the next ten minutes chatting with and petting him and Winona.

As I see Claire bring a horse in to groom, she walks right past me without a word. Maybe she didn't see me. She moves to the area next to me, and I decide to greet her.

"Hey Claire."

"Hey," Claire responds curtly, not even glancing in my direction.

"How's it going out here?" I try again, hoping to break through her aloofness.

"Brad's over in the office," she nods toward the far end of the building.

"Okay," I respond, sensing her irritation but not understanding its source.

"He'd already be out here if he knew you were here."

"Is everything okay?" I ask, confused by her demeanor.

"You know, he's never cooked for anyone before. He doesn't walk around like a giddy schoolgirl with anyone else after spending time with them. And from the looks of your finger, it seems you'll be marrying Mr. Everett. I don't know if you're leading Brad on or if he's delusional enough to think he has a chance with you, but everything he does is in hopes that you two will be together. If this is innocent on your part, then set clear boundaries with him. If it's not, then you two should just leave together. Mr. Everett has been miserable for years until you came along. Now you have both of them wrapped around your finger, and it's not just them you're hurting. There are people who truly care about Brad and don't want to see him get hurt," she says with an uneven tone.

"Brad and I are just friends," I tell her firmly, though I feel a pang of guilt.

"I don't treat my friends the way he treats you," she accuses.

"Do you have a thing for Brad?" I ask, still very much confused by her hostility.

"Does it matter? If I told you I did, would it make a difference? Brad wants you, Kalyn. For a while, I foolishly believed he was starting to want me. Then you came along, and I realized he never looked at me the way he looks at you. I can't even get him to have a conversation with me because all he wants to do is have sex and go on about his day as if we didn't just share an intimate encounter. I used to think you were just a talker and that's how he always wound up trapped in conversations with you. But I realized pretty quickly he talks just as much, if not more, to you. And you both are people with little to say. Your chemistry is palpable. Mr. Everett isn't blind and can see it from a mile away. But for some reason, he allows you and Brad to prance around like secret lovers. Just don't hurt him. Don't hurt either one of them," she warns.

This is the most I've ever heard Claire say, and she seems genuinely upset. I see her look behind me, her eyes seeming to harbor a lot of pain in them.

"Welcome back, pageant queen. Where are your giddy-up boots?" Brad asks, setting a heavy bag down next to the stall with a loud thump.

"Thanks. I didn't wear them out here since we aren't staying. Are you almost done?" I attempt to keep my tone light despite the tongue-lashing Claire just gave me.

"Ready when you are."

"Should you wash your hands before we go?"

"For what?" he wipes his palms down the front of his jeans.

"We need to go shopping," I remind him.

"Shopping for what?"

"Food ingredients."

"I've already got everything I need at the house. Ready?"

"Ready," I reply, wanting to get as far away from Claire as possible after that odd conversation. Maybe she's right; perhaps I should take a step back from my friendship with Brad.

He waves cheerfully and says, "See ya, Claire." She waves back, but her response seems so incredibly pained.

I awkwardly wave bye to her, noticing her expression drops as she watches us leave together. We head out the back door and make our way to the parking lot. When we reach his truck, he opens the passenger door for me.

"Thank you, sir."

"Can we roll the windows down?" I hover over the button, waiting for him to give me the go-ahead.

"Windows down it is," he replies, lowering his window.

I buckle my seatbelt and glance at him. "Buckle up, Bert," I tell him. He laughs and reaches behind him to fasten his seatbelt.

He sends off a text and then puts his phone between his legs as he backs up. I glance over and see Claire watching us from the window. My heart breaks for her; she's so quiet and reserved that I wonder if she's ever told him how she feels.

We head through town, and Brad leaves out a back road.

"I didn't think this road led to anywhere?" I say.

"Just to people who live here," he replies, taking a turn down a dirt road lined with trees.

When we reach a clearing, there's a large farmhouse-style home with a lot of yard. He parks in the driveway and gets out of the truck.

As we walk to the front door, he just pushes it open and walks in.

"You're gone for days at a time and don't lock your house?" I ask, shocked that he literally just left it unlocked.

"Yeah, if someone broke in, they'd need to be able to make themselves at home," he says.

"You'd let them just walk on in?" I glance around, noticing he has a lot of really nice things. He'll probably end up getting robbed eventually.

"Absolutely. I'd snap their neck when I found them, but at least they'd be comfortable for a bit," he walks to the fridge and begins taking out food.

I laugh, thinking he's joking until I see his face is completely serious. "Well, okay then. I'm questioning whether I'm going to be strung up in a cornfield like a scarecrow for stepping through your door," I jokingly say.

"You're safe. Anyone who hurts you, however… they'll find themselves in a cornfield."

"For some reason, I feel like you're not lying when you say that," I widen my eyes sarcastically.

"I'm not," he closes the fridge door with his foot.

I walk to the counter, pulling out a chair on the other side of the island and watch as he starts prepping the food.

"Do you like being out here all alone?" I stare out the large window to the back patio. It's really pretty, but I'm willing to bet it's creepy at night. Looking at the window frame, I notice he doesn't even have blinds or curtains, so anyone could literally just look right inside the house.

"Yeah, I hate people, I told you that. Hence, working with horses," he smirks.

"You've always hated people, or did your past make you hate people?" I question.

"I've always hated people."

"So, I take it you don't have people locked in a secret cellar or something here?" I tease, trying to lighten the mood.

He looks up at me from cutting potatoes, pausing for a moment before continuing.

"You're so creepy, Bert," I laugh.

He puts the potatoes in a pot and hands it to me, then grabs the rest of the food and walks to the back door. I follow him out onto the back patio. It's a large wooden deck with a rug and nice patio furniture. At the far end of the deck, there's a stone wall with a built-in grill kitchen, complete with a fridge, a large grill, a sink, and a TV. There's even a bar with seating and shelves stocked with alcohol.

"Looks like every man's dream," I say, impressed by his set up.

"Want a drink?" He points to the alcohol.

"So you can roofie me?"

"Maybe," he winks.

"I'll take water, please. Roofie on the side."

He sets the food down and takes the pot from me, filling it with water before placing it on the stove and turning it on. Then, he turns to the grill, firing it up. Opening the fridge, he pulls out a water bottle, twists the lid open, then retightens it and hands it to me. "Water with a roofie on the side."

He starts preparing the steak with an assortment of seasonings before placing it on the hot grill. The sizzle of the meat hitting the heat fills the air. He flips the steak with practiced ease, ensuring it cooks evenly.

Once the steak is perfectly seared, he transfers it to the cutting board. I watch as he cuts my steak into thin, small pieces, and I don't know why it makes me smile, but it does.

We sit on his porch swing, holding our plates. I take a bite of my delicious-smelling steak, and my eyes roll at the exquisite taste. This man DOES know how to grill—damnit.

An exaggerated moan escapes my throat. "Damn, Bert, this is terrible," I say, taking another bite. "Let me save you. Put your steak on my plate; you shouldn't have to suffer through this deliciou—I mean terrible food," I hold my plate out to his.

He has a piece of steak on his fork and holds it in my direction, offering it to me.

"Oh no you don't. I want the whole thing. I'm saving you from the embarrassment of bragging about your grilling skills when it's this bad."

He laughs and takes the bite off his fork. "Wanna see something pretty cute?" he asks, pulling out his phone from his back pocket.

"If you show me a dick pic, I will stab you in the eye with my fork," I threaten, clutching my fork as if ready to stab at him.

He swipes over his photos and turns his phone to show me a picture of a puppy. It's an Australian shepherd with a painted blue merle coat, light gray and dark gray coloring it's fur, a white chest, and a white stripe up his nose that ends between his ears, with light blue eyes.

"Is this yours?!" I exclaim, taking his phone from him and zooming in on the adorable little face.

"I pick him up in two weeks," he says proudly. "His name is Hank."

"He's so cute. Did you name him?"

"I did. Why? You don't like the name?" he asks.

"Just wondering. If I got a dog, I would name him Sir Charles Barkley and call him Barkley for short."

"You gonna get a dog, Wanda?"

"Probably not ever. So if you choose to rename Hank Sir Charles Barkley, I won't complain. It sounds like a sophisticated gentleman."

"It sounds like he would need to always wear a bowtie."

"How cute! I'll find him bowties while I'm gone," I exclaim excitedly.

"I feel like your entire goal is to embarrass my new buddy."

"A bowtie is not embarrassing," I argue. "It's distinguished."

"Is that what it is?"

"Name a single time you've seen someone in a bowtie and thought they didn't have their shit together," I challenge.

"You're right. A bowtie definitely gives off 'shit together' vibes," he agrees, laughing.

When I finish eating, he stands up, takes my plate, and walks over to his grill area to wash them.

"You're like a domesticated housewife, Bert," I rock back and forth on the swing as I watch the sunset. "I love sleeping outside. It would be so peaceful out here at night. What kind of wildlife is out here? Bears? Coyotes? Moose? Wolves? Like, would I wake up to something eating me?"

"You'd wake up being eaten, but not by an animal."

"You'll have a napkin wrapped around your neck and every-thing," I laugh.

"I don't need a napkin—I love getting dirty when I eat," he sits down next to me and leans back in the swing.

"Do you know how to swim?" I ask.

"Who doesn't? We all started off as swimmers," he laughs.

"Ew, were you a sperm?" I scrunch my nose.

"I was. I'll bet if we were racing, you'd still be lost in the fallo-pian tube, and I'd already be in the comforts of the egg."

"If we were sperm together, you'd be the one swimming in circles," I retort.

"Circles around your slow ass," he shoots back.

"Who mows your grass?" I ask, pointing to his perfectly maintained lawn.

He turns his head to look at me, raising an eyebrow. "What did you just ask?"

"I asked who mows your grass," I repeat, noticing his amused expression.

He tilts his head back and starts laughing. "I do, Wanda. You wanna help next time?"

"What did you think I asked?"

"That's exactly what I thought you asked, but I thought you were meaning something different," he clasps his hands together and rests them on his stomach.

"I don't care about none of your dirty business," I motion my hand in a circle to insinuate I'm talking about his privates.

"You love my business," he retorts without missing a beat.

The sun is almost completely down, and every star in the sky is visible. Standing from the chair, I walk down the porch steps and into the grass, looking up at the beautiful twinkling colors. Moments later, Brad joins me with a blanket in hand. He spreads it out on the grass and lies down, placing his hands behind his head. He stares up at me, waiting for me to join him. I lie down next to him and turn my eyes to the stars.

"It's incredible out here," I say.

We lie there quietly, absorbed in the view. I think about how it feels endless out here yet so small at the same time.

"What would you do if we suddenly saw a giant eyeball in the sky staring at us, like a giant looking at us under a magnifying glass?" I ask.

"I'd tell you to take your top off," he whispers out of the corner of his mouth.

"What would that do for him?"

"It wouldn't do anything for him, but it would keep me calm," he says.

"What if he wanted to see your chode instead of boobs?" I counter.

"Good thing he came prepared. He'd need that magnifying glass real close to see my little weiner."

"That's probably a sore subject, huh? Everyone you sleep with probably says that to you all the time: 'Where is it?' Every time you pull it out."

"Yeah, it's a sore subject. I'm popular with women because they all want a look at the little dick."

"Do you think that's why you also have little dick energy?"

"Is that the energy I give off?" he asks, smiling at me.

"You give off big dick energy, but no way you of all people could have one of those," I hit his arm playfully.

"You give off big dick energy too," he replies.

"Elaborate," I laugh, curious to hear his reasoning.

"Like you take really big dicks," he says, as if it's obvious what he means.

"Ohhh, like throwing a hotdog down a hallway?"

"I wouldn't know for sure without testing that. But I'd imagine they still manage to fit."

"All those suckers who've had to endure the trenches of my musty swamp," I joke, rolling my eyes.

"I just want to put this on the record: if I could, I would take one for all of mankind and wife you, just so no other poor sap had to potentially deal with the abyss that is your vagina. I know, it's noble of me, but I care about my fellow people." He holds his hand over his heart, like he's really being kind here.

"Bless your heart," I place my hand over his.

"Thank you, Wanda. It would be a tough job, but I'd be up for the task."

"Lucky for you, Jonah stepped up to the plate first and took one for the team instead."

"And I've been cursing his name since—I mean—Wait, what?" He looks at me, and we both start laughing.

"I see why all these women fall head over heels for you," I admit, turning to look at him.

"Please, tell me more," he smiles wide.

"You're funny and easy to talk to," I say, noting his smile slowly fading away as he realizes I'm being serious.

"I don't have conversations with any of them," he says matter-of-factly.

"Oh, whatever."

"I don't."

"Why wouldn't you talk to any of them. You're sleeping with them."

"Exactly. I'm not looking to get to know them," he clarifies.

"What are circumstances under which you decide someone is worth getting to know?" I always assumed he and Claire had some sort of close friendship since she was bringing him lunch one day. But then she says that he basically beds her and leaves like he does with everyone else.

"When they're always on my mind."

"What if you met your dream girl and she was absolutely not interested in you? Would you cry?"

"I didn't cry. Just jerked off a lot and had sex a lot to get her off my mind," he confesses.

"Ooh, this is juicy." I turn onto my side, propping my head on my hand, nudging his leg with my knee. "You said you didn't cry, as in it already happened. Why do you think she wasn't interested?"

"Because I was sleeping with too many people," he replies.

"See! Stop doing that!"

"I would have never slept with another woman again if she were mine," he says.

"Do you think you ever have a chance with her again?"

"Nah, I never did to begin with," he responds pensively, his eyes scanning the night sky above.

"I don't believe that for a second. If we scrubbed up your image and you quit being a man-whore, she will gladly take you," I assert confidently. "If not, find someone better."

"She's getting married."

"Oh. Sorry," I murmur sympathetically, though I can't help but feel he brought this on himself. Even I've told him he sleeps with too many women. Unfortunately, it caught up with him. But he still does it, so he obviously never learns.

"You should be. You wrecked my world, Wanda," he laughs.

"Shut up," I retort, then steer the conversation towards a lighter topic as I roll onto my back again. "We need to find a porch swing or yard swing that lays fully flat and can still rock so we can gaze up at the stars all night. This would be so much better if we had something soft to lay on verses us laying on the hard ground."

"Noted," he nods, his gaze fixed on me.

"What?" I whisper, turning to look at him.

"Nothing."

"Then watch the sky, because I just saw a shooting star and you made me miss my chance to make a wish." When he looks back up, three shooting stars fly across the sky, and I point at them. "Look, that one's mine, you take that one," I say, closing my eyes and making my wish.

We settle into a comfortable silence, watching the stars twinkle and listening to the crickets chirp. The night air grows cooler, and my shorts and tank top from earlier don't seem nearly warm enough. When the chill in the air becomes more pronounced and I feel the stiffness in my back from lying on the ground for so long, I sit up and stretch.

"We should head back," I suggest, turning to face him. "Are you going to stay here tonight or at the apartment? I can have Jonah come get me if you want to stay home tonight."

"I brought you here; I'll bring you back. I'll just stay at the apartment tonight."

We walk back to the house, and I help him bring the dishes inside. He puts them away, and I head toward the front door. He retrieves his coat from the hook and holds it open for me.

"I'm okay," I assure him.

"You always do that—accept an innocent gesture when it's offered," he remarks, smiling as he continues to hold it open.

Rolling my eyes, I slip my arms into it. The initial chill fades as I feel the warmth of his coat enveloping me. "Since you're not staying here tonight, lock your damn doors."

"Yes, mother," he says, locking his front door securely.

The drive back is quiet. I pull my knees to my chest and zip his coat around me. He looks over, watching me, and smiles. Since he doesn't make any comment about it or give me shit, I don't say anything.

As we pull up to the front of the mansion, he gets out and walks around to open my door. "Thank you," I say, shaking his coat off and handing it back to him so he can put it on. I start my way toward the stairs, and he turns to head back to the driver's side of his truck. "Oh, and Bert… you have a piece of pepper in your teeth," I wink at him and walk up the front steps, hearing his laughter as I open and close the door behind me.

CHAPTER
Thirty-One

JONAH

I know how Brad feels about Kalyn. I see it in his eyes, the way he watches her. He's respectful, but not in the usual way women expect. He knows she's in a relationship and won't cross that line. He's a smooth talker, though. I've heard how he and Kalyn banter. I should put an end to it, but I can't bring myself to do it. Part of me thinks she might have a crush on him, like all the women do, but she'd never act on it. If she did, perhaps I'd deserve it for not treating her like the queen that she is.

I like that she opens up to him. She's always gotten along better with men than women. I've never asked, but I'll bet she dealt with jealous girls growing up. Someone like Kalyn, with her natural beauty and kindness, is bound to stir up envy. It's probably why her best friend growing up was a guy. It's good she has someone to hang out with while I'm working. Shay and Jonathan are so obsessed with each other, she follows him around constantly, and he eats it up. I know my job gets to her sometimes, but she never complains. So how could I make a big deal about her spending time with Brad? What I'm starting to realize is I could end up losing her to someone like Brad because he feeds her emotionally in a way I've never known how.

"Kalyn and Brad have been gone a really long time," Shay says, glancing at her phone again for what feels like the hundredth time as we sit in the chairs by the windows in my office.

"Stop looking at your phone if it's bothering you," I tell her, trying to mask the fact that it's starting to bother me too.

"How do you not care that she's with another man? You aren't having intrusive thoughts like 'what if they're fucking?'" she asks.

"I satisfy her," I respond coldly, unsure if I'm trying to convince her or myself. Maybe both. Do I satisfy her enough to keep her from sleeping with him?

"Brad satisfies the entire town. And they've been gone long enough that he may have been laying it down with her," she looks at her phone again.

"They're not," my tone grows louder than it should have, catching Jonathan's attention.

"Hey, Everett," he raises his hand as if to protect Shay. "Why don't we just call her? Just to make sure she's having a nice time," he offers, trying to ease the tension.

"We don't need to call," I say with finality.

Shay abruptly stands from her chair. "How do you not even care? Why would you agree to her leaving with him? Don't come crying to us when she comes back having been fucked by someone else."

"Honey, calm down," Jonathan says. "She's bothered because she thinks Brad is trying to take her place. Plus, he has a penis, and we know Kal likes those since she lives on yours," Jonathan quips, tossing my small football back to me.

"I'm just going to call her," Shay looks at her phone again.

"Chill, honey," Jonathan reassures her.

"No, this is pissing me off," she says, still standing there.

"I'm gonna take her to bed. I can think of something that will calm her down," he says, taking her hand and pulling a very irritated Shay out of the room as she glares at me. Shay is making it very known how possessive she is over Kalyn. And here I was thinking I was the only one.

I can't let Kalyn leave with Brad anymore. My mind is made up. This was too much—hours of them bonding alone. My leg shakes as I lean on my elbow, sliding my finger between my teeth. What would I do if she did sleep with him? I'd kill him. And her… I'd have to try harder to make her love me more. Why am I even thinking like this. He wouldn't do that. He DIDN'T do that.

I retreat to my room and try to lie down, but it's futile. I can't relax, and I certainly can't sleep. When I close my eyes, I see her beautiful smile in the sunlight, and then my mind shifts to me on top of her, both of us naked while I fuck her. The image morphs into Brad being the one between her legs.

"Fuck!" I slam my hands down on the bed, my frustration boiling over. I rip the bedding away, feeling suffocated by the thoughts in my head, and walk to the bathroom. Maybe a shower will clear my mind. I turn on the water and step in, hoping the heat will wash away the gnawing unease.

As the water pours over me, I lean against the shower wall, letting my head hang. I try to focus on the water, but my mind keeps drifting back to Kalyn and Brad. Why the hell did I agree to them being alone? He has a dick, after all—one that he uses frequently.

And her pussy might just be the most appetizing one he's never been able to have, becoming a challenge he can't resist.

I scrub my face vigorously, attempting to erase these thoughts. I think about how freely she laughs with Brad, how comfortable she seems around him. Brad's smooth-talking ways, his charm… could she be tempted? I know she wasn't tonight, but possibly in the future.

I ball my fists, water dripping from my knuckles. I need to do better—be better. I have to show her that I'm the only one she ever needs or wants to be with.

I crank the water hotter, the physical discomfort is a welcome distraction from the chaos in my mind. I need to talk to her about how tonight is making me crazy, and I never want to experience these feelings again. If that means cutting off her friendship with Brad... I will. As I rinse off, an idea comes to mind. It might come back around and bite me in the ass, but at this point, I don't care—I have a phone call to make. I'll do what I need to do to protect my relationship, even if that means involving others. Turning off the shower, I step out, wrapping a towel securely around my waist.

I sense her presence before I see her. Glancing in the mirror, I watch as Kalyn walks through the doorway. She turns on the shower, beginning to undress. Each movement is graceful, almost hypnotic, and I can't tear my eyes away. She slips off her shirt, her skin glowing in the soft bathroom light, then unbuttons her shorts, sliding them down her legs.

Before she can step into the shower, I grab her hand. She turns to look at me, curiosity and desire mingling in her gaze. I gently pull her hand, leading her away from the shower, towards the large tub in the corner. She follows without hesitation. We stop by the tub, and I guide her to sit on the stairs. She bites her bottom lip, watching me intently.

I kneel before her, my hands pressing her legs apart. Leaning in, I bury my face between her thighs, tasting her sweetness. She gasps, her hands finding their way into my hair, pulling me in. I revel in the feel of her soft skin against my lips, her wetness against my tongue. Her breath hitches, and I can feel her body responding to every move.

I take my time, exploring her with my mouth, tracing circles and flicks that elicit soft moans from her. Her hips begin to move against me, urging me to go deeper. I slide my hands up her thighs, gripping them firmly as I intensify my efforts, focusing on the spots that make her gasp the loudest.

"Don't stop," she whispers, her voice trembling. *I have no intention of stopping.*

I quicken my pace, creating a rhythm that has her writhing beneath me. With one final, deliberate motion, I sink two fingers inside her. She cries out, her body shuddering as waves of pleasure wash over her. Her hands tighten in my hair, pulling me closer, as her body trembles. Finally, she collapses back against the stairs, breathing heavily.

I rise to my feet and look down at her, admiring the sight of her relaxed and content. She opens her eyes and looks up at me. I extend my hand, helping her up. "Let's get in the shower," I suggest, my voice low and husky with desire.

She nods, still catching her breath, and places her hands in mine. I bend over, wrapping my arms around her waist and lifting her up off the stairs, carrying her to the shower. The heat surrounds us, and this shower feels a thousand times better than the shower I took before, washing away the worry I was feeling. I place her on her feet and can't take my eyes off her as she moves closer, the steam enveloping us in a hazy cocoon. She presses against me, her hands sliding down my chest.

Her touch is gentle, almost teasing, as her fingertips etch patterns down my torso, stealing my breath. She looks up at me, her eyes dark with desire. Slowly, she reaches down and wraps her hand around my cock, moving with slow, deliberate strokes. I can feel my pulse quickening, my body responding to her touch. She leans in closer, her breath warm against my skin, and then she kneels in front of me, the sight of her on her knees is incredible.

She starts with a soft lick at the tip, her tongue barely grazing the sensitive skin. The sensation is mind-shattering, and I grip the shower wall to steady myself. She takes her time, savoring every moment.

I drink in the sight of her, mesmerized by the way she peers up at me, her eyes filled with desire and mischief. She knows exactly what she's doing and enjoys every second of it. She wraps her lips around the head of my cock, applying gentle suction, and a groan rips from my throat as my head lolls back. It's a slow, torturous delight, building with each passing second.

She takes more of me into her mouth, working her magic, and I feel I'm about to lose control. My thoughts are a jumbled mess of desire and need, my body on fire with the pleasure she's giving me.

"Baby," I mewl, my voice barely more than a whisper, filled with raw desperation as her mouth remains warm and wet around me. Her hands grip my thighs, steadying herself as she takes me deeper, her movements deliberate and intoxicating. My hand finds its way into her hair, tangling in the wet strands as I hold on for dear life.

She looks up at me, her eyes locking onto mine, and it's that connection—that look—that pushes me over the edge. The feeling is intense, all-consuming, and I give myself over to it completely, letting her take me to places only she can. My hips thrust against her movements, striving not to hurt her while competing with my imminent release. Her hand and mouth work faster until my release spills from me, spurting ropes of semen down her throat. Her lips form a seal around me, capturing every droplet.

When she finally withdraws, her lips leave me with a final, teasing kiss. She rises to her feet, and I pull her close, holding her against me as the water continues to pour over us. For a moment, nothing else matters but the two of us, lost in the heat and steam, reconnected in a way I was trying to convince myself was gone.

Tilting her head up, I pull her into a deep kiss, tasting the water and myself on her lips. My hands roam over her wet body, feeling the slickness of her skin. It's electric, and the need to be inside her becomes overwhelming. I scoop her up, her legs wrapping around my waist as I press her back against the cool tiles of the shower wall. The contrast of the cold wall against our heated bodies only intensifies the moment.

I hold her close, our eyes locked as the water cascades around us. I feel her shiver, her hips arching toward me. Her nails bite into my shoulders, her breath coming in short, shallow gasps as I slowly begin to push inside her. The tightness of her around me is incredible, and I move with deliberate slowness, feeling every inch until she has taken all of me. Her moan is soft at first, a whisper of pleasure that grows louder with each passing second. I can feel her body adjusting to me, welcoming me.

I begin to move, starting with slow, deep strokes, feeling the way her body responds to mine. I pick up the pace, my hips pressing into her with a rhythm that speaks of our need for each other.

Her fingers claw at my back, her legs squeezing around me as I push deeper, harder. Her cries become more urgent, more demanding, and I match her intensity, giving her everything I have. Her walls clamp me in a vice hold while she cries out my name. "Jonah," her voice filled with desperation. "Don't stop."

I plunge into her with a relentless rhythm. Her body trembles against mine, her cries turning into screams of ecstasy as I hit that precise spot inside her that sends her hips rocking with need.

I can feel her tightening around my cock, her body tensing as her orgasm builds, her hips gyrating more urgently against my pelvis. I hold her close; the look in her eyes is pure, unfiltered pleasure. My lips capture hers in a searing kiss, her screams muffled against my lips, and I swallow every whimpered exhale.

She comes undone around me, her body shaking with the force of her climax. It's too much, and I feel my own release building. I let myself go, thrusting hard into her one final time, our bodies locked together in perfect harmony. We stay connected like this, the water washing away the sweat and remnants of our passion. I hold her against the wall as I wait for my body to relax.

I love this woman.

I slowly ease out of her, seating her gently on the shower bench. She leans against the wall, her breath coming in ragged gasps. Kneeling on the floor before her, I rest my chin on her knees, and her hands comb through my hair. Her chest rises and falls, giving me the best view of her gorgeous tits.

"Welcome home to me," she whispers.

"You're incredible. I showered before you got back. I'm going to get out and let you finish up." I climb to my feet and lean down, pressing my lips to hers.

She nods as I step out of the shower, quickly wrapping a fresh towel around my waist while my mind races. The revelation of how wet she was when I just went down on her—drenched, if I'm being honest with myself—irks me. Shay's words still echo in my head, her remarks managing to get under my skin despite my attempts to brush them off. The thought of Kalyn and Brad together gnaws at me.

What would I do if they had slept together? I glance back at the shower, seeing Kalyn rinsing off, completely unaware how bothered I am. I went down on her not just to get her off, but to check if there were any traces of him on her. The thought sickens me, but I needed to know. And there weren't. In fact, I could still smell the lingering scent of myself on her from our encounter the previous night. It's a small comfort, but a comfort nonetheless.

I step out of the bathroom, leaving Kalyn to her shower. Shay's accusations were baseless—I know that logically and factually—but they've planted a seed of doubt that I can't easily shake. I hear the water shut off, and fifteen minutes later, she walks into the bedroom, a towel wrapped around her. She looks refreshed and happy.

I sit on the edge of the bed, my hands clasped together as I watch her enter. She walks over and climbs into my lap, a mischievous glint in her eyes. "Waiting for me, Mr. Everett? I know what you sitting here means, and we just had sex. Did you already forget?" Leaning in, she bites my lip and sucks it into her mouth. "Do you need more?" she whispers, her teeth grazing my neck in the same way they did on my lip.

"I just wanted to hold you," I murmur, tightening my arms around her waist.

She sits up and looks at me. Her eyes shift, noticing something, and I can see emotions transforming her eyes. She seems bothered, but quickly plasters on a fake smile. "Ready for bed?" She climbs off my lap, dropping her towel to the floor, and pulls back the comforter on her side of the bed, slipping under the covers.

I watch her, realizing she knows I'm bothered. She's not mentioning it, so I won't either. I join her in bed, wrapping my arms around her and pulling her to me, nuzzling my nose into her nape.

The more I think it over, the more I realize I can't tell her she isn't allowed to hang out with someone—that's a dick move. He's her friend, and the fact she asked me so easily if she could go to his house made me feel a bit more at ease with the situation. What she wasn't aware of, and what Shay wasn't aware of, is that Brad has security cameras with sound hidden all over his house. Before they left, he sent me a single text, "See ya later, Wolf Warrior," giving me permission to watch the cameras. I watched the entire time until Jonathan and Shay came into my office—those were the only moments I became overly concerned with. Perhaps he knew I quit watching and that's when he made his move.

Years ago, when we were training, Brad taught a course about teamwork and the importance of having a code word only the team would know for different tasks. One of the missions we did for ops training had us teamed up with Jonathan, Dame, and Brandt. Brad led the team and said, "Cameras are in each corner of the room; we need to take them all out," pointing as he spoke. He said the head trainer, "Wolf Warrior," was the one monitoring the cameras and would do anything to sabotage our training as part of his own job. Once the last one was taken out, Brad called out, "See ya later, Wolf Warrior," and our team completed the training in record time. From that moment on, we referred to security cameras as "Wolf Warrior."

One time, Brad got arrested, and his one phone call was to me. When I got there, I asked if there were cameras in the interrogation room where he was being held. Hearing them say there were no cameras, the first thing he said when I entered the room was, "What's up, Wolf Warrior," and I knew they were lying about the cameras not being in the room.

I understand Shay's concern. She started to fuck with my head too. But given the fact Brad gave me permission to watch them, I realize he didn't have any plans on trying to make a move on Kalyn.

Over the next half hour of holding her, my mind runs rampant, feeling the need to protect what's mine. She shifts slightly, her breathing steady and calm. I try to match my breathing to hers, hoping it will calm my mind, and it works. Eventually, my racing thoughts begin to slow, and I drift off into a restless sleep.

I stir when I feel her hands rubbing my cock, groggily opening my eyes to meet hers.

"Hi," she whispers.

"Hi," I whisper back, my voice still heavy with sleep.

She pulls the covers down to mid-leg and pushes on my chest, guiding me onto my back. Straddling me, she looks down. I'm hard—I'm always hard when I see her naked, or really, any time I'm around her. I've grown accustomed to my body's reaction to her, the constant arousal she evokes in me.

Her hands continue to move over my length, and I groan softly, my hips instinctively pushing up into her touch. She leans down, her breath warm against my skin, as she kisses a trail from my neck to my chest. Shivers weave down my spine, and I reach up, running my hands along her sides, feeling the smoothness of her skin beneath my fingertips.

"Did you have a nice evening?"

"I did. He grilled steaks. Did you know he lives so far out that you can basically see all the stars with no lights around?"

He cooked dinner for her. That requires time, preparation, and planning. He did all of that for her. For as long as I've known him, he's never done that for a woman before. Yet, he did it for my fiancée. "If you want complete darkness, baby, I'll turn off every light here anytime you want to go stargazing," I offer. I would do anything for her.

"How much property do you own?"

"Here or in general?" I probe.

"Well, I didn't think my question would need clarification, but it's you, so of course you would own more property than just here. But the property that your castle sits on—how far does it extend?"

"A little ways."

"Well, we should build a house far enough out that we can be in pitch dark and fall asleep under the stars. But preferably off the ground."

"So, a house where we can stay, but with easy access to the roof, and a bed for stargazing and sleeping under the stars?" I seek confirmation.

"Yes," she confirms with a nod.

"Tell me your specs," I prompt.

"Well, it will be an open concept for the living room and large kitchen, with a huge center island, and two master bedrooms," she outlines happily.

"And that's it?"

"That's it."

"K, explain the two master bedrooms."

"Umm, isn't it obvious? One is mine and one is Shay's."

"Oh? Are you forgetting anything else?"

She taps her finger on her chin. "No, not that I can think of. Why? Is there something else you can think of?"

"Mmm, a Jonah and perhaps a Jonathan," I suggest with a playful grin.

"I mean, I guess you guys could come and visit," she jests.

"Visit? Do we need to be penciled into your calendar?"

"That's a really good idea. However, sometimes, you're good for other things," she murmurs as she leans down and presses her lips to mine.

"Let's discuss those," I draw her in closer.

"Let's," she whispers, biting my lower lip, before releasing it. Her hand navigates between us, stroking me, then slowly lowers herself onto me, working me inside her tight channel.

"What's a unique way an animal gives birth?" she murmurs amidst her moans.

My breathing turns labored, as I struggle to collect my thoughts. Her movements stop once she has the entire length of my cock inside her. "Umm..." I stammer, my voice laced with the strain of my rapidly growing pleasure. "A... a kangaroo gives birth in a unique way."

"Tell me more." Her voice drips with seduction, her inner muscles tightening around my shaft rhythmically.

"They give birth to an embryo the size of a lima bean," I begin, gasping as she undulates her hips provocatively. "Then, the embryo has to climb through the mother's fur to reach the pouch, which takes about three minutes. Ah, fuck, baby, don't—"

"Keep going," she insists, her whisper a velvety command.

"Once inside the pouch, it finds the nipple and feeds for the next thirty-four weeks. Then it's mature enough to leave mom's pouch, though it returns to feed for another four months." I barely finish, my hands desperately grasping at her round ass.

"That's really cool. Do the embryos look like baby kangaroos?" she asks, rolling her hips again. My eyes flutter back, my hips lifting, and I need her to ride me. But her movements seize. "Baby," she purrs into my neck before biting down gently.

I respond through clenched teeth. "Not really; it looks like a pink mochi toy Adeline likes to play with."

"Tell me another random fact," she demands, biting gently into my side.

"I'll tell you as many random facts as I know if you fuck me," I groan, the plea rough in my throat.

"That's what I'm doing," she clenches her core again.

"If you want to know whether an egg is fresh, put it in water. If it sinks to the bottom, it's good—if it floats, you shouldn't eat it," I pant, the lines between pleasure and conversation blurring.

"Sometimes I wonder if you just make things up and I just believe every word," she chuckles, her tongue teasing my nipple.

"I read a lot—doesn't mean it's all true, but I still find it all interesting," I tell her, attempting a smile amid my heavy breaths.

"How do you find time to read with the amount you work?" she moves to the other side, softly biting, then sucking.

"Maybe I pretend to work, but I really spend all my time reading interesting facts just to impress you."

"At this point, I'm going to look up random facts and ask you questions just to see if you know the answer."

"Maybe you can teach me something I don't know," I push her hips back on me. A moan leaves her throat, replaced with a wide smile as her head falls back.

"What makes a fact a fact?" she asks, as her hips move in a slow, tantalizing circle.

"Is this my first test?"

"Maybe," her hands move to her breasts, pinching her nipples.

"A fact is… a statement that can be proven," I answer, focusing all my effort on maintaining a coherent sentence amidst the rising tide of pleasure from watching her touch herself and her squeezing my cock.

"Are mermaids real?" she asks, her voice a sultry whisper.

"As far as I know, there's no evidence of mermaids existing. But if you want to see one, I'll drain the ocean looking for one," I reply, struggling to keep my voice steady.

"I was really hoping you knew that a mermaid was actually real," she says, her movements making it increasingly difficult to think.

"There's so much hidden from the human population. I'm sure mermaids, megalodons, Bigfoot, and aliens are all here on Earth with us," I manage to say, barely. "Time's up, baby," I declare, flipping her onto her back. She giggles briefly before I pull out and grind back into her, her pussy enveloping my cock and turning her giggles into moans.

She grabs the sheets, her head thrown back as I work myself in and out of her. The feeling of her stretching around me is almost too much to bear. I lean down, capturing her lips in a searing kiss, our tongues tangling as our bodies move in perfect harmony.

Her nails dig into my back, and the slight pain only adds to the intense pleasure coursing through me. I increase my pace, each thrust more powerful than the last. Her moans crescendo, her breath now ragged gasps. I feel her walls contracting around me, and it's all I can do to restrain my own release. Burying myself one final time, she cries out, her body shuddering, and I follow her into bliss.

Collapsing on top of her, breathless and sated, I can feel her heart racing against mine, and for a moment, the world outside ceases to exist. It's just us, lost in the aftermath of our incredible connection.

"Tell me something that isn't a fact but is still interesting," she whispers, her breathing steadying.

"The body you occupied in a past life is buried somewhere on this earth… next to mine," I murmur into her neck.

"Eww, Jonah, that just gave me chicken skin," she says, holding up her arm to confirm the goosebumps covering her flesh.

A laugh escapes me, and my dick slips out of her slightly. "Do you know where the term 'scapegoat' came from?" I ask, propping myself up on my forearms to gaze down at her.

"Uhhh… nope, sure don't," she replies, her eyes sparkling with curiosity.

"Some ancient tribes used to tie up a goat and whisper their sins to it," I explain. "Then they'd let it 'accidentally' escape, believing it would carry their sins away and absolve them of guilt. Hence, it being their literal 'escape goat.'"

"That's cool. You're pretty cool too, Mr. Everett," she bites my nipple.

"You're pretty cool too," I kiss her.

CHAPTER
Thirty-Two

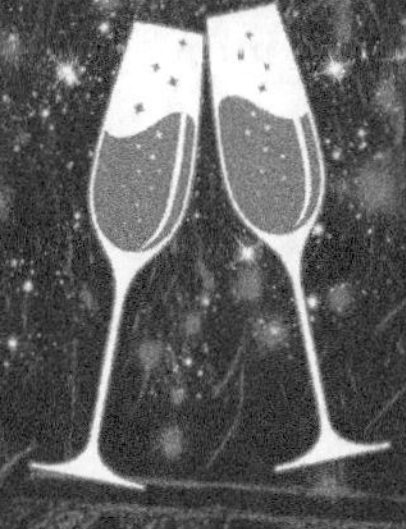

KALYN

The fall festival is happening in town, and everyone from the Mansion is invited to attend, courtesy of Jonah. The entire town is decorated with hay bales, food trucks, game booths, bounce houses, and fair rides. Laughter fills the air as kids dart around, having a blast while we roam through the festive scene.

"I want—"

"Cotton candy," Jonah finishes my sentence, a knowing smile on his lips.

I look at him and grin. "Yes, actually, that's exactly what I want."

"That's where we were headed," he points, leading the way toward the cotton candy booth.

The girl operating the booth notices his approach and gives him a beaming smile.

"Mr. Everett, sir. Hi, how are you? What brings you here? Are you enjoying yourself? It's a really nice day out today. Do you plan on going on any—"

"Two cotton candies, please," Jonah interrupts her rambling.

"Right, of course," she quickly grabs two bags and hands them over to him.

"Thanks," he says, slipping a fifty into her tip jar and handing Shay and me a bag of pink cotton candy each.

"It's free, sir... You paid for the entire festival," she informs him, looking slightly flustered. "I appreciate it, of course; anything that you're willing to give me, I would gladly accept. You are—."

He ignores her and starts to walk away.

"It was for your excellent service," I say, looking at her with appreciation.

"Thank you so much, Mr. Everett's wife," she responds eagerly.

As we walk away, I playfully whisper to him, "Did you catch that? I'm *WIFE*."

He whispers back, "The only thing making that untrue is a piece of paper."

I give his hand a gentle squeeze as we continue strolling around, exploring the various booths. Some are filled with beautiful artwork and handmade crafts, while others showcase clothing and toys.

"Mr. Everett, sir. I'd be thrilled to sketch you and the Mrs.," a man calls out from behind an easel, ready to draw us.

"Can you do four?" Shay asks him, gesturing to the group.

"Sure thing, go ahead and have a seat," he points to the chairs on the other side.

We sit down, and for the next forty-five minutes, he skillfully draws and airbrushes the portrait while engaging in an enthusiastic conversation with Jonah. The locals in town really do treat him like a celebrity, oohing and aahing whenever they get the chance to talk to him.

When the man finishes the drawing, he turns it around to show us, and I'm completely blown away by how incredible it looks. The cartoon characters resemble us so accurately. Shay and I have hearts in our eyes, and he drew big hearts connecting Jonah and me, as well as Shay and Jonathan.

"Oh my gosh, I absolutely love it!" I exclaim, standing up to take a closer look at it.

"That's amazing," Shay says, joining me to admire it.

"I can hold onto it for you, and you can pick it up before you leave, if you'd like," the man suggests.

"That would be wonderful," I say, handing the artwork back to him.

"Do you mind if I hang it up for others to see?"

"Please do," I encourage him, feeling proud of the beautiful depiction.

We spend the next few hours wandering around the festival, sampling various foods, and chatting with the friendly locals. As the sun sets, the town is illuminated by twinkling string lights, and the rides glow with vibrant colors.

"Can we ride the Ferris wheel?" Shay asks excitedly, tugging Jonathan towards it.

He chuckles and agrees, following after her.

I glance up at Jonah, giving him my best puppy-dog eyes.

"Lead the way, *wife*," he says, and I eagerly drag him towards the line.

Shay and Jonathan hop on ahead of us, and soon we're next in line for the Ferris wheel. As we start ascending, I take in the picturesque view of the town, capturing the moment in my mind. When we reach the top, the ride pauses, and I peer down as the worker lets another couple off. Jonah's hand gently lifts my chin, turning my gaze towards him.

"Hi," I whisper, feeling a flutter in my chest.

"Kiss already," Jonathan calls out from the seat behind us.

I grin at his comment as Jonah leans in, our lips meeting in a sweet, lingering kiss. The world around us seems to fade away as his lips move gently against mine, and I lose myself in the warmth and tenderness of the moment. His hand cups my cheek, and I feel a shiver of excitement run through me.

The Ferris wheel begins to move again, breaking our kiss, and we continue to exchange soft, loving glances. Each rotation of the ride gives us a new view of the festival—children darting around with glowing sticks, couples holding hands, and families enjoying the various attractions. Jonah's arm is wrapped around my shoulders, and I rest my head against his chest, feeling the steady beat of his heart. One day, it could be Jonah and I with our kids wandering around the fall festival. The thought of kids was never anything I would have ever considered, but with Jonah, the thought of kids feels right.

By the third rotation, the excitement of the festival below merges with the intimacy I feel being with him right now. The gentle breeze carries the scent of fried dough and sweet treats, mixing with the distant sound of cheerful screams from the roller coaster. Turning to look at him again, our eyes lock, my gaze drifting to his lips before returning to his eyes. His hand caresses the back of my neck, sending sparks down my spine. Our lips part and meet again, and I savor the taste of him, a mix of sweetness and longing.

"Better put your tongues away since you get off next," Jonathan calls out, and we pull our mouths apart to see we are the next ones getting off. I glance at them as they stand by the gate waiting for us.

When we finally step off the ride, Shay links her arm with mine, a mischievous glint in her eye, and whispers, "I just got fingered on the ride."

"Shayla!" I exclaim as I turn to look at her. Her cheeks are certainly flushed. Glancing back at Jonathan, he has a satisfied smirk on his face, knowing she told me.

"I need to use the restroom," she says, leading us in that direction.

"Do you really need to go or just clean yourself up?"

"Both."

While waiting in the short line inside, I ask, "How was it?"

"Amazing. You should give it a try," she laughs.

"Weren't you worried about people knowing what you were doing?"

"No, why? Should I be? Plus, it's thrilling to be spontaneous sometimes."

The guys headed to the men's room at the same time we went to the ladies' room, but it seems the line was shorter for them. When we exit, Jonah and Jonathan are seated on a bench outside, chatting with a brunette with purple streaks in her hair, hanging to the middle of her back.

Before we can make our presence known, Jonah speaks up. "This is the lady of the house; she's the one you need to talk to," he says as we approach. Sometimes I wonder if this man has eyes on the back of his head. He seems to always know when I'm close by.

"Hi, Mrs. Everett," she turns to me. She's quite attractive, with dark brown eyes, sporting short shorts, a cropped white tank top revealing her midriff and pierced belly button, along with cowboy boots.

"Hi, what can I help you with?" I ask, curious who she is or what she's wanting and why Jonah would tell her she needs to talk to me. He's the one in charge, after all—I don't typically make any decisions.

"I recently moved here and wanted to talk to you about potentially working at the stables. I grew up on a farm, adore horses, and I'm willing to do anything you need me to do," she says enthusiastically.

"Are you currently working here in town?"

"No, I've been living off my savings, but I'll eventually need a job," she replies.

"Do you live here locally?"

"I live with my aunt and uncle," she answers. "They've been kind enough to let me stay with them while I get settled."

"Are you wanting to stay living there, or would you be coming to live at the Mansion?"

"Is that possible?" Her eyes light up with excitement at the thought. "I'd love to be closer to the horses and the work."

"Why don't you come by tomorrow, and I can give you a tour? We can discuss everything in more detail," I suggest

"Really?! Thank you so much!"

"Of course. Have a great night," I tell her.

She smiles and waves as she walks away.

"She seems nice," I comment to the others, nudging Jonah's foot, which is crossed over his knee. He puts his leg down, and I take a seat on his lap, leaning back into his chest and resting my head on his shoulder.

"Jonathan finger-banged Shay on the Ferris wheel," I glance up at Jonah and then over at Jonathan, who grins widely.

Since my legs are already spread apart, I can't help but wonder aloud, "Why am I not getting finger-banged?"

Jonah casually responds, "I don't want anyone to see you turned on."

"That's such a lie! Because one, I'm already turned on right now, and two, those two have practically seen us in action as many times as we've done it," I point out, gesturing towards them.

"Yeah, but 'those two' are our best friends, and will be the only ones who witness our intimate moments," Jonah says softly, leaning in to nibble on my ear.

"But I'm feeling horny, and if you don't take care of it, I might just have to do it myself or ask Shay for some help," I say playfully.

Jonah's laugh vibrates against my neck, and I can feel the warmth of his breath. "You're impossible," he says, tightening his arms around me.

"Shut the fuck up… Kal, do you see that?" Shay asks, her mouth hanging open as she stares off in the distance.

Confused, I follow her line of sight to see what she's looking at, and then I see it too. Theo just won a stuffed teddy bear and is handing it to… Lilly!

"Are they on a date?!" I exclaim.

"Who?" Jonathan asks, looking between us and then off into the distance.

Shay stands up, grabbing my hand and pulling me off Jonah's lap. She pulls me toward the games, rounding the corner to make sure we will run into them. We stop just in time to avoid a collision.

"Sorry," Shay says, pretending not to know who we almost bumped into. Then she feigns surprise. "Lilly! Hi," pulling her into a hug.

Lilly blushes, clearly excited.

"Theo?" she greets him. "Great to see you outside work. Are you two here together?" she questions, acting like she hadn't already seen them together.

Lilly looks up at Theo, gauging his reaction.

"We *are* here together," he says, taking her hand in his.

Jonah and Jonathan approach, and Jonah casually drapes an arm around my shoulder. He extends his hand to Theo and says, "Theo."

"Mr. Everett," Theo responds, shaking Jonah's hand.

"Are you guys enjoying the festival?" Jonah asks.

"Very much, sir," Theo replies.

I love that Theo has ditched his hat and styled his hair. Lilly is wearing one of her brightly colored, poofy dresses, and her hair is pulled up into an elegant updo.

"Who's this little guy?" I ask, pointing at her teddy bear.

"Theo just won it for me," Lilly beams.

"Wow, great job, Theo," I praise.

"Thank you, Miss Kalyn. I hear congratulations are in order," he adds, glancing down at my hand.

"Thank you," I follow his gaze to my hand for a moment, not wanting to make a big deal about it. I never quite know how to handle it when a man comments on my ring. Women tend to get all giddy and demand to see the ring immediately, while men often just acknowledge it with a simple, 'Wow, okay, it's just a ring.'

In truth, I can't help but feel the swell of pride when I look at my ring. It's the most beautiful ring I've ever seen and my most prized possession. Its significance goes beyond its beauty; it symbolizes that I get to spend my entire life with Jonah. Plus, he picked the diamond himself and designed the entirety of the ring himself.

"May I?" he asks, gesturing to see my ring up close. I hold out my hand, smiling proudly.

He lets out a long whistle, holding my hand and admiring my ring. "Gorgeous ring for a gorgeous woman. Congratulations to you both."

"Thank you, Theo," I feel a warm blush rise in my cheeks. "You will be invited to the wedding—both of you." I wink at Lilly.

"Do you have a date set yet? Theo asks as he gently releases my hand.

"Not yet," I admit.

Jonah interrupts smoothly, "I've got it all under control," his tone confident. I turn to look at him, one eyebrow raised in curiosity. He meets my gaze and smirks.

Before I can probe further, Lilly pipes up, "Have you tried the pitas yet? They're amazing!"

"Those are my favorite!" I exclaim, turning to her. "The ranch one."

"Wanna go get one?" Lilly offers excitedly. "I've been eyeing them since we got here."

"I'm not hungry, but we can go with you if you'd like," I offer.

"Oh, we're going," Shay insists, waggling her brows at Lilly.

We stroll with Lilly to the food stalls, the guys following behind us. "You have so much explaining to do," Shay whispers out the corner of her mouth to Lilly, who walks between us.

"I'll tell you every detail," Lilly replies, her excitement evident as she raises her shoulders to her ears, trying to contain her joy.

After Lilly and Theo each get a pita, we find a stone bench to sit down. I attempt to sit next to Jonah, but he places his hand in the spot I was aiming for. "You think that will stop me? I've sat on your hand more times than I can count," I challenge.

Jonah laughs and grabs my hips, shifting me to sit on his lap.

"Mr. Everett," a gentleman approaches us with his wife and three small kids in tow. "I just wanted to come and thank you for all you do for the community, sir. The fall festival has become our favorite time of year, and every year it gets even better."

"Can we do this more times a year too?" a little girl says excitedly. She looks to be about Adeline's age.

"What a great idea," I smile at her.

"Look what my daddy won me at the ring toss," she proudly walks to me showing me her little stuffed cat.

"Wow," I exclaim, widening my eyes. "She even has a princess crown that looks just like yours," I point to the crown on her head.

"And I have a cat painted on my face," says the second little girl, who appears to be a year older.

"Oh wow, it looks amazing! If I got my face painted, what do you think I should get?" I turn my face side to side.

"You look like a princess, so maybe like, umm, a unicorn around your eyes," the first little girl suggests.

"Yeah! With wings right here," the second one adds, softly touching her hands on my cheeks.

"Do you want to come play with us," the younger one asks, grabbing my hand.

"No, sweetheart, as much fun as Mrs. Everett would have playing with you both, she's here with her friends," the mom says, smiling at me.

"Thank you all for coming. I'm glad you had a nice time," I tell them, waving at the little girls and the little boy as they go to leave.

"Thank YOU again for funding the festival," the gentleman says before they walk away, waving.

"Kal, kids love you," Lilly observes with a warm smile as she finishes the last bite of her pita.

"Smile!" Shay directs, holding out her phone to take a picture.

Jonah and I turn toward her, and I lean into him. Theo wraps his arm around Lilly, and we all beam for the picture.

"Cute!" Shay exclaims, sending it to each of our phones. "I don't have your number, Theo, but Lilly can send you the picture."

As soon as Lilly gets it, she saves it and announces she's going to upload it to her Instagram.

"You ready to go home, baby?" Jonah murmurs into my neck.

"Yeah, we can get going," I turn to smile at him. It's way past his bedtime, and he's been such a good sport about everything we've done tonight.

We all stand, and Lilly hugs Shay and me. "See you later," she says, and we wave goodbye to Theo.

As we walk away, Shay links her arm in mine. "Holy shit, it's about time," she says, echoing the words I was thinking.

"She must be so excited," I say, genuinely happy for both of them. Lilly has liked Theo for years, and I'm glad she finally got her date with him.

We pass by the game booths, and Shay turns to Jonathan, "If you think we're leaving now without you winning me something, you're cray," Shay declares.

Jonathan laughs and walks her to the basketball hoop game, which is notoriously difficult to win.

"Nobody can win on these," I comment.

Jonah scoffs. "Wanna bet," he says, fully confident Jonathan will in fact win.

"Yeah," I challenge him, but before we have a chance to place a bet, Jonathan shoots, and the ball goes in.

My mouth hangs open in astonishment as I watch Jonathan dominate the impossible basketball game. I always thought nobody could make a basket, given the hoop's oval shape designed to make scoring difficult. The man running the booth tells Jonathan that if he makes another shot, he can upgrade his prize to the next size. Jonathan shoots and sinks it again. Shay jumps up and down, clapping her hands in delight and cheering him on. On the next attempt, the ball bounces off the rim and falls to the side.

Shay immediately picks a big, colorful jellyfish for her prize and hugs it as soon as the man hands it to her.

"What do you want, baby?" Jonah asks, scanning the prizes around us.

I spot a fluffy pink llama stuffed animal at the balloon-popping booth and point excitedly. "I want her!"

The man tells us we can basically have any of the prizes we want, but Jonah insists on winning it for me the proper way. The booth attendant hands Jonah eight darts, explaining that if he pops eight balloons, he can get the pink llama.

With the first dart, Jonah throws it sideways and pops three balloons in a row. We watch him throw the second dart and pop three more. By the third dart, he expertly pops the remaining two balloons he needed to get my llama.

"That was hot, babe," I tell him as the booth attendant looks impressed and hands me the llama. "Thank you," I tell him, grinning wide as I squeeze my new stuffed animal. "Her name is Penelope."

These aren't your average fair toys that feel cheap and filled with Styrofoam. These feel like high-quality stuffed animals from the store. My guess is Jonah made sure all the prizes are top-notch.

Jonah pulls me close and kisses me. "I love you, baby."

We walk back to the truck, and I revel in the amazing time I had today. Jonah and I climb into the backseat, while Jonathan and Shay take their spots in the front. We haven't even left yet, but Jonah's mouth is already on mine, his kiss deep and demanding.

His right arm wraps around me, his elbow resting on the back of the seat, while his left hand deftly finds the button of my shorts and pops it open. He wastes no time as his hand slides down the front of my shorts, seeking out my already wet slit and beginning to rub tantalizing circles.

"You good, Jonathan?" Jonah asks, his voice husky as he pulls away for a moment.

"My full attention is on the road, Boss. You're good to go," Jonathan confirms, his eyes flicking up to the rearview mirror briefly.

I don't fully grasp Jonah's question at first, but it dawns on me he's ensuring Jonathan will stay focused on the drive back since we aren't wearing seatbelts.

A gasp leaves my lips, and my head leans on Jonah's arm as he works his magic. I hadn't realized how turned on I was until his touch ignites a fire within me. His lips move from mine, trailing hot kisses down my jawline and to my neck, where he begins to suck gently.

"I'm gonna fuck you with my fingers, and then my cock," he whispers in my ear before softly biting the curve.

When he starts to slide lower, I arch my hips forward, desperate for him to penetrate me. The anticipation is unbearable, and I'm eager and ready. He slowly slides down my soaking wet slit and pushes inside me, my hips rocking in rhythm with his movements.

I look down, trying to watch his hand, but my shorts obscure the view. All I can see is his forearm flexing, the muscles bulging as he moves his fingers inside me.

"Yes," I pant, feeling him hit my most sensitive spot.

Slipping my hand inside my shorts, I begin rubbing my clit, knowing my orgasm is imminent. As he rocks faster, my hips lift off the seat. My moans grow louder, and I shift my leg over his to spread myself wider, giving him even better access.

Jonah's hot breath against my neck and his whispering in my ear drive me wild. "You like that, baby? You're so fucking wet for me."

My hips buck and rock in time with his fingers, and I can feel the pressure building, my entire body tingling with anticipation. The combination of his fingers thrusting inside me and my hand working my clit sends me spiraling. My body trembles, and I clutch onto him, riding out the waves of pleasure as they wash over me.

I moan as my free fingers dig into his forearm, feeling it flexing with his movements, my chest rising and falling as I come down from that high. Jonah

slows his pace, gently easing out of me. He kisses me softly, both possessive and demanding. We nestle closer together, the truck's movement lulling us into a comfortable silence.

As we pull into the garage and the truck comes to a stop, we all get out. Before Jonah can even start to walk, I push him back against the truck.

"I like where this is going," he murmurs, his voice filled with desire as he gazes down at me.

I drop to my knees, the concrete cool against my skin. My hands deftly work on the button and zipper of his shorts, freeing his impressive erection. The sight of his massive cock makes me salivate. I lean in and lick the tip, savoring the salty taste of his pre-cum. His hands immediately tangle in my hair as he pulls me toward him.

Opening my mouth wide, I take his tip between my lips, hollowing my cheeks as I slowly pull off. Jonah's grip on my hair tightens, a low groan escaping his lips. Encouraged, I take him back into my mouth, moving slowly and deliberately, letting him feel every inch I take.

My hand slides up his thigh, feeling the tension in his muscles as he fights to stay still. My other hand wraps around the base of his cock as I bob my head, taking him deeper each time. The taste of him is intoxicating, the feel of his throbbing cock against my tongue sending waves of arousal through my body.

His breathing grows heavier, his hips subtly inching forward, urging me to take him deeper. I relax my throat, taking him as far as I can. His guttural moan reverberates through the garage, echoing off the walls. I pull back, gasping for breath, then dive back down, increasing my pace.

He guides my movements, controlling the rhythm as he shoves into my mouth. I look up at him, my eyes meeting his, and the raw desire I see there fuels my own arousal. His eyes are dark with lust, his lips slightly parted as he pants with need. I feel his cock twitch and I know he's close.

I pull back slightly, focusing on the tip, my tongue dancing around it while my hand strokes his length. "Fuck, baby," his voice thick with need.

Encouraged by his reaction, I suck harder, creating a tight seal around him. My hand moves faster, matching the rhythm of my head bobbing. I can feel his cock pulsing, his orgasm building until his hot cum spills into my throat. I swallow, savoring the salty taste as he empties himself.

His breathing is ragged, and I gently release him, licking my lips then wiping them with the back of my hand. He pulls me to my feet, murmuring, "Your ass is mine," as his hands roam my body, pulling me close. His lips claim mine, his tongue exploring my mouth with renewed hunger. "Let's get you to bed," he whispers against my lips.

As we head inside, I catch sight of Shay still on her knees in front of Jonathan. The realization that she was doing the same as I had been with Jonah sends a thrill through me—I find it so hot I want to stay and watch, but Jonah keeps pulling us to the house. "Have fun, you two," I call out to Jonathan with a playful grin.

We stumble through the door, our hands all over each other. The door closes behind us with a thud, and Jonah's hands are on my hips, lifting me. He carries me up the stairs, his lips never leaving mine, until we reach the bedroom.

He lays me down on the bed, his eyes raking over my body with unrestrained desire. "You're so fucking beautiful," he breathes, his voice filled with awe. Then he sucks on my neck gently. His hands explore my body, peeling off my clothes piece by piece.

CHAPTER
Thirty-Three

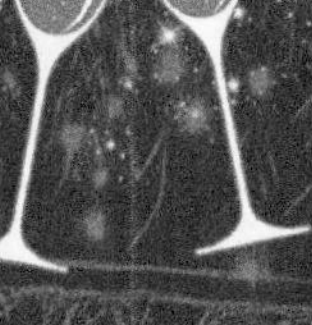

KALYN

I'm sitting in Jonah's office, deep in conversation with him, when there's a knock on the open door. Jonah glances toward the doorway, giving a brief nod in acknowledgment, and I turn to see Giles standing there. "Miss Kalyn, Emma Martin is here to meet with you," he announces.

"Who is Emma Martin?" I ask, utterly confused as I glance at Jonah.

"I believe she's the woman from the festival last night looking for a job," he replies.

"Ohh, right. I never did catch her name. Thank you, Giles," I respond, sliding off the edge of Jonah's desk. Before I can take a single step, his hand encircles my waist, gently pulling me back toward him. With a playful smile, I lean down, and our lips meet briefly in a sweet kiss. "Love you, handsome."

"Love you, baby," he replies, as I head out to meet our random festival interview. I'm already intrigued by Emma, who boldly approached Jonah yesterday to inquire about a job. Especially since he's quite intimidating.

As I greet Emma in the foyer, her enthusiasm is palpable. "Hi, Emma. Thanks for coming by," I say, extending my hand.

"Thank you so much for having me," she meets me with a firm handshake.

"Let's head out to the stables," I suggest, gesturing for her to walk with me. We stroll along the sprawling corridors of the mansion, and Emma's eyes widen in admiration.

"It's even more incredible inside than it is on the outside," she comments.

Her reaction brings back memories of my own first day here, when the grandeur of the estate left me just as speechless back then as it does now. So much has changed since Jenevieve left. We have a new head housekeeper, Yesenia, who has been with Jonah for twelve years. Although she doesn't reside on the premises, she lives nearby in town with her daughter and three grandchildren. Yesenia is a gem—sweet and incredibly hardworking. She not only assigns tasks to the maids but also rolls up her sleeves and works alongside them instead of just supervising. Though I always think Jonah is the perfect example of "lead by example," Yesenia also has this same great trait.

The staff working in the stables now have been given a more relaxed dress code, allowing them to wear either shorts or pants with a T-shirt embroidered with "Everett Stable Staff." Throughout the day, people come and go, eager to ride the horses. This place has become a destination, attracting visitors from far and wide who stay in town just to experience riding the trails that wind across the surrounding forest. Elites from around the world seek out this hidden paradise.

The stable lounge also gets used more frequently, as those who want fresh lunch can have kitchen staff deliver meals directly there. This allows the stable workers to not have to walk through the mansion smelling like the stables, something I always hated doing.

We haven't hired anyone new for a while, as far as I know, because our staff turnover has been non-existent since Jenevieve left. When we do hire, we allow new employees to let us know their preferences, offering them roles where they'll be happiest. We do genuinely want happy staff.

"What kind of stable work are you looking to get involved in?" I ask Emma.

"Anything you have available. I just need a job and love horses. I know how to muck stalls, feed and bathe horses, groom them, and train them. I'm specially trained as a farrier, and I know how to maintain and repair saddles, bridles, and harnesses. I'm also skilled in office and reception work. Really, anything you need, I can do," she says confidently, her passion evident.

"Well, let's go find Claire. She's our go-to for everything out here. She manages the stables and handles the horse grooming. We'll see what she thinks," I suggest as we enter the main building. Despite my cheerful facade, I really don't want to talk to Claire, and I know for a fact she certainly doesn't want to talk to me. I've made a mental note to avoid coming out here when I know Brad and her are both here since she's already mad at me for hanging out with him. Even Jonah seemed slightly off when I got home from Brad's. Not to mention the plethora of texts I got from Shay on our drive back. It appears mine and Brad's friendship isn't well-received by anyone.

The stables are always busy with workers bustling about. The scent of hay and horses fills the air, mingling with the sounds of hooves clopping and soft nickers. We finally find Claire, brushing one of the horses. I introduce Emma to her, and Emma repeats everything she told me.

Claire listens attentively, her expression slowly shifting from neutral to surprised.

"You sound like exactly what we need around here. Can you start tomorrow?" Claire asks, and Emma eagerly accepts. Not that she would really need my permission to hire her because I trust Claire's judgment, and I also agree that Emma would be a great addition to the staff. But, it bothers me that Claire is acting like I don't exist.

"Wonderful, I will see you tomorrow then," Claire says, then gets back to brushing the horse she was grooming.

I take Claire's statement as an end to the conversation and guide Emma out of the building. One thing I never knew, because Jenevieve did a poor job of orientation, is that the maids have their own quarters, while the stable hands have separate housing out here.

We walk down a paved path to another seemingly ordinary stable building adjacent to the staff parking area. Unlike the maid quarters, which are more secluded within the mansion, this building stands alone and opens into a spacious living room with rooms lining the edges. A large staircase leads to more rooms upstairs.

"Upstairs or downstairs?" I ask, knowing there are two empty rooms on the main floor and one available upstairs.

"Upstairs?" she says hesitantly.

I lead her upstairs, guiding her around the balcony that overlooks the living room area, until we reach the farthest room at the top. The key is already in the door, and I twist it open, letting her step inside. As I watch her take in the space, a wave of nostalgia washes over me, making me feel like I've stepped into Gladys's role my first day at the mansion.

"This is your stable apartment if you choose to live here. It's free, and you will still be fully compensated for your work. You can come and go as you please, and there are no curfews. The walls are decently soundproof, but not entirely, so be respectful of your neighbors when it comes to loud music or TV late at night. When you meet with Claire in the morning, she'll get you work shirts," I explain.

"This is amazing, thank you so much, Mrs. Everett," she beams, looking around her new apartment.

"Your keys are in the door. You can leave your door unlocked if you'd like or lock it up. We have carabiners and other key holders for you if you want one. You can also leave the extra key at the stable office in case you accidentally lock yourself out," I tell her.

"Thank you so much for the opportunity. I promise I'm a hard worker, and you won't regret hiring me," she says excitedly.

I walk her back to the mansion around the side of the house to the front where she is parked, as she mentions she's going to go back to her aunt and uncle's to pack and will return after dinner. I show her that when she comes back, she should turn down the left driveway, follow it through the open bridge between the house, and then take the road to the left, which will bring her down to the stables where there is staff parking in the back.

I also inform her that Claire will have sign-on papers for her to fill out in the morning. She thanks me again, and waves as she walks to her car.

It's been a week since Emma started, and she seems to have settled into her new role at the stables, working diligently alongside Claire and the rest of the staff. As I walk out to check on her, I remind myself of my decision to stay out of her personal life, especially concerning Brad. I debated whether I should warn her about him, but I can't imagine telling anyone to avoid him now. Though I acknowledge my relationship with him is unique—different from the fleeting flings he has with other women—it's not my place to interfere with what he does. I just hope he doesn't sleep with her and cause her to quit.

"How's it going?" I ask, stepping into the main stable building where Claire and Emma are grooming a horse.

"Really good," Claire replies. "She is very skilled when it comes to horses."

Emma looks up, clearly pleased with the compliment.

"Do you want to go for a walk?" I ask Emma, noticing she seems eager to take a break. I want to check on her to make sure everything is going as she had hoped.

"Sure," she replies, putting down the horse brush and following me out of the building.

As we stroll along the paved path around the racetrack, I take the opportunity to learn more about her experience so far. "How are you finding everything?"

"It's been fantastic," Emma responds enthusiastically. "Everyone's been so welcoming, and the work is exactly what I hoped for. I'm really grateful for this opportunity."

"I'm glad to hear that. You've certainly impressed Claire, and that's no small feat. She's very particular about who she works with."

"I've noticed. She's a great mentor though, and I've already learned so much from her," she says softly.

As we saunter around the racetrack, Brad interrupts us by stopping the golf cart merely three feet from where we're walking. "I was starting to think you were trying to avoid me, Wanda. You haven't been coming out to see our son."

"I come out every evening to see my son," I retort.

For a moment, he seems bothered, but his smile never falters. "Scared you won't be able to resist me after I cooked you dinner?" he winks.

"You better put the pedal to the metal, Bert, before I rip you out of that golf cart and hulk smash you up and down this entire stable," I playfully threaten, and he laughs.

"Always a pleasure, Wanda. Let me know when you want to join me in anger management," he calls before driving away.

I roll my eyes and continue walking, noticing Emma staring after the golf cart. I call her name, bringing her attention back to me, and she apologizes, hurrying over. We chat for a bit, but I can tell her mind is elsewhere. Stepping on the seat of a nearby shaded picnic table, I take a seat on the table, and she follows, sitting next to me.

"Brad isn't a relationship-type man," I advise her, air-quoting "relationship." "If you get lonely and want a good lay, look no further. But if you're wanting a real relationship, you're not going to find it with him."

She momentarily pretends not to know what I'm talking about. When I don't say anything else, she says, "That won't be a problem. He doesn't even notice me."

I'm taken aback by her response. She's stunning, and I know for a fact Brad would absolutely sleep with her, even if she didn't show any sort of interest in him. Pussy means dick gets wet, to

Brad. And she has the plumbing he's looking for. But then again, he never made a move on me when I started, and he said it was because he thought of me as more than just a fling. Maybe that's the reason he hasn't tried having sex with her?

"Did you and Brad date?" she asks.

"No," I answer honestly.

"You guys have a son together, though?" she questions.

I'm confused why she would think we had a kid together, then remember him mentioning Kodiak. "No, have you met Kodiak?" I point back to the building he's in.

"Yeah! He's the most beautiful foal I've ever seen. Claire said he's yours."

"Brad helped with his birth, and we take him for walks together. Brad likes to say he's our son," I clarify.

"Ohh, okay, that makes more sense," she looks relieved.

"Brad doesn't have kids, though he would be such a great dad," I say with a smile. I realize Emma is watching me intently, and I can almost hear her thoughts trying to figure out if I'm having an affair with Brad. It seems every person comes to the same conclusion, and it pisses me off because I instantly want to blame it on him being a man whore. "How long have you been in town? You were staying with your aunt and uncle?"

She seems tempted to press the topic of Brad but decides against it. "Yes, only about a couple of days. They called out of the blue and practically begged me to come. I really love it here." Her smile reveals her genuine affection for the place. People come to visit from all over and never want to leave. While nobody talks about expanding the town, it grows slowly with new babies and family members moving here to escape their previous lives.

It's like you carry all this tension and stress until you come here, where the atmosphere lifts away all those worries. Some have moved away only to return within a year or two.

On one of my trips to town with Shay and Lilly, we were cruising around, and I noticed a new development being built. It's a subdivision with expensive-looking houses, reminiscent of movie suburbs where men leave for work at the same time and their wives wave from their front porch, perfectly dressed and coiffed.

Lilly said it was Jonah's land, and enough people wanted houses on the property that a hundred homes were pre-sold. About ten are nearly ready for residents, and they are stunning, custom mansions with a pool and a huge park in the center.

"What brought you here?" I ask.

"It was time for a change in scenery. My boyfriend dumped me. Well, actually, he said he wanted to experience everything college had to offer, so I told him he absolutely should and moved here. He has a small penis, so I think he'll quickly realize he doesn't have much to offer college girls, especially when he doesn't know how to use the single inch he was given," she says, and we both start laughing.

"Does he know you're here?"

"Nobody does. Well, my mom and stepdad do, but they never cared for him, so they were more than happy I wanted to get away for a while."

"Are you going to attend the community college in town?"

"No, I have an associate degree in Liberal Arts. College really wasn't for me, though. I grew up on a ranch and love animals. I wanted to be a veterinarian but didn't want to go through that much schooling."

"Do you ride horses?"

"I've been riding since I could walk," she says confidently. "I was the rodeo queen five years in a row. There's nothing like the thrill of the rodeo and the bond you form with your horse."

"Rodeo queen. Wow, that's amazing."

"Let me guess, you were for sure prom queen probably all four years of high school and pageant queen or something similar?"

I let out a laugh. "Not even close."

"Really?" She seems shocked.

"Really."

"It's funny because my aunt and uncle have been trying to get me to move here for years. They always said, 'The man who owns the town is an eligible bachelor and so handsome; you two would make the perfect couple.' When they randomly called to get me to move here, they let me know that Mr. Everett is no longer available; he's engaged to be married, but they think I should come work at his stables. And all I thought was 'Okay, and?'

Then I saw him and was shocked at how young and attractive he is. I thought for sure he would be married to a beautiful, blonde who was stuck-up and treated everyone like gum on her shoe. When I met him at the festival and he told me I needed to speak with you, I was bummed when I saw you walking over because you were everything I expected—until you started talking. I was taken aback by how kind you were. You're well-loved around here. I haven't heard a single bad thing about you," she smiles, and this is probably the most kind and open thing someone has said to me, aside from Shay, who has always been candid with her thoughts.

"Thank you," I reply. "That was very open. I'm glad I met your expectations, and you don't find me stuck-up."

"Sorry, I probably shouldn't have said all that to you."

"No, it's completely fine. I like honesty."

"Claire said you used to work out here. Were you an employee before you and Mr. Everett started dating?"

"Yeah, I was a maid. But the head housekeeper didn't care for me, so she sent me to work in the stables as a punishment. Brad was honestly the only thing that kept me sane during that time. I couldn't stand him at first because he always seemed to harass me. I figured maybe the head housekeeper was paying him to do it or something. Until one day, he told me he was going to talk to her about the way I was being treated. I told him to just stay out of my business and keep his mouth shut."

"How did you and Mr. Everett start dating?"

I sigh, a hint of amusement playing on my lips. "Where to even begin? That's quite the story. I'll tell you what: I'm sure working here, you'll hear all sorts of stories about how we started dating. We're going out of town for a couple of weeks for work. If you hear anything juicy, let me know, and we can swap stories. I'll share the real story with you, and you can see how they compare. For now, I'll let you get back to it. If you need anything, don't hesitate to ask."

"Thank you, I won't," she says as we both stand.

I take the longer way around the stable because I see Brad standing at the fence watching riders on the track. I walk over to him and lean my arms on the fence next to him. Reaching over, I hold the back of my fingers to his forehead. He lets out a laugh, grabbing my hand and staring into my eyes.

"Ignore me one week and get all handsy with me the next; you're gonna give me whiplash, Wanda," he grins, kisses the back of my hand, and lets it go.

"Just checking if you have a fever."

"I look that shitty today, huh?" he muses.

"When was the last time you had sex?"

"You offering?" he smirks.

"Nope, just curious," I respond, lifting a brow.

"I don't know, I wasn't keeping track. Didn't think I'd be quizzed on it, but a week or so. Does that turn you on?"

I knew it. He likes Emma.

"Have a good rest of your day," I say, turning to walk away.

"Come watch the riders with me," he calls after me.

"Nope, you stink," I call back without turning around, already knowing he's smiling.

"You stink too. Get back here," he shouts.

I turn, walking backward for a moment, grinning, then spin back around and keep walking.

CHAPTER
Thirty-Four

KALYN

The city's usual lively energy is always such a stark contrast to the serene countryside that I've grown so accustomed to. Even after a week here, my body isn't used to the constant liveliness. By the time this week is over, and we're headed back to the mansion, my body will just be getting used to being here. It's the start of the second week away on business, and Monday rolls in at a slow pace. I've been in my office, the early morning light filtering through the windows behind me, meticulously reviewing quarterly reports for several companies on probation for altering their submissions. Each line of data requires careful attention, but the slow trickle of information leaves my mind wandering.

Shay sits in her office next door, going over different reports. I wonder if she's just as bored as I am. I also wonder what Jonah is doing. Bridget keeps walking past my office to his and then back to her desk, so I know she's getting more work information to give him. The windows in here are soundproof, but I can almost imagine the outside noise. I peer out the window, my eyes landing on the adjacent buildings as I reminisce about the amazing morning sex Jonah woke me up to. He was sweaty from his workout, and I licked up every bit of sweat I could reach as he had his way with me.

My computer pings with an incoming message, pulling me back to the present. I turn toward my monitor and see an instant message from Shay appearing on my right screen.

Shayla Harper: I want to fuck my husband

> **Kalyn Bell:** Me too. I mean… I want to fuck your husband too… in case I wasn't clear 😜

Shayla Harper: *giggity* I sent him a picture… up my dress… he hasn't even opened it.

Shayla Harper: … he just opened it *swoon*

> **Kalyn Bell:** …. Isn't he in a meeting? LOL

> **Jonah Everett:** Yes, he's in a meeting.

> **Kalyn Bell:** Babe, get out of our PRIVATE chat.

Shayla Harper: You act like you own the company or something 👩

Jonah Everett: Something like that.

Jonah Everett invited Jonathan Harper to the conversation
Jonathan Harper accepted invite

Shayla Harper: This is an A and B conversation, both of you better C your way out.

Jonah Everett: @JonathanHarper Our wives are being naughty

Shayla Harper: 🙀

Kalyn Bell: 👱‍♀️ 🧑‍🦱

Jonathan Harper: Come fuck me wife

Kalyn Bell: 👅💦💦

Shayla Harper: Is your meeting over?

Jonathan Harper: My part is. Camera off.

Kalyn Bell: Lucky….

Jonah Everett: I'm not in a meeting, baby. Come here.

Kalyn Bell: 🐼👉👌 cumming

We exit our offices simultaneously, exchanging knowing grins. Shay heads to Jonathan, while I make my way to Jonah.

Entering Jonah's office, I find him leaning back in his chair, his chin propped on his knuckles, his pointer finger resting against his cheek as he leisurely swivels back and forth. His eyes lock onto mine, exuding a mixture of authority and desire that would be intimidating if this was my first time ever encountering him.

My grin widens as I approach, noticing his other hand drifts down toward his erection straining against his pants. The sight sends a thrill through me. As I approach, I reach behind me to unzip my skirt, the sound of the zipper echoing in the room. Stopping in front of him, I slowly lower it, letting it pool around my feet before placing it neatly on his desk. Standing before him in just my thong and blouse, I feel his eyes devouring every inch of me.

I slowly pull my blouse over my head and unsnap my bra, letting my breasts spill free. The way his eyes light up as he gazes at my body makes me feel powerful and irresistible.

"I hear you need some special attention, sir." I bite my lip as I straddle his lap; the heat from his body radiates into mine. My hands move to his pants, and I take my time undoing his belt, button, and zipper until I can wrap my fingers around the hardness of his throbbing member, and the way he twitches in my grasp.

His hands slide up to my hips, caressing my skin. I shift my thong to the side and glide him along my slit, teasing us both. The sensation of him pressing against me is intoxicating, and I savor the feeling before finally positioning him to fill me.

"You're so sexy," I whisper as I begin to lower myself onto him. He lets out a shaky exhale, his grip tightening on my ass. The sound of his breathless response fuels my need, and I move slowly, relishing every inch as he fills me.

"Thank you. I think that's all for now," I murmur, feigning an attempt to rise, teasing him with the possibility of leaving.

Before I can lift off him, he secures my hips with a desperate need. He pulls me down hard, burying himself deep, and I gasp at the stretch while he groans, our bodies locking into rhythm.

The world outside ceases to exist as we move together, his hands roam my body, exploring, caressing, claiming me.

I begin unbuttoning the bottom of his shirt. His hands move to his tie, loosening it, before he starts unbuttoning the top of his shirt. Our hands meet in the middle, a brief but electrifying touch. As soon as his shirt is open, my lips find his chest, sucking and kissing his skin as I continue to ride him. My hips move in slow, sensual circles, swaying and bouncing.

Sitting up, my fingers slide into his hair. I pull him closer, guiding him to my breasts, craving the feel of his lips and tongue on my skin. As soon as he latches onto me, a rush of heat floods through me. I bring my hands behind me, resting them on his knees, giving me leverage to gyrate on him. My eyes fluttering closed as I rock my hips.

"You feel so good," I moan, pulling him deeper into my chest while my other arm supports me on his knee.

Minutes stretch into an eternity of bliss as we ride the waves of our desire. Finally, with a shuddering release, we collapse into each other, spent but deeply satisfied.

Reluctantly, I extricate myself from his embrace as he watches me with a satisfied smile. "Thank you for filling me with all that," I laugh, glancing down before reaching for some tissue on his desk.

I fasten my bra and slip on my blouse, enjoying Jonah's eyes watching me intently. As I pull up my skirt and tuck in my top, Jonah straightens his shirt, tucking it back into his slacks and adjusting his tie.

As I'm finishing tucking in my blouse, the door swings open, and Bridget steps in. Her eyes briefly widen at the scene before her, but she quickly composes herself. Jonah reaches for my zipper, closing it smoothly and letting his hand linger on my backside.

"These are the documents for your next meeting. I've highlighted the areas needing correction and just need your signature," Bridget says, handing him a stack of papers.

With a final smooth of my hands down my skirt, I prepare to exit. Jonah snakes his arm around my waist, pulling me back against his chest. He leans around me, pressing his lips to mine.

"Bye," I step away from his embrace. "Bridget, since I know you keep tabs on everyone who enters and exits this office, please knock and wait to be invited in when Mr. Everett and I are alone in here." I shoot her a pointed look, then glance at Jonah. His grin tells me he finds the situation amusing as he settles back into his chair, while Bridget gapes at me in disbelief before continuing with her update.

As I pass by Jonathan's office, his door is open, and he's leaning back in his chair, deep in conversation on the phone. I smile at him, and he winks in return while continuing his call.

Just as I reach my door, Miles approaches. "It seems like the audit did some good. Numbers appear to be coming in accurately now."

"Unfortunately, they should have been the entire time," I remark as I settle behind my desk.

Miles takes a seat across from me. For the next hour, we chat about how weird it was for companies to try to steal by reporting false numbers. Miles tells me he went to a concert on Saturday, and the band invited him to hang out on their tour bus. It was a band I've never heard of, and he said I should listen to some of their music because it's a "vibe." Miles is so professional at work, but I get the feeling he's super laid back and fun to hang out with outside of work. He's always a welcome distraction every time he comes to chat.

Eventually, he returns to his desk, and I sign back into my computer, and a new message box pops up.

Shayla Harper: I started a new conversation without....

Kalyn Bell: How was your "meeting" with the hubby?

Shayla Harper: Very productive. How was yours? I saw you got called into the BOSSES office!!!

Jonah Everett: She is definitely getting a raise.

Kalyn Bell: Babe! Get out of our chat! Creeper.

Shayla Harper: Don't you have work to do, Mr. Everett?

Jonah Everett added Jonathan Harper to the conversation
Jonathan Harper accepted invite

Jonah Everett: Don't YOU have work to do?

Kalyn Bell: We just put in a lot of work. My legs are still shaking.... Was my work not good enough, Mr. Everett?

Jonah Everett: Now that you mention it, take the rest of the day off. It is well earned.

Jonathan Harper: @ShaylaHarper Talk more about how productive your meeting was (Include pictures)

Kalyn Bell: I'm going to send a picture of my butthole if you don't get out of our private chat.

Jonah Everett: (loosens tie and kicks shoes off) Let the show begin

Shayla Harper: Perverts. Both of you.

Jonathan Harper: You married me

Kalyn Bell: I'm rethinking this whole marriage thing. I'm never getting married.

Shayla Harper: *Grabs popcorn*

Jonathan Harper: Any last words Kal? You just fucked up, love.

CHAPTER

Thirty-Five

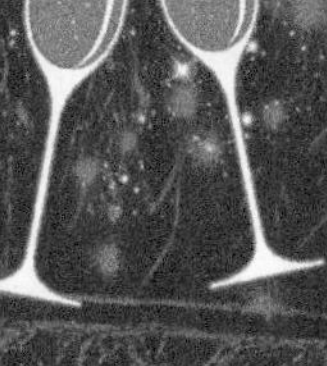

JONAH

I read the words "never getting married" repeatedly, doubting my ability to read correctly. For a brief moment, I think I may have forgotten how to read. I wonder if I'm experiencing a bout of dyslexia, mixing up the words. Even though she has already accepted my proposal, and I know she's just fucking with me, my brain finally registers that I *AM* reading the words correctly, and it compels me to get up from my chair and head toward her office.

I hear Jonathan laughing as I walk past his door. I stride to her office, shove her door open, and carelessly slam it shut behind me. She looks pleased with herself, fully aware of what brought me here. Without even looking up, she continues to focus on her screen.

Standing behind her, I lean over her chair, sliding my hands under hers as they hover over the keyboard.

Kalyn Bell: Kalyn is busy. - Everett

"Never getting married, huh?" I spin her chair around, leaning over her.

"Yep, I don't need a contractual bind to anyone," she replies confidently.

A wicked grin spreads across my face as I gently brush my fingertips down her cheek, along her jaw, and around the back of her head. I grip her hair firmly and pull her up from her chair. "Get on your knees, baby," I command. Arousal lights up her eyes, and she immediately complies, pulling her skirt up over her knees as she lowers herself down, sitting back on her heels and staring up at me. Our gazes lock, and I can't help but notice how painfully stunning she is as she waits for my next instruction.

The office door opens, and without looking, I know it's Shay. From the corner of my eye, I see Jonathan standing behind her, likely coming to investigate why her last message appeared to be from me. Now they know.

"Undo my belt," I command.

Without breaking eye contact, her hands move to my belt, quickly undoing it. Then her small fingers work on the button of my pants. My hold on her hair tightens.

"Did I give you permission to unbutton my pants?"

She bites her lip and subtly shakes her head no.

"Is there anything you have to say? Anything you want to correct?"

She hesitates for a moment, contemplating how to respond, before a devilish smile spreads across her face and she shakes her head no again.

She wants to play.

"Undo my pants and pull my cock out. Now," I order.

Her red lips part as she begins unfastening my pants. When she pulls my cock out, her eyes widen, and she unconsciously licks her bottom lip. She stares up at me, waiting for instructions.

I know what she wants, and she knows what to do. I pull her head towards me while moving my hips forward, feeling her lips part as she takes me into her mouth.

"Fuck," I groan as her soft tongue caresses the underside of my shaft. Her head and hands move rhythmically, back and forth, and I can't tear my eyes off of her. The way she moves, the way her lips wrap around me, is intoxicating. Her eyes close, and a look of pure pleasure crosses her face as she hollows her cheeks and sucks slowly.

Holding her head steady, I begin thrusting. She wants to hold our marriage hostage. Let's see how "bad" she feels when my cum fills her mouth.

The sight of her on her knees, taking me so eagerly, is utterly sexy. Her hands move to my thighs as she deepens her rhythm, her head bobbing up and down at a tantalizing pace.

"Look at me," I command. Her eyes flutter open, locking onto mine. The intensity in her gaze, mixed with the lust and sub-mission—so good. Her breath is hot and ragged around me. Her tongue swirls around my tip, teasing and coaxing. My hips bucking as I lose control, driven by the need to claim her.

"You're so good at this," I rasp, my voice raw with arousal. She responds by sucking harder, her cheeks hollowing with the effort, and her eyes never leaving mine. The pressure builds, my body tenses, and my muscles coil. Holding her in place, I glide into her relentlessly, each time deeper and more urgent. She continues sucking even as saliva begins to leak out of the side of her mouth.

"You like that, don't you?" I murmur hoarsely. Her hands dig into my thighs, her nails peeling the skin back as she urges me to let go.

I can feel it building—the intense, unstoppable force of release. "I'm going to fill your mouth, and you're going to swallow every drop," I growl. Her eyes darken with desire, and she works me with renewed vigor. The sight of her, so eager and willing, is all it takes. With a shuddering release, I spill into her, shoving as far into her throat as I can go, even if it cuts off her oxygen—she will swallow everything I give her.

She takes it all, her hands coming to my hips and pushing against me as I choke her with my cock. Tears pour from her eyes as she struggles to breathe, but she doesn't stop. When I finally release her hair, she pulls off me, gasping for air and swallowing before she's back on me, milking every last drop. I watch, mesmerized. Her eyes find mine again, filled with satisfaction and a hint of defiance, showing she won't give up even if I try to choke her.

"Fuck," I groan. She pulls back slowly, her lips letting go of me with a soft, wet pop. She sits back on her heels, wiping the corner of her mouth with a finger, her eyes glinting with triumph.

"You think that's going to change my mind?" Her voice is husky. I reach down, pulling her up to her feet, my hands sliding over her body, feeling every curve, every soft inch of her.

"We'll see," I murmur, capturing her lips in a fierce, possessive kiss, tasting myself on her tongue. Flopping down in her chair, I breathe heavily. She takes a step closer and sits on my lap, resting the back of her head on my chest as my arms encircle her. We sit in silence for a while until she breaks it.

"Thank you, husband, that will be everything. You are dismissed," she says as she stands.

"Now you accept the idea that you *will* be my wife?"

"I never doubted that I would be your wife. In fact, I demand it. I just wanted my face fucked. You'd have to cut my finger off to get this ring back. Now go," she sits on the edge of her desk, waiting for me to stand.

"Thank you for that incredible blow job; you can expect to see it reflected on your paycheck." I fasten my pants and lean in for a kiss.

"What would you have done if she passed out from you choking her?" Shay asks, sitting in one of the chairs across from the desk. Jonathan occupying the other.

"I would keep fucking her face until I was satisfied."

"If you don't fuck my face like that, I'm getting our marriage annulled," Shay tells Jonathan.

"Your threats are useless, honey." Jonathan reaches over, pats Shay's leg, and gives it a squeeze. "I'll fuck your face like that. Senpai teaches good."

Shay laughs, then informs me that my "shadow" was searching for me. "Bridget tried walking by. We told her you had Kalyn's mouth busy, and she stopped and walked away. She'll be looking for you if she's not standing outside the door waiting."

Kalyn's eyes widen, "Did anyone see?"

"We closed the door," Shay winks.

"With us inside," Jonathan adds proudly.

"Yeah, I can still see your boner, pervert," Kalyn says, leaning back on her desk, noticing Jonathan is pitching a tent.

"In his defense, watching you being dominated was fucking hot, Kal," Shay chimes in.

"Maybe I want to watch you get dominated," Kalyn retorts.

"Dominate me," Shay challenges Jonathan.

Kalyn looks expectantly at Jonathan. "Well?"

He laughs, then stands. "We have a meeting in ten minutes," he points out, gesturing toward me. I glance at my watch and reluctantly stand.

"Keep it up, and I will take you to the courthouse and marry you," I threaten.

"Maybe I would prefer that," she lifts a brow.

I lean in and kiss her, then stride out of the office with Jonathan following behind. "That should have been recorded, Kal. I half wanted to watch and half wanted to finger myself," Shay says as we leave.

"Be good, honey," Jonathan tells her before we round the corner.

We stride down the hallway, assuming our professional roles. Yet, all I can think about is how I want to turn right back around and go fuck Kalyn. Jonathan checks his watch, prompting Bridget to glance over at him as we quicken our pace.

Straightening my tie one last time, I enter the conference room. The key executives from Cromwell Capital Group already fill the space, their faces etched with concentration. The older gentleman at the opposite end of the table appears confident, but his demeanor will matter little if he fails to provide the information I requested.

Now that Kalyn is aware of my past with Bridget, it sharpens my senses, making me hyper-aware of everything Bridget does. She stares longer than she should, especially during meetings, her eyes flicking between me and Jonathan with a hint of longing. A single glare is enough to make her shift uncomfortably, adjusting her posture and refocusing.

This interminable meeting drags on, and I struggle to stay engaged, unable to stop staring at Jonathan's ring finger. As the older Cromwell executive addresses the room, Jonathan dutifully jots notes on his pad. It still feels surreal that he is finally married. I always knew he would marry Shay; *he* always knew he would marry Shay. But now that it's official, it still feels surreal.

I remember the day he returned home from visiting his family. He told me he had met "the one" at the airport. Half-expecting him to have brought her back with him, I asked where she was, thinking they'd spend a week together in bed before he would send her back to wherever she came from. But he didn't have her with him; he didn't even have her phone number—just a first name.

For the next three weeks, he obsessively scoured the Internet, searching for every possible spelling of "Shay," desperately trying to find his mystery woman. Then, business obligations took us out of the country, forcing him to shift his focus back to work.

When we finally returned home, I had barely made it to my office, removed my jacket, and sat down when Jonathan burst into the room, his eyes wide with excitement.

"What?" I wondered if someone died.

"She's here…" he breathed out, flopping into the chair opposite my desk.

"Who's here?" I asked, still not understanding.

"Shay," he replied breathlessly.

"Bring her in," I said, confused as to why she isn't with him.

"She doesn't know I'm here. What if she doesn't feel the same about me? She might not even remember me. Maybe she was just looking for a hookup on the plane."

"Back up. Two questions: is she not here for you? And you hooked up with her on the plane?" Now I'm really confused.

"No, I never found her, and yeah, in the bathroom," he admitted.

"Good," I nodded, processing the fact that he had sex with her on the plane. "Is she an employee?"

"Maid."

"Okay, that's easy enough. Housekeeping is wrapping up for the day. I'll send her to your office to clean tomorrow, and you can act like you didn't realize she worked here. It's not a big deal, Jonathan. She'll love you," I assured him. And I meant it. Jonathan is a ladies' man because he's good-looking and the funniest guy I have ever met. But he's never had it this bad for anyone before. I think he literally fell in love with her at first sight.

Now, I often catch him glancing down at his ring finger with a contented smile on his face. He's a proud man. Watching him, I realize I don't want to wait to marry Kalyn. I want her to be mine now. *I need her to be mine.*

"Wanna wear it?" he whispers, smirking at me.

"Let's take the girls on a vacation this weekend," I whisper back.

"Hell yeah. Where to?"

"I'm marrying Kalyn." The declaration is firm, ignoring his question.

His grin widens. "Does she know?"

"She will when we get there. Think she's talked to Shay about dresses?"

"If she has, I doubt she envisioned a wedding with just the four of us. I can have Shay take her shopping to get some ideas."

"Yeah."

"Done."

The thing about Kalyn is she *would* prefer an intimate wedding over a big one any day. The only reason I'd consider a large wedding would be for my mother, since she would be the only mother Kalyn has. It could have been special, but my mom has chosen to be impossible, so I won't subject Kalyn to that.

"Think she'll care Sam isn't invited?" he whispers cautiously.

"I'll give her a real wedding later. This is just to make her my wife."

"Tie her down now before she changes her mind about marrying you." He playfully nudges my shoe.

"She can change her mind all she wants, but she won't ever get away."

"She won't want to get away—she likes your cock."

He pulls out his laptop and starts typing, the bluish hue on the screen casting a glow on his face. My leg bounces with impatience, a mix of the dragging meeting and my eagerness to marry Kalyn.

Jonathan's face brightens as he turns his laptop around. The screen shows a secluded beach—the very image of a tropical paradise. Crystal-clear turquoise waves gently brush the shoreline, the almost-white sand glistening under the sun. Palm trees sway in the breeze, their shadows dancing on the sand. In the center is an elegant wedding setup with an arch adorned with white roses and trailing ivy. Delicate petals of pink and white form a floral path leading from the edge of the beach to the archway. Lanterns hang from shepherd hooks lining the aisle.

"Book it," I tell him, staring at the picture and imagining Kalyn standing there in a dress, saying her vows.

He clicks on another tab. "He should be able to officiate the ceremony and handle all the legalities, including the marriage certificates. You'll just have to pay for his trip and time. I've sent him an email and will let you know when I hear back. I know he'll agree." Another click reveals a third tab. "A private band that will play an acoustic set, if that's what you want. Or we can have music from a speaker. They seem set up for both."

"Yeah, that sounds good. Have it all ready for Friday."

"Your official wedding day will be October 23. That's nice." He pulls his computer back and resumes typing.

CHAPTER
Thirty-Six

KALYN

"That caught me off guard. I didn't know what I should be doing," I tell Shay, recalling Jonah barging into my office. I knew I'd get some sort of reaction out of him for saying I didn't want to get married; I just didn't know what reaction I would get. "It might be one of my favorite times I've ever given him a blowjob. Who knew pretending to not want to get married would have such a sexy effect on him."

"I almost intervened when he wasn't letting you get air," Shay chuckles. "What'd you expect was going to happen teasing him like that? You had my heart lurching in my throat when I read it."

"You think that man would let me die? I could die, and he'd find a way to the afterlife just to drag me back," I retort, knowing damn well Jonah would never do anything that would actually hurt me.

"Or you'd think you were finally getting a break from him, only to find him hot on your heels, cutting in line to stay right behind you, because heaven forbid you do anything without him," laughter ringing in her voice. "Let's grab a snack," she suggests, rising from her chair.

Grabbing my purse, we walk to the elevator and go down to the food court. After she gets an ice cream cone, we settle on a couch by the large bay windows to enjoy the view.

"Have you ever considered having a threesome with Jonathan?"

"Are you asking because you're down?" She licks her ice cream cone, looking in my direction.

I let out a laugh. "Quit seeming so eager—I'm asking in general."

She pauses, considering her answer. "Yeah, I've imagined it a lot."

"Do you think it would affect your relationship afterward?"

"Not in the slightest. You and Mr. Everett are the only people I'd let in our bed, and I refuse to let anything come between our relationship," she asserts, her eyes sincere.

"Have you ever thought about it? Us?" I probe.

"Kal, I've touched myself thinking about you being the one who did it. I've had Jonathan go down on me while fantasizing it was you, even coming to your name. If Mr. Everett weren't so possessive, I'd have already suggested we explore that," she confesses with remarkable openness.

"How do you think Jonathan feels about that?"

"Hun, Jonathan wants to fuck you, but he likes his dick and knows Mr. Everett would probably cut it off if he voiced it," she remarks knowingly.

"How do you feel about that?"

"I want to watch Jonathan fuck you so bad. I want to replace the image of our guys fucking Bridget with them fucking you."

"I have to be honest about something," I begin.

Her smile grows wider. "Do tell."

"After you mentioned Jonathan and Jonah having sex with me, I found myself dreaming about it that night," I hesitate, wondering if I should continue. "I woke up so wet I had to sneak into our closet just to play with myself."

"Annnnd…" she encourages, leaning in closer.

"And I used that vibrator you mentioned, imagining it was you and Jonathan with me," I confess.

"And did you imagine Mr. Everett watching?"

"No, I… fingered myself… from behind, imagining it was Jonah."

"Okay, so you fantasized about all three of us having you?" she seeks clarification.

"Yes, and I'm sorry I did that," I admit, feeling ashamed now that I said it out loud.

"Sorry?! For what? We can make that happen right now if you think Mr. Everett would be on board. Well wait, has he put his dick in your booty?"

"No, I'm too scared," I confess.

"Maybe once you guys can successfully do that, we can come back around to this. Both of them taking you, with their size, would really hurt if it's his first time in there. And since I know Jonathan has wanted to bed you longer than I have wanted to, I'm not sure he could restrain himself enough to be gentle the first time. I want it to be good for you, not something that leaves you traumatized," she leans in so our shoulders touch.

"I think that's why I got so mad about Bridget. Right after I'd imagined the scenario, I found out they took her exactly how I envisioned them having me, minus you being in my fantasy. It made me furious that she got to experience them both, and I wanted that."

"Yeah, fuck her," she dismisses briskly.

"Would you want to have sex with Jonah?" I ask, realizing I've never considered that possibility. If I'm going to be with Jonathan, she might expect the same with Jonah, and the thought makes me feel queasy. How hypocritical to want Jonathan to pleasure me, but not want Jonah to do the same to her.

"I'm drawn to people for who they are. For the most part, I find men off-putting. I've been in more relationships with women than men. I prefer a woman's body over a man's. And I prefer Jonathan over any other person on this earth. If I get a threesome with someone, it sure as fuck won't be with another man. Jonathan would agree. We can happily spend forever just the two of us. But if we're spicing things up, we both want you. Mr. Everett would gladly only ever have his dick in you, and I'm good with that. To answer your question directly, Mr. Everett is sexy as fuck, but he has the same anatomy as Jonathan, so I'm not interested."

"You don't want what Bridget had?"

"Two big-ass dudes fucking me? Hell no. I want my big-ass dude and a dildo, plus you."

"What's the difference between a woman going down on you versus a man?"

"Have you ever kissed a woman?"

"No," I answer truthfully.

"That's okay," she reassures. "Women are gentle, soft, and sensual. Men can be more intense. Their kissing is hard and passionate, while women have softer skin; their touch is more delicate. I've watched Mr. Everett eat you, and he leaves no crumbs. He devours you, buries his face in your pussy like he's in a full-blown make-out session with it. Women know how to touch a pussy, knowing precisely how to be tender in all the right ways. Plus, our hands are smaller, and while men can reach deep, sometimes the gentle precision from a smaller hand can be just as satisfying, if not more so. So, have I sold you on hooking up with me yet?" She lets out a laugh.

"You never had to sell me on it. I've been down. It's my partner that we have to convince," I share with a conspiratorial grin.

We grab smoothies and make our way back to the elevator. Thankfully, it's empty when the doors open—a rare blessing, given how crowded they usually are. As the elevator ascends, I repeatedly press the "door close" button, hoping to avoid any additional stops, but the doors stubbornly open on the next floor.

Shay and I exchange amused glances, as the doors part to reveal two incredibly attractive men. Jonah steps inside, a smirk playing on his lips. "Baby, were you trying to make the elevator skip this floor?" He wraps his arms around me. My hands instinctively move up to his shoulders as he kisses me.

"I was trying. It obviously didn't work. I wasn't expecting my stalker to be standing at the door."

Jonah chuckles, then places his lips around the straw of my smoothie and takes a sip. "Strawberry banana?"

"Do you like it?"

With a low, seductive tone, he asks, "Yeah, can I have more?" Rather than take another sip, he leans in and kisses me deeply, his tongue exploring my mouth as I was trying to offer him the cup.

The intimate moment is interrupted by a gentle pat on his back. Glancing up, I see Jonathan smirking at us as he walks by, with Bridget waiting outside the open elevator doors. Shay and Jonathan stroll down the hall, their arms wrapped around each other.

Smiling, we exit the elevator, his fingers laced with mine. "So you didn't actually want more of my drink," I clarify, taking another sip.

"I wanted to taste it on your tongue," he murmurs, giving my hand a squeeze.

When I get back to my office, my phone has a missed voicemail. I smile when I hear the Scottish accent. "Call me back, Lass. It's strictly work-related. I don't want to know how you and Mr. Perfect are doing. This is fancy toes, in case you forgot. Call me back." The message ends with a click.

Aware of the time difference, I know it's late evening where he is, but he called just an hour ago, so he's likely still awake. I pull up the video call on my computer and dial him. He answers on the second ring, and I'm greeted by the sight of the ceiling as he walks around.

"Give me a second to put a shirt on, Lass," he says, setting his phone down. Moments later, he picks it up again, now fully dressed and grinning wide. "Good afternoon. Did you get in some afternoon delight?" He winks, and my eyes widen. "Aye, you did." He seems quite pleased with himself.

"What can I do for you, Mr. McIntosh?"

"Show me your finger," he responds.

I try to maintain a serious face but can't contain my smile and hold up my hand.

"Get that back from the camera, lass. You both can't fit in the frame," his eyes widen. "I'll bet Britches loved seeing that," he grins.

"Everyone should love seeing it; it's a pure form of commitment and happiness." I beam with pride.

"Aye, don't forget my invite to the wedding. I know someone who could do your nails."

We talk for the next thirty minutes, covering everything from work to personal anecdotes. His daughter even joins the call, and I gush about the amazing pedicure she did on her dad, which makes her eyes light up with excitement. He even introduces me to his wife, who is an absolute doll.

"Before you go, is there anything work-related that I can help you with?"

"I had a naggin' feelin' you had a new piece of jewlery; I needed to see if my suspicions were true."

"Are you a clairvoyant too?" I roll my eyes, unable to hide my amusement.

"I've got all kinds of talents up my sleeves. I'm like a magician with a hat full of tricks."

I laugh and shake my head. "Well, I'll keep that in mind if I ever find myself in need of a magic show. Have a good evening, Mr. McIntosh."

"You as well, Lass." Then the call ends.

CHAPTER
Thirty-Seven

KALYN

Some days, I just need to be near Jonah, overwhelmed by my love for him, and come to hang out in his office just to be in his presence. He never seems to mind; in fact, he always looks so happy when I walk in with my arms piled full of papers and silently take a seat across from him at his desk. Most days, he just smiles and keeps on working. Other times, he says something like, "Took you long enough, I needed something pretty to look at."

Today, I sit comfortably in his office, immersed in the stack of reports spread out before me. So far, everything appears to be good. It seems these companies are finally understanding that Jonah won't tolerate stealing. It's surprising that, despite Jonah's reputation for being a hard-ass, some people still felt ballsy enough to try and be sneaky.

"Stop staring at me, Mr. Everett, or I'm going to tell on you," I grin, keeping my focus on the reports.

"Who will you tell?" he asks casually, swiveling lazily in his chair.

"Keep it up and you'll find out," I peek up from the papers to meet his gaze.

"I can't help it. You're so beautiful."

His phone suddenly rings, slicing through the quiet hum of the rustling papers. He picks it up, his eyes still fixed on me. He answers in his trademark authoritative tone, "Everett." I continue scanning the reports, listening to his commanding voice. He's so intimidating on the phone. I wonder if people ever get nervous having to make a call to him, especially when they're giving bad news.

"Who authorized that decision?… Then perhaps you should consider working for him if you prefer taking orders… Close the deal, or are you suggesting it's beyond your capabilities? … Call me back when you have actionable updates." With a decisive click, he ends the call.

While I would dread being on the receiving end of that call, being his fiancée on the other side of his desk makes me want to climb over it and devour him right there.

"Come on, Kal, we're going shopping," Shay announces, breezing into Jonah's office.

Jonah looks up from his computer, his fingers still moving across his keyboard as he watches her approaching.

"*WE* are working, Shay," I grin, casting a look over my shoulder at her.

"No, we *were* working. Now we're going shopping. I want to get out of the office. Mr. Everett, I'm stealing your fiancée, and we're going shopping," she declares, grabbing the papers off my lap and placing them on the corner of his desk. She holds out her hands to me, helping me up, then holds her hand to Jonah.

He shakes his head in defeat. Opening his desk drawer, he grabs his wallet and pulls out a black card, handing it to her. "Have fun," he chuckles.

She snatches it out of his hand. "We will. Let's go, hun."

Walking around the desk, I wrap my arms around Jonah and kiss him. "I feel so naughty playing hooky from work. Don't tell my boss. See you in a bit, lover face," I murmur against his lips, stealing another kiss before hurrying after Shay.

"See ya later, sucker," Shay says to Jonathan as we pass him in the hall. He just laughs and keeps walking.

We meander through various stores, browsing the racks for new lingerie, and she takes me to a boutique specializing in dresses. "Did you ever go to prom?" she asks.

"I did."

"With Sam?" Her curiosity is evident.

"Yes, with Sam."

"I need pictures," she insists.

"Sam actually has them. I don't have any copies."

"Have you talked with either of them since the bachelorette party?" she asks.

I hesitate, unsure of how to respond. "No, I feel super betrayed by Amber, and I don't want to hear Sam's excuses for her weird behavior." My frustration is still fresh, especially since Sam took her to my family's graves without talking to me about it first, and then she continued visiting them on her own. This topic is definitely dampening my mood.

As she continues rifling through the dress racks, she casually asks, "What kind of dress did you wear to prom?" Oblivious to my growing irritation. Not with her, but with how easily Sam tried replacing me with the first woman who came along. And I mean literally replacing me because he's taking her to my parents' grave. It's so disrespectful.

"An all-black one."

"I can't picture it. I imagine something sexy and skin-tight, maybe a sparkly red one, like the dress you wore at the Gala. Ooo, look at this!" she exclaims, holding up a short white lace dress with delicate shoulder straps. "My wedding dress was so poofy; I fantasized about Jonathan lifting it up in the limo and having sex right after the wedding, but there was too much material. I wish I had chosen something like this. Easy access."

"I want a form-fitting dress, but now that you mention it, that might make it hard too. Jonah loves to rip my clothes off," I muse.

"At least he can afford to replace all the clothing he destroys. Find a short dress. We're trying them on."

We both select dresses and head to the dressing rooms. After trying them on, we step out into a room with an entire wall of mirrors.

"Wow, Kal, that dress is sexy," she says, eyeing me up and down.

"I was going to say the same about yours. I thought we were picking out white ones. Why is yours pink?"

"It's blush pink, your favorite. Bend over," she instructs.

I comply. "Do you like the view?" I tease.

"Your panties definitely won't stand a chance with Mr. Everett," she observes.

"Mine is over-the-top, and yours is modest. Let's switch. I want to see you in this one."

"No way! Your tits look amazing in that dress," she compliments as she continues taking in my appearance. She appears deep in thought but doesn't say anything more.

I turn towards the mirror, admiring how the dress accentuates my figure. "Do you think Jonah is more of a boob or ass man?" I examine the back of the dress, trying to decide if I were getting married, which feature would I try to highlight. My boobs do look really good in this dress, but it's so short in the back my entire ass almost hangs out. It definitely seems slightly inappropriate for a wedding. But for just Jonah, he would love it.

"Mr. Everett is a YOU man."

We remove the dresses, a little reluctant to part with them, and hand them back to the woman at the front of the store. "Is there a restroom I could use?"

"Of course," the woman replies, pointing me in the right direction. "Just down the hall to your left."

When I return, Shay is chatting with the saleswoman. As soon as she catches sight of me, she immediately wraps up their conversation, thanks the woman, and turns to face me. "Shall we?" She links her arm with mine and guides me out of the boutique.

We find a café on the corner and settle into a booth by the window. Shay and I both like to people-watch, and this allows us the perfect view to do just that.

"Does it feel any different being married?" I ask.

"I didn't think it would, but yes. It feels amazing," she admits.

I mull over her words. I've always viewed marriage as somewhat pointless. If you're already committed to one person, why go through the hassle of a wedding and the name changing just so people know you're married? Then there's the mess of divorce if things don't work out. The only thing I have left of my parents is their last name. Sometimes when I think about having Everett as my last name, I get overly excited, but then I remember that changing my name to Everett means giving up Bell, and it always makes me want to drag out our engagement forever.

Some days, when I feel overwhelmed by the thought of marriage, I will overly call Jonah my husband in hopes that he will forget that we aren't actually married. Maybe if we get him a wedding band to wear, he will completely forget all about the formalities of legalizing our marriage. Then, years down the road, when he realizes, I can just be like, 'At least you know you won't have to give me half of everything if we get divorced.'

"Marriage suits you so perfectly, Mrs. Harper."

"Sometimes I stare at Jonathan and can't believe he's mine. He's MY husband."

We finish our lunch and decide to indulge in a little pampering. Our next stop is a spa, where we treat ourselves to manicures, pedicures, and a relaxing massage. The tension from the past few days melts away under the skilled hands of the masseuses, and by the time we're done we're both feeling rejuvenated.

As we step out of the spa, the late afternoon sun is beginning to dip in the sky. By the time we arrive back at the office, we realize it's almost time to go home. The building is quieter now, with most of the staff having left for the day. As we enter Jonah's office, he and Jonathan are lounging on the couch, talking, and tossing a football back and forth.

"Well, how was ditching work?" Jonah asks, looking in our direction.

"It was good—so good, in fact, I think we'll do it again tomorrow," Shay replies with a playful glint in her eyes as she hands Jonah back his card.

"Thanks for the invite," Jonathan quips.

"It was girls only," Shay says, sitting next to him and casually draping her legs over his lap.

I walk around the coffee table and tap Jonah's shoe for him to put his leg down. He obliges, and I settle comfortably onto his lap.

"Shay took me to get my nails done," I announce, kicking my heels off and extending my hands and wiggling my freshly polished toes.

"They look beautiful, baby" he presses a kiss to my jaw.

IT'S NOON ON FRIDAY WHEN JONAH WALKS INTO MY OFFICE, HIS GRIN lighting up the room. "Hi, baby."

"Hi," I set down the folder I've been working on. It's crazy how I still get butterflies when he unexpectedly appears.

"Can that wait until Monday?" He walks over and casually perches on the edge of my desk.

"Sure. You taking me home to bed?" I bite my lower lip as I rise from my chair and step between his open legs, wrapping my arms around his neck.

"I was thinking we could get out of here—maybe go somewhere nice for the weekend," he suggests.

I pinch my lips between my teeth, trying to hold back the excitement. Quickly, I shut down my computer and tidy my desk. I file away my papers, lock my desk drawer, and grab my bag and coat. "Ready!" I beam.

Jonah stands, laughing softly, before leaning in to kiss me.

"Let's go, lovebirds," Jonathan calls out from the doorway.

"Are you guys coming too?" I ask excitedly, turning to see Shay and Jonathan standing there.

"Duhh," Shay replies, extending her hand towards me.

I hurry over to her, grabbing her hand as we walk together, the guys following behind.

CHAPTER
Thirty-Eight

KALYN

When we arrive at the resort, we're ushered to our suite and greeted by a beautifully decorated space with elegant furnishings. The suite has two master bedrooms, each with a king-size bed and en-suite bathrooms. Billowing white curtains sway in the breeze at the far end of our rooms, where the double doors stand open. Outside, the back patio is complete with a cozy firepit, a relaxing jacuzzi, comfortable lounge chairs, and a cute mini tiki bar.

Beyond the patio, a staircase descends to a meticulously landscaped walkway that meanders toward paved paths connecting directly to the incredible beachfront. We haven't even settled into our rooms or had time to relax from the flight or from work today when the guys tell us to start getting ready for dinner.

In the bathroom, Shay expertly curls my hair and pins a section above my right ear, adding a beautiful pink flower for a special touch. Once our hair and makeup are complete, I dress in a light pink, flowy dress, while Shay opts for a short sundress.

Stepping out of the bathroom, I hear the men talking on the patio. "Can we wear sandals?" I ask Jonah as I approach.

They both turn around, and Jonah's eyes light up as he takes me in, rising from his position by the balcony edge. "Wow, baby, you look incredible. We're heading down to the beach, so feel free to go barefoot if you'd like." He gestures behind him, indicating the direction we're going.

"What are you going to wear?" Shay asks.

"I'm going to wear the sand on my toes," I tell her.

"Sounds good to me," she drops her sandals in a patio chair and takes Jonathan's arm. "Shall we, husband?"

As we make our way down the patio stairs, I can already see the table and lights set up on the beach, with a server waiting for us. Jonah makes everything seem so effortless. While his wealth certainly helps, I know he and Jonathan handle most of the planning themselves. This beach dinner, however, is undoubtedly Jonah's idea. He knows it's one of my favorites—dinner while we watch the sunset.

After we've finished our meal, Jonah looks at me with a tender smile. "Want to take a walk?"

"Are you going to say it's so we can leave these two alone to make out and then propose again?"

"If that's what you want," he stands and offers his hand to me.

"I'd love to," I stand, placing my napkin on my empty chair. He takes my hand, leading me closer to the water. As we walk along the shoreline, the sand feels like a cloud beneath our feet.

It's almost as if my feet can't fully register they're touching the ground.

When we return, Jonathan and Shay are sitting together on the beach, with Jonathan motioning his hands animatedly as he tells her a story. Jonah sits down beside them and opens his arms for me to join him. I settle between his legs, feeling his hold around me. I hold onto his arms, squeezing them gently as I look up at him. He leans down, and our lips meet in a lingering kiss.

We spend the next hour simply embracing each other until we all agree it's time to go inside and head to bed.

The following evening, we receive the same instructions to prepare for dinner. Excitement bubbles up as we head straight to my bathroom.

"What's todays date?" Shay asks, rummaging through her makeup bag.

I tap my phone screen and lean over to see the date. "Uhh, October 23rd. I'll do my own hair and makeup tonight," I inform Shay, wanting to give her a break from doing both of ours as she usually does.

"Sit your cute little butt down. I'm taking care of your hair and makeup, and you have no say in the matter," she already has a brush in her hand and strands of my hair in her grasp before I can fully sit.

Every time Shay finishes dolling me up, I feel like a movie star ready for the red carpet. Admiring my reflection, I marvel at how flawlessly she enhances my features. "I'd fuck me," I laugh.

"I'd fuck you too," she says as she finishes the final touches on her own hair and makeup and looks stunning—a perfect complement to her natural beauty. "Tonight will be full of surprises. Look at these shoes," she says, holding up a pair of white, glittery heels.

"Those are amazing!" I exclaim, my eyes widening.

"I got them for you. And I also got you a dress. It's over there. This one's mine." She holds up a garment bag.

Opening mine, my mouth drops open. Inside is the gorgeous dress I tried on a few days ago. "You got me the dress!" I squeal.

"Not just yours; I got mine too. Figured, after dinner, we'll for sure get some action."

"We need to be extra careful; what if we spill something on them?"

"We can just get them dry-cleaned. Then again, knowing Mr. Everett, he will probably just tear the material off. You'll probably have to toss it or donate it after tonight."

We leave the bathroom and step into my dimly lit room, where flower petals are now blanketing the floor. Shay moves around me and says, "Oh yeah, one more thing." She grabs a bouquet of white and pink peonies and hands them to me.

"These are my favorite!" I exclaim, staring down at them.

"I know." She smiles, tears welling in her eyes. "Come on," she says, pulling me along.

As I walk with her, I take in the flower petals scattered on the floor. At the back door, I stand frozen, my eyes meeting hers, both of us tearing up. Lanterns line a pathway in the sand, with pink flower petals creating a delicate trail.

A white altar stands elegantly against the sunset backdrop, with a man in a tuxedo at the center, Jonah by his side, and Jonathan next to him. It's a mirror image of Shay and Jonathan's wedding, but now Jonah stands at the center. To the left, a band begins to play as soon as Shay and I appear in the doorway.

"Shay…" I whisper, my words trailing off as the first tear escapes my eyes.

She turns to me, wiping it away. "Don't you dare ruin your makeup. I only want to see tears when your *husband* lifts up your dress and consummates your marriage."

I let out a laugh, but the tears keep coming. "Did you know?"

"Yes," she whispers, her voice filled with emotion.

"Us ditching work?"

"We needed to find you a dress."

"I love you so much," I turn to her.

"I love you more. Let's get you to your husband." She takes my hand and laces her fingers in mine.

We walk across the sand in our heels, which proves to be a big mistake, but I don't even care. Thankfully, there's a flat surface for us to stand on when we reach the altar. As we walk, I notice Jonathan placing a supportive hand on Jonah's shoulder.

When we arrive, Jonah has tears streaming down his face, his eyes filled with pure love and happiness. I smile wide at him, my own tears flowing freely. The music quiets as the officiant begins to speak, his words blending into the background of my thoughts. When he finishes, Jonah takes a deep breath and begins, his voice steady yet filled with emotion.

"My life felt meaningless, dark, and miserable. The first night I saw you, you became a light so bright in my life, I knew everything I had been through, the twists, the turns, all led me to you. I will give you the wedding of your dreams, but I can't wait any longer to be your husband. I love you, Kalyn Wrenley Bell. I will love you until the day I die and continue loving you in every life we enter after this. My soul belongs to you as yours belongs to me. I will forever take care of you and love you with everything in me."

His words crash over me like a tidal wave, and my tears come even faster. "I didn't know we were doing this, or I would have prepared something. I love you so much," more tears stream from my eyes as I speak from my heart. "Thank you for showing me what true love is and loving me when I didn't think I deserved it or would ever know what true love meant. You are my everything, and you complete me in every way I never knew someone could. I will gladly follow you into every life after this, and I'm so glad we found each other in the deepest, darkest sea, with my bioluminescent light. You will forever be my anglerfish, baby."

He lets out a laugh as more tears stream down his face.

"Now the rings," the officiant says.

Jonathan hands Jonah a ring as Shay softly taps on my arm, placing a ring in my hand. I stare down at it, my heart swelling with a rush of emotions. It's solid black, but on the inside, it's inscribed in gold script: 'Jonah & Kalyn Everett.' The lettering sparkles in the light. My eyes are transfixed, marveling at the beauty of this perfect circle. Forever, my husband will wear this ring. It's more than just a piece of jewelry; it's a symbol of our forever commitment—the promise we are making to each other. It represents the love that we share and the bond that will hold us together through the ups and the downs. Forever, this ring will link me to him and him to me. Women will see this ring and know there is a woman who put it there, marking this moment when it became a permanent fixture on his finger.

"With this ring, I thee wed," Jonah says as he gently slides the diamond band onto my finger. The ring catches the light, sparkling as brilliantly as the love shining in his eyes.

I take a deep breath, my heart pounding as I hold his ring in my fingers, ready to place it on his hand. I feel the bond weaving us together in this moment. "With this ring, I thee wed," I repeat, my voice trembling slightly as I slide the band onto his hand. It's there—a ring on Jonah Everett's finger. He is officially a married man. *MY* married man.

We say, "I do," in unison, our voices blending together in perfect harmony, sealing our vows with those simple but powerful words. We gaze into each other's eyes, the world around us fading away as we become lost in this moment. The officiant's voice is a distant murmur as he pronounces us husband and wife.

Jonah's hands find my waist, and he bends me back in a passionate kiss. The warmth of his lips against mine sends a shiver down my spine, and I melt into his embrace, feeling the strength and all-consuming power of his love. "I love you so fucking much, baby," he murmurs against my lips, his voice husky with emotion. He brings me back up, his lips reclaiming mine, his kiss more fervent, more desperate, as if he's trying to pour all his love into this one moment.

"I love you so fucking much, too," I manage to say, my voice breaking as tears of joy spill down my cheeks.

The night I was leaving Jonah, we made love in a way that was slow, sensual, loving, soft, passionate, and everything in between. After the ceremony, he took me to bed and made love to me again—tenderly. Then rough, and fast, the entire night. He was between my legs in one way or another.

I'm not sure who the officiant was, but he took all our documentation to legally change my name. He even promised to have my new ID and passport delivered to the office on Monday. When I asked how he would do that without me being there for a photo, all the guys smiled at me like I was missing some big secret. I even questioned Jonah on whether our marriage is even deemed "legal" with whatever they were doing, and he very seriously assured me he would never mess around with something as important as me being his wife.

WE ENJOY DINNER AT A RESORT RESTAURANT, AND SHAY AND I HAVE A few cocktails to celebrate Mr. And Mrs. Everett. By the time dinner ends, we're slightly tipsy and full of giggles. As we walk back to our suite, Jonah holds my hand, his touch grounding me when my legs want to fail me.

I'm dressed in a sexy pencil skirt that hugs my curves, accentuating my hourglass figure, the hemline skimming just above my knees. The lace top I chose is quite revealing, designed to showcase my chest with a plunging neckline that's enticing. I caught not only Jonah staring at my tits but Jonathan and Shay too, so it had the desired effect.

As we enter our suite, I kick off my heels, ready to get out of clothes. Jonah usually helps me out of my skirts, but he's leaning against the doorframe between our bedrooms, watching. I'm about to tell him to get his cute butt over to help when Shay's hand finds my zipper and starts lowering it.

"Glad someone decided to help," I cast a glance in his direction as I pull my top off, letting my breasts fall free. The cold air in our room instantly peaks my nipples, and I let my skirt fall to the floor. In my buzzed state of mind, I wonder why Jonah is just standing there, but if he doesn't want to come touch his wife, fine by me. I'll get in bed, and I'm sure he'll follow. I wait a moment longer to see if he'll move, but he remains rooted in place.

As I turn to walk to my side of the bed, Shay is right there, her face serious. She's completely naked, her eyes filled with desire while Jonathan is sitting in a chair right next to the corner of the bed.

"Hi," I giggle softly.

"Hi," she whispers, her eyes flaring with lust.

"What's happen—" my words die on my tongue as her soft hands move to my hips, pulling me closer. Her lips brush against mine, delicate and wet, tasting like strawberries. Her kiss is different from Jonah's—more tender.

"Are we—" my breath hitches, my chests heaving, causing our breasts to press together.

She smiles and slides her hands up my body, caressing the curves of my breasts before moving to the back of my neck. One hand pulls me deeper into the kiss as our tongues intertwine. My senses explode from her touch, and my body relaxes as my hands instinctively go to her full, round ass, pulling her closer.

She grins and pulls away momentarily. Her hands slide down to cup my breasts, squeezing gently before leaning down to pull one into her mouth. My head falls back, and I tangle my fingers in her hair, pulling her closer. My arousal heightens when I glance over at Jonathan. He watches us intently, his feet propped up on the bed, his hands on top of his erection, pushing it down as if he doesn't want to be bothered by it or have it getting in the way of the show.

"Mr. Everett," she says, her voice laced with arousal, "come sit next to my husband. Both of you, move to the couch." Jonah obeys, pushing himself off the wall and taking a seat next to Jonathan on the white couch. She takes my hand and moves me toward them, positioning me right in front of both men. She moves behind me, wrapping her arms around me and kissing my shoulder. Her hands cup my breasts, then one slides down my stomach, and I watch her hand as it moves closer to my panties.

"Do you want to watch me fuck your wife with my fingers," she asks Jonah.

"Yes," he says, his voice low and seductive.

Her fingers delicately brush over the top of the material, slowly tracing my slit. I let out a shaky exhale as her hand slowly moves lower between my legs. She puts her foot between Jonathan's legs, widening them, and looks at Jonah, her eyes commanding him to do the same. Both of them sitting with their legs open.

"Scoot closer," she demands, and Jonathan scoots closer to Jonah. "Good." She smiles, her hand softly rubbing up and down my wet folds. "Put one of your knees between each of their legs," she instructs, and I comply, placing one knee between Jonah's leg and the other between Jonathan's, hovering above their laps.

Her hand slides to my neck, pulling my head back to meet her eyes as she kisses me again. Her other hand moves back down my belly to my panties. When I think she will playfully torment me again, her hand slips beneath the fabric, and her fingers find my swollen clit, rubbing tantalizing circles.

"Do you want me to finger her?" she asks, turning her gaze to Jonah. "Tell me to fuck your wife with my fingers," she demands.

"Fuck my wife with your fingers," Jonah murmurs in a gravelly tone.

Her fingers slide lower, and my head tilts back on her shoulder as she moves toward my center. "Are you sure?" she questions again.

Jonah leans forward, his eyes blazing with raw desire, and rips my panties away. "Fuck my wife with your fingers, now," he commands Shay.

She grins wickedly as she presses two fingers inside my channel. "Oh my god," I cry out, captivated by the sight of her fingers plunging in and out of me.

"Do you like that?" she whispers in my ear.

"Yes," I breathe, my hand sliding over hers, urging her to keep going. My hips move against her hand as I meet Jonathan's gaze. The burning desire in his eyes makes me even wetter.

She continues moving her fingers, then withdraws them, tracing a teasing path from deep inside me, up my slit, rubbing tantalizing circles on my clit before sliding back inside. Her fingers move with deliberate, sensual strokes, my hips syncing with her rhythm.

"Do you want her to come?" Shay's voice is sultry, cutting through my heated moans.

I don't know who she's asking, but Jonah is the one to answer. "Yes."

Her fingers pick up speed, finding that precise spot that sends my body into overdrive, causing my toes to curl. She pinches my ear between her lips, then whispers, "Do you want to come?"

"Yes," I pant, and my orgasm crashes over me like a tidal wave. My cries grow louder, my body convulsing around her, craving more. Her fingers continue their relentless rhythm, pushing me past my limits. I lean forward, grabbing a fistful of Jonah's shirt for support, my hips moving in shallow, desperate thrusts.

When Shay finally withdraws her fingers, they glisten with my arousal. She admires her handiwork, and then brings them to Jonathan's mouth. I watch, breathless, as he licks them clean. Shay smiles, and she pulls them away with a satisfied praise, "Good boy." Her attention returns to me, her eyes burning with renewed hunger. "But I want to taste you," she murmurs, grabbing my neck and pulling me into a deep, demanding kiss.

"Lie on the bed," she orders, and I rise on unsteady legs, moving to the bed. Jonah and Jonathan stand, moving chairs to the end of the bed at Shay's direction.

Shay climbs onto the bed, crawling towards me; her movements are predatory and full of intent. She pushes my legs apart, her eyes lighting up as she takes in the sight of my exposed body. "Honey, can you see her pink pussy?" she asks Jonathan, ensuring he has an unobstructed view.

Then she settles between my legs, her breath hot against my sensitive skin. Her arms wrap around my thighs, pulling me closer, and her tongue softly touches between my lips. The experience is electric; shockwaves rippling through my entire being as her tongue flicks and swirls.

Her fingers dig into my thighs as she delves deeper. My hands thread through her hair, tangling in the silky strands as I urge her closer. Her mouth moves with expert precision, and I'm completely swept up in the sensation, my hips bucking against her. Every flick, every languid lick propels me higher, her throaty hums vibrating against my skin.

"God, yes," I cry out, my body bowing off the bed, greedy for more of her touch. She hums in response, the sound sending shivers through me. She finds my sweet spot, circling it with agonizing slowness, then flicking it with rapid strokes. I can feel the heat coiling in my belly, ready to explode.

Shay works me over, relentless and skilled. She knows exactly what she's doing, and she's taking her time. I can't hold back any longer. With a final, desperate cry, I shatter, my body shaking with the force of my release.

She doesn't stop, drawing out my orgasm, forcing me to ride it out until I'm a trembling, breathless mess. Finally, she pulls back, her lips glistening with my arousal, a satisfied smile on her face. She looks up at me, her eyes dark with desire and triumph, and I can barely form a coherent thought, much less speak.

She climbs to her knees, crawling up my body and pressing her mouth to mine. "You taste incredible," she breathes against my lips.

"I want to try," I whisper, my voice trembling with a mix of excitement and nerves. Shay's lips pull away from mine, a knowing smile spreading across her face as she offers a slight nod. She lies back, her thighs falling open in invitation, and I'm mesmerized by the sight of her. My mouth waters just looking at her beautiful pussy. I've never been with a woman before, and the anticipation makes my heart race. I need to explore her, feel inside her.

Moving between her legs, I lay on my belly, mimicking her earlier position. I wrap my arms around her thighs, pulling her flush against me as I take a moment to drink in the sight of her. Tentatively, I trace my tongue along her seam, coaxing a throaty whimper from her lips. The sound emboldens me, spurring me on. Placing my mouth against her clit, I flick it, and she cries out again, her hips undulating in response.

Releasing her left leg, I use my right hand to explore further. Lifting my face, I watch her eyes close. Her moans grow louder, and I know I've found a rhythm she likes.

Confidently, I slide my fingers down her folds, pressing two inside her. It's incredible, different from when I touch myself. I move in and out of her, feeling her warmth and wetness, then start to rock against her interior wall. Her hips buck in response, and I know I'm hitting the right spot.

I lower my face back between her legs, my lips fastening around her nub as I lash and stimulate the sensitive flesh. Her pornstar whimpers fill the room, making me feel like I'm doing everything right. Her responses fuel my desire, and I continue my ministrations, wanting to reciprocate the same pleasure she gave me.

As I lavish attention on her, I feel her inner muscles ripple around my fingers. Her hips buck against me, and I match her intensity, meeting her thrust for thrust. Her cries of pleasure become more insistent. My fingers curl deep inside her while my tongue dances over her clit.

Her fingers tangle in my hair, anchoring me closer. I feel her body tensing and her breath coming in short gasps. She teeters on the precipice, and I don't let up, giving her everything I have. With a final, deft stroke of my tongue and a deep, measured thrust of my fingers, she shatters, her body convulsing as her legs vise-like around me.

Her moans crescendo into an ecstatic wail, and I prolong them for as long as possible. Her body shudders, her thighs quivering around my head. Gradually, I ease my fingers out, treating her clit to one final, tender caress before sitting up. Our eyes lock, both of us panting, and she greets me with a languid smile, her chest rising and falling as she recovers.

Sitting up, Shay instructs me to lean back on my hands, and I comply willingly. She repositions herself, sliding one leg beneath mine and draping the other over top of mine. We inch closer, our bodies melding together until the warmth and moisture between our legs blend seamlessly. She bites her lower lip, her gaze smoldering as she leans back on one hand. Her other grasps my upper thigh, drawing me nearer as she begins a sensuous roll of her hips against mine.

"Go get my toy, honey." Shay's voice is thick with desire as she pants. Jonathan stands, his movements deliberate and returns shortly with a pink double-sided dildo. Shay takes it, and I quickly piece together how this is going to work.

I make eye contact with Jonah; his expression is intensely aroused. Briefly, I wonder if he's okay with this, and I don't know if the man can literally read my mind, but he subtly winks at me, and I melt. Anticipation courses through my veins as I crave Shay in every sense of the word.

She repositions herself, turning her hips towards the guys so they have a perfect view of our bodies intertwined. "Want me to explain what I'm going to do?" she asks.

"I've got it," I smirk.

"Good," she murmurs. She carefully places one end of the dildo at my entrance, gently circling it as she coats it with my arousal. When it stops, she begins to push it in slowly. I adjust my hips, giving her the space she needs to slide it in deeper. It's exquisite, filling me up completely and stretching me perfectly. She slowly drags it out, then pushes it back in. Her rhythm is initially languid, but soon she quickens, the dildo moving in and out with a growing urgency as I meet each thrust with my own movement.

When she slows again, my breath hitches as she positions the other end against her own center. She gradually eases herself onto it with measured care until our bodies are pressed tightly together.

My breath catches in my throat as she starts to move. My mouth forms an open "O" of surprise as I begin rocking back against her. The toy connects us intimately, each movement between us sending pleasure through both of us. Shay's eyes lock onto mine, a mixture of lust and affection in her gaze.

I lean forward, our breasts brushing against each other as our hips move in a synchronized dance. Her skin against mine, combined with the fullness inside me, is almost overwhelming. I moan, my hands gripping her thighs as we grind harder.

"Do you like that?" she murmurs.

"Yes," I respond, my hips moving faster. The dildo slides smoothly between us, creating a delicious friction. Shay's hands roam my body, caressing my breasts and pinching my nipples.

Her movements become more urgent, her hips grinding against mine with increasing intensity. I match her pace, feeling the tension build inside me, ready to explode. She reaches out, pulling me to her as her lips crash against mine. Her hand slips between our bodies, finding my clit and rubbing circles.

The added stimulation sends me over the edge. "Oh my God, Shay," I gasp, my body convulsing as my hips buck wildly against hers. Shay follows soon after, her cries of pleasure so sexy that I grasp her thigh tightly until our movements come to a slow stop. Leaning back on my hands, I tilt my head to the side, my eyes roaming over her sexy body.

"I'm gonna pull it out, okay," she whispers. I nod, watching as she eases herself off the dildo and then pulls it out of me. She tosses it to the end of the bed as I collapse on the pillows. She looks back at me, kisses my shoulder, then rests her head in the same spot.

We watch as the guys stand from their chairs. Jonah pulls off his shirt, tossing it into the chair he was just sitting in, and slowly stalks toward my side of the bed. I lean in toward Shay as he pops the button on his shorts. "Babe, no," I laugh as he moves closer.

He nods slowly, climbing onto the bed, pulling the back of my knees toward him. "Shay got you warmed up for me," he lowers himself on top of me. "Wife," he murmurs.

"Husband," I respond skeptically as he reaches between our bodies. Usually, he takes his time working himself into me, and I revel in every inch he gives. But like he said, 'Shay got me warmed up for him,' and he doesn't give me an inch, or even two. He gives me the entire thing in one thrust of his hips. My body nearly launches off the bed, and I keen out as he fills me, my body slumping back as his hips begin working me over.

My hands move above my head, one landing on top of Shay's. I glance up, and our fingers lace, both hands palm up, her fingers squeezing mine. Jonah slams into me repeatedly, and I clutch the large hand that intertwines with mine, my hand sandwiched between them.

I moan loudly as Jonah penetrates deeper. My legs fall open wider, brushing against Shay's soft leg, and I clutch her hand. When I look up, I see the tattoo-covered arm on top of mine and realize it's Jonathan's hand I'm squeezing—Jonathan and Shay's hands. We're all deep in the moment, and I try to pull my hand from theirs, unsure if he knows it's my hand he's holding. I hear him rasp, "No," and both of their hands tighten around mine.

Jonah's pace quickens, his body driving into mine with an intensity that leaves me breathless. My wails blend with Shay's soft sighs and Jonathan's low growls. Without warning, my orgasm crashes over me, freezing my body as pleasure radiates from my core.

I feel him still using my body to get himself off. He sits up on his knees, lifting my hips off the bed. His grunts grow louder and sweat pours down his chest. With a final, deep push, he buries himself inside me, his cock flexing as he releases, filling me completely.

"Since Shay and I have had sex with each other and been railed numerous times tonight in this bed, can we move to their bed to sleep?" I suggest feeling the wetness of the bedding beneath me.

Jonah nods. "Yeah, or I can have someone change our comforter."

Jonathan stands, lifting Shay and slinging her over his shoulder. "Our bed is fine," he says, carrying her to their room.

I crawl to the end of the bed, then run and jump into theirs. We all climb in, the space both too cramped and somehow just right. Jonah adjusts the thermostat before joining us.

"What did you do?" I ask, curious.

"It's going to get hot in here with both of us," Jonah says, gesturing between him and Jonathan. "I don't want you getting uncomfortable." He grabs my side and draws me in.

CHAPTER
Thirty-Nine

KALYN

Back at the office, we're greeted by the receptionist, Sadie, as soon as we get off the elevator. With a bright smile, she hands Jonah a manila folder.

"For you, Mr. Everett. It just arrived ten minutes ago."

"Thank you," he nods, then turns to me, holding it out. "Open it."

Skeptical, I take the folder from his hands and slowly open it. My breath catches when I see the contents inside: an official marriage certificate, a passport, and a new driver's license. I stop walking, staring at the name printed on them: Kalyn Wrenley Bell Everett.

My eyes well up with tears. Jonah hyphenated my maiden name. *He kept it.* The gesture overwhelms me. He never knew how much my last name meant to me, how it was the last remaining connection I had to my parents. *And he kept it.*

I also notice the updated address—*our* mansion. My smile grows even wider.

Jonathan and Shay stop beside us, and I see Bridget standing just behind. I look up at Jonah, my eyes shimmering with gratitude.

"I love you, *wife*," he drawls, leaning in to kiss me.

The binder in Bridget's hand slips from her grasp and crashes to the floor. We all turn to look at her as she hurriedly picks it up, her face pale. She looks like she's seen a ghost, her eyes wide and fixated on the marriage certificate in my hands. It dawns on me that she's completely shocked Jonah called me his wife and has seen the proof right in front of her that we are, in fact, now married.

As we reach my office, my eyes immediately notice the new nameplate on the door: Kalyn Everett. It feels like I'm on a rollercoaster, my belly flipping with excitement.

"Why are we all gaping at her door? She's always been Kalyn Everett," Shay smirks, heading back to her office.

Stepping inside, my gaze is drawn to the massive flower bouquet sitting on the conference-style desk to the right of the room. A hundred red roses, with petals carefully scattered around the table, form a breathtaking display. I walk over and pick up the card, neatly scrawled in Jonah's handwriting.

To my wife,

I will spend the rest of my life showing you how much you mean to me.

Love you for always,
Your anglerfish,
Jonah

I smile and place the card back down, then notice a crystal snow globe. Inside, a bride and groom who look just like us stand together. The bride's dress is exactly how I envisioned mine would be if we had married the old-fashioned way. The front of the globe reads "Jonah and Kalyn Everett" with our wedding date beneath it. I flip the globe upside down and back again, watching the snow swirl around before winding the knob underneath to play music. The melody, reminiscent of "Once Upon a December" from *Anastasia,* sends chills down my spine. I admire the beautiful globe, the couple forever captured inside the glass, feeling my love for Jonah deepen even more.

His arms wrap around my waist, and I look up at him, tears already spilling over.

"Do you like it?" he asks.

"I love it," I whisper, setting the globe down with shaky hands.

I turn to the smaller of the two bags and find a jewelry box inside. Opening it, I discover a delicate bracelet with a charm that says "Jonah."

"Cute," I laugh.

"You're wearing it," he insists, taking the box from my hand and fastening the bracelet around my wrist. It's classy, tasteful, and I know I never want to take it off.

Finally, I reach for the last bag and pull out lingerie. There are three outfits inside, but with Bridget standing in the doorway, I quickly put them back in the bag. "We can explore that bag later. Thank you, baby," I kiss him again, feeling overjoyed by his thoughtful surprises. I wonder how long he must have been planning all of this. Just the effort alone seems like it would have taken weeks.

I sign into my computer, and immediately a message from Shay pops up.

Shayla Harper: Check your email AND the company website!

Shayla Harper: Mrs. Everett. Does this mean you are technically... my boss?

Confused, I check my email and find the most recent one from Jonah.

Subject: Exciting News!

Dear Team,

I hope this message finds you all in good spirits. As many of you know, I am typically a quiet and reserved individual, preferring to keep my personal life private. However, there is one piece of news that I simply cannot keep to myself.

This past weekend, I had the immense joy and honor of marrying the love of my life, Kalyn. It was a beautiful and intimate ceremony, and I am thrilled to introduce her as Kalyn Everett.

Many of you have probably seen Kalyn around the office, assisting with auditing our quarterly reports. If you see her walking around, don't hesitate to say hi. She is as gentle and kind as she appears, and she has brought incredible happiness and inspiration into my life.

Thank you for your continued hard work and dedication. Here's to new beginnings and the wonderful days ahead.

Warm regards,

Jonah Everett

With a picture of us on the beach. My heart races, and tears well up for a second time because he amazes me even more every day. Knowing how private he is, this gesture means a lot. He even included our photo in the email. The same picture is featured on the website's opening page, with "CONGRATULATIONS MR. AND MRS. EVERETT" displayed proudly.

> **Kalyn Everett:** Is it bad that I want to just spend all day messaging everybody and sending pointless emails just so I can see Kalyn Everett pop up on everything.

Shayla Harper: I spend all day writing my name on everything just so I can write Harper over and over. I've been practicing my signature. Which do you like best?

The picture she sends makes me laugh out loud because it's her name at least a thousand times with different styles of writing "Harper." I send her a picture of doodles all over a piece of paper with Kalyn Everett scrawled everywhere.

> **Kalyn Everett:** I have no idea what you're talking about.

Shayla Harper: 😄

> **Kalyn Everett:** Imma be honest, this isn't my first time LOL

> **Jonah Everett:** That looks beautiful, baby.

> **Kalyn Everett:** Babe, you're so nosy.

> **Jonah Everett:** You're my wife, I like to make sure you are good.

Shayla Harper: Awww, why does my hubby not spy on me. : (

Jonah Everett invited Jonathan Harper to the conversation
Jonathan Harper accepted invite

Jonathan Harper: I will always spy on my honey.

> **Kalyn Everett:** You can't spy on her. She is MY wife. :)

> **Jonah Everett:** Wrong.

> **Jonathan Harper:** Fuck yeah! Can I watch.

Jonah Everett removed Jonathan Harper from the conversation

Kalyn Everett: 😉

Shayla Harper: 😂😂

Jonathan walks by my office, laughing. "Your husbands a dick," he says as he continues to Shay's office.

I lock my computer and walk to Jonah's office.

He smirks as I walk in. "That wasn't very nice, husband," I cross the room to him. He turns in his chair to face me. I straddle him, settling my knees between the opening in his chair and wrapping my arms around his shoulders.

"It was the nicest thing I could have done in the moment."

"Not nice," I repeat, kissing him.

"Is this what happens when I'm not nice," he questions, his voice lowering.

I shake my head slowly as I reach between us, grabbing his belt and begin to undo it.

There's a knock on the door, followed by another. "Jesus Christ," Jonah mumbles under his breath. "What?" he barks out.

Bridget opens the door, momentarily looking annoyed at me being in here. "Mr. Collins is here to meet with you, sir," she stands in the doorway.

"Bring him back in five," Jonah instructs her, turning his attention back to me. He brushes his hand through my hair, tucking it behind my ear.

"Get out!" he barks again, hurrying her out the door. She quickly exits, closing the door behind her.

"We will resume this later… Mr. Not Nice Husband," I lean in and bite his lower lip, sucking it into my mouth before releasing it. "I'm going to eat you up," I climb off his lap.

The rest of the morning flies by. I'm mid-dialing Miles' extension to ask for more files when Jonah opens my office door. My fingers freeze on the button pad as I see the annoyed look on his face.

"We have a meeting. Come on," he pushes my door open wider and waits for me. Bridget stands beside him, trying not to make eye contact.

I hang up the phone and quickly stand, trying to keep up with Jonah's brisk pace, confused about this unexpected meeting. "I didn't realize we had a meeting. Sorry," I stammer, hurrying out the door. Jonah's demeanor is stern, and I can't fathom why. What did I miss? I know I checked my schedule and all my emails today. He hadn't said anything about a meeting.

When we arrive four floors down, Jonah stands in front of the elevator door, holding his arm out for me to go first. As he makes eye contact with me, I start to walk, but Bridget cuts me off, further irritating me. I try to let it go, focusing instead on Jonah's growing impatience.

As we walk down the hall, passing offices and glass conference rooms, a childhood memory flashes in my mind. I'm walking into a house and running toward the couch when the couple there turns and smiles wide. The tall man scoops me up and squeezes me tightly. The memory dissipates, and I nearly stop in my tracks when I see the room we're heading to is full of Everetts. Antoinette, Beaumont, and even Eliza is there. My stomach churns, realizing this must be business-related. I didn't know Jonah and his father did business together, and I worry this might somehow not be about business at all, and about me and our marriage instead.

Praying we keep walking, but realizing I won't get that lucky, I continue forward. My heart sinks even deeper when Jonah pushes the conference room door open and holds it for Bridget and me.

Jonah takes the lead, walking around the table. Antoinette looks up, does a double take at me, her expression softening only momentarily before her scowl returns. He pulls out a chair for me. "Baby," he gestures for me to sit. I take a seat confidently, even though my heart is racing. Jonah sits next to me, with Bridget on his other side, setting up her laptop. The room is uncomfortably silent.

Eliza breaks the silence first. "This is a business meeting, Jonah. You didn't need to bring—"

"Finish that sentence and see what happens," Jonah interrupts sharply.

She narrows her eyes at him, clearly baiting him. "It's business. You didn't need to bring two of your flings with you."

Jonah reaches across the table, pulls the phone towards him, and presses several buttons. "Everett, twenty-four, Discovery," he says before hanging up.

Within a minute, four security guards enter the room. Jonah stands as everyone turns to look. The guards step forward, and Jonah points to Eliza. "Escort Miss Eliza out of the building, and don't let her back in."

Simultaneously, Antoinette and Eliza react with disbelief, their voices overlapping. "Are you joking, Jonah?" "What are you doing? You dick."

"Get her out of here," Jonah snaps, and security immediately moves toward Eliza.

"Jonah, stop it," I interject, standing up and gently grabbing his arm. "She's fine." I turn to the security guards. "We're fine here. Sorry."

They look uncertain who's orders to take. "Sir, do we take your orders or Mrs. Everett's orders?"

At that, Antoinette's head snaps in their direction and slowly turns back toward us, glancing between my hand and Jonah's. Her chair starts to slide back slowly, and her hands sprawl flat on the table. She looks like she's summoning every ounce of calmness from every human on earth. "What is on your hand?" Her words are slow and venomous.

"Mrs. Everett?" the guards ask, unsure how to proceed.

"Did you marry this woman?" Antoinette snarls.

"Yes," Jonah replies sternly.

"For God's sake, Jonah, did you sign a prenup?" Antoinette demands.

"You married a broke whore?" Eliza sneers.

"Get her out of here now!" Jonah barks.

"Stop." I hold up my hand to everyone.

Jonah looks at me. "Give us a minute," he tells the guards, taking my hand and leading me out of the office just outside the door. I feel all eyes watch us as we walk out of the room.

"I'm not going to let anyone disrespect you," he speaks before I can.

"I appreciate you, babe, but I can just go back up to my office and work. I don't need to be here for whatever this is." I offer.

"You're staying."

I pause, trying to understand why he wants me here. He knew my presence would upset his family. He's purposely trying to upset them by having me stay. Antoinette has never apologized for what she did to me, and I don't want to be anywhere near her. Jonah refuses to answer her calls because of it, causing a landslide of issues between her and us. Now, he's trying to throw his sister out, which will inevitably make everyone hate *me* even more. "Okay, and I will stay, but she stays too."

"Babe—"

"*My* sister-in-law stays. Take it or leave it." I reply firmly, leaving no room for argument.

My words seem to deflate his anger. He lets out a sigh, leaning in and softly pinching my chin between his fingers, tilting my head up and pressing his lips to mine. "Okay."

"Thank you." I whisper.

He kisses me once more, then slides his hand to my lower back, guiding me back into the room. Everyone watches as we walk around the table.

"Thank you, gentleman. If you can wait outside, we should be okay for now, per Mrs. Everett's orders."

Eliza scoffs.

"Unless you'd rather go with them," Jonah bites out.

I'm halfway frozen between trying to sit and unsure if I should stand back up.

Eliza stands. "I'd—"

"Enough!" Beaumont shouts, causing everyone to freeze. Eliza immediately sits back down. Jonah adjusts his tie and sits down, and I quickly follow suit. If looks could kill, I'd be in pieces on the floor from Eliza's glare.

"Get to the point. I'm sure you didn't come all the way here just to judge my marriage," Jonah says to Beaumont.

"I have a business proposal that I want us to collaborate on. It will draw in more revenue for both of us," Beaumont says.

"I'm not hurting for money," Jonah replies bluntly.

"Honey, this will be a great opportunity for you and your father to work together again," Antoinette says, reaching her hand out on the table as if trying to get him to understand.

Jonah remains impassive, and I can sense his reluctance. I place my hand on his forearm and give it a gentle squeeze, trying to encourage him to at least listen. "What's the project?" Jonah asks, his tone giving nothing away.

"I have preliminary plans," Beaumont slides a leather binder across the table to Jonah.

Jonah reaches over for the binder, opening it and flipping the pages. "A golf complex?" he questions, looking up at his father with a mixture of curiosity and skepticism.

I peer over to the binder at the plans provided. Though I've never been golfing, this is a brilliant concept. Golf does seem to be something so many people love to do. I used to hear customers at the diner complain about the weather not being suitable for them to go golfing.

"The golf industry is experiencing a remarkable surge," Beaumont begins, his voice confident. "A growing demand for facilities that offer not just an exceptional playing experience, but also a premium level of luxury and comfort. As the landscape of leisure evolves, high-end luxury golf complexes are emerging as the future, redefining the very essence of opulent recreational pursuits."

Beaumont's plans are detailed and thoroughly thought out. "We propose an expansive property that transcends the conventional boundaries of golfing paradigms. Our vision encompasses meticulously crafted grass golf areas, providing enthusiasts with an authentic experience. Complementing this, our comprehensive amenities will include golf carts available for seamless mobility across the course."

Jonah listens intently to his father speak, his eyes narrowing in consideration. Beaumont continues, emphasizing the facility's adaptability. "Recognizing the variability of weather conditions and our clients' diverse preferences, we will integrate covered and air-conditioned areas. These provide sanctuary from the elements, ensuring enjoyment of the game regardless of conditions. Our complex will offer an unparalleled experience, from the thrill of competition to the camaraderie among players, all elevated to new heights of luxury."

Jonah continues flipping through pages and stops on one that discusses the business structure, scrutinizing the details. I try to discern if the deal seems fair, but Jonah abruptly shuts the binder and drops it onto the table.

"These are great plans; this could be very profitable for you," his tone polite but firm. "At this time, I will pass on the opportunity. I wish you the best, sir."

I'm taken aback by Jonah's decision. Though I don't know the full extent of the issues between him and his father, he never initiates conversation to talk about them, so I never bring them up. But Jonah is a businessman, so it seems odd that he's turning down a great opportunity like this. However, I know it's not my place to question his decision. So, despite my disagreement, I remain silent, trusting his judgment.

"Son, at least think about it," Antoinette urges.

"You know this is a phenomenal proposal, Jonah. Put your pride aside and consider it from a business standpoint," Eliza adds.

Jonah pauses, then grabs the binder from the table, flipping back to the last page. He crosses out sections and writes in new terms. Jonah is a master negotiator, skilled at getting his way but equally ready to walk away if he doesn't. Whatever he's writing now will either secure a deal with his father or lead us to leave the room, likely with them somehow hating *ME* more.

When he finishes, Jonah leans forward, placing the binder in the middle of the table, then reclines in his chair. The tension in the room is palpable as Beaumont picks up the binder, flips to the last page, and immediately scoffs. "Goddamnit, son—"

"Take it or leave it," Jonah interrupts. "I'm not doing business with Cedric Campbell."

Who is Cedric Campbell? I thought this was a business deal with his father?

"It's business only, son. Nothing else," Beaumont insists.

"I'm not playing these games," Jonah retorts, narrowing his eyes at his mother.

She scoffs condescendingly. "There are no games, Jonah."

"I wasn't born yesterday."

Okay, I am clearly missing something here and it feels like it's something crucial.

"What about a 40/30/30 split, you 40," Beaumont counters.

"I wouldn't do it for a 99/.5/.5 split," Jonah replies. "This meeting is over." He pushes his chair back.

"You know this is a good business plan," Beaumont barks.

"I also know how to read, and your contract states that I must personally be involved in the project, while Mr. Campbell will have a partner stand in for him. Let me guess—that partner is his daughter? Am I right? My wife is right here. This is insulting."

Ohh, this is getting interesting.

They all seem momentarily stunned. Did they forget that Jonah works in their world and he's brilliant at it?

"Jenevieve is overly qualified to take on a business venture like this and has agreed," Eliza states confidently.

What. Did. They. Just. Say? Jenevieve? Jenevieve's last name is Campbell? Of course she would have a basic name. She's a basic bitch. Yet, it doesn't stop my fingers from trembling.

"Sorry you wasted your time. Thank you for the offer, but I'm confidently declining."

"We will discuss this, son," Beaumont stands, his chair rolling backward. The room grows even more charged as they both stand, exchanging the most professional argument.

I notice how much Jonah resembles his dad. They also both have incredibly deep, soothing voices. As I watch them, a fleeting memory flashes in my mind of a boat—my dad chasing me with a worm, a tall man picking me up protectively, everyone having a good time. Just as quickly, the memory fades.

"Can we speak privately," Beaumont requests firmly, leaving no doubt that a private conversation *will* be happening.

Jonah responds condescendingly, "I think I'll pass." He holds his hand out to me.

"We will discuss this, son," Beaumont insists. "Everyone out," Beaumont commands, and Antoinette and Eliza stand.

Jonah stares at his father for a few beats before sighing. "Give me a minute. Wait by the door," he instructs, leaning down to kiss me.

"Yes, sir," I feel uncomfortable but comply with his request.

I walk to the door with Bridget right behind me. She crosses the hall and waits while I stand by the door as Jonah asked. Security stands nearby as Antoinette and Eliza exit the room.

"Mrs. Everett, should we wait?" the head of security asks.

"No, we are okay, thank you," I reply.

They nod before walking away, which makes the hall turn automatically tense. Bridget looks just as uncomfortable as I feel, while Antoinette and Eliza give me dirty looks on the opposite side of the door.

"Hi, Mrs. Everett, I'm so sorry to bother you. Can I get your input, please?" A girl from accounting approaches, holding out a stack of papers.

"Of course. What's the issue?" I take the papers from her hand.

She hesitates for a moment before explaining, "I'm having trouble reconciling these expense reports with the budget allocations for last quarter. Specifically, there are discrepancies in the travel expenses. Could you take a look?"

I nod, flipping through the pages. "Alright, let's see. Ah, here it is. It looks like the travel expenses for the marketing team were coded incorrectly under administrative costs. You'll need to reallocate these entries to the correct budget line."

We discuss the necessary adjustments, and I suggest, "Also, double-check the receipts to ensure all expenses are accounted for and match the reported amounts. This should resolve the discrepancy."

"Thank you so much, Mrs. Everett. I'll make those corrections right away," she says, taking the papers back and walking down the hall.

"I bet you're pretty proud of yourself," Antoinette says nonchalantly, glancing behind her into the conference room.

"About as proud as you should be embarrassed for what you did," I reply just as nonchalantly as she did.

"Was it the money?" she questions.

"Is that all you see your son being good for? His money? No wonder he can't stand you."

"I know what a wonderful man *my* son is. But women like you are only after one thing," she says calm as ever.

"You caught me. I guess I should thank you since you are responsible. He has the biggest penis I've ever seen, and it feels incredible," I retort with a smile.

"You are trash."

"Will you be saying that when I have your grandbabies?" I glance in her direction.

"You wish."

"Your son does refuse to wear a condom."

"You're only further proving my point that you're trash," she says casually.

"Well, your son married me, so I guess he's trash too."

"I will have this marriage annulled by the end of the week," she says, meeting my gaze.

"Cute thought. I wouldn't waste your time. Plus, it's rather embarrassing that you'd try to control your grown son's life decisions."

"What's embarrassing is a low-life like you somehow managed to brainwash my smart boy. You won't win," she narrows her eyes at me.

"I already did," I meet her gaze.

I smile when Shay walks up. "Can we get lunch already?" she asks. "Where's Mr. Everett?" She glances at Antoinette and Eliza as if she has no clue who they are, even though she absolutely knows who they are. Then back to me and behind me to the glass office. "Think he would care if we got lunch without him?"

"My purse is in my office. Let's go grab it and we can go."

"No need, I'll pay," she offers.

"Okay, sounds good."

"It was lovely seeing you again, Mom. Sister," I smirk, then turn and walk away with Shay hooking her arm in mine. We don't make it ten steps before we're stopped.

"Babe," Jonah calls from the door to the office, leaning out. "Get back here," he directs, and Shay and I exchange a glance.

"Damn, guess not," she pouts, and we turn and walk back to the office.

I approach Jonah to whisper our plans. "Shay and I are going to go to lunch. I can bring you back something," I offer.

"No, you can wait for me," he whispers back, but his voice carries, and everyone can hear what he's saying.

"I don't want to rush you, and Shay and I are hungry now."

"Five minutes," he responds.

I sigh, not wanting to wait but not wanting to argue in front of any of them.

"Let me get my coat," he says.

"No, go finish talking with your dad," I encourage.

"No need. I'll be right back, baby," he insists.

"We'll wait. Go finish," I sigh again.

"Five minutes," he repeats.

"Okay," I turn to walk back to Shay.

Jonah grabs my arm, pulling me back for a kiss. "I love you, baby. I'll be right back."

Standing next to Shay, I give her a 'get me the fuck out of here' look, and she offers an apologetic smile. "Do you need anything from your office before we go? I can run up and grab it," she asks quietly.

"If you think you're leaving me, you're sadly mistaken. I'll put you in a headlock right here and give you a noogie if you even try," I threaten playfully then turn to face Shay with my back to Antoinette and Eliza. Shay glances into the office where Jonah and his father are talking. "Mr. Everett Sr. is kinda sexy," she says, grinning.

I turn and follow her line of sight. "Yeah, I'd let them both tag team me," and we both start giggling. I'm so uncomfortable that inappropriate things start to fall out of my mouth. Though Beaumont is handsome, I feel dirty for even saying something so gross. "Don't tell Jonah I said that," I laugh.

"John is like 5'9, and Jonathan is 6'5. Maybe he's the milkman's. Mr. Everett looks like Sr. Everett copy and pasted himself into a young version of himself," she muses, still watching them until her eyes subtly start to move.

The door opens, and Jonah's arm wraps around my shoulder before I hear him approach. He kisses the side of my head and pulls me to walk with him. His hand moves from my shoulder to lace his fingers with mine as we head to the elevator. When he pushes the button, I notice his family waiting behind us.

As the elevator opens, we all get in, the air thick with tension. "Is Jonathan coming?" Jonah asks Shay without looking at her.

"He wasn't going to, but I let him know you insisted on coming, so he's waiting downstairs for us," she replies.

As we exit the elevator, his mom slows her pace, seemingly wanting to say goodbye. "Jonah," she calls.

He keeps walking, but I stop, tugging his hand. He pauses briefly, glances at his mother, then lets go of my hand, grabs me by the waist, and keeps pushing me toward the door. "I think she wants to say goodbye," I tell him.

He remains silent, continuing to guide me outside.

CHAPTER

Forty

JONAH

We head home in the morning. Tonight, I'm taking Kalyn on a dinner date in the city and told her to dress nicely. It's been a while since she and I went out to dinner alone, and I'm really looking forward to spending time alone with my wife. I put on a black suit and stand in the kitchen talking to Jonathan while Kalyn and Shay are in the bathroom.

"Think your parents showed up after seeing the website?" Jonathan asks.

"That's what I assumed. But my mom was genuinely shocked when she saw my ring. She definitely didn't have any warning."

"What's the deal with the golf complex? That's a good idea."

"The idea is solid, but the intentions are shit. It's another attempt to get Jenevieve and me together. They clearly planned it before I got married. My marriage probably threw a wrench in their plans."

"Does Jenevieve know you got married? Or her family?"

"No clue. I'm sure word will spread fast. I don't care if she knows or not."

"Maybe we should send a wedding announcement to her and her family," Jonathan grins wide.

"That's not a bad idea."

Kalyn enters the room in a short black dress that hugs her body. Great—now I have a boner. She's stunning, so utterly breathtaking. She does a slow twirl, and my jaw feels like it's on the floor. Her ass is mouthwatering. Her heels are sparkling, and she wears a simple diamond necklace and earrings, and still has on her bracelet.

She walks over, wrapping her arms around my shoulders, and I lean in to kiss her. "Nothing to say?" she asks.

And I don't. She has left me speechless. My hands roam down her hips to her ass, and I can feel she's not wearing panties. Fuuck.

She smiles up at me, her hand rubbing over the outside of my pants. "What's happening here, husband?"

"My wife is incredibly sexy." I don't even want to go to dinner now. I want to eat her for dinner.

"You look great, Kal," Jonathan says, his eyes fixed on her ass.

"Thanks, I was hoping to catch your boss's attention," she replies.

"You got two out of two guys' attention that have seen you. You've succeeded," Jonathan smirks.

We're out front of the restaurant, and my fingers are buried inside her. I can feel she's close to coming, but I intend to keep her wanting more. I withdraw from her, grab my pocket square, clean her up, and fold it back into my suit pocket.

"Are you kidding me?" she asks, looking shocked.

I push the door open and extend my hand to her. She huffs but takes it. As we step inside, the maître d'hôtel is waiting to guide us to our table. We're led across the restaurant to a more secluded, premium area reserved exclusively for those who value privacy. Though still open, it's much quieter.

"You're an asshole," she whispers, nudging her elbow into my stomach.

"I'm going to take care of you at the table," I wrap my arm around her neck and pull her closer to kiss her forehead. Her irritation is palpable. Good. Her pending orgasm will be even more intense.

"My thighs are soaked."

Moving my hand down, I slide it up the back of her dress until I feel the wetness she mentioned between her legs. "Mmm," I murmur.

"I was seconds away from finishing. Now you can use your mouth," she grumbles.

I groan in approval, the sound rumbling in her ear. She giggles, looking up at me, and I lean down, capturing her mouth with mine, slipping my tongue in to deepen the kiss.

"LYN-E!" Adeline's voice rings out as she runs toward us. Kalyn pulls away, and just as Adeline is about to leap onto her, I intercept, picking her up so she can wrap her arms around Kalyn instead. "I missed you!"

"What about me?" I protest, tickling her side.

Her little arms wrap around my neck, hugging me. "Adeline, dear, come sit down," my mother calls, standing from her chair and beckoning Adeline back.

Walking back to their table, I try to set Adeline down, but she clings to me. "You need to eat, Bug," I tell her gently.

"Lyn-E, will you eat with us? Please?"

"We have our own table, Bug," I kiss her cheek.

"Can I have dinner with you?" she begs, looking at Kalyn. "Please, Lyn-E, I'll be good."

"Can we get two more chairs, please," my dad tells the waiter.

"That's not necessary," I interject.

"Son," my mother says sternly, indicating not to argue.

I look at Kalyn, and she offers a reassuring smile. "Looks like we're having dinner together after all," she tells Adeline.

"Baby," I pull out Kalyn's chair, and she sits gracefully.

I set Adeline down at her chair, and she instantly goes to Kalyn, climbing in her lap. Adeline slides her hands into Kalyn's and then notices her ring, touching it gently. "Are you married to my brother?"

"I am," Kalyn replies warmly.

"That's a really big diamond," Adeline says, pinching the diamond between her tiny fingers. "We really are sisters now, huh?" Her eyes widen. "Mommy said my brother Ethan has too many girls to make my sisters," she adds innocently.

"Ads, come over here," Eliza says, smiling at Adeline.

"I want to stay with Kalyn. Liza has a new boyfriend," she points. I realize she just redirected the conversation off herself, and I want to high-five her for being so smart.

"Big dick? Would explain you acting like you have a stick up your ass," I mumble under my breath to Eliza, who's sitting next to me.

"Very big dick. But the stick up my ass is because my brother IS the biggest dick," she smiles condescendingly.

"I can't wait to meet him. I wonder how much money it would take to get him to leave you. After all, this family likes to break up couples. Maybe when he's done with you, Mom can play match-maker and try to marry him off to—"

"Fuck you, Jonah. Shut the fuck up," Eliza hisses under her breath.

The waiter comes and takes our order, and just as I'm about to make another snide remark, Adeline interrupts.

"Can I have a spend-over?"

"Not tonight, Bug," I say to her.

"I want to stay with you," she says to Kalyn. "Want to spend the night with me?"

"We can plan something. Kalyn and I leave in the morning to go back home," I tell her, my arm resting on the back of Kalyn's chair as I lean over.

"Can I come?" Adeline asks eagerly.

"Adeline, that's enough, dear. Come sit," my mother says.

"She's not a bother. If you're okay with her sitting here, I don't mind," Kalyn says.

"I do mind," my mom snaps, and Adeline scurries off Kalyn's lap and into her own seat.

I start to stand, not willing to put up with this bullshit. "Son," my dad says in a low, stern voice. He doesn't like anybody making a scene in public, and that was my warning.

"Babe, sit, please," Kalyn takes my hand before I can speak.

Our food arrives, and I sigh, remaining in my seat. Dinner goes by, and it's awkward to say the least. Not only did I give my-self blue balls, I also probably gave Kalyn the female equivalent to blue balls, and the mood is complete tanked. She'll probably want to go to Shay the second we get back. If my dick falls off, I deserve it.

None of us eat much, and when the waiter asks if we want to take our food to go, we all decline.

"Will you be joining us for Thanksgiving?" my mom asks in a clipped tone. "I know you received the invite. I just can't figure out why you're choosing to ignore me."

I stare at her, unsure if she's fucking with me or just that clueless. When I come to the conclusion it's the latter, I let out a breathy laugh. "You don't know why I'd ignore you? You tried having my girlfriend leave me in the middle of the night."

"Jonah," Kalyn says quietly, hinting for me to shut up.

"You didn't talk for days after. You cried non-stop."

"And this isn't the time to talk about it," she eyes me.

"Who made you cry?" Adeline asks. Without waiting for an answer, she says, "Can you take me potty?"

"Good idea," Kalyn says, glaring at me as she stands and places her napkin on the table. "I'll take Adeline to the restroom," she narrows her eyes at me as if to say, *Deal with this before I get back.*

She walks away hand in hand with Adeline, and once they're far enough away, I turn back to my mother. "You should be embarrassed and disgusted with yourself. You're despicable."

"You threw away everything that was planned," she spits out.

"That was *your* plan, not mine. And since you're so obsessed with love connections, let me remind you that Jenevieve was as appealing as watching paint dry. If you want boring, by all means, but keep that shit out of my life. And she was shit in bed. You wanna fuck a board?" I aim the question to my dad.

"Watch your mouth," he warns, glancing around to make sure no one else hears.

My mom's eyes are wild with anger. "Oh, yes, don't settle down with someone with class. Of course you'd settle with the one who has tons of experience," she snaps, insinuating Kalyn has slept around.

Leaning forward, I narrow my eyes at Eliza. "Kalyn has slept with as many men in her entire life as your daughter here used to fuck in one night regularly in college. Or are you still spreading your legs for the entire football team?"

"You son of a bitch," Eliza hisses.

"I sure am," I respond.

My mom's eyes flare with anger at that remark.

"You're one to talk. You screw anything with a pussy," Eliza retorts.

I shrug. "I'm not dwelling on the past. I'm married now."

"Can't wait for her to meet Ethan. I know someone who's slept with both of you and prefers Ethan. I wonder what the legal process would be for her to change the name on the marriage certificate to Ethan—"

My hand is on Eliza's throat, squeezing before she even finishes her sentence. I could snap her neck right now.

"Jonah," my mom says, her voice sounding like it's in a tunnel. I hear the blood pumping in my ears, and all I want to do is kill her. I'll kill anyone who tries to take Kalyn from me.

"Watch your tongue, bitch," I growl as her face reddens and she claws at my hand to release her.

My dad stands between us, his hand on my arm. "Son," he says, calm but firm, "your wife is coming back." With that, I release Eliza's neck.

She sucks in air, and I turn to see Kalyn and Adeline talking and pointing at a water fountain. Kalyn is bent over, explaining something to Adeline, who is jumping with excitement as they continue walking.

"Either of you ever threaten my wife, try to interfere in my marriage, or make lewd comments again, I'll cut your tongues out. Kalyn has the biggest heart and will forgive what you did to her.

For some reason I can't comprehend, she doesn't have any qualms with you. You want a relationship with me, it's through her." I stand needing to get the fuck away. "Ready to go, baby," I smile at her.

"Yes," she replies.

"You'll join us for Thanksgiving this year, won't you?" my mother asks Kalyn with a truly convincing smile.

Kalyn looks between my mother and me, then nods. "I'd love to." Her response is so genuine, and I fucking hate that I know she's happy about the invite.

"Wonderful, I look forward to seeing you in a couple of weeks," my mom croons happily. She should've been an actress; she's truly believable.

When we arrive back to the condo, Kalyn still looks happy. Now I have to find a way out of this. There's no way I'm taking her to my parents for thanksgiving.

CHAPTER
Forty-One

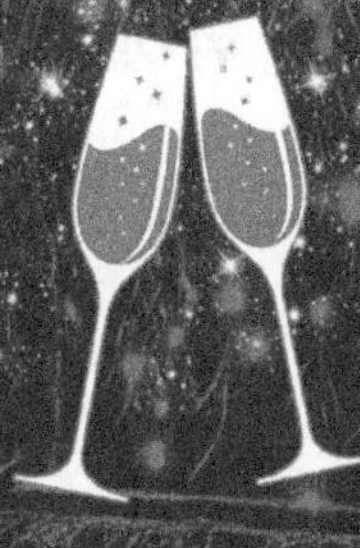

KALYN

My palms are sweaty, and it feels like my entire body is vibrating with nerves. I'm still surprised Antoinette invited me to have Thanksgiving with them. I swipe my hands down my lap, hoping Jonah assumes I'm just smoothing out my dress. He reaches over, laces his fingers in mine, and gives a reassuring squeeze.

We arrive at his parents' beautiful mansion. It's not as big as Jonah's but still massive. My first impression is that, although it looks warm and cozy, it seems like it would feel stiff and cold. If I were driving by, I'd imagine a husband who's always away on business, a wife who spends her days at the country club playing tennis while the nanny takes care of the kids. It's funny how, when you're raised with nothing, you dream of living in a big mansion with toy rooms and tricycles you can ride around every room. But as I stare at this home, I think of Adeline and how lonely she must feel, being the only small child here. Even with her nanny, she's not around kids all the time. Or maybe she is. I don't actually know.

Jonah parks at the front of the house and climbs out, walking around to open my door. I take his hand, and we walk up the stairs arm in arm. The door opens as we approach, by a butler wearing a tuxedo. Other staff members, also dressed in uniforms, move about. I even spot a maid in none other than the same maid uniforms as those at Jonah's house, scurrying away. A familiar scent greets me as we enter the house. Is it the smell of Thanksgiving? It feels different, more nuanced. A woman in a black dress approaches, taking my purse and helping me out of my coat before I'm ready. I try to unfasten the button before she rips it off me. Without my red peacoat, I feel exposed in my red glitter flare cocktail dress, which, although modest in the picture, is slightly more revealing than I'd like due to my breast size, even though they're completely covered.

"Lyn-E!" Adeline comes running up, happily right into my arms.

"Hi, LeeLee," I beam, scooping her up and giving her a bear hug.

Jonah wraps his arms around both of us. "I see how it is. Have I been replaced as your favorite, bug?" he plants a kiss to her forehead.

She giggles, "Lyn-E is my favorite, but I can have two this one time." She unwraps one arm from my neck and wraps it around Jonah.

"Sweetheart, so glad you made it," Antoinette croons as she walks to Jonah and hugs him.

"Mother," he says curtly.

"Kalyn," she acknowledges me just as curtly as he did her.

"Antoinette, thank you for having us. Your home is beautiful," I offer my best smile as I adjust Adeline on my hip.

"Come, dinner should be ready soon," Antoinette replies, gesturing gracefully from where she just came.

Jonah gently places his hand on my lower back, guiding me forward. I set Adeline down, and she takes my hand as we walk. The house is stunning, every corner steeped in the elegance of Jonah's upbringing. I imagine a young Jonah running through these very halls. Lost in thought, I instinctively lead us to the formal dining room.

"How did you know where to go?" Adeline giggles.

I hadn't even realized I did it until we entered. "I don't know. I just assumed."

I don't even have time to dwell on it or think any further into it when we enter the room, and my gaze lands on a man who looks remarkably like Jonah, like almost a spitting image of him, leaning in the doorway, engaged in a conversation with a woman. The resemblance is uncanny; they could almost be twins, though I think Jonah might be slightly taller. The man is at least 6'5". I glance between Jonah and the man, taken aback by their likeness.

The man grins at the woman he's speaking to but turns and does a double take when his eyes meet mine. Jonah pulls me along, not acknowledging the man, though he must have noticed me staring. As we move to our chairs, Jonah, ever the gentleman, pulls out my seat, then sits next to me.

"No, I want to sit by Lyn-e, Jonah," Adeline pleads, standing between our chairs.

"Adeline, sweetheart, take your seat." Antoinette points to a chair on the opposite side of the table.

"Jonah," she begs once more.

"Babe, scoot down one chair so Adeline can sit here," I suggest, tapping Adeline's nose playfully.

She giggles and looks at Jonah with her little blue doe eyes. He stands up and moves to the next chair. "You can take my seat, and Adeline, you can take Kalyn's."

Adeline's smile grows even wider as I stand and offer her my chair. I notice the man still watching me. His mannerisms are eerily similar to Jonah's as he pushes himself from the doorway and joins us at the table, sitting across from me.

"Baby?" Jonah asks, his tone more questioning.

"Sorry," I reply, settling into my seat.

Eliza enters the room with a man, and everyone greets her. She glares at Jonah but still hugs him, whispering, "Don't be a dick," to which he responds, "Don't be a bitch."

I find it slightly odd that nobody is introducing anybody; but it appears nobody likes anybody here.

Turning to me, she says, "Hi, sis, glad you could make it," and surprisingly hugs me. She feels oddly familiar—perhaps the hug feels like hugging Shay?

She then moves to Adeline, kissing her on the cheek before doing the same to each of them. When she reaches the man across from me, she kisses his cheek, saying, "Ethan," then gives a condescending smirk to the woman next to him. The woman returns a disgusted look, rolling her eyes before looking forward again.

My heart nearly stops when I realize this is the man that fucked Jonah over in every disgusting way possible. Now, when he turns his gaze back to me, it makes me mad.

"Do you want to color with me after dinner?" Adeline whispers.

"I would love to. We'll just have to see what your brother says," I smile at her.

The room falls into chatter, and I can feel Ethan's eyes boring into my face. I can also see Jonah glaring at him from my peripheral. Five minutes pass, and Jonah turns in his chair, his large hands grabbing my face and pressing his mouth to mine, his tongue pushing inside.

"Jonah!" Antoinette cuts in. "It's Thanksgiving—that's so inappropriate."

"You're right. Come on, baby, let's go upstairs so I can fuck you in private," he says, glaring at Ethan.

"Jonah," Antoinette snaps more harshly.

"Can I not have sex with my wife?" he retorts, emphasizing "wife" while glaring at Ethan.

"We are having a nice dinner," she insists.

Dinner progresses, filled with awkwardness. Afterward, Adeline leads me to her room to color, and I couldn't get out of the dining room fast enough.

"That looks really good, Adeline," I admire her drawing.

"Hi, baby," Jonah's voice murmurs in my ear as he pulls out the tiny chair next to me. He leans over, his hand on the back of my chair, inhaling the scent of my neck.

"Hi, Ethan. Do you want to color with us?" Adeline asks, not looking up from her page.

Ethan?!

My head snaps in his direction, locking eyes with Ethan's intense gaze. "I'd love to color with you," he tells Adeline, never breaking eye contact with me.

I glare at him, willing my eyes to somehow set his stupid face on fire.

"Where's the page I get to color?" he asks Adeline.

She scoots a blank piece of paper across the table to him. He picks it up and inspects the back. "This is blank," his voice is deep like Jonah's.

Adeline giggles, grabbing a marker and placing it on his paper. "You have to draw a picture."

"What should I draw?" He yanks the cap off the marker.

"Us… as princesses," Adeline's eyes widen with excitement.

He proceeds to draw three princesses, making sure to get our likeness in the drawing, each of us wearing big dresses. I fight the urge to smile at his sweetness, getting angry with myself for finding anything he does endearing. I look away, refusing to acknowledge the drawing.

Adeline starts giggling when she sees his picture. "We need princess crowns."

"How could I forget?" He playfully taps his forehead and adds a crown to each of our heads.

"You're a boy. Why are you wearing a dress?" She giggles again.

"You said we were princesses. I look nice in a dress," he points at himself on the paper in the biggest, poofiest dress.

"You could have been a prince. Where's that girl you brought?" Adeline asks Ethan, switching topics.

"Dad's talking to her."

"Is it because she's mean?"

"She's not mean," he chuckles.

"Does she know you have a different girlfriend too?"

"What are you drawing?" he diverts the topic, looking at the butterflies on Adeline's paper.

"Did you know Kalyn is our sister now?" Adeline asks Ethan, smiling broadly.

"That's what I hear," he says, fixing his gaze back on me. "How did everyone manage to keep you a secret?"

"Jonah married her in a secret," Adeline replies. "Mommy is mad. She said Jonah should have married Jenevieve."

Adeline gets up to grab another box of markers from across the room.

"My mom can be nasty when she doesn't get her way. If you want to stay in the family, I can make that happen," Ethan says quietly.

"You're disgusting. I wouldn't let you touch me with a ten-foot pole. You wanted Jenevieve, go get her," I whisper, stopping coloring to glare at him.

"Meh, she was a lousy lay," he shrugs.

"And you shouldn't have any knowledge of that," I retort.

He looks at me with interest. "Are you and her chummy?" He looks amused.

"I'm married to Jonah. Do you think that would equal her and me being chummy?"

"You just seem to think you know everything about something you know nothing about," he says, clearly entertained.

"Even if the entire thing was exaggerated, the fact that you're in here trying to flirt with me while you have a date downstairs tells me everything I need to know about you."

"What if I told you the story you were told was the other way around and your beloved husband was the one who was screwing my girlfriend?"

There's no way. No possible way. Jonah isn't that kind of person. "I'd say you're full of shit."

He quirks a brow as if challenging me, and it catches me off guard. He can't be serious.

"Why are you in here?" Jonah barks from the doorway.

"Hi babe, I was just coming to find you. Adeline and I were coloring."

"You're not who I was talking to," Jonah growls, his glare fixed on Ethan.

"You never introduced me to your wife. I figured I should get to know my sister-in-law," Ethan says, leaning back, completely unbothered.

Jonah looks ready to tear Ethan apart.

I walk to Jonah, smiling up at him and pushing on his hips. "Baby, show me your room." He doesn't budge. "Jonah, now. Don't do this in front of Adeline," I urge, and the mention of her name catches his attention. He turns his gaze to mine, and I take his hand, pulling him out of the room.

He takes the lead and pulls me toward the stairs, opens the closet, and slips on his coat before holding mine open for me. Taking my hand, he guides me toward the door.

Antoinette hurries after us. "Sweetheart, where are you going?"

"We're staying at a hotel." He jerks open the front door.

"Oh Jonah, stop. We're having such a nice gathering."

"No, you didn't tell me he would be here." His voice is so dark it makes me flinch. Then I think back to what Ethan said: 'What if I told you the story you were told was the other way around and your beloved husband was the one who was screwing my girlfriend?' Chills race through my body.

"It's Thanksgiving, Jonah. Of course he would be here. He's not here to try to sleep with your date." She refuses to refer to me as anything more than Jonah's dinner date, and that irritates me.

"Let's go, baby." He turns his back to her and pulls me away.

WE ARRIVE AT OUR HOTEL ROOM, AND JONAH IMMEDIATELY HEADS TO the bathroom. I thought I was making progress with his family, but the tension between Jonah and Ethan is far worse than I imagined. Ethan was clearly trying to get under my skin, and I trust that Jonah would never sleep with another man's girlfriend—especially his brother's. I can't fathom what Ethan's angle was in suggesting otherwise—unless he's telling the truth.

I hate when Jonah is in these moods—when he shuts me out. He didn't say a word on the drive to the hotel; he didn't even turn on the music. We rode in complete silence, and I could almost feel the storm of thoughts swirling in his mind.

I've spent so many years feeling sad about not having a family—feeling alone. But seeing how dysfunctional Jonah's family is, I almost feel like I'm better off. It's awful to think, but it's true.

His shower lasts longer than usual. When he's really mad, he stays in the shower until he "cools off." He must be fuming because the shower has shut off and turned back on twice now.

I don't know how to help him. I feel so uncomfortable—wanting to ask him about what Ethan said but not wanting to reignite his anger. As the water finally shuts off, my palms grow clammy, and I fidget with my fingers, trying to think of how to approach the conversation.

The bathroom door opens, and steam billows into the bedroom. Jonah steps out, looking like a god with just a towel wrapped around his waist. All my previous thoughts evaporate.

"Hi, baby," he says, stopping in front of me and staring down with an intensity that makes my heart race.

"Hi," I whisper back, feeling a mix of anxiety and longing.

He extends his hands and gently pulls me to my feet. Slowly, he turns me around, moving my hair over my shoulder before unzipping my dress. I step out of it and turn back to face him, feeling his eyes on me.

"I was going to offer to help you out of your heels, but I think I want you to keep them on," a grin spreads across his face. The shower has clearly done wonders for his mood.

Our eyes remain locked as he lets the towel fall to the floor. Slowly, he lowers himself to his knees, his hands reaching for my panties. He presses a kiss just above my slit before sliding them down my legs. I step out of them, feeling the anticipation build.

His lips touch my hip, and he drags his tongue sensuously across my skin to the other side, kissing my opposite hip. He moves a hand between my legs and wraps it around my thigh, lifting it over his shoulder. My fingers tangle in his hair to steady myself, our gazes remaining locked.

He leans in, placing a delicate kiss on my slit. As his tongue starts to massage me with firm, deliberate strokes, my hips instinctively rock against him.

I can't look away. The sight of him between my thighs is intoxicating. His hands grip my ass, one hand loosening to slide across my flesh. I know exactly where that hand is headed. It moves to my thigh, squeezing hard before slipping between my legs, his fingers sliding down my wet folds and pressing inside me.

A moan escapes my lips as he begins to move in and out, rocking them back and forth. My limbs tense, my skin prickling with the impending orgasm. It surges through me, and I come apart, my body shaking as it ripples along every nerve ending. My hips move against his him, his rhythm relentless as my climax peaks and then slowly subsides, leaving me panting and trembling.

He gently lowers my leg from his shoulder, his arms wrapping securely around me as he lifts me off my unsteady feet. Untucking the blankets, he lays me down with care, then removes each of my heels, placing a kiss to my toes as he does. Finally, he pulls the blankets up over me, his touch tender and reassuring.

"Ready for bed?" he asks, his smile warm and inviting. "We'll head home early in the morning." He leans down and presses his soft lips against mine.

I would normally not let the night end with only my satisfaction, but Ethan's words still echo in my mind. I know we need to discuss it, but not here, not now. I won't sleep, but I'd rather save the conversation for when we're home. There, if things get tense, I have plenty of places to retreat to: our bedroom, Shay's room, the stables, a walk, Estelle, or even a drive into town.

Jonah flips off the lights, climbs into bed, and soon falls asleep. I, however, am left to replay the evening's events. Ethan's insinuations, and Jonah's reactions. My thoughts swirl until Jonah's alarm jolts me awake in the morning. It feels like I never truly slept, which might make for a quick flight home, as I'm sure I'll nap on the way.

As we pull into the driveway, the setting sun casts a warm glow over the mansion, and I instantly feel a sense of relief. Being home eases some of the tension. Jonah and I haven't talked much, but I'm not in the mood for an argument.

Shay and Jonathan aren't home yet from their Thanksgiving, and Jonah has retreated to the gym. Wrapped in a blanket, I sit by the window in the second-floor living room, watching the first delicate snowflakes fall. The sight is truly breathtaking—a light dusting that dances from the sky.

My phone pings at my feet, and I reach for it, expecting a message from Shay.

UNKNOWN:

Sorry if I got you in trouble

I stare at the unfamiliar number, unsure of who it could be. Ignoring it, I place the phone back down and pull the blanket around my shoulders, trying to recapture the serenity of the moment.

"Did you have a nice Thanksgiving?" asks Gia, one of the maids who started working here the same time I did, as she enters the room to dust.

I return her smile. "I did, Gia. How was yours?"

"It was nice. I'm seeing Carl, the owner of Carl's mechanics in town. I had dinner with him and his family, and I met his daughter."

"Oh, Gia, that's great. How old is his daughter?"

"She's 10. His entire family is really great. You and Mr. Everett spent Thanksgiving with his family?"

"We did. We got home yesterday evening."

My phone pings again, breaking the conversation, and I open the message.

UNKNOWN:

You never did take the drawing

It's Ethan.

KALYN:

How did you get my number?

ETHAN:

We're family now, wouldn't you say?
Why wouldn't I have my sister's number?

KALYN:

Quit texting me.

TWO DAYS HAVE PASSED, AND JONAH AND I STILL HAVEN'T ADDRESSED what Ethan said. It's been gnawing at me, and I'm even more frustrated by how much I think about him. Not in a sexual way, but I need Jonah to confirm that Ethan is full of shit.

When I enter Jonah's office, I'm surprised to find it empty. Sighing, I walk in further and notice the bookcase at the far end of the wall is slightly ajar. Pushing it open, I head into his secret area. Opening the door to the living room, I find him sitting on the couch, his head leaned back against the cushions.

I walk around the couch and sit, leaving one cushion between us.

"Penny for your thoughts, Mr. Everett," I say after a prolonged silence.

He lets out a long sigh and looks in my direction, just staring without saying a word. I guess I'll have to start.

"I already know the answer, but I still need to ask… Ethan said he was the one dating Jenevieve and that you slept with her."

Jonah doesn't respond. He doesn't even appear shocked by what I'm saying. He just stares.

"Well?" I prompt.

"Well, what? You just said you didn't even need to ask. So why are you asking?"

"I didn't think I did, but now I'm starting to feel like maybe it's a good thing I'm asking," I can feel a knot forming in my stomach.

"What are you expecting from this conversation?"

"For you to tell me that Ethan is full of shit. For you to ease my nerves. For you to make me feel better." I'm dumbfounded that he even needs to ask that.

"Ethan is full of shit," he says nonchalantly.

"Is he?"

"You tell me. It seems you already made up your mind."

"Jonah, this isn't a joke. Please answer the question. Was Ethan the one dating Jenevieve?"

He stands, looking at least ten feet tall, imposing and towering over me. He walks over, leaning down until his face is an inch from mine. "No," he drawls out, then stands and walks away.

I'm momentarily stunned, only snapping out of it when I hear the door slam behind him.

What just happened?

He seems mad at me just for asking a question that his brother planted in my mind. I really don't think I'm in the wrong here. And yeah, I don't trust the words from a man I met for all of five seconds before he begins spewing bullshit. But I had hoped Jonah would just tell me Ethan is a shit-starter and there's nothing more to it than that. But he doesn't even give me that. Instead, he storms off, which, to me, makes him look pretty guilty.

I leap off the couch and race after him, not sure which way he went. I close the bookcase behind me and pass through his office. Maybe he retreated to our room. As I walk up the stairs to our wing, I catch sight of him disappearing into our bedroom.

"Jonah!" I shout just as the door slams shut.

Jonathan and Shay stand in their doorway, looking confused, but I don't stop to talk to them or even welcome them home. My fury propels me onward.

I follow him into our room. He's settled on the bed, the TV flickering to life as he reclines against the pillows, one leg bent on the bed, the other still planted on the floor.

"Jonah Joel Everett, how dare you walk away from me while we're talking."

He has the audacity to flip through TV channels like I'm not even here. Walking over to him, I rip the remote from his grasp and shut off the TV, tossing the device back on the bed. "You have my blood boiling right now. Talk to me!"

He stares at me, his face devoid of any emotion.

"Are you schizophrenic? Bipolar? What's happening?" I demand furiously.

Without a word, he stands and attempts to walk away, but I reach out and grab his arm. He easily shrugs me off as he exits the room. This is the first time I've wanted to slap the shit out of him. Maybe Ethan really was telling the truth?

I glance over and see Jonah's phone on the nightstand. Grabbing it, I scroll his contacts, letting out a sigh as I hover over the FaceTime button contemplating whether I should make this call. Finally, I hit the FaceTime icon on one of the last people I thought I would ever reach out to for advice.

She answers on the second ring. Her wide smile falters when she sees me.

"Hey, Eliza."

She stares momentarily, appearing stunned, "Why are you calling me from Jonah's phone?"

"I didn't have your number. He's fine... actually, no, he's not. I don't know what's wrong with him. He won't talk to me." My voice wobbles on the last words.

She lets out a long sigh. "I'll be back," she says to someone offscreen, then goes to another room, closing the door. "What happened?" she asks.

"I don't know. I was coloring with Adeline, and Ethan came in and started coloring with us. Ethan insinuated that he was the one dating Jenevieve and Jonah cheated with her. Jonah came in, got mad, and said we were leaving. When I asked Jonah about what Ethan had said, he didn't even deny it. He's literally avoiding me, slamming doors and leaving every time I try to talk to him. He all but ripped his own arm off just to get my hand off of him a minute ago."

"For starters, Ethan is goading you. Jonah *was* the one dating Jenevieve, and Ethan slept with her." She doesn't get any further before I burst into tears, relieved Jonah wasn't the cheater. The mere thought had made me feel like my insides were going to fall out of my butt.

"Oh, Kalyn," she says sympathetically.

She lets me cry until I finally calm down.

"I don't even know why I let him get in my head, Shine," I admit, hating that I questioned Jonah's integrity.

Eliza sits quietly, just watching me, and I start to feel so foolish for even calling her.

"In high school, Jonah had a crush on the head cheerleader, and she obviously liked him back. Ethan managed to talk her into sleeping with him by telling her Jonah didn't date virgins and he would help her get him. Then, after Ethan slept with her, he told her Jonah would never give her the time of day now. He then told Jonah he could have his leftovers. Jonah was so mad that he found out who Ethan was taking to prom, slept with her, and then told Ethan the same thing. They fought, Jonah beat the crap out of Ethan, and Ethan never let it go. Jonah refused to date anyone afterward because he feared Ethan would try to sleep with her. Jonah didn't want to date Jenevieve, but our parents pushed it. Her family initially rejected Ethan because he slept with Jenevieve's cousin. They shifted their focus to Jonah, who eventually gave in and started dating her to make everyone happy.

During a summer vacation, Jonah walked in on Ethan having sex with Jenevieve. Jonah just walked away, and Ethan laughed.

But then our families insisted they stay together and make it work even though she cheated on Jonah with his brother. Jonah couldn't stand Jenevieve, and I was furious at her. She complained about Jonah being rough with her in bed, which secretly made me happy because she fucking deserved it for what she did to him. She deserved any sort of punishment he gave to her for it. At a family gathering, she couldn't even sit, and when I asked, she said she and Jonah liked it rough. I knew it was his way of punishing her. He continued being rough with her in hopes she would get sick and tired of it and leave, but I'll give it to her—she was in it for the end game.

Jonah sank into a deep place. Even though he never loved Jenevieve, it was another thing Ethan took from him. You know the rest. If Jonah isn't talking to you, he's sinking back into that dark place, and you need to pull him out. Seeing you with Ethan probably triggered all those old wounds. I've never seen him love anyone the way he loves you. You're the only one who could destroy him. He might not want to listen, but make him. Let him know how much you love him."

"I love him so much, Eliza. More than I ever thought possible."

She sighs. "I know you do." After a moment, she adds, "Save my number in your phone. We should get to know each other; we're sisters now, after all."

"Thank you," I wipe away my tears. "I will."

"Let me know how it goes," she says before we end the call.

We talked for over an hour, and I hope Jonah has had time to calm down. I walk to his office, hoping to find him there. He is, along with Jonathan, Shay, Brandt, and Dame. At least he's talking.

"Hi," I say, wrapping my arms around Shay from the back of her chair and kissing her cheek.

"Hi," she smiles, wrapping her arm around me.

"Hey, Kal," Jonathan greets me as I do the same to him, wrapping my arms around him from behind.

Jonah glanced at me when I walked in but hasn't acknowledged me since. I stand behind Jonathan's chair, leaning on the back as everyone chats. The courage I had when I walked in fades. I had hoped it would only be Shay and Jonathan here, but with everyone else present, my confidence wanes.

Going back to Shay, wrapping my arms around her, I whisper, "I'm going to bed. Love you," and quietly head out, hoping no one notices.

I softly close the door behind me and am heading toward my room when I hear the door to his office open and shut. I turn and see Jonah following me. He remains silent, matching my pace, maintaining a constant distance. I continue to our room, opening the door and holding it for him.

"I'm sorry for even questioning you. I'll do anything to make it up to you. I feel awful for doubting you." I'm rambling when he lifts me off my feet and kisses me, carrying me to our bed. "I'm so sorry, babe."

"I'd never lie to you," he whispers, laying me down and climbing on top of me. "When I saw him with you, I wanted to kill him. I imagined every way I could hurt him." His lips find mine again. "Thinking about him with you made me want to skin him alive." His words are pained.

I push him onto his back and climb on top of him. "He will never know what I feel like. Ever. You are my husband. You're all I will ever need." I sit up and unbutton his shirt, then lean down, kissing across his bare chest and abs, taking my time as I let my lips and tongue enjoy him. Sitting up, I pull off my shirt and toss it behind me. He flips me onto my back, removes my shorts, and tosses them over his shoulder the same way I had just done, then sheds the rest of his clothes.

"I was planning on giving you a blowjob since you got me off last night," I whisper as he settles between my legs.

"Nice," he smiles, positioning himself at my center and presses in.

My smile instantly transforms into pure arousal as he works himself inside me.

An hour later, we lie entwined, our fingers interlaced, as I trace patterns between his. "I called your sister," I admit softly.

He turns his head to look at me. "Liza?"

"Yeah. You left your phone in here, and I didn't know what else to do. I think it helped. She told me to save her number so we can talk again... since we're sisters now. Her words, not mine."

"She's a good person," he says.

"She told me about you and Ethan. I'm not Jenevieve. I'd never cheat on you."

"Yeah," he responds, but it doesn't sound convincing.

"Jonah," I wait until he meets my gaze. "I would never cheat on you."

"Nobody plans on cheating."

"Are you saying that because you think I might find you in bed with someone else?" My voice tinged with concern.

His eyebrows knit together as he turns fully toward me. "Fuck that. I'd rather rip my own dick off than ever put it in anyone else."

"Good. Because I'd rather you rip your dick off than you ever put it in anyone else. Speaking of... did you know after a male octopus mates with a female, she will eat him? So, male octopuses started detaching their dicks and throwing them at the female to impregnate her that way in order to survive." I grin so wide, because I started looking up random facts too, and I can't believe how perfectly this random TikTok fact I saw is coming in handy.

He lets out a laugh. "Something like that."

"Well, regardless if that's true or not, I'll rip your dick off if you put it near anybody else."

"It's partially true, and my dick will never be near anybody else ever again," he leans in and kisses me.

He lays on my chest, his arms wrapped around me as I softly run my fingers in his hair. He feels so good. His body relaxes, and I can feel the delicious weight of him on me as he falls asleep. Picking up my phone, I take a picture and send it to Eliza.

KALYN:

> All better. Thank you for talking to me.

ELIZA:

> Aww, he looks so peaceful. Anytime.
> Thanks for calling me.

WE STAY AT THE MANSION FOR TWO BLISSFUL WEEKS BEFORE RETURNing to the city. Although I don't want to disrupt Jonah's work schedule, I wish we had a different arrangement: three weeks at home, and one in the city each month. I'm so much more relaxed at home, but I understand Jonah has to work, so I don't complain.

While Jonah is in meetings all day, I busy myself in reports to stay occupied.

My phone pings, breaking my concentration.

ETHAN:

> Is cereal considered soup?

KALYN:

Quit texting me. I won't tell you again.

ETHAN:

Think about it, it's in liquid, that's soup, right?

KALYN:

If you text me again, I will tell Jonah.

ETHAN:

Ahh, I see. You aren't allowed to talk to other men. That's a little controlling, wouldn't you say?

Without hesitation, I block his number and set my phone down. Barely five minutes pass before it pings again.

UNKNOWN:

Really? Ouch.

KALYN:

Do you not know how to listen? Leave me alone.

I don't want to talk to you. I don't want you texting me.

ETHAN:

I wonder which lies you are referring to.

ETHAN:

Hmm

I spend the rest of the day pondering whether to tell Jonah. The decision becomes easy when I see him enter the bedroom after working out with Jonathan. As he starts to undress, I walk over and hand him my phone.

"What's this?" he asks, puzzled by my gesture.

"Read them," I reply, feeling a knot of nervousness constricting in my stomach.

His smile fades as he scans the messages. "I obviously blocked him, but he persisted by using another number."

Jonah hands my phone back and kisses me gently. "You handled that well, baby. Come shower with me." He reaches over, lifts my shirt over my head, and tosses it into the laundry basket. I finish undressing and follow him into the bathroom, feeling my concern dissipate.

I assumed he would have been incredibly mad over the texts, but he appears to not care at all, which catches me off guard. But I'm not going to worry about it. Our talk must have eased his mind, and that makes me happy.

In the morning, I wake to find he's gone. It's Saturday, so I know he will either be in the gym or his office, but my gut instinct points me toward the latter. As I approach the door, I can hear the murmur of his voice, and my initial thought is that maybe Jonathan's joined him. However, the door is cracked open just enough for me to peer inside. His office at the condo is much smaller than his office back at the mansion and I can see he's pacing back and forth, one hand shoved deep in his pocket, the other holding his phone to his ear.

"It was hardly a threat," he says into the phone.

After a moment of him listening he speaks again. "He did this. Not me. But if he thinks he can pull the same bullshit again with Kalyn, I'll kill him."

He listens again. "Get it through your thick skull, Mother, I never wanted Jenevieve. YOU forced that. Ethan sleeping with her sealed her own fate. I would have never married her. If he thinks trying to get with Kalyn will have the same outcome, you all are so sadly mistaken, I will burn—"

"Good morning, babe," I enter his office, pretending I haven't heard anything.

"I'll talk to you later," he abruptly says and hangs up.

"Good morning, baby," he puts his phone on his desk and walks over to me. He picks me up, and my legs wrap around his waist as I bring my lips to his.

"Who was on the phone?"

"My mother," he kisses me again.

"Everything okay?"

"Everything is perfect. How'd you sleep?" he asks as he sets me down.

"Good. I hoped I'd wake up with you next to me, but you snuck away."

"Let's go back to bed and start over."

"Fine by me," I giggle as he scoops me back up and takes us right back to bed.

CHAPTER
Forty-Two

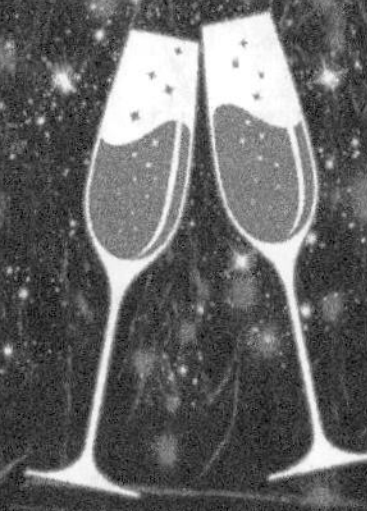

JONAH

Commotion in the hallway interrupts my morning meeting. I abruptly end the call and get up from my chair to see what's happening.

"Bridget, stop. This is Mr. Everett's father, Sr. Everett. Show some respect," Kalyn is holding her hands up as she tries to get Bridget to step aside.

My father is stopped near my office door, looking utterly irritated with Bridget blocking his way, while Kalyn tries to de-escalate the situation.

"Bridget, you can go back to your desk. Thank you for escorting my father," I say, dismissing her, though I had no idea he was coming by.

"Thank you, dear," my father says to Kalyn before walking into my office.

"What can I do for you?" I ask, not wanting to waste time. I can't imagine he would pop in for a casual visit; and I'd rather not deal with him bringing up the golf contract again.

"Can we sit?" he gestures toward the couch instead of my desk, which surprises me.

I stare, then nod, gesturing for him to take his seat of choice. We sit in silence for a moment too long before I begin to speak, but he beats me to it.

"I want to start by apologizing. I didn't realize how serious things were with Kalyn. I'm sorry you felt you needed to marry her privately. I've amended the contract and would like to partner with you on the golf complex," he says, reaching into his briefcase and handing me a new contract, fully amended to include just our two companies.

"Why the change of heart?" I ask simply.

My father lets out a long sigh. "Plain and simple, I see the error of my ways. I messed up. My first child to get married did so without their family present because of how we behaved. Your mother and I were making decisions for your life solely based on business gain, and I'll never do that again. If you can clear some space in your schedule, I'd love to take you and Kalyn to a couple of spots where I've reserved land for possible development. We can also grab lunch."

I stare blankly ahead, leaning forward in my seat with my elbows resting on my knees. "And Cedric?"

"We have already discussed it," he says, offering nothing more.

"And?"

"He feels as I'm sure you can imagine," my father says, leaning back and rubbing his palms down his slacks.

"Does he know I'm married?"

"He does," he nods.

"Are we going to play 20 questions?"

"We don't need to. I don't want to talk about him or his feelings towards your marriage or this deal. It's all done in that sense. My priority is my family, my business, my son, and my daughter-in-law." I'm surprised he seems to be taking the news of my marriage so well.

"Let me talk to Kalyn."

"Please," he urges.

Her door is open, and she's typing on her computer. "Hi, babe, got a minute?"

"Hey," she smiles, turning toward me. "Is everything okay?"

"He apologized," I sit on the edge of her desk.

"Okay? That's good, right?"

"I think I'm going to proceed with the business plans. The contracts are amended to include just our companies. He wants to show us some land and have lunch. Are you comfortable with that?"

"Absolutely, Jonah, this is great," she stands and wraps her arms around my neck. "Plus, your dad called me 'dear.' I think he's starting to accept me as his bonus daughter."

I smile and touch my lips to hers. Leaning over, I grab her desk phone and dial Bridget's extension.

"Bridget," she answers with a sigh after a few rings, as if this call is somehow bothering her. Her tone pisses me off, especially since she thought it was Kalyn calling her.

"It's Everett. Clear my schedule this morning. I'll be back this afternoon."

"Yes, sir," she responds, her voice immediately shifting as she realizes it's me on the line, not Kalyn. I hang up, deciding I will address this later.

Standing, I take Kalyn's hand, pulling her to the coat hanger and help her into her coat. Then we head back to my office.

My father is standing by the window, peering out, but he turns as we enter. "Ready if you are," I say, grabbing my jacket.

Kalyn's smile is so bright it makes my chest clench.

"How are you, Kalyn?" he asks as he approaches.

"I'm well, Mr. Everett. Thank you for inviting me along," she replies with a smile.

"Please, we are family. Call me Beau, or Dad if you'd like," he offers, and from here it almost looks like she's tearing up.

"Ready?" I ask, smiling at her.

My dad takes us to an open field, a prime location just outside the city limits, yet close enough for convenient access. Tall trees border the property, forming a natural barrier from the nearby road, and the air is filled with the scent of fresh cut grass.

"Perfect for a large parking area right here," he points to a flat, open expanse near the entrance. "We can easily accommodate a hundred cars. And over here," he gestures to the gently rolling hills further in, "that's where we'll build the golf complex. There's plenty of space for multiple 18-hole courses, all on real grass. We can maintain it to the highest standards, making it a top destination for golf enthusiasts."

I nod, agreeing with his vision. "I have to admit, it's a good spot."

As we continue walking around the property, he details his plans for each section. "This area will be perfect for the driving range," he points to a slightly elevated section. "And we can put a practice green over there, near those trees."

Kalyn's excitement is infectious as she hangs on to every word my dad says, her interest in what he says makes him more eager to keep talking.

We spend another hour exploring the property, discussing potential details. When we finish and head back to the car, my dad asks what we think.

"I don't personally know much about golf, but I think this is well thought out. This is going to be amazing," Kalyn says, making my dad look even more pleased.

"It's great, Dad. The location seems perfect."

KALYN AND I SIT ACROSS FROM MY DAD FOR LUNCH, AND HER EYES sparkle with excitement as we talk about the new golf complex. My dad leans back in his chair, a contented smile on his face as he listens to her talk.

We finish eating, and Kalyn excuses herself to go to the restroom. I watch her walk away and still can't believe she's my wife. When she returns a few minutes later, Dad does a double take, his face momentarily paling as if he's seen a ghost. I blink, wondering if I imagined it, but then he recovers and greets Kalyn warmly.

As we move off the topic of the golf complex and show my dad the video of us getting engaged and married, he seems overjoyed. I'm surprised to see how much his attitude has changed. Throughout lunch, I notice him glancing at Kalyn as if lost in thought, only to shake it off and return to the present.

On the drive back to the office, he continues staring at her. I can't quite place the look. Is it recognition? Joy that he has a new family member? But it's more. I just don't know what.

We're dropped off at the front of the building. My father gets out, shaking my hand and doing the same to Kalyn's. Only he holds her hand for a moment longer.

"Kalyn, your last name was Bell? Yeah?"

"Yes," she smiles. "Well, still is. I'm hyphenated: Bell-Everett."

"Is… is your father's name Konrad?"

Kalyn's smile grows wider. "Yes."

"And your mother," there's a long pause before he says, "Katrina?"

"Yes," she nods again.

My dad's eyes well with tears as he grabs Kalyn and pulls her into a hug. She hugs him back, her eyes closing as she relaxes into him. When he releases her, he wipes away a tear and gets back in his car.

"Okay, your dad is either the best actor or he absolutely accepts me," she says, watching after the car, then turning toward me.

I have no idea what just happened, but Kalyn's happiness has me not giving it a second thought. She kisses me, and I kiss her back. Not caring that we are in public, I kiss her passionately. She is still radiating happiness when we get home, and I love this side of her. Kalyn feeling loved, looks good on her.

At the office the following day, Kalyn is still glowing with happiness. She walks into my office, appearing as if she's floating on a cloud as she hands me a folder. I stand, grab her arm, and draw her to me until she's flush against my chest. Accepting the folder, I toss it on my desk before claiming her mouth. Her hand presses into my pants, and a guttural rumble builds in my throat, urging me into her touch.

"Do you want me?" she whispers, and I nod, capturing her lips with mine again. She pushes on my chest, and I stand upright, giving her room to turn around and present herself to me. "Then take me."

I unzip her skirt, only wanting to untuck her shirt so I can feel her bare tits. I jerk my zipper down, releasing my dick, then slide her skirt up over her ass. She widens her stance and pushes her ass out toward me. My fingers trace her slit, confirming her readiness. My naughty girl is soaked for me.

My palm cracks against her ass; she jolts, a sharp gasp ripping from her throat. I bend down, my cock gliding up her drenched folds before notching at her entrance. With one forceful thrust, I'm buried to the hilt. A raw exclamation rips from her mouth. I cup her breast before releasing it, my hands clamping her hips. I yank her into me, my pace merciless.

Her legs begin to tremble, a sure sign that she's close. She collapses onto my desk, reaching her arms above her head to grab the edge for support. I slip my hand between her thighs, my fingers tracing circles on her swollen nub.

My phone rings, and I ignore it. It's silent for a mere second before it rings again. And then again. As I release inside her, it rings a fourth time.

"What!" I bellow into the receiver.

"There is a woman here demanding to see you. Her name is Jenevieve."

I stiffen. *Why the fuck is she here?*

"You can't go back there!" Bridget voice rises, and then the phone drops onto her desk.

"Fuck," I mutter, pulling out of Kalyn and grabbing tissue, handing a pile to her and wiping myself off.

She quickly stands, wiping herself up, tossing the tissue in the trash, and adjusting her skirt. She's tucking her shirt in when the door swings open wide, and the unmistakable stomp of Jenevieve's heels echoes right on in.

She's… blonde—very blonde—almost Kalyn's color except Kalyn doesn't have to pay money for hers. Her scowl is plastered across her face, growing even more displeased when she sees Kalyn.

"You have five seconds to explain why you're in my building before I throw you out," I bite out.

"Babe," Kalyn says, holding her skirt in place behind her. I reach down and zip her.

"Two seconds earlier, you would have walked in on us for a *third* time having sex. It's starting to feel kind of pervy at this point," Kalyn says to Jenevieve.

Jenevieve's eyes flare before narrowing again.

"Thank you, husband. That felt incredible," Kalyn turns to face me, grabbing my face with both hands and pressing her mouth to mine. Then walks around the desk. "Jenevieve, it's never a pleasure," she says and walks out.

Flattening my tie against my chest, I sit and shift toward my desk. Opening Messenger, I type a quick message to Jonathan, instructing him to have security ready. Jenevieve just barged into my office, fuming over, I assume, her dad being cut out of the deal.

"Husband? Is this like a new nickname?" she scoffs, advancing toward my desk.

"No, it's the proper term for her to refer to her husband," I reply.

"As in…" she trails off, her eyes flicking from my ring back to me in shock.

"As in Kalyn is my wife," I finish her sentence.

She falters, her gaze lingering on my ring. "Jonah, you can't be serious."

"Get on with it, Jenevieve. I can't imagine you came here just to walk in on me having sex with my wife and then question the validity of my marriage," I say, irritated.

"You can't cut my father out of the golf deal just because you married the hired help," she scoffs.

"You can't cut someone out who was never included," I raise my brow at her to show my boredom. I can see her brows furrow with anger, and it brings me joy to know I'm getting under her skin. How did I ever fuck her?

"Is this because of… her?"

"My wife? This has nothing to do with her. Though she has been a huge part in helping find the land we'll use to develop the establishments," I smile proudly.

"You will reconsider," she demands.

I laugh dryly. "Get out."

"When did you become so heartless, Jonah?" she narrows her eyes.

"I've always been this way toward you. You just never paid attention. But after I found out you put your hands on Kalyn, you don't deserve even an ounce of respect. I should have pressed charges against you."

"You think that cheap whore will stay faithful? Jonathan probably has sex with her behind your back. And Ethan, it's only a matter of time before he fills her the same way he used to fill me."

"Jonathan doesn't need to do it behind my back. Kalyn and I don't mind getting adventurous with him," I grin, knowing this will really chap her ass. "As for Ethan, she met him, wasn't a fan," I shrug.

"Let's see how Shayla feels about that," she smirks.

"She loves it. It was her idea, actually."

Her jaw clenches as she realizes she has absolutely no control here.

"That seems fitting. Brad too, I guess, since he's always been so fond of her."

"Like an orgy," I raise my brows to bait her. The pulse in her neck throbs, and her jaw flexes as her attempts to provoke me fail.

"I sure hope nothing happens to the group's bicycle," she sneers. "It would be such a shame for her to go out the same way her parents did."

In an instant, my hand clamps around her throat, and she smiles, which only fuels my anger. "Get the fuck out of my office, you disgusting, filthy tramp." I release her.

Her hands go to her throat before bursting into laughter. "You always did like it rough. I guess you still enjoy having me the way you always did."

"You're an embarrassment. The business plans were accepted and signed this morning. Unless you happen to share the last name Everett, you're not part of them. I'd offer Ethan as a way to stake a claim on the Everett name, but he's currently fixated on my wife, and, well, he didn't want you in the past, he certainly won't want you now. Get out of my office."

"You think you're some big shot—"

"Jenevieve. Get out. I was done with you years ago. I wanted you dead the day you put your hands on my wife. I will kill you myself if you don't get the fuck out of my building and leave me, my wife, and my family alone."

Jonathan walks in with security. "Time to go, baby deer," he says, motioning for her to leave.

"Excuse me?" Her head snaps in his direction as she glares.

"Oh, because you look like a newborn deer trying to walk in heels. Gotta go." He crosses his arms over his chest and gestures toward the door with his thumb.

"Nobody has ever liked you," she snarls.

"Aww," Jonathan pouts mockingly.

Security approaches her, and she rips her arm away, even though no one has touched her. She storms past them, and Jonathan cackles as she walks by.

"Fuck off," she bites out, and he watches as she leaves.

"Toodles," he wiggles his fingers after her.

Without turning around, she flips him off.

She has my blood pressure so high I'm probably on the cusp of a heart attack. I shove open Kalyn's office door, finding Shay and Miles on the opposite side of the desk, with Shay mid-sentence.

"Get out," I bark, closing the distance between Kalyn and me in five quick strides. They immediately stand and retreat.

"Is everything okay?" she asks, rising as I approach.

Grabbing her, I lift her onto her desk by her waist and tug her skirt up.

"Babe, what happened?" she asks, watching me as I jerk my pants open.

I pull her legs toward me, and she nearly loses her balance, her hands catching behind her as I impale her. She whimpers in pain, but I need to get off.

"Jonah," her eyes fill with worry. "Jonah, that hurts," she winces, pushing her hand against my pelvis. I grab it, pinning it behind her back while holding her lower back with the other hand, pulling her against me with brutal force, thrusting in and out. This is about me—about my anger and needing to release it. Not her. Not Jenevieve, and sure as fuck not Ethan.

I drive into her harder. She isn't wearing a bra; her tits are so perfect she doesn't need to wear one. Letting go of her hand, I rip her shirt up and bite down on her nipple, sucking it into my mouth. She cries out in pain, and I don't care. She grabs my hair, trying to pull me off, but that only fuels my need. Standing upright, I grip her hips tighter, watching her glorious breasts bounce. She pushes on my jaw, but I easily move my head back. When she pushes on me again, I grab her hands and pin them behind her back once again.

"Jonah, stop," she begs. All I can picture is walking in on Ethan and Jenevieve, and my mind distorts those images to Ethan buried inside Kalyn. I fucking hate it. I need those images gone.

I groan as I reach orgasm. Pulling out, I come on her dress, wanting to defile her as the image taints my mind. Breathing heavily, I begin buttoning up my pants as my breathing steadies.

"What the fuck, Jonah?" She slaps me and shoves my chest, forcing me away as she climbs off her desk. She grabs tissue from the box, wipes the come from her dress, and adjusts her clothes to look somewhat presentable.

"Fucking prick," she says, storming out of her office.

I stand there, leaned over her desk. Did I seriously just do that?

Fuck. I angrily run my fingers through my hair.

Walking back to my office, I follow through the large mirror on the right wall that opens up to a hallway with a bathroom on the left, a closet on the right, and a bedroom at the end of the hall. Some days I used to work so late that I would just stay. Not many people know I have an entire bedroom here, but she certainly does because I've taken her to it a couple times. My bathroom is also more convenient than the employee bathroom, and she doesn't need to share a bathroom with the employees.

In the large walk-in closet, Kalyn has a side with entire outfits. They weren't intended for this purpose, but they're certainly useful right now.

She's already undressed and pulling on a new outfit.

"Sorry," I apologize.

She turns and throws her skirt at me. "What the fuck was that?" she bites out as she zips up another dress. "I told you that hurt, and you went even harder."

"I'm sorry," is all I can get out.

"You're sorry? I told you it fucking hurt, and you didn't stop. I wasn't ready, and you shoved your big-ass dick inside me. Then you just fucking tried to bite my nipple off. And all you can say is you're sorry? You literally didn't even get me off! So now that's twice today you got off and I didn't—because of Jenevieve."

"Jenevieve got under my skin."

"So you hurt me?" she questions.

When I remain silent, she glares and storms past me, shoulder-checking me as she mutters, "Fucking dick."

As we head to the elevators, Jonathan and Shay clearly sense the tension, but they keep quiet. The ride home is the same—nobody says a word.

Once we're in our room, Kalyn changes clothes. I see the bite mark on her breast where I made her bleed around her nipple. I don't have the reaction I probably should; instead of feeling remorse, my dick springs to life and I want her again. As soon as she's dressed, she walks over to Shay's place, which makes me jealous. I access the camera feed from their condo, switching between screens until I find footage of Shay and Kalyn in the kitchen and click to watch.

"Did he say what Jenevieve wanted?" Shay asks.

"No clue. He stormed in my office as you saw, split me in half, and tried biting my nipple off."

"Who's biting nipples?" Jonathan asks as he enters the kitchen.

"Your asshole best friend," Kalyn replies. "Will you look at it?"

Shay's eyes widen. "Did it break the skin?"

Kalyn lifts her shirt, and Shay's mouth drops open as Jonathan steps in to examine the mark. He leaves and returns with a first aid kit. He prepares supplies from it, glancing at Shay, who turns back to Kalyn.

"I'm going to play the best friend role here, even though I find this hot. Did he say why he did this? Heat of the moment? Thank god he has straight teeth."

"No, I told him it hurt when he rammed his giant-ass dick in me before I was even ready, and when I tried pushing him away, he bit me." She winces as Jonathan applies alcohol to the wound. "Jesus Christ," she mutters, looking down as he makes quick work of trying to clean it.

"Where is Mr. Everett now?" Shay asks, trying to distract her.

"Don't know, don't care. Keep your first aid kit handy because I'm going to bite off something much bigger than his nipple," she retorts.

Over the next three hours, they sit in the living room watching a movie. Kalyn lies in Shay's lap while Shay plays with her hair, and her legs rest on Jonathan's lap, where the lucky asshole is massaging her foot. His other arm stretches over the back of the couch, his fingers lightly tracing Shay's neck and shoulder. Kalyn's shirt is still pulled up to avoid staining it with the ointment Jonathan applied. I'm actually impressed that Jonathan isn't blatantly staring at her tits, even though they're impossible to ignore. I just know if she moved her leg back a bit, she'd feel he's pitching a tent.

Kalyn stays over there for the next three hours, and I take the coward's way out when she finally comes back by lingering in my office, hoping she'll be asleep by the time I come to bed. To my surprise, she's still awake when I enter our room. I shower, and when I come out, she remains lying there, eyes closed but not asleep.

I feel like shit. I heard her say it hurt, and I didn't care. Her body wasn't ready, but I forced myself in anyway, consumed by rage at Jenevieve's words. She implied that Kalyn might meet a similar fate to her parents, suggesting some sort of untimely demise like a car wreck. That was the breaking point for me. Everyone probably thinks my anger was solely about Jenevieve flaunting her affair with Ethan, but that wasn't it at all. Walking in on Jenevieve and Ethan in my bed didn't even surprise me; it was the audacity of them doing it there. They could have done that bullshit in his bed, but instead, they chose mine.

I sit on her side of the bed, elbows on my knees, and my hands in my hair. "I'm sorry, baby. I really messed up." I struggle to find the right words to properly apologize to her. "Jenevieve is mad I cut her father out of the deal," I explain, but she doesn't move. "I lost control. I can't promise it won't happen again, but I'll try to be better, to be everything you deserve and more."

"What could she have said that made you that mad?"

I let out a sigh, not even wanting to repeat the words. Knowing I won't get out of this without just being upfront I let my hands hang. "She insinuated that you were going to meet the same fate as your parents."

I feel her shifting, and then she's pushing on my shoulder until I sit up. She straddles my lap and wraps her arms around me. "Jenevieve is a miserable bitch."

"Yeah," I agree.

"And you're an asshole," she murmurs.

"I know. I'm sorry."

"Jonah, you're my husband. I don't care what Jenevieve, Ethan, or anyone else says. Nobody will ever come between us. Even her lame attempt at threatening my life. Do you understand?"

"Yes," I kiss her gently, trying to make amends for my mistakes.

"I demand at least four orgasms now since I was gypped all day on them."

"I'll give you ten," I kiss her and flip her over on the bed.

IT'S JUST AFTER LUNCH, AND KALYN AND I HAVE JUST FINISHED A quickie on my desk when Jonathan and Shay walk in. Though we're finished, I'm still buried inside her.

"Well, that looks fun," Jonathan comments, taking a seat in a chair on the opposite side of my desk.

"The office is a terrible place for sex," Kalyn laughs. "Hours go by without interruptions, but the second we start, someone walks in."

"Nuts. We don't have that problem," Jonathan says. "But you guys do remember you have a bedroom right there." He gestures toward the mirror.

"Yeah, we don't have that problem only because you answer the phone while we're having sex or you start your meetings while we're doing it," Shay gives him a playful shove.

We make quick work of cleaning ourselves up mere seconds before Bridget knocks on the door, opening it and peeking in. Everyone turns to look. "Your 2:00 PM meeting has arrived, sir." she says quietly, looking embarrassed.

"Thank you, Bridget," I nod. Kalyn, Shay, and Jonathan exit as Ivan Collins and Pierre Quiff enter.

As they take their seats at the conference table, Ivan begins to lay out the golf complex plans. "Mr. Everett, thank you for meeting with us. We brought mock plans with the dimensions of the land Beaumont sent over. Nothing is set in stone; this is just a rough idea," he says, unfolding the blueprints.

I nod appreciatively, focusing on the plans. "I'm looking forward to seeing what you've come up with," I reply.

Pierre points to different sections of the blueprints. "We've proposed several key areas for development here," he explains, indicating various elements of the layout. "We believe these will maximize the land's potential while maintaining a balanced and sustainable environment."

Ivan adds, "Our next step will be to create 3D models. These will provide a more comprehensive view of the project and help you visualize the final product. We can make adjustments based on your feedback before moving forward with any final decisions."

I lean in, examining the plans intently. "I appreciate the detail you've put into this. The 3D models will be incredibly useful for making sure everything aligns. So far, we're on the right track. Thank you for bringing this by."

Ivan smiles, "Of course, thank you for trusting us with this project. I also hear congratulations are in order, Mr. Everett! That's wonderful news."

Pierre nods in agreement. "Yes, congratulations. It's always nice to hear about such happy occasions."

"Thank you," I reply. "It's been an exciting time. My wife, Kalyn, has been incredibly beneficial through all of this. I'll introduce you to her before you head out."

I knock on Kalyn's open door, and she stands. "Come in," she waves, and I walk in, feeling incredibly lucky to introduce her as my wife.

"Kalyn, I'd like to introduce Mr. Ivan Collins and Mr. Pierre Quiff. Gentlemen, this is my wife, Kalyn Everett," I announce proudly. "Mr. Collins and Mr. Quiff are from Collins and Quiff Odysseys. They are leading the design team for Everett Pines Golf. We'll be working closely with them as we begin the design stage. They worked up the mockups and now will create 3D models to show us."

Kalyn shakes each of their hands. "I look forward to working with both of you. We're really excited about this new venture, and

I think golf lovers will be thrilled with what you come up with," she says with a smile.

"Thank you for allowing us the opportunity to work with you," Mr. Collins replies. "We will keep you up to speed every step of the way."

"If you need anything at all, feel free to reach out," Kalyn says, handing them each one of her business cards. "Mr. Everett is incredibly busy, and we work side by side. I'd be more than happy to assist in any way I can."

"Walk with us," I offer.

We walk to the elevators while they continue chatting. As we wait, they discuss different features of golf. I've never been much into golf, and Kalyn has never been golfing before in her life. She finds the topic rather boring, but she can tell I'm excited to work with my father, and that makes her happy for me and for the project.

"It was wonderful to meet you, Mrs. Everett. Take care and talk soon," Mr. Quiff says.

"Lucky man, Mr. Everett. Congratulations again on the marriage," Mr. Collins adds.

"Thank you," I say, and we wave goodbye.

As soon as the doors close, I wrap my arms around Kalyn, kissing her passionately. When I pull away, she wipes my lips. "You took the gloss off my lip stain," she smiles. Then she glances over at the receptionist desk and all the three women behind the desk glare at her.

"Can I help you with something?" she asks.

"No, ma'am," Sadie responds, and they all look back down at their computers and continue typing.

"Mrs. Everett," I correct her, "You will refer to her by her name. Mrs. Everett."

"Yes, sir. Sorry, Mrs. Everett," she says, looking uncomfortable.

I shake my head and grab Kalyn's hand, walking her down the hall toward our offices.

"When do we meet with your father again?" she asks.

"Work-wise, in a couple of weeks or so, depending on how long the plans take to draw up. My mom called to invite us to Christmas at their house." I make sure to leave out the part where she called numerous times, left several messages with Bridget, and threatened to continue calling every number in my office, leaving voicemails with my staff until I called her back.

"And? We're going, Jonah," she insists.

"Yes, baby, we're going."

"Well damn, I thought I had myself a fight," she grins.

We spend three more days in the city before wrapping up to head home. Kalyn is so antsy to get back she packs her bag and wheels it into the bedroom.

"Going to work tomorrow doesn't sound very fun," she huffs. "But I can adjust quickly. Wanna leave at noon tomorrow?" her expression almost pleading as she walks to the bed.

"And my afternoon meetings?" I hug her to my chest when she lays on top of me.

"Reschedule?" She bats her lashes at me. "I'll give you three really good reasons: Kodiak. Kodiak, and I'm dying to see Kodiak," she says, raising a finger each time she mentions her horse's name.

"And if I say no?"

"You don't tell me no," she taps her finger on my nose and rolls over onto her side of the bed.

She's right; I don't. Grabbing my phone, I shoot off a quick text to Jonathan to rearrange our flight to leave at two instead of seven as planned. I also check in with Gladys to ensure the Christmas decorators will arrive in the morning as they do every year. She replied almost immediately, confirming, and knowing how much Kalyn loves Christmas and how excited she'll be to see the house getting decorated makes me eager to go home too.

The morning flies by, and we have to be on the road in 15 minutes to get in the air on time. I make quick work of gathering all the work documents I'll need for the next three weeks, and we set off for home.

CHAPTER
Forty-Three

KALYN

Home sweet home. We arrived in the late afternoon yesterday, and I'm so happy to be back. I sit on the other side of Jonah's desk, leaning over and batting my lashes at him. He's reclined in his chair with his feet propped up on his desk, tossing his little football straight up in the air and catching it.

It's December 1st, and the entire mansion is transformed into a Christmas winter wonderland. It's truly to die for, and I don't think I've shut up about how excited I am.

"Can we put a Christmas tree in our bedroom?" I ask him, then correct myself. "I'm going to put a Christmas tree in our bedroom." I smile, reminiscing. "My mom and I used to decorate a tree together. She would let me put real candy canes on it and then cover the tree in tinsel. It never went on very pretty, but by the time I came back, it would be flawless. I would think, 'Wow, I did so good,' and now that I'm older, I realize my mom fixed it when I wasn't around, so she didn't hurt my feelings. I'm going to put so much tinsel all over our tree."

"My mom did the same thing. My childhood cat used to tear it off the tree, and my mom would get so mad," he says, tossing the ball up in the air.

My eyes unfocus, lost in a memory. "Pawing the glass ornaments under the couch."

He catches the football, looking surprised. "Yeah, actually," then his eyes shift to the window as his feet come off the desk. "It's snowing, baby," he adds, holding his hand out to me. I stand and eagerly take it.

We watch through the window as the white fluffy balls float from the sky, a light dusting of white beginning to coat the ground below.

"Come on," I say, grabbing his hand and pulling him out of his office. He follows me to the back patio, and I fling the doors open and run out into the falling snow.

"Baby, you're not wearing a coat or shoes," Jonah calls out from the doorway.

"Live a little, Jonah," I reply, spreading my arms out wide and spinning in circles, tilting my head up to catch the snowflakes.

He steps outside, scoops me up, and I wrap my arms and legs around him, squeezing tightly. "I love you," I whisper.

"I love you," he says.

Snow is already covering his hair, and I gently brush the flakes away.

"Can we go inside yet?" he asks, his breath visible in the cold air.

"Yes," I give him another kiss. "Will we get snowed in? I want to go to town and get snow gear."

"Tabitha got you some. It should be in the closet," he says, closing the door behind us.

"You both are going to catch a cold if you go outside without a coat on," Gladys says, entering the room.

"The Mrs. went out without shoes," Jonah points out, placing the blame on me.

I jokingly drop my chin, showing him my shock. "Did you just tattle on me, Mr. Everett?"

"I can't possibly have Gladys upset with me," he teases.

"Both of you better go dry off," she places her hand on her hip.

"Yes, ma'am," Jonah replies, carrying me out of the room and back to our bedroom.

As we pass Jonathan and Shay's room, they are both on their way out.

"Why are you both so wet?" Jonathan stares after us.

"It's snowing!" I exclaim excitedly as he keeps walking.

"She darted out in the snow barefoot."

"You're such a tattletale, babe," I laugh as he pushes our bedroom door open and strides on in.

It's not until I look in the bathroom mirror that I see how soaked I am. I peel off my clothes and put them in the hamper. Glancing over at Jonah, I admire his sculpted backside. "That's a nice ass you have there, baby."

"So is yours," he looks over his shoulder and grins. "I'd take a bite right outta that bubble butt," he snaps his teeth at me.

I change into a tank top, matching sweatpants, and zip-up sweatshirt, then put on slippers and toss my hair up in a messy bun. Jonah is wearing sweatpants, a T-shirt and a zip-up hoodie.

"I need your phone. I have to call the cops. It's illegal to be that sexy," I say, pretending to be annoyed as I playfully hold out my hand.

"You'll be getting arrested too," he slaps my butt and then squeezes it. "But if you want to be in handcuffs, I have some in my nightstand we can get out right now," he smirks.

"Can you be the one tied up?" I smile wide.

"If that turns you on, I'll gladly let you," he drapes his arm over my shoulder as we leave our bedroom.

"Do you mind if I move one of these chairs next to the window?" I ask, pointing at the four leather chairs in his office we always sit in.

They are near the window, but I basically want to be one with the window and be smashed up against the glass.

"Where do you want it?" he asks, grabbing the chair and moving it.

"That's perfect, thank you," I say.

As I watch the snow blanket the landscape in white, I feel so at peace. I only realize I was lost in the view when Jonah puts a blanket on my lap and then moves another chair next to mine.

I look over at him as he grabs his laptop from the chair he just moved and sits down beside me.

He gives me the most beautiful, sweet smile, and my heart flutters.

"Hi," I whisper.

"Hi, baby," he whispers back.

My attention lingers on him as he begins working again, then I look back out the window.

"Do you think Kodiak is warm?" The serene moment disappears by the thought of my little baby being cold.

"He's fine, baby," Jonah reassures me, looking up from his laptop.

I begin fidgeting with my fingers, worrying if he's really okay. My phone beeps from my pocket, and I pull it out to see I have a new message from Jonah. When I pull it open, it's a single text with Brad's contact information.

Instantly clicking on it I text him.

KALYN:

Bert, is Kodiak warm? Does he need a heater? Or a blanket?

I anxiously wait, checking my phone repeatedly. Our chat is blue, so I'll know when he's typing back. I sure hope he has his read receipts on.

Eight long minutes go by before my phone beeps with a new message. He sent a picture of him sitting next to Kodiak, who is lying down. He has his arm around Kodiak's neck, gives a thumbs up, and wears a big grin.

BRAD:

Walked all the way out here just for this picture. You're welcome, Wanda.

KALYN:

Give my baby a kiss from mom

He sends a picture of him kissing Kodiak.

BRAD:

KALYN:

Thank you

BRAD:

Oh sorry, Wanda. I was rubbing it in that I get to kiss our boy and you don't

KALYN:

I'll come out there and punch your lips off your face.

BRAD:

Let me know if you want me to drive up there and pick you up. My lips haven't been punched off my face in awhile

KALYN:

Have you ever had an Indian burn?

BRAD:

Like the ones kids would give each other on the playground in elementary school?

KALYN:

Yes!

BRAD:

I never participated in purposely causing myself pain. So no, Wanda, I've never had an Indian burn

KALYN:

How's that fun?

BRAD:

Do you want to give me an Indian burn?
I feel like you want to give me an Indian burn

KALYN:

> I was going to say since your lips take so much beating, we will give them a break and I will give your balls an Indian burn until they are removed from your body...

BRAD:

> If I'm deciphering that correctly, you are offering to give me a hand job

KALYN:

> Yes... a "hand job," and afterward I will have two little nuggets I will place in your palms 😁

BRAD:

> Wow! Sign me up! Merry Christmas to me

KALYN:

> Like a jingle and bells. Except without the bells. You'll only be left with the jingle part.

BRAD:

> Alright. Show me how you'd jingle it

"Scooch," Shay says, walking up to the chair and motioning for me to make room for her.

Smiling, I scoot, and she lifts the blanket and climbs in with me.

"It's so beautiful out," she says, staring out the window. "Have you had a chance to see the decorations throughout the house?"

BRAD:

> ???

KALYN:

> We can discuss me burning your dick n' nuggets off later. Shay just got here.

"Earth to Kalyn," Shay swipes her hand back and forth in front of my phone.

"I haven't. When Jonah finishes working, I'll drag him around to look with me," I push my slipper into his knee, rocking it back and forth. "He's gonna let me handcuff him to our bed," I turn my head to look at Shay.

"Ooo, first time?" she quirks a brow.

"Yep, got any tips?"

"Mmhmm. Make sure he's bent over. Makes ass play more fun," she winks at me.

We both glance over at Jonah, who is smiling and shaking his head as he keeps typing.

"Make sure your nails are trimmed," she adds.

"Done," I hold up my short, red-polished nails.

"Put those fingers in my ass, and my dick is going in yours," he chimes in without looking up from his computer.

"Anything I put in your ass, you can put the equivalent in mine. And vice versa," I hold up my pointer and middle finger to show him.

"I'm not concerned over those little fingers," he smirks.

"We can get a mold of your dick, and then you can really feel what Kal feels," Shay tells him.

"Ooo, I like that. Then I can also have sex with myself with it," I smile.

"You don't need a mold of my cock; it's here whenever you need it," Jonah replies, his fingers still flying across the keyboard.

"It's for your pleasure, babe," I try to sound convincing.

"If shoving a mold of my dick in my ass is going to please you, then I'll get you one," he looks up from his screen. My stomach does flips when we make eye contact. How does he still manage to give me butterflies like this?

"You guys wanna come see the decorations?" Jonathan eagerly asks from the doorway.

"Yes!" Shay and I exclaim simultaneously.

Standing, I hold my hands out to Jonah. He puts his laptop in the chair I was just occupying and takes my hands as he stands. We walk to the front of the house, where a massive Christmas tree stands in the large entryway. Christmas garland wraps around the staircase banisters, and red and white striped décor decorates the trees. Wrapped boxes, made to look like presents, are perfectly situated underneath.

We walk room to room, admiring all the Christmas decorations. Massive ornaments hang from the ceilings, making it look like the North Pole has completely set up shop here in the mansion. It feels like this would be any kid's dream.

"Do you have any Santa fetishes?" Jonah asks as we keep looking around.

"You're the one with fetishes," I quip. "… the maid uniforms," I mock.

"You did look sexy in your maid outfit."

"If I say I have a Santa fetish, will Santa find his way into our bedroom to punish me for being a naughty girl?" I ask him.

"He might," Jonah replies.

"In that case… I have to fetish with Santa. But that feels creepy to have him sneaking around in our room," I widen my eyes.

"Santa can come in my room, big boy," Jonathan winks at Jonah.

"You make up the entire naughty list," Shay tells him.

"What would you do if you woke up getting a blowjob—" I am mid-sentence.

"I like this already," Jonathan says as I look at him while asking the question.

"What would you do if you woke up getting a blowjob, then you cum, and I stand up and say, 'See ya later,' and walk away?" I laugh.

"Do I know it's you during?" he asks.

"Give reactions for all scenarios."

"Well, blowjobs feel good, and you both are practically the same person at this point, so I'd just tell you to get your ass back in bed so I could lay down pipe like a gentleman," he says.

"What would you do if you walked in and saw me giving Jonathan a blowjob?" I ask Shay.

"I'd sit on his chest and scoot down until my pussy is in your face and have you go down on me instead. I will talk all of you into an orgy one day," she points to all of us.

"Do we get a round two of their wedding weekend?" Jonathan asks biting his lip.

"Yes. Can we make a fun room for the four of us?" Shay asks Jonah.

"Sure," he shrugs.

"You ready?" Jonah asks, turning to look at me. We're both geared up in full snow attire—pants, coats, boots, gloves, and beanies.

"Ready," I reply excitedly.

As we make our way down the back steps of the mansion, I hold onto his arm to prevent myself from accidentally slipping and falling down the stairs. I'd probably end up breaking all my bones and ruining Christmas. Once we reach the bottom, we survey the area.

"Okay, don't laugh, but I've never made a snowman before, so I have no idea where to start," I admit, looking at the untouched snow around us.

Jonah kneels down, scoops up some snow, and begins forming a compact snowball.

"Just scoop up some snow like this, pack it together, then place it on the ground and start rolling," he explains, waiting for me to follow his lead.

Side by side, we begin forming our snowballs.

"Why is yours growing so much faster?" I ask, noticing that his snowball is rapidly expanding while mine is only the size of a basketball. I keep pushing my ball and glance over to see him further away, his ball growing quickly.

"Can I ditch mine and help you?" I ask, walking towards him.

"Get on in here, big guns," he grins, and I join him in pushing the gigantic ball.

"Do you guys realize you still need to add two more balls on top of that?" Shay questions as we turn and see her and Jonathan completely decked out in snow gear too, coming to help.

"And?" Jonah retorts sarcastically.

"That's already huge. You should probably consider stopping there," she chuckles.

"Well, no need to fear; I already made the head," I joke, pointing to the beachball-sized snowball I made. "I know, I know, it's impressive." I hold my hands up as if acknowledging I did something spectacular. "Let's keep rolling and build an igloo!" I suggest, excitement evident in my eyes.

"That's a great idea," Jonathan agrees, looking at each of us to confirm we agree with changing the plan.

"Let's finish our snowman first," Jonah suggests.

"My baby can't start a project and not see it all the way through. He'll go mad if we don't complete the snowman," I say, knowing it's the complete truth.

Over the next hour, laughter fills the air as we struggle to lift the heavy second snowball. Even with the combined strength of Jonathan and Jonah, it proves to be quite a challenge. However, we are soon joined by additional helping hands. Theo, Brad, Lilly, Brandt, Giles, and Gladys all come out to lend a hand. Even some of the mansion staff, dressed in snow clothes, join us. I step back to get out of the way and am blown away by the beautiful sight.

Everyone gathers around the snowball, working together to lift it onto the first one. I clap with excitement when they get it perfectly placed on top. "Yay," I exclaim, jumping up and down.

"One more to go," Jonah announces. "We'll need a ladder for that."

"I'll go get one," Brandt offers, making his way back towards the mansion.

"Here you go, sweetheart," Gladys says, extending a carrot and a bag of coal toward me.

My face instantly lights up upon seeing the items in her hands. "Thank you, Gladys! Look, Jonathan, we are using part of your Christmas present for the snowman," I hold up the bag of coal to show him.

"You think that's funny," he softly kicks snow at my legs, then playfully wraps his arm around my neck and squeezes as we all laugh.

Brandt comes back with the ladder, and Jonah takes the big ball and starts climbing.

"Someone better catch him if he falls," I say, feeling nervous as I watch him holding on with one hand.

"Oh, so you don't want us to push the ladder over?" Jonathan quips, his hands planted firmly on the base.

"I'll kick your dick so far in your stomach you'll never be able to use it again," I playfully threaten him.

I see Barkley hopping around in the snow, so I bend down. "Barkley, come here, baby," I say, holding my arms out to him. He happily wags his tail and comes over to me, hopping like a bunny. Brad decided to go with the name I suggested after all, and it's absolutely fitting for this precious little guy. "Hi," I smile, picking him up as he licks at my face. "Oh, you are so cute, aren't you? Oh, yes you are," I coo in a baby voice.

He's a nice distraction because Jonah is safely back on the ground and looking proud.

"That's the biggest snowman I've ever seen," Shay says, staring up at it while petting Barkley.

"Here, baby, the carrots and Jonathan's coal are right there," I tell Jonah, nodding to the snow next to my feet.

He leans in and kisses me, then bends down to grab the items off the ground. Before Jonah comes back down from the ladder, Lilly takes off her scarf and hands it up to him. "So he can be fashionable."

"What about a hat?" Shay ask.

"It won't be mine, I already lost half my Christmas present to Olaf," Jonathan says.

Brandt takes off his beanie and packs it with snow before handing it to Jonah. "I'll take one for the team."

Jonah plops it on the snowman's head, and we all burst into laughter at how funny it looks. But I absolutely love it.

As soon as Jonah comes back down, Gladys tells everyone to stand in front of the snowman so she can get a picture.

"I suppose you can have your baby back," I tell Brad, handing him Barkley.

We all huddle together for the picture while Gladys takes at least fifty.

"You two, stay put," Gladys says, pointing to me and Jonah.

Everyone clears out of the way, dispersing and beginning to do their own thing, like snow angels or making their own snowmen.

Gladys takes another picture of just me and Jonah, then says she wants one of us kissing. I stand on my tippy toes to meet Jonah halfway, and he grabs me by the waist, twists, and bends me over to kiss me. My foot lifts off the ground as our lips meet, then he pulls me back up to a standing position.

Not even moving yet, I'm pelted in the back by a snowball. Turning to see where it came from, I spot Brad scooping up another snowball.

"Oh, that's real cute, twerp," I call out, bending down, scooping up snow, and packing it into a snowball as another one comes barreling toward me. Rushing toward him, I throw it; my aim strikes true and smacks him on the side of the head. His mouth falls open animatedly.

"You done messed up, Wanda. It's on now," he says, gathering another snowball.

I scoop up more snow and throw it at him, then take off running to try and get away before I'm hit. Jonah, Jonathan and Shay are standing there laughing as they watch. Grabbing another snowball, I throw it right at Jonathan's face. Well, that was the goal—it hits his shoulder, and he bends down to grab snow at the same time Jonah and Shay all take off running in opposite directions, grabbing snow and hurling the balls at us.

We're running around, trying to dodge flying snowballs, and I find a statue of a naked woman to hide behind. I can see Jonah quickly making a snowball a couple yards away.

"Baby," I whisper. As soon as he looks at me, I chuck the snowball in my hand at him, and it hits him right on the forehead.

He lets out a sinister laugh, and I take off running when I hear snow crunching behind me. I know I'm really in for it now.

I squeal when strong arms encircle my waist, and my feet lift off the ground. I kick as he lays me on my back and straddles me.

"Open your mouth, bad girl," a devilish grin spreads across his face.

"No," I wriggle, trying to break free. "Truce… truce," I repeat.

"Okay," he says, leaning down and kissing me. "Because you're so cute," he climbs off me.

I grab a pile of snow, chuck it at him again, and then attempt to crawl away.

He grabs my ankle and pulls me back to him.

"No," I laugh as he grabs snow and pushes it in my face.

"You like that," he asks, laughing, then softly brushes it off.

"I do," I smile up at him, then flinch when a snowball hits him on the side of his beanie. We both look up to see Jonathan taking off running.

Jonah is off me in an instant, chasing after Jonathan. I roll over on my stomach and watch as they throw snowballs at each other, with Brad, Theo, and Brandt joining in.

One by one, they all start to give up.

"Hot chocolate, chicken noodle soup, grilled cheese and fresh cookies are ready," Gladys announces, and we all begin to stand and make our way back up the patio toward the back door.

Everyone strips off their snow clothes, leaving them on the marble floor by the back door, and heads to the dining hall where all the food is already set up for us.

After we eat and hang out for a bit, we return to our room. I see a bare Christmas tree has been set up in the corner on my side of the bed. The room is so big, the tree is still pretty far away, but I'm excited for it to be decorated. I told Jonah a while back that I like Christmas trees that are all red and white, with mixes of peppermint-looking ornaments and garland.

One by one, Jonah and I fill the tree with ornaments.

"Oh, I forgot, I have one more thing," he says as he walks to the closet and then comes back with a box of tinsel.

"Jonah," I stare down at the box in disbelief.

"Get it on the tree," he gives me a playful spank. I giggle as I open the box.

It doesn't look as perfect as the trees my mom used to decorate, but it's beautiful nonetheless.

I sit on the edge of the bed, the room is dim except for the glow of the tree lights. I stare in awe at how magical it all feels, though a pang of sadness tugs at me, wishing my mom and dad could see that everything has turned out okay.

Jonah was right. *I am* right where I belong.

We decide to host a Christmas party at the mansion before the actual holiday so that everyone can spend Christmas with their families. The party's dress code is Christmas-themed, and I choose a short Santa dress, complete with a Santa hat and high-heeled black boots. We playfully suggest that Jonah should dress as the Grinch, but he goes for a more refined look with black slacks, a white dress shirt, a candy cane-striped tie, and a Santa hat.

Over five hundred people—family, friends, and all the mansion staff—fill the house. The energy is electric; kids run around with excitement, their joy echoing through the halls. The *real* Santa Claus even makes a grand entrance, arriving with a sleigh full of gifts for all the kids and bringing Christmas bonuses for all the employees.

The kids have their own special activity to keep them busy: a cookie decorating station. They eagerly decorate cookies with colorful icing and sprinkles, with Santa's elves helping them.

A photo booth was set up so everyone could take as many pictures as they want with their friends and family. Jonah and I got in on it and are soon joined by our two favorite humans when Shay and Jonathan come over.

Dinner is a highlight of the evening for me, with a feast that leaves everyone satisfied and content. There's an array of delicious dishes and desserts, all beautifully presented. I ate so much that I don't think I could eat anything else for a week. Jonah will probably have to roll me back to our room.

All the mansion staff receive an extra Christmas bonus from 'The Everetts' as a small token of our gratitude for their hard work and dedication throughout the year. As the night winds down, the mansion is filled with the warmth of holiday spirit.

By the time everyone is gone and we're in bed, Jonah and I exchange a look and simultaneously shake our heads. Neither of us has the energy for intimacy tonight. And with that, we both drift off to sleep.

CHAPTER
Forty-Four

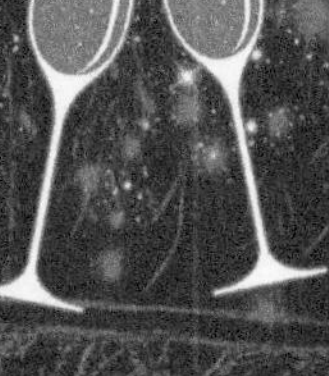

KALYN

Christmas with Jonah's family has been… odd. Antoinette still hates me, glaring at me every chance she gets. Ethan couldn't travel due to treacherous snow conditions preventing his flight from taking off. Eliza and Beaumont, however, have been genuinely gracious and welcoming, while Adeline is perfect as always.

Once dinner concludes, Beaumont's invitation to move to the living room hangs in the air. The nanny whisks Adeline away, leaving an unsettling silence in her wake. As Jonah and I settle onto the couch, a direct line of sight forms with Beaumont and Antoinette across from us while Eliza claims a solitary armchair. Adeline's absence gnaws at me; her lively presence often diffuses moments like these. Antoinette's erratic behavior throughout dinner set my nerves on edge. I'm not sure if she's about to skin my hide, unleash a verbal tirade, throw a drama party where she lays blame for Jonah's actions at my feet, or will be decent to me. The heavy silence suggests civility might be a distant hope.

Beaumont clears his throat, his eyes glistening with tears. "I, uh, have something I'd like to say," he stammers.

Antoinette shoots him a worried glance, her brow furrowed. "Dear, is everything alright?" she questions, her hand fluttering to his back in a comforting gesture.

Beaumont's chin quivers, and he hastily dabs at his brimming eyes with a crumpled tissue. "Kalyn, sweetheart, there's a photo... on that wall," he chokes out, his trembling finger pointing to the collage of framed memories on the far wall, just behind Jonah and me. I twist around, scanning the array of pictures, then turn back to him, skeptical. "The one in the gold frame, can you...can you bring it here?"

I pause, half-expecting him to crack a smile, to reveal this is some kind of joke. But his gaze clings to mine, his eyes glassy with unshed tears. "You want me to take it off the wall?"

"Yes," he manages a weak nod.

"Beaumont? What's going on?" Antoinette asks, concern etched on her face.

I dart a glance at Jonah, then release his hand as I rise, my heart pounding. I walk to the wall, my eyes fixed on the gold-framed picture. I can feel everyone's gaze on me as I carefully retrieve it and carry it back to Beaumont. I hold it out to him, and tears well up in his eyes as he stares at me, frozen, making no move to take the frame from my outstretched hands. Now I start to second-guess myself—had he actually asked me to remove the frame from his wall? His eyes shift down to the photograph, and mine instinctively follow, then flick back to him before snapping back to the picture. A chill runs through me, my heart thundering in my ears. As I slowly turn the picture toward me, bringing it closer, my eyes widen in shock.

The photo shows Antoinette, a wine glass in hand, her arm wrapped around a woman who looks exactly like me... *my mom*. My hands tremble as I take in the image of my dad standing next to my mom, his arm around her waist while Beaumont stands next to Antoinette. On the floor is a young boy with a white-haired girl in his lap and another little girl pointing at him with her head tipped back and crying. It's Jonah holding—*me*.

I remember this picture. Eliza didn't want Jonah to sit next to us, but I insisted on sitting in his lap, and she cried when he let me.

"Liza, let Kalyn sit with her boyfriend," Antoinette had teased, making Eliza cry harder while the adults posed for the photo.

I trace my fingers over the familiar faces and the names written on the photo: Beaumont, Antoinette, Katrina, Konrad, Ethan, Shine, JoJo, Moon.

"It's not possible," Jonah says, bringing me back from the memory. I hadn't realized that he stood behind me, looking down over my shoulder at the picture. He looks as stunned as I feel as he takes the picture from my hand. "How did I forget?"

"What? Forget what?" Antoinette asks.

Jonah stares at the picture for so long in shock until Antoinette stands and takes the picture out of his hands. Beaumont smiles. "All the jokes you and Kat used to make about Moon and Jojo getting married... Katrina was determined to make it happen." We all watch Antoinette's face, waiting for it to register. Her expression shifts from confusion to grief, and finally to recognition. Her eyes snap up to me, and she practically tosses the picture to Beaumont before crashing into me, sobbing.

"Oh, Moon, your mother must hate me," she cries, pulling back to examine my face. "You look just like her. How did I not realize?" and starts kissing all over my face. "You can slap me right across the face," she says so serious that I laugh again.

"We have a lot to catch up on," Beaumont says, gesturing for us to sit.

Antoinette holds me so tight I can barely move. "You are sitting with me," she declares. She laces her fingers with mine, sandwiching my hands between hers.

"Does my wedding ring look a little more appealing on my hand now?" I joke, holding it up. Antoinette grabs my hand, admiring the ring for the first time. She traces the diamond, and pulls my hand to her face, holding it as if she can't believe I'm really here.

"Did you already know?" Jonah asks Eliza, his voice a mix of curiosity and trepidation.

"I started to suspect it after we FaceTimed," she admits, her eyes locked on mine. "She called me Shine, and the memory of us playing hide and seek came flooding back. I could hear her whispering, 'Shine, come over here,' and when my gaze refocused on her, I mentally aged her over the years and realized who she was. When I came home, I went to the basement to find pictures from when we were little. Geoffrey said boxes from the basement had been moved to Dad's office. I was going through them when he walked in. I asked how long he'd known, and he said he just realized at lunch with you both the day before," Eliza explains, her words tumbling out.

"How could we have forgotten?" Antoinette sounds so frustrated as she stares at me, taking in every detail of my face, her eyes scanning every feature as if searching for the reason behind forgetting me.

"It was my fault," Beaumont replies somberly, his voice heavy with regret. "We tried to get custody of you, and your grandmother was irate, then refused to let us see you. We begged, offered her money, and she changed her number. At your parents' funeral, Jonah wouldn't let you go, and she called the cops. They forced you both apart, and that was the last time we saw you. She moved to the middle of nowhere and kept you both hidden. Liza cried nonstop. But Jonah took it the hardest. He was so serious all of a sudden. He was so angry and wouldn't talk to anybody about it. To cope with the trauma, I made the decision to put us all through intensive therapy. The goal was to bury the most painful memories, particularly those involving Kalyn. The therapy was meant to help us forget you, to ease our pain by removing those memories from our minds. Jonah became determined, studied all the time, learned all sorts of skills, and never got serious with anyone. But now, those buried memories are starting to resurface. You might be experiencing fragments of the past, and it's because our minds are beginning to recall what we tried so hard to forget."

"You put us through therapy to forget her?" Jonah's tone is angry, his eyes blazing with fury his words can't fully capture.

"I had no choice, son. You weren't sleeping, your mom wouldn't get out of bed, and Liza cried nonstop. I searched for her and found her, but her grandmother got a restraining order against me. I was losing everyone I loved, and I had to do something," his voice cracks, the raw emotion evident in his trembling words.

I reach over and take Beaumont's hand. "I think you did the right thing. My grandma would have rather seen me dead than living with anyone from my mom's past." I squeeze his hand again, turning to face Jonah. "He did the right thing, Jonah."

Tears streak down Jonah's face as he processes my words. He stands and kneels in front of me, placing both hands in my lap and resting his chin on my knees, looking up at me with eyes filled with a mix of sadness and longing.

"Nothing would have kept us apart, baby," I whisper, my fingers intertwining behind his nape as I rest my forehead against his. "I remember Christmas night. My mom and Mama Ettie had too much 'juice.' In her tipsy state, my mom accidentally spilled her red juice all over the white sofa. You and my mom found it hilarious," I share with Antoinette. "My dad said it was bedtime, but my mom was resistant. However, after he whispered something in her ear, she giggled and eagerly followed him. Dad told me it was time for bed too, but Liza was already fast asleep. Jojo volunteered to sleep with me in the guest room," I gently caress Jonah's cheek. "We snuck Mr. Jiggle's into the room, and I forced him to hide under the blankets with us. When he tried to escape, I clung to him. He scratched me in the process, but you placed your hand over the wound, downplaying the injury, saying it was nothing. You wouldn't let me look at the cuts, even though we both knew it was bleeding. I didn't cry, fearing we would be separated, and I didn't want you leaving me. Even back then, I knew you were mine," I smile, my eyes welling up with tears. He kisses the scars on my arm, remnants of Mr. Jiggles' claw marks, and I run my fingers through his silky strands.

He gazes up at me, then shifts his attention towards Eliza. "Finish that story, tattletale."

She chuckles. "I was waiting for that. You tell *your* truth, Jonah."

"We were asleep when you came in, woke me, and threatened to tell Mom and get me grounded if I didn't leave. Kalyn was sleeping on my arm, and I said that I didn't want to wake her. You said that you would wake the entire house if I didn't get out now. That's not merely *my* truth; that's THE truth."

"I woke to find you cuddled up with my best friend. The excuse 'she was sleeping on my arm' would have been plausible if you weren't spooning her with your arms wrapped around her. You clearly had a crush, and you had cooties, and my best friend let you sleep in the same bed as her. I was mad. Plus, anytime she was with us, you followed us around, and it was really annoying." She playfully rolls her eyes.

"You were encroaching on my bonding time with my future wife," Jonah smirks, planting a kiss on my knee.

She shoves his shoulder playfully. "Everyone always predicted you two would end up married. But I would be damned if I ever let that happen. How dare you have sex with my best friend, you perv."

"Mmm, she's good too," Jonah says, earning him another playful punch on the shoulder.

"Were you okay… for the remainder of your childhood?" Antoinette inquires gently.

"Everything was fine," I respond vaguely, not wanting to delve into how difficult growing up actually was after my parents' death.

"All this crying has me exhausted," Antoinette admits, dabbing at her tear-soaked eyes.

"It's getting late. Perhaps we should retire for the night and resume our reunion in the morning," Beaumont recommends, clapping his hands on his thighs.

"Will you lie with me for a bit?" Antoinette requests.

"I'd like that very much," I reply, my voice cracking.

Jonah rises, pulling me into his embrace as he clings to me. He then shakes his head, as if he can't believe anything that's happened tonight. "I love you to the moon and back," he murmurs, his lips brushing against mine. He says the saying my parents used to say to me… the origin of my once cherished nickname. "I really loathe the idea of separating right now," he admits, stalling.

"I know. We have all the time in the world. I'll join you in a bit," I console him.

He purses his lips, clearly tempted to linger, before exhaling a resigned sigh and agreeing.

Everyone begins to disperse, and Antoinette and I settle onto the couch together. For the first time since my mom's passing, it feels like I'm being held by her again. It feels nice.

"Lyn-E, do you want to have pancakes with me?" Adeline whispers, her small voice filled with excitement as she leans over my shoulder. Antoinette and I are still on the couch, and I can see the sun beginning to creep through the windows.

"Good morning, LeeLee. I'd love to," I respond, gently peeling myself off the couch and draping a blanket over Antoinette.

Adeline's face lights up as I take her hand, and we walk to the kitchen together.

A chef is already busily preparing breakfast, and she greets us warmly as we enter.

"Good morning," I return her greeting as Adeline and I settle onto the stools at the counter. We engage in quiet conversation while our breakfast is expertly made.

"Why were you sleeping with Mommy? Are you sad?" Adeline inquires, her brow furrowed in concern.

"No, honey. I'm so, so happy," I reassure her, gently brushing a stray strand of hair behind her ear.

"How come everyone cried last night?" she presses on, appearing puzzled.

"Because we were happy," I explain patiently. "Sometimes when adults are really happy, they cry happy tears."

"Does Jonah like Mommy again?"

"He loves Mommy. And I can promise things are going to be a lot better between everyone," I tell her, wrapping my arms around her small shoulders in a comforting embrace.

"I wish you were my mommy."

"Well, you know what's better than me being your mommy? Sharing your mommy. Did you know when I was your age, my mom and your mom were best friends? And you know what I called your mom? Mama Ettie," I reveal, holding my hands out as if to say, who knew?

"Where's your mom now?"

"My mom and dad passed away in a car wreck," I explain, trying to keep my voice steady.

"And now we can share my mom and dad," she suggests, her eyes shining with innocent optimism.

"You know what? I can't think of two people on this entire planet my parents would have rather had step in and take their place."

"Can you have a baby already?" she asks abruptly, catching me off guard.

At that moment, the chef places our food in front of us. "Wow, that looks delicious!" I exclaim, widening my eyes in gratitude, silently thanking her for the impeccable timing.

After we finish eating, Adeline asks if I'll play with her in the snow. I agree, feeling a sense of nostalgia wash over me. We go upstairs, and my memory guides me straight to where they keep the spare snow gear. Once we're bundled up, I follow her outside.

CHAPTER
Forty-Five

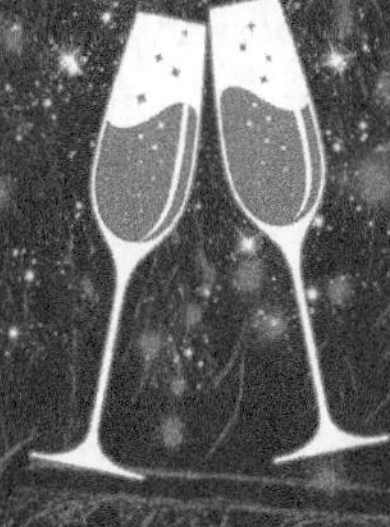

JONAH

I expect to find Kalyn in bed with me when I wake, but an empty expanse of sheets greets me instead. Her side of the bed is still untouched. I'm surprised I slept in until 9 in the morning, considering she never came to bed last night. Downstairs, my mom still sleeps on the couch where we left her, but there's still no trace of Kalyn. I make my way to the kitchen, and Mary, our lifelong chef, gestures toward the backyard.

At the window, a smile spreads across my face. Kalyn pushes Adeline on the swing, their laughter and chatter carrying on the breeze. I pull out a chair, transfixed by the heartwarming scene. Their cheeks are red from the cold, but they are fully bundled up in snow gear, so they must be decently warm.

"I thought it was a dream," my mom murmurs, joining me at the window. I know exactly what she means. Kalyn's reappearance in my life has always held a dreamlike quality. The potent, inexplicable pull I feel toward her still takes my breath away.

"When I first saw her at your house, I thought she was Katrina," my mom continues. "I even asked Jenevieve her name, and she said she couldn't remember. Later, when I pressed the matter, she said it was Kara. Then, Kalyn appeared out of nowhere in the lineup when my necklace was stolen. I saw her bandaged hands and wanted to hug her and apologize. She tripped while carrying my tray of tea and was injured. But then she was accused of being the one to sneak into my room and take the necklace, and you made it clear to everyone that you two were intimately involved. I was so mad this Kara girl was with my son. Do you know how embarrassed I am for trying to talk her into leaving you? I could puke I'm so disgusted with myself."

"Good thing I'm slightly obsessed with her," I reply, holding my fingers slightly apart to illustrate.

She laughs and wraps her arm around mine.

"I visited their grave. Uncle Konrad and Auntie Kat. I followed Kalyn there. I introduced myself to them, and they probably sat there laughing at me." I watch Kalyn chasing Adeline around the swing set and my chest tightens with my love for her. "I went to their funeral. I remember their funeral, but I don't remember being there. Well, I do, it's just all different. I think my memory isn't as great as I like to think it is," I admit.

"Your memory is intact, sweetheart. Konrad's wretched mother moved them to where they are now a month after they were buried. Don't tell Kalyn that. Your father was at the cemetery yelling at everyone, but she had the right to move her son, and she did. The only small blessing in that is she had the decency to move his wife with him. I figured for sure she would have left Kat and taken Konrad alone."

"I guess it was good Kalyn got to grow up close to them," I sigh.

"Was she okay? Growing up?"

I don't know how to answer that, so I sit here quietly.

"We'll save that for another time," she gently pats my hand. "When we were in the hall waiting for your dad and you to finish talking about the golf contract, Kalyn and I had a civil argument. I called her trash, and she said, calm as ever, 'Will you be saying that when I have your grandbabies?' I couldn't even stomach the thought of her having my son's child. And now all I want is to see her belly swollen, carrying my grandbaby. God, she looks just like Katrina. She's so beautiful."

"She's the most beautiful woman I've ever met. And I'm not ready to share her yet."

"Don't be selfish. Kat and I already planned on you two having four kids," she leans into me.

"Think her body can handle one of my big-ass kids?"

"You two are a perfect match; her body can definitely handle your big-ass kids. I assume she's on birth control? She must be since I overheard your filthy mouth talking about filling her with your babies, and she's not pregnant yet."

"I don't think that's what was said," I grin.

"I'm not repeating what you said."

"She is on birth control, and we haven't discussed her stopping it."

"I'd like to start making amends by planning a wedding ceremony and reception for you both. You deserve to be celebrated, and I want the world to know you are married. After that, we can discuss the birth control."

Kalyn locks eyes with me, and a smile tugs at me as she and Adeline head toward the house.

"Good morning," she greets as they walk in then she leans in for a kiss. "How long were you two gawking?" she questions, helping Adeline out of her coat.

"We were discussing grandbabies. Jonah doesn't think your body can accommodate his big-ass babies," she laughs.

"My body has accommodated every big-ass part of you, a baby will be a piece of cake," Kalyn remarks. "I'm going to shower, would you like to come?"

I'm already on my feet before she finishes her sentence.

"Can I come?" Adeline asks, trying to follow.

"No, sweetheart. Jonah and Kalyn want to be alone," my mom says, grabbing Adeline by the hand and stopping her from following us.

"Why? I'll be good," she protests.

"They are going to go work on making me a grandbaby."

CHAPTER
Forty-Six

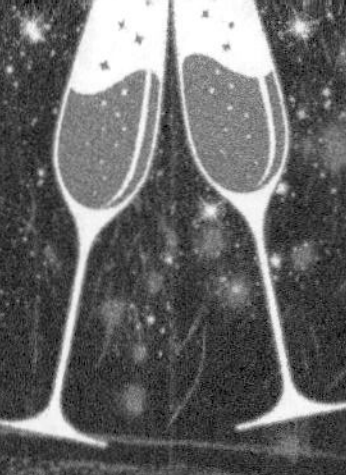

KALYN

Work after the new year feels busy, but everyone seems to be in a good mood. We just got word that the golf models are complete, so we're meeting on Wednesday to review them.

I miss Jonah today more than usual, even though I've seen him off and on all day. I know he's on the phone with a client right now, but I want to touch him. I make my way to his office, catching Bridget's gaze down the hall. She offers a smile before refocusing on her computer.

I knock softly on Jonah's door as I enter. "Hi," I mouth, approaching him. He's on the phone, leaning back in his chair, watching me.

I settle onto his lap, crossing my legs and wrapping my arms around his neck. I don't really need anything—just wanting to unzip his skin and snuggle inside. My fingers delicately weave through his hair as he continues his call, his hand coming to rest on my hip, his thumb lazily tracing patterns.

We remain like this until he concludes his conversation. Then, he scoots his chair to the desk, his long legs pulling us forward as he hangs up. Wordlessly, he turns my chin towards him and kisses me. I expect a brief peck, but when I attempt to pull away, he shakes his head, and threads his fingers in my hair, pulling me back for a deeper kiss.

"How many blender blades did you lick to master that kind of kissing?"

"A few," he winks.

"You'll have to demonstrate for me one of these days. I want to watch you lick chocolate from one."

"I'll lick chocolate off of you," he counters, biting his lip as he leans in for another kiss.

"I'm his mother," Antoinette announces, bursting into the door and halting Bridget in her tracks.

"Sorry, sir, she didn't give me a chance to call," Bridget apologizes, appearing flustered.

"Hi, honey," Antoinette greets me, disregarding Bridget as she envelops me in a hug, placing a kiss on my cheek before repeating the gesture with Jonah.

"It's fine, Bridget, thank you," I assure her with a smile and a wave.

She nods and leaves, closing the door behind her.

"Is everything okay?" I ask, noticing her freshly touched-up makeup, hinting at recent tears.

"I'd like to show you both something," she says, holding up a disk.

"Please," I say, inviting her to proceed.

Jonah accepts the disk, inserts it into his computer, and press-es play.

The camera jostles, then the curtains part with giggles. "Liza is so mad, look at her," Antoinette whispers. A very angry Liza flings sand from the sandbox while five-year-old me lies on a blanket playing Barbies with nine-year-old Jonah.

"How mad do you think Liza will be when JoJo marries her best friend?" my mom's beautiful voice asks. This is the first time I've heard her voice since her passing, and it brings tears to my eyes.

"She'll be mad now, but one day, she'll accept it. They're so cute," Antoinette replies.

"Twins run on my side of the family," my mom laughs, Antoinette joining in.

"One for each of our arms," Antoinette adds.

The video ends, transitioning into another.

It's Jonah's tenth birthday, the room filled with presents and chaotic with kids. Everyone sings "Happy Birthday," and Jonah clutches my hand as he blows out the candles. Following cake and gifts, the kids are eager to play with the birthday boy and his new toys. He graciously allows them to join in, while he silently watches from his spot on the floor.

"What's wrong, buddy?" my mom asks.

"Nothing," he replies, glumly.

"Well, Moon is outside swinging alone if you want to see what she's doing," my mom suggests.

His face lights up, and he rushes to join me.

"Did you see how fast he ran out to his girlfriend?" Antoinette observes.

"She's not his girlfriend, she's MY best friend," Liza corrects from behind them.

The camera lingers on Jonah as he approaches me. I'm swinging and smiling, looking carefree.

I could watch videos of my mom all day long. It's almost eerie how much we look alike in videos. She even has her hair braided and over her shoulder. We could pass as sisters, if not twins.

Rising from Jonah's lap, I envelop Antoinette in a comforting hug, aware of the pain it must bring her to watch these videos of her best friend. Sobs rack her body as she dabs tissues to her eyes.

"Oh, Kalyn, I miss her so much."

"Me too," I whisper, my hold on her tightening.

"I am so sorry, sweetheart," she apologizes, pulling back to study me. Her fingers graze my face as if reacquainting herself with my mother's features after all these years. Taking my hand, she guides me to the couch and sits beside me. Jonah observes from his chair, a look of quiet understanding on his face.

She cradles my hands, her thumbs rubbing the tops. "We counted how many freckles you have in the exact same spots as your mother," she reveals, tracing the two freckles on my hand. "You have 14 on your arms and hands, the single one on your cheek, and two behind your ear that your mother always said were your vampire bites." She gently sweeps my hair aside, and fresh tears cascade down her face as she spots them. "But there was one freckle you didn't share with her, but you did with someone else," she says, her gaze shifting to Jonah. She delicately turns my wedding ring, exposing the freckle on the inside of my finger, hidden beneath the band. "This freckle… the only person who shares this freckle is Jonah," she smiles, rotating my ring back into place.

I remember Jonah playing with my hands one night, talking about putting a ring on my finger. I told him I couldn't wear a ring because then our ring finger freckles couldn't kiss anymore. He would say our ring freckles will get to kiss our wedding rings all day, which is even better.

"I know my grandmother kept you from me, but I want to thank you for my parents' beautiful headstone. It was really thoughtful," I express, avoiding eye contact, focusing on my wedding ring instead.

"Of course," she replies, giving my hands a squeeze. "The first day I saw you at Jonah's, my heart nearly stopped. I thought I was seeing Katrina. I was trembling so badly, and it never registered that it was because you were her daughter. It made me so angry that you looked like my best friend. I hated the sight of you because of it. But that's one thing about the universe—you can try to keep some things apart, but they will drift back together if they are meant to. There wasn't any force on this earth that was going to keep you two apart. Not even Jonah's crazy mother," she laughs, and I join in.

CHAPTER
Forty–Seven

KALYN

I love being home. Time in the city makes me appreciate it even more. We've discovered a crazy amount about our past, and I haven't even told Shay about it yet. Antoinette and Eliza text me all day, and I've changed their names in my phone to "Mama Ettie" and "Shine," because it feels more fitting. Antoinette broached the subject of planning a formal wedding for Jonah and me, and I said I would really like that. Though the prospect of being the center of attention unnerves me, I know it's something both she and my mom would have wanted, and I'm happy and honored to do it for her.

There's still snow on the ground and the air is crisp, but it's beautiful. We arrived home late last night, but first thing this morning, I layered up in winter attire and headed out to the stables to see Kodiak.

I feel a rush of excitement when I see him. "Hi, baby," I coo softly as he trots to the gate. "Hi mama," I stroke Winona's muzzle when she stands beside him.

I lean in, touching my forehead to his, and pour out how much I missed him.

"She missed you, Buddy, but came out to see me," Brad says, ambling up to me.

"Oh no you don't. This is *my* time with my son," I say, reluctant to relinquish my hold on Kodiak.

"Good. You can spend time with both of us," he playfully flicks my leg with a towel.

"Why do you always do that?" I sway to the side even though he already got me.

"To hear you laugh," he replies, joining me at the gate, resting his arms on the top and stroking Winona.

"Give me the towel so I can whip you back."

He pulls the towel from his back pocket, holding it out to me. "I guarantee I will thoroughly enjoy it."

"I'm not touching your dirty towel," I scrunch my nose in exaggerated disgust.

"It's clean... ish," he holds it out and examines it before stuffing it back in his pocket.

"Next, you're going to hand me handcuffs and want me to cuff you to the gate and whip you... freak."

"You want to handcuff me to the gate, I'll comply," he winks.

"You'll comply with what?" Emma asks, walking up. "Hey Kalyn," she smiles, and her hand softly brushes Brad's back in a more-than-friendly greeting, which I immediately act like I didn't notice.

"Hey Emma, how's it going?" I greet her.

"It's going really good. This is about the time Brad and I take Kodiak for a walk," she says, holding his harness.

"Oh," is all I manage. This shouldn't bother me, but I instantly feel jealous that she's spending so much time with my horse, forging a bond with him that I should be forming with him, and I hate that I feel this way.

Brad, never missing anything, pushes himself off the gate and takes the harness. "Let's go, Wanda, our boy needs a walk."

"I can get him ready," Emma says, trying to reach for the harness again.

"I've got it," he tells her, more curtly than she's apparently used to, because she flinches and stares at him in disbelief.

"Have a nice walk, baby. I'll come see you in a little bit," I stroke Kodiak's muzzle before turning to leave.

"Nice try, Wanda, you're coming," Brad says, taking the towel from his pocket and playfully flicking my leg again. Emma looks between us, appearing...jealous? Confused?

"I'll take him for a walk myself if you don't mind. I'd love to spend time alone with him," I say, reaching for the reins.

"Nope. Because I do mind, and I'm not done harassing you," he walks past me.

I take my usual spot on the opposite side of Kodiak, and Emma falls into step next to Brad.

I feel like an intruder, and it's incredibly awkward.

"How long are you home?" Brad breaks the silence.

Even though I know he's addressing me, I glance over to confirm. "A couple of weeks," I reply, as both he and Emma look at me.

"Do you want to finish season 4 tonight?" Emma asks Brad, taking his attention back to her.

Uncertain if I should pretend not to hear them, I decide to quietly continue walking. I can't catch Brad's response because they're whispering, but I can feel tension, and I know it's because of me.

We complete one lap, and I'd much rather be mucking horse stalls than enduring this uncomfortable walk.

"Are you going to keep walking him?" I ask Brad.

"We usually take him for at least three laps," Emma responds.

"Okay, well, I'm going to head back," I say, handing the reins to Brad.

"Let me drive you," Brad offers.

"No thanks," I blurt out a little too quickly.

As I stride away from the track, I can feel their gazes on me, and a wave of discomfort washes over me.

I deliberately wait until after 8 to go out and see Kodiak, knowing Brad and Emma will be gone from the stable. Jonah and a group of other guys are playing poker, and I don't want to just sit idly by and watch. He offered to teach me how to play, but it always looked boring.

A sense of relief floods me as I find the stable mercifully empty. I enter the enclosure, sink down next to Kodiak where he's lying, and begin to pet him.

After an hour, I head back to the house.

For the next week, I only visit the stables in the evenings to avoid any more awkward encounters. I'm sitting by the window, having set aside my book, and lean against the glass, staring out at the snow-covered landscape. I see Emma walking toward the house, probably heading to lunch. She flashes a warm smile at someone, and then I see Brad emerging from the direction of the house. They wrap their arms around each other and share a kiss.

That solves the mystery—they are definitely seeing each other. Brad is usually a hit-it-and-quit-it type of guy and wouldn't display such public affection after a casual hookup. They turn and walk away, her arm around his waist and his around her shoulder. I feel a pang of sadness seeing that, because while I want him to be happy, I fear no woman in a relationship with him will want him to have a friendship with another woman. And I am a woman. I'll just do my best to avoid him.

I managed to succeed for a total of eight days. I take my usual walk to the stables at 9 in the evening today, settling in beside Kodiak. I bring a horse brush and softly talk to him while brushing his mane.

The gate unlatches, startling me from my tranquility.

"Sorry," Brad says quietly.

"You're off work," I note as he sits down in front of Kodiak.

"It's dark, and Abel mentioned you come out here every night. I figured I'd corner you and find out why you're avoiding me."

"I'm not," I lie.

"Oh yeah? Then why do you come out at night when we always take Kodiak for walks during the day?"

"Because I want to visit my horse without others around," I say defensively, which is mostly true.

"Okay, is this the time you always come out?" he asks.

"Just whenever," I reply vaguely.

He flashes a knowing smile. "I can't harass you if you don't tell me what time to meet you out here."

"I come this late so I can be alone," I say bluntly.

"I only get to see you a couple of times a month, if that. Work with me, Wanda."

"Jonah and I got married," I say abruptly, and Brad's face freezes, all color draining from it. "And I know you and Emma are kind of dating, or maybe you're exclusive, I don't really know. It's not my business. But I saw you kissing the other day. She seems great, so I'm happy for you," I ramble, the words spilling out. I don't even know why I'm telling him all this.

He sits there for a moment, looking flabbergasted, then gets up and walks away without a word.

I have no clue which part upset him, and I spend the next hour replaying our short conversation, trying to figure out what made him so mad.

The next night, I'm back in the stables when I hear footsteps, different from Brad's. I can't pinpoint whose they are.

"Hey, Kalyn," Emma says, standing at the gate, a look of concern etched on her face.

"Hi, Emma."

"Did something happen with you and Brad?" she asks.

"When?"

"Last night?"

"No." Nothing really happened. He walked off before we could even start a conversation, so I don't know what his problem is.

"Do you have feelings for him?" she asks, catching me off guard with the directness of her question.

"I'm married?" I say awkwardly.

"That wasn't really my question," she says. I remain silent, unsure what to say. I can't see how any of this is my fault, so I keep brushing Kodiak, focusing on the soothing pace.

"Did you guys ever date?" she asks after a moment of prolonged silence.

"No," I say again, unsure where this line of questioning is coming from.

"Brad and I have been seeing each other, and it's been amazing. But he got weird when you got back. Last night, we were supposed to watch our show, but he completely shut me out, took a shower, and then went to bed."

I can't fathom why that would be my fault. So again, I remain silent and keep brushing Kodiak.

"Kalyn, please talk to me," she pleads, her voice filled with desperation.

"I have stayed away during the day when all I want is to come see Kodiak. I only come out here late at night so I can spend time with my horse. I don't know what more you want from me. Nothing happened between me and Brad," I confess.

"What did you guys talk about?"

"Excuse my directness, but that's none of your business. Conversations you weren't part of aren't meant to be gossiped about. Go ask him. Go interrogate him. I'm trying to spend the little time I have with Kodiak while I'm home. I don't need the third degree from you or Brad or anyone else."

"I see," she says, and when I turn, she's dabbing at a tear rolling down her cheek.

Standing, I sigh and wipe the back of my pants. "All I can say is if you haven't slept with Brad, it's because he likes you, really likes you. And if you have slept with him and he's still talking to you, he also likes you. Any way I look at it, Brad likes you, Emma. Quit making me out to be the bad guy. Maybe ask him what's wrong." I open the gate, then secure it behind me. "I like you, Emma, and I think you and Brad could be great together, but please don't bring your relationship issues to me and accuse me of being the cause of your turmoil."

As I head back to the house, I see Emma walking back to hers, her shoulders slumped in defeat. Deciding at the last minute, I walk to Brad's apartment, climb the stairs, and try the door. It's unlocked, so I walk in without knocking.

"I'm not in the mood for visitors," I hear him call from his bedroom, his voice gruff.

Ignoring his words, I stride to his bedroom, prop myself in the doorway, cross my arms, and stare at him. He's folding laundry and lets out a heavy sigh as he looks over his shoulder. Then his face relaxes, and he abandons the folding.

"I'm married... I... am... married. In another lifetime, Brad, you and I would have set the world on fire. But not in this one. This one is me and Jonah. And I feel the ache in your chest. Because sometimes—sometimes I stare at you and wonder, *what if.* Sometimes I think it's not fair that I met Jonah and fell in love with him as deeply as I did and still somehow—sometimes... I get butterflies when I see you. Jonah is my life. My whole world. And you and I, all we get is a friendship, and maybe it's not fair, maybe all we needed was one night together to know we would never have worked. But I think we both know that wouldn't have been the case. But you can find happiness, Bert. I promise. And I know someone really great who really likes you."

He lets out a ragged sigh, his expression etched with so much pain, as he collapses onto his bed and hangs his head, his palms resting on his forehead. I walk to him, kneel on the floor between his legs, and look up as I watch tears stream down his face in rivulets.

Reaching up, I swipe them away with my thumb, but before I can pull away, he grabs my hand, pressing a tender kiss to the inside of my wrist and holding it there. He begins to cry harder, his shoulders shuddering violently. I stand and climb into his lap, wrapping my arms around his shoulders. He squeezes my waist and cries, and I let him. I let him cry the way he let me cry in the stables the day Claire walked up with a lunch tray. I don't know how long we stay like this, but I don't move until his tears subside into sniffles and his body starts to relax.

"Because I'm such a gentleman, I'm going to pretend I can't feel your boner right now, because this is the first time you've ever shown any emotion other than being a total cocky asshole," I tease. "Have you slept with Emma?" I whisper.

He shakes his head.

"Well, if I were you, I would walk right over there and ravage her because she has a banging ass and amazing tits." I squeeze him again before leaning back.

He slowly shakes his head no, and his eyes well with tears again. "I'm in love with you, Kalyn," he whispers. "I'm so fucking in love with you, and I'll wait forever for you." His voice is choked up.

"Don't," I whisper back. "My heart belongs to Jonah, and you know that."

He nods. "I know."

"Don't put your life on hold waiting. Share that cockiness with others," I tell him.

He chews on the inside of his cheek, clearly lost in thought. "What?"

"I can't just be your friend," he admits, his voice wavering for the first time since I've known him.

I nod slowly, letting him know I understand. "It's okay." My stomach constricts, and it feels like we're breaking up, which is absurd. But if the way for him to get over this is for me to stay away, then I'll do it, no matter how much it hurts.

There's a long pause before he speaks. "What now?"

"Well, I continue being married, and you continue being your usual cocky, arrogant self." I figured my jab would at least put a smile on his face, but his eyes look so pained my heart breaks. "Well, Brad," I intentionally use his name, the lack of his nickname sealing the fate of our friendship dissolving. "Maybe I'll see you around." I shift uncomfortably on his lap, preparing to get up.

He pulls me back into a desperate hug. His arms wrap around me, holding me close in a way that feels final. *This is a goodbye kind of hug.* We sit there for a moment, clinging to each other as the reality of this sinks in. Finally, I feel his arms loosen, and I know it's time to go.

"Bye, Brad," I whisper, my voice barely audible. He looks up at me, our eyes meeting one last time before he nods and looks away.

There's nothing left to say, so I leave, feeling like I'm leaving a part of myself behind. It was Brad who made my first weeks and months tolerable here. It was Brad who kept me fed when Jenevieve refused to let me go to lunch. And Brad who did my work for me when my brain was smashed around in my skull from Jenevieve knocking me out with a bucket. It was Brad who delivered my horse and Brad who took me for walks with Kodiak.

I walk back to the house, my head hanging as I try to hold on to my emotions. Yet each step closer to my husband, to my life, has my chest feeling like it's crumbling—leaving Brad behind as well as all thoughts of him.

CHAPTER
Forty-Eight

JONAH

"For someone with such a pretty face, you sure have a resting bitch face," Kalyn nudges me playfully as we stroll down our favorite morning trail. It's a beautiful day; the sun is shining and it feels warm despite the snow. I'm grateful Shay and Jonathan decided to join us today. I've been worried about Kalyn—she's been a mess since coming home from the stables, her eyes red from crying. Her tears continued throughout the night, and she told me she and Brad ended their friendship. She hadn't divulged very many details, and when I would ask follow-up questions, she would start crying harder. It was clearly tearing her apart, but being out here in the fresh air, surrounded by our friends, seems to be doing her some good.

"I agree. You can be kind of scary, Mr. Everett," Shay remarks, eyeing me teasingly.

"I am not," I defend myself, laughing. "I'm a perfectly nice person."

"Sure you are," Kalyn says, her voice dripping with sarcasm. "That's why all the staff are scared of you."

"They are not," I insist.

"Oh really? So you've had long, heartfelt chats with them? Aside from Gladys, of course. And let's be real, men don't count. They all think they're your bros," Kalyn fires back, raising an eyebrow.

"Not exactly," I admit, feeling a twinge of guilt. I haven't ever really taken the time to talk with my house staff.

"Exactly," Kalyn retorts, smirking at me.

"You really think they're scared of me?" I ask, starting to feel a little defensive.

"Yeah, dude, they totally are," Jonathan chimes in, letting out a hearty chuckle.

"Whose side are you on?" I demand, feigning offense.

"I'm on no side. But the staff is definitely intimidated by you," he clarifies, holding up his hands in a peaceful gesture.

"Then we are all peas in a pod together because you nearly gave Mr. Thomas a heart attack that time you yelled at him," I point out. "And you two," I turn to Kalyn and Shay, "are just as bad. Kalyn, you had Bridget to tears in the bathroom, and Shay, you have every woman in the office quaking in her boots when you walk in."

Jonathan lets out a loud laugh. "Fuck that guy. I forgot all about him."

"I had to put her in her place," Kalyn says. "She grabbed my wrist the first week I was there, and she's lucky I didn't deck her. Then she has the nerve to cut me off every time we're going through a doorway, glare at me all day, and when I finally called her out in the bathroom, she had the balls to tell me all about how you and her used to have sex 'often.' So yeah, I made her cry."

I didn't realize that much had happened without me knowing. Now I'm feeling like a total dick. "Well, we've established I clearly suck as a person. Anything else I should know I suck at?" I jest.

"Are you feeling sensitive today, baby?" Kalyn asks, stepping in front of me and wrapping her arms around my waist.

"I'm feeling some type of way," I tease, scooping her up in my arms.

The rest of our walk is filled with easier conversation, but I can't shake what they said about the staff being scared of me. There's no way that's true. Maybe they're a little intimidated, but if I make an effort to be friendly, surely they'll see I'm not so bad. I make a mental note to try harder with them, to show them I'm not the brooding, terrifying boss I'm being accused of being.

I make it my mission today to try to interact with my staff so they don't feel uncomfortable. I'm determined to be friendly and approachable. I'm presented with the perfect opportunity when a maid dusting a hall table is standing there, her back to me.

"Good afternoon," I say to her as I walk by, trying to sound as non-threatening as possible.

Her head shoots up, and the crystal vase in her hand crashes to the floor, shattering into a million shards. Her face flushes, and she looks like she's going to be sick. Her eyes go wide, and she stares at the mess.

"Oh no!" she gasps, her voice trembling.

I stand frozen, confused about what just happened.

Gladys, hearing the noise, comes peeking around the corner to see what all the ruckus was, then rushes over. "What in the world…?" she trails off. "Is everything okay?" she asks, eyeing the broken vase.

The young maid bursts into tears, and I'm really confused now. *What is happening?*

"Am I fired?" the young woman asks me like I'm about to pronounce her doom.

"No, of course not, it was an accident," I assure her, holding up my hands. "Accidents happen. It's okay."

But she just erupts into tears again, and I blink in utter astonishment at this unfolding situation. Then she takes off down the corridor, still crying. I watch her go, feeling bewildered.

"Well…that was interesting," Gladys says, staring after her, then looking at me. "What was that about?"

I shrug. "I have absolutely no idea."

"Did you say anything to her?"

"I said good afternoon."

She stares at me for a moment, then bursts out laughing. "Go on, charmer, I'll get someone to clean this up," she shoos me away with her hands as she shakes her head.

I'm not going to let that one incident deter me from making a point that the staff isn't scared of me. So what if one person got frightened? I've never actually seen her before, so she probably didn't even know who I was.

I turn and walk away, heading in the direction the cleaners are working today.

There are two maids wiping windows in the living room, so I stop.

"Are you both having a nice day?" I ask.

Their talking stops abruptly, and both their heads whip in my direction, eyes wide as they stare.

"Your day?" I ask again.

"Do you need something, sir?" the taller one asks.

"Just asking how your day is going," I say politely.

They glance at each other, looking genuinely perplexed.

"Hi Andy, hi Tara," Kalyn says as she approaches.

"Hi Kalyn," they both greet.

"Did you guys have a nice weekend?" she asks easily.

"I did; I went ice skating," the girl she referred to as Andy says.

"I just stayed home because it's too cold to go out," the other girl, Tara, says.

"She doesn't like the cold," Andy explains.

"So, no snow angels in your future," I ask Tara, and she stares at me like I grew three heads.

"Oh come on, you've never made a snow angel?" Kalyn asks Tara.

"When I was younger," she admits.

"Live like you're little again, Tara; make a snow angel," Kalyn encourages her. "Come on, baby, let's let them get back to work." Kalyn takes my hand and pulls me away.

"They are genuinely terrified of me," I say, disbelieving.

"You're sexy, and it's intimidating. There's a difference. Maybe don't stop and pierce them with your stunning eyes. Just walk by and offer a greeting, like 'good morning,' and keep going. Eventually, you can stop and chat," she explains.

"I did that this morning, and a vase got shattered all over the floor," I tell her.

"I know; Gladys came and got me. I'm proud of you for trying."

"Why would someone work for anyone they were scared of?" I voice my thought.

"You pay way more than you should, they get to work in a beautiful home, you don't micromanage or yell about everything. You aren't yelling at anyone. You're not even home half the time. There are a million reasons someone would want to work for you.

But honestly, you don't have to be everyone's friend. You just have to be pleasant and approachable. If you walked around saying hi and greeting everyone, eventually they would relax," she explains.

"They're relaxed with you," I note.

"Yeah, because I was one of them," she nudges me with her elbow.

THE MONTHS PASS IN A BLUR OF THE SAME OLD ROUTINE. DAY IN AND day out, life continues without much change, except for the tireless efforts of my mom and Shay as they pour their energy into planning our wedding. The anticipation builds, but I can sense Kalyn's underlying impatience.

Just the other day, she had another dress fitting. She seemed reasonably happy about it, but I know her well enough to see the fatigue in her eyes. She just wants the second wedding to be over and done with, to move past this chapter of planning and preparations.

With the big day less than a week away, she's a bundle of nerves, unable to sleep as she tosses and turns relentlessly. Her beloved books, usually an escape, now lie forgotten as she can't focus. "What can I do to help, babe?" I ask with concern as she slams her wedding book shut and hangs her head over the arm of the chair she's sitting in.

"Why did we agree to this? We're already married. Did you know your mom told me she's already had over 200 people RSVP… that's not including their plus ones. Who invites that many people to a wedding? And I'll be in heels. What if I trip?" Her worries spill out in a frantic tumble, and I absorb each one, trying to think of any sort of solution to make her feel better.

"I don't know, the last time we got married, I remember a really sexy show you and Shay put on," I wink at her.

"Yeah, Shay and I had sex. What's going to top that this time? Better be something good since I want to call out dead the day of the wedding," she retorts, her nerves getting to her.

I wheel my chair to face her. "I'm sure we can think of something," I grin.

"Like?"

"Like a repeat of you and Shay. Like you letting me in," I suggest, my hand sliding between her legs, past her core, to her back entrance.

Her eyebrows shoot up. "So, you get the majority of the fun," she playfully accuses.

I shake my head, my mouth a whisper from hers. "No, because it will feel better if you're stimulated multiple ways." I softly nip at her lip.

"I'm listening," her eyes locked on mine.

I inch closer, my words whispered against her lips. "My best man would like to help with that." I shift to her ear, my teeth grazing her lobe before my tongue traces a path down her neck.

"Have you guys talked about it?" she breathes, her words barely audible.

"We have," I confirm, my touch never leaving her skin. Jonathan and I have discussed this numerous times. I've known he's wanted to have sex with Kalyn since the first time he saw her at the diner. I watched his jaw fall open when I pointed her out. Shay's even poked fun at him before, saying they always have even better sex after they've been around Kalyn because they are both so turned on. I've also noticed him watching her anytime we have sex within eye distance. When I mentioned a threesome on our wedding night, he could barely contain his eagerness. When we mentioned it to Shay, she was equally enthusiastic as she clapped and jumped up and down.

"And?" she pants.

"And I want you from behind… and he wants you from the front, and Shay wants to watch, but we both know she'll be touching you in some way." I continue my sensual assault on her neck, my lips kissing down her chest, freeing one breast to draw her nipple into my mouth. I release her, moving to the other side, my question a taunt. "So, wife, how does getting married again sound now?"

"Fucking amazing," she breathes, pulling her shirt down over her other breast and drawing my face back to her.

CHAPTER
Forty–Nine

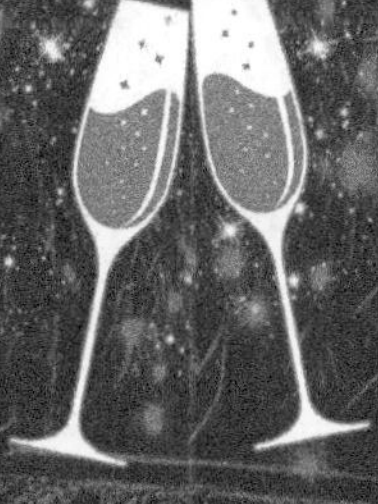

KALYN

I'm getting married... well, I'm getting married again. Jonah and I's official wedding date is October 23rd, but our wedding date for all our loved ones will be on March 4th.

As I sit in my wedding dress, the team of stylists works their magic on my hair and makeup. They curl my locks and create a partial updo, weaving in pearls for added elegance. Suddenly, Gladys appears in the doorway, her face lighting up with joy as she takes in the sight of me. Tears well in her eyes, threatening to spill over.

"Oh, don't you dare, Gladys," I say, turning to her.

She rushes over, her hand stroking my cheek affectionately, then pulling me into a warm embrace. "You look absolutely stunning, Kalyn," she gushes.

"Thank you, Gladys," I reply, squeezing her hand.

"Well, since we're here, I have a confession to make," she continues. "I'm the one who put the flyer on your door, dear. Mr. Everett was so smitten with you it was driving him mad. I couldn't bear to watch it any longer. I tracked you down and asked the diner owner where you lived, then taped it to your door. I hope you're not upset with me for interfering," a hint of worry creeping into her expression.

"Oh Gladys," I hug her tightly. "We kind of suspected it was you. Thank you," I say sincerely, knowing I probably wouldn't be with Jonah if not for her.

"I couldn't have imagined a more perfect match for that big lug. I knew you would be something special just from how enamored he was by you, but you've exceeded every image I had of who you would be. I've always served you, Kalyn, but from the bottom of my heart, I gladly, appreciatively, and dedicatedly serve you just as much as our beloved Mr. Everett."

Now my own eyes start to brim with tears.

"Don't you dare," I warn, fanning my face as I fight to maintain composure.

"Sorry sorry," she replies.

"Are you ready?" Shay asks, standing. She looks gorgeous in a blush pink satin dress that accentuates her curves, hugging her hips, waist, and breasts while flowing out to her ankles, with a flattering slit up the right leg.

I'm wearing my dream dress. The mermaid style delicately frames my shoulders, accentuates my breasts, and hugs my figure. The back is daringly open all the way down to the top of my rounded cheeks and comfortably snug around my thighs, fanning out at the bottom. The train isn't super long, but it's beautifully dramatic.

Our wedding is in a stunning venue at a winery overlooking the town. Antoinette planned everything, basically throwing the wedding she thought Jonah and I would love, and since this is our second wedding, I'm happy with whatever she chose.

We got a peek at the ceremony room where we'll exchange our vows, and there are 300 chairs elegantly set up with white cloth draped over them and a blush pink bow tied to the back. It's indoors, but almost the entire room on the front and sides are windows offering a breathtaking view of the beautifully landscaped grounds.

I really hate being the center of attention. Like really hate it. The thought of all those eyes on me, witnessing my vulnerability, is almost too much.

"Mr. Everett is all that matters," Shay reassures me, standing steadfastly before me. "When those doors open, no one else in that room matters. Focus on Mr. Everett. One foot in front of the other until you reach him."

I inhale deeply, seeking to anchor my fraying nerves. My hands quiver as Shay takes them in hers, her grip warm and firm.

A soft rap on the door signals our time to go. It swings open to reveal Antoinette beaming at us, Adeline cute as a button beside her. "Ready, darling?"

"No, but we're already here," I admit, honestly.

"You look so pretty," Adeline's eyes wide as she takes me in, her tiny hands clutching her white basket bursting with rose petals.

"You look just as pretty," I smile back.

Antoinette offers an encouraging smile and we glide out together to the waiting room.

It's a space dominated by expansive mirrors and flattering lighting, an opportunity for one final admiring glance before the grand entrance. Or to make sure you don't look green from needing to vomit. Jonathan and Beaumont await by the doors, resplendent in their tuxedos, their handsome faces a comforting sight.

"You are breathtaking, sweetheart," Beaumont murmurs as he envelops me in a gentle hug, placing a soft kiss against my cheek.

Jonathan presses a kiss to Shay's lips before turning to me, his arms wrapping around me in a warm embrace, "I would say you look more sexy, but breathtaking works too," he whispers in my ear.

"Your husband is being a perv," I whisper to Shay with a grin.

"I said she looked sexy," he counters mischievously.

Shay merely shrugs. "It's true, you do," she agrees.

"It's time," Gladys announces.

Shay and Jonathan position themselves before the doors, poised for their grand entrance. Shay blows me a kiss and mouths, "I love you," before Jonathan escorts her down the aisle. An endless moment stretches out before the doors swing open once more.

"Come on, Adeline," Gladys encourages. "Your turn, sweet girl."

"Can I walk with you?" Adeline asks, her voice trembling slightly.

"You need to go first so I can walk on the flowers you lay down for me," I reassure her with a wink.

"Oh, okay!" She exclaims and skips in before they close again.

I wish I could watch her delicately scattering the petals. I can picture how precious she looks.

"Are you doing okay, sweetheart?" Beaumont offers his arm for me to take.

"I'm nervous," I admit. "That's a lot of people out there."

"I've got you. Imagine Konrad and Katrina here with us. It feels like they are," he smiles down at me.

"I feel them too," I agree, smiling back.

When the doors open again, he gently places his hand over mine. The entire room rises. My gaze finds Jonah's, and like before, Jonathan's hand goes to his shoulder in a familiar gesture.

"I love your son so much," I tell Beaumont as we step forward.

"I know you do," he chokes out.

We walk down the aisle, my heels carrying me gracefully. Though surrounded by faces, Jonah is all I see. When we reach him, our officiant from our first wedding asks, "Who gives this woman to this man today?"

It's in this moment, I know my mother would want Antoinette by my side as well.

"Wait," I whisper to Beaumont, glancing over his shoulder to the right, "Mom," I call, beckoning her with a nod. Her face lights up as she hurries to join me, claiming my other hand and the bouquet in it.

"Even more perfect," the officiant remarks, his expression warm and approving. "Ready?"

We exchange nods of agreement, and he launches into the ritual once more. "Who presents this woman to marry this man today?" he asks. Beaumont and Antoinette respond in heartfelt unison, "We do."

The remainder of the ceremony blurs by in an instant, a beautiful whirlwind of words. Jonah cracks a joke about it being easier to recite his vows when there were only four of us on a beach, prompting laughter from everyone in the room. His promises this time are more conventional and elegantly composed.

As we stroll back down the aisle, now hand in hand with my husband, an overwhelming wave of relief crashes over me. The moment we clear the doors, instructions ring out directing everyone to proceed to the reception. We duck into the bridal suite, where Jonah greets me with a tender kiss.

"That was so scary," I giggle as Jonathan readies shots of tequila for us.

"We're almost done," Jonah reassures me, his eyes crinkling at the corners.

"I just want some cake," Jonathan chimes in, passing us each a shot.

"Mmm, cake sounds so good," Shay agrees, her eyes wide.

"I want some of that turkey," I counter, and we clink glasses before downing the liquid.

"Ughh," I shudder at the burning sensation that courses through me.

"Is the makeup still in here from earlier?" Jonah asks, scanning the room.

"Yeah, do you need to fix your makeup, Mr. Everett?" Shay chides.

Jonah turns his head to me, his lips meeting mine as our tongues begin to dance.

A tap on the door precedes Antoinette's entrance, signaling our cue for the grand entrance of Mr. And Mrs. "She'll need that lipstick now," Jonah tells Shay with a smirk.

The DJ's voice booms out from the speakers, "Please give a warm welcome to Mr. and Mrs. Jonah Everett!" The doors swing open, and a torrent of cheers and applause greets us.

Friends and family take their time on the mic, sharing stories of how they know us and expressing how happy they are for us. Sam's family attended, despite my not extending an invitation to him personally. I'd confided in his mother about the situation, and while she was understanding, she also expressed hope that I would include him, though she didn't pressure me. Mr. Milo surprised me by showing up when he had originally said he wouldn't be able to make it. Lilly and Theo make their debut appearance as an official couple—YAY! Miles put in an appearance, along with a hand-ful of other colleagues. I'd basically mandated his attendance, joking that it fell under the purview of his duties as my unofficial assistant, plus he got an all-expenses-paid vacation. I intend to for-malize that title upon our return to the office. Mr. McIntosh, his wife, and two beautiful kids are here as well. He even made sure to show me his flashy pink nails—correction, his flashy pink nails and fingers his daughter polished just for the wedding. Jonah was confused why I invited a client, and I finally told him how Mr. McIntosh and I had actually met at the hotel.

We spend the next while smiling at the heartfelt words and anecdotes shared about us. Of all the people gathered here to-day, I never expected to be so deeply touched by Antoinette's speech, while simultaneously, I completely expected her to deliver a tearjerker.

We all watch with bated breath as she walks to the front of the room, taking the microphone off the stand. The image of Jonah and me on the massive screen behind her dissolves into a video I had no idea existed. I'm captured on film outside the diner, lean-ing into Jonah's open car door as I hand him a bag of food. "I put napkins in the bag. Silverware too, if you need them," I say. "I don't bite." Then I poke his chest. "Hard anyways." I smile before straightening and shutting the door.

I glance at Jonah admiringly, and his eyes are glassy. Then I turn back to the screen behind Antoinette, and the image changes to the first picture Jonah took of us on the couch at the rundown mansion.

"Many of you know my son as a very serious individual. He works hard—well, all he ever used to do was work. And when he puts his mind to something, he succeeds, but almost two years ago, that all changed, didn't it? The somber man fell madly in love, and the Jonah I knew and raised began to reemerge. Kalyn has changed Jonah's life in more ways than anyone in this room realizes. And it wasn't six years ago that he began his pursuit of her outside her workplace."

She dabs at the corners of her eyes, the microphone momentarily at her side as she composes herself. "I told myself I wouldn't get emotional," she admits, prompting a round of sympathetic laughter.

The backdrop behind her transitions to an image of my mom cradling newborn me in the hospital, while Antoinette supports her own baby, and a young Jonah sitting on his knees on the bed kissing my newborn head. "It began here," her voice trembles. "The day my dearest friend Katrina gave birth to a beautiful baby girl named Kalyn." The room erupts into a collective gasp, even Shay and Jonathan's jaws dropping in surprise.

She continues with her heartfelt address as photos and videos play behind her, illustrating her words. I allow tears to silently trail down my cheeks, dabbing at them with a tissue.

"Jonah, my sweet, happy, loving little boy was forever altered the same night our lives were all upended. Our best friends were driving home with their six-year-old daughter after having spent a wonderful holiday with us, when they perished in a car accident, leaving only one survivor." She manages, her gaze locked on me as she wipes away tears. "We didn't just lose our best friends that day; we lost our beautiful white-haired little girl when she moved away to live with her last remaining relative. But that wasn't all. Our beautiful baby boy was lost without his counterpart. He became driven, angry, and emotionally numb. He became the man everyone here knows. Because half his heart had been torn away when he was only ten. Years later, a chance detour on a rainy spring evening led him to an unfamiliar town, where every piece of his shattered heart began to mend with a single glance at a white-haired blonde, crying as she walked home in the rain. Call it fate, call it destiny, I call it the legacy of Katrina and Konrad. Jonah found the missing half of his heart twenty-three years later. My baby boy is back, and though they both took a scenic route to get here, they've arrived at last. Kalyn, Katrina, and Konrad would be so proud of the incredible woman you've become. We always knew you two would end up together, and all those years ago when we made that prediction, we never realized we'd be celebrating this moment. Welcome home, honey. We're over the *moon* to have you back where you've always belonged."

WE PULL UP TO A BEACH HOUSE JONAH RENTED FOR US.

It's late. Really late. Probably 1 AM, yet I'm buzzing with a second wind of energy after the wonderful night with our loved ones. As we ascend the stairs, my excitement only builds.

"The door should be unlocked," Jonah advises, and I twist the knob to find it is in fact open.

He catches my arm, halting me from stepping across the threshold, and sweeps me up in his arms, carrying me inside in traditional bridal style before kicking the door shut behind us.

As we enter, a large mirror immediately catches my entire re-flection. I take in my appearance and am relieved to see my hair and makeup have remained immaculately in place despite the evening of dancing at the reception.

I catch sight of Jonah approaching me in the mirror, a slow smile spreading across my face as he positions himself behind me. His fingers delicately trace the straps of my gown down my shoulders, peeling the fabric away until I stand before him in nothing but my sparkling white heels and silk panties.

He gently kisses my nape, and I watch in the mirror as he works to free himself from his pants. Then, he aligns his body with mine, pinning me against the cool glass of the mirror as he shifts my panties aside and sinks into me. A moan tears from my throat as he withdraws, then thrusts in once, twice, before pulling out again.

"What are you doing?" I gasp, craving so much more of him. He flashes a smirk as he steps back, and I turn to assist him in shedding his remaining clothes. I'm captivated by the sight of him, his chest rising and falling with labored breaths.

He gestures towards the living room, and I grin, poised to lead him there, but my feet falter as I take in the scene before me. The room is bathed in the soft, warm glow of candles, and Shay sits on her heels, back straight, wearing a provocative lingerie set. Jonathan reclines on the floor in only his boxers, propped against a mountain of pillows, his head resting against his bent arm as he grins at me with uncontained excitement.

"Come here, bride. You've got a wedding to celebrate," Jonathan invites, curling his finger at me.